D

The
rea

k Times, number one bestseller **P.C. Cast** is an award-
fantasy, paranormal romance, and young adult author.
a teacher for many years, but now concentrates on
and public speaking full-time. Currently she divides her
ween Oklahoma, Grand Cayman Island, and Scotland.

website at www.pccast.net

CP/494

Goddess of Troy

P.C. Cast

piatkus

PIATKUS

First published in the US in 2008 as *Warrior Rising* by The Berkley Publishing Group
A division of Penguin Group (USA) Inc., New York
First published in Great Britain as a paperback original in 2011 by Piatkus

7 9 10 8 6

A CIP catalogue record for this book
is available from the British Library.

ISBN 978-0-7499-5361-4

Typeset in Jenson by Hewer Text UK Ltd, Edinburgh
Printed and bound by CPI Group (UK) Ltd, Croydon, CR0 4YY

Papers used by Piatkus are from well-managed forests
and other responsible sources.

MIX
Paper from
responsible sources
FSC® C104740
www.fsc.org

Piatkus
An imprint of
Little, Brown Book Group
Carmelite House
50 Victoria Embankment
London EC4Y 0DZ

An Hachette UK Company
www.hachette.co.uk

www.piatkus.co.uk

This one is for friends everywhere!

Acknowledgments

As always I'd like to thank my agent and friend, Meredith Bernstein. Your consistent belief in me means more than I can express with these few words.

Thank you to my new Berkley editor, Wendy McCurdy, who made the scary process of changing editors practically painless. You are a pleasure to work with!

And a big THANK-YOU to all the fans of my Goddess Summoning series who have sent wonderful letters sharing with me how much my books entertain and empower you. Hope you enjoy this trip to my version of the Trojan War!

Prologue

Thetis of the Silver Feet rose from the depths of the hidden cove. Her son was already there, awaiting her arrival. With that odd, almost preternatural sense of calm that had been his to command even as a babe, he stood on the beach staring with quiet intensity at the distant, watery horizon. He had not yet noticed her, so she took the opportunity to study him carefully.

Though he had barely lived sixteen summers he more closely resembled the man and warrior he would become than the child she'd held at her bosom what seemed but a moment ago. He was magnificent – her golden eaglet, her pride, her heart – her Achilles. And today her soul wept for what Zeus's oracle had revealed to her. Thetis wished she could deny the truth of it or even simply run from the choices the great god had revealed. But she, too, was a deity, born of the water, daughter of Nereus, an ancient sea god, and she knew all too well that the prophecies of the gods could not be avoided – that to run from them left only chaos and heartbreak and ruined lives in the wake of consequences. Fate could not be avoided, so it must be endured.

At least Achilles had been given a choice.

The small splinter of hope that thought gave Thetis was short-lived. It worked itself free of her heart as she continued to gaze at the wondrous man her son was becoming.

Before his conception the oracle had foretold that her son would be greater than his father – thus freeing her of the tiresome courtships of Zeus and Apollo. Neither god would ever have suffered a son to outshine him. She had eventually married Peleus, King of the Myrmidons. A slight smile touched her shapely pink lips. Peleus had desired her so desperately that compared to her smooth, white thighs the oracle's predictions were inconsequential. Thetis tossed back her silver-blonde hair. She hadn't, of course, been able to settle permanently with a mortal, king or not, but she did think of him fondly and often. Perhaps she would visit him later that night. He always welcomed her joyously into his bed and she would need the distraction of passion after hearing Achilles' choice. Sadly she knew her son too well; what the oracle at Dodona had prophesied for him would, indeed, come to pass. Thetis drew in a deep breath and readied herself.

'Achilles!' she called to him.

His response was instantaneous. He turned toward her with a dazzling smile and a formal bow so deep and respectful that Hera herself would have been pleased.

'Mother, what news from Dodona and Zeus's oracle?'

Thetis glided to him, extending her soft hand. 'Not even a hello for your mother? Are oracles and prophecies all you care about, my son?'

Achilles' blue eyes, which were the exact color of the turquoise depths in which his mother had been born, sparkled with mischievous humor. 'Forgive me great goddess of the sea!' He took her hand, kissed it fondly, then tucked it around his already well-muscled arm as he led her from the warm Aegean waters. 'And how is your health, Mother? Has it changed in the two days since last I saw you?'

She pushed at his shoulder, which felt even more rocklike than it had two days before when they'd taken lunch together in this very cove. 'My health is perfect, as you very well know. And I am but a lowly sea goddess, not one of the Divine Twelve, so there's no need to flatter me as such. As you also know very well.'

Achilles bent and kissed her quickly on her cheek. 'You are *my* goddess, Mother, and more divine to me than any of the Twelve.'

Instead of replying with her usual good-natured banter Thetis met her son's sparkling eyes and said sharply, 'Do not jest about the gods. Were I to usurp one of the Twelve Olympians, even just in your mind, it would be a grave insult and my hubris could be punished severely.'

Achilles frowned. 'What has happened, Mother?'

Thetis sighed and unwound herself from her son's arm. Silently she walked to a chair-sized rock and sat. Then she looked up at her son. Where he was standing, with the sea at his back and the sun caressing his youthful body with its golden rays, he seemed for an instant like a gilded statue of himself, like something a great people – perhaps in the distant future – would erect of him to memorialize the remembered exploits of a warrior whose life had blazed like a comet and then burned out much too soon.

A shiver passed through Thetis's body.

'Mother?' Achilles repeated. He began to walk toward her, but her upraised hand stayed him.

'This will be easier if you remain there.' Then she wouldn't be tempted to clutch him to her as if he were still a babe, and beg him to be wise ... to consider ... Thetis drew another deep breath. When she finally spoke, her voice was emotionless, as if she were an oracle herself. 'Zeus's oracle presented two choices for you, Achilles.' She closed her eyes and recited: 'One path to the future will lead to a long, prosperous life. The Myrmidons will flourish under your rule. You will have a fruitful wife who will bear you many sons and daughters. You will know peace and tranquility and love. Your long life will be full and rich and you will die quietly in your bed when your beard is white, surrounded by those who love you. You will be deeply mourned, but eventually your name will be forgotten as just a speck in the countless sands of history.' Thetis drew another deep breath and continued, still not opening her eyes.

'Another path to the future will lead to acclaim that will outshine all other kings and warriors. You will lead the Myrmidons in battle with a red ferocity that will burn everything before you. Your fire will rage hot and high so that your name will be remembered for thousands of years in lands past the edge of the world. But like a fire that burns too hot too quickly, you will be consumed, and never see the close of thirty summers. Rage will destroy your life. You will only glimpse peace and love and tranquility – you will never know them.' Thetis paused long enough to ready herself for what she knew she would see, and then she opened her eyes.

Achilles was already blazing. She'd known it when the oracle had spoken her son's choices, but she couldn't help the small hope she'd nurtured. Now, like a snuffed candle, hope was extinguished.

'You must choose, my son, but take your time. Reason carefully. Remember, once your choice is made, Zeus had decreed your fate and your path will be set.'

Achilles' grin was young and untamed. 'I already know my choice, Mother!' He lifted his arms to the sky, threw back his head, and shouted his decision to Olympus as a fierce prayer to the gods. 'Divine Zeus, I honor you for the choices you have given me. I choose the life of a warrior and eternal fame!' At that instant the heavens above him were split by a deafening crack of

4

thunder and a massive lightning bolt, jagged and glowing, shot from the sky into Achilles' body, driving the boy to his knees and filling him with a red, raw power that literally changed his visage, hardening the smooth cheeks. It seemed he actually grew, becoming taller and broader, becoming *more* of what he had once been. His eyes glowed with the rust color of old blood and his lips pulled back from his teeth in a feral snarl as, once again, he shouted his decision in a voice unrecognizable as his own, 'I choose the life of a warrior and eternal fame!'

Tears spilled silently down Thetis's cheeks as she watched her son choose to end his life too soon. He looked like a shining golden godling, her wonderful eaglet. Proud, beautiful, fierce and immortal.

But he wasn't immortal. He would die in barely a breath of time. And she would watch as he blazed and burned out.

Bowing her head, Thetis sent up her own prayer to Olympus – not shouted with words, but spoken with the power of a mother's broken heart.

'Hera, Goddess of All Mothers, take pity on me. If it is possible, let my beloved son know love and peace before he dies. Athena, Goddess of War and Wisdom, I ask with my immortal soul that though he has chosen a warrior's life, you give Achilles the wisdom to outlive his own youthful foolishness . . .'

Thunder clapped through the clear Greek sky and Achilles laughed with fierce joy, not noticing the lovely peacock who suddenly appeared beside his mother. The bird stretched out its royal neck to lay its sapphire head against the sea goddess's thigh. Then, on the other side of her, a magnificent owl appeared, ethereal in its white feathers. The owl's wise gaze met hers, and it regally bowed its head to Thetis. Then both divine birds disappeared in a glittering of diamond dust.

'I have to tell you darlings, the Trojan War is making my ass hurt,' Venus said, glancing at Athena with one perfectly raised brow.

'I don't know why you're looking at me like that,' Athena bristled.

'Athena, my friend, it could have something to do with the fact that you are Goddess of War,' Hera said.

'Add to that your obsession with Odysseus and his safety, which doesn't help matters over there in Troy,' Venus said. Then she lifted her empty goblet and called, 'I'm out of ambrosia!' Instantly a satyr galloped in with a glistening pitcher of the golden wine of the gods. Venus blew two kisses at the very male, very enthusiastic beast who wriggled appreciatively at the goddess's attention, bowed low, nuzzled her feet and then trotted reluctantly from the room.

'You spoil those creatures,' Athena said, frowning after the satyr. 'And you're the one who instigated Odysseus's affection for me, remember?' The gray-eyed goddess tossed her golden hair. 'So our relationship is really your fault.'

'If you weren't so uptight maybe you would have a *relationship* instead of decades of sexual frustration and obsession,' Venus mumbled.

'What was that?' Athena asked, narrowing her eyes.

'I'm just saying—'

'That the Trojan War has become entirely too tiresome,' Hera interrupted neatly. 'I'm especially disgusted by the new rumors. It was bad enough that Agamemnon and Menelaus blamed poor Helen for starting the war when it was their greed for the riches of Troy and their overblown male pride that was really responsible.'

Athena gave Venus a considering look. 'Didn't you have something to do with Paris's infatuation with Helen?'

The Goddess of Love sniffed delicately. 'Menelaus didn't appreciate Helen's beauty. The man was boorish and inconsiderate. All I did was create a little love spell to make the dolt jealous. I had no idea Paris would be so susceptible and Helen would be so needy.'

'Whatever the cause,' Hera said, 'it is silly that the Greeks are blaming an entire war on one straying wife and the man who stole her away.'

'Man? Paris is little more than a lust-filled boy, which is exactly why I didn't think my tiny, inconsequential spell would create such a problem.'

'As ridiculous as one woman causing an entire war, that rumor is nothing compared to what they're saying now. Have you heard that the Trojans have proclaimed that the three of us instigated the entire Helen/Paris debacle? And I don't mean a simple jealousy spell that got out of hand,' Venus said.

'Not that apple thing again? I heard that outlandish story months ago. I can't believe it's caught on and is being repeated,' Athena said.

'As if the three of us would actually participate in a beauty contest!' Hera scoffed.

'It's Discord's fault, you know. She was angry at not being invited to Peleus and Thetis's wedding, so she started the rumor,' Venus said. 'I know it was her because in all the gossip I'm called Aphrodite. Discord knows I prefer my Roman name. It's just like her to start rumors about me using the name I like least just to irritate me. I wasn't even at that silly party!'

'Discord does know how to annoy,' Hera said.

'No wonder she doesn't get invited to many parties,' Venus said.

'The rumor is that Venus, or rather Aphrodite' – Hera paused and smiled apologetically at Venus – 'gave Helen to Paris as reward for his choosing you as the fairest of the three of us,' Hera said.

'I've heard that nonsense, too. Which is the main reason the war is making my ass hurt. I'm so done with the Greeks and Trojans blaming everything on women – goddesses in particular. Darlings, we really must do something to encourage this little war to end. Now.'

'It's been almost ten years. As far as I'm concerned that is nine years too long,' Hera said.

'Exactly,' Venus said.

'Agreed,' Athena said.

'So what do we do about it?' Venus sighed. 'They blame it on the women, but it's the damnable men of the ancient world with their archaic attitudes that actually keep everything stirred up.'

'You know it's really not Odysseus's fault.' Athena spoke up quickly, as always, defending her favorite.

Venus snorted.

'I believe you're right, Athena,' Hera said, nodding slowly. 'Achilles and his rage is at the heart of the war.'

'Yes,' Athena said. 'He's definitely the problem. Take him and his Myrmidons out of the equation and the Greeks would probably lose heart and not be able to keep up the siege on Troy.' Clearly annoyed, the goddess tapped one slim finger against the glass of her wine goblet. 'We should have known he would come to no good all those years ago when Thetis invoked our aid. Had we acted then it would have saved us a lot of irritation.'

Hera sighed. 'We didn't act then because of the problems it would have caused between Zeus and me. Again.'

'Would you please explain what you two are talking about?' Venus said.

'You know Thetis went to Zeus's oracle at Dodona asking about her son's future, don't you?' Hera asked the Goddess of Love.

'Vaguely. Wasn't it something about Achilles having a choice between fame and a long life?'

'Yes, the impetuous boy chose fame, of course,' Athena said. 'And when he did, Thetis begged our aid. We heard her, and I know I for one meant to act.' The goddess shrugged her lovely rounded shoulders. 'It just never seemed the right time. And I will admit that it simply slipped my mind.'

'I, too, meant to act. I suppose I allowed the trouble it would cause with Zeus to dissuade me. And then there is that terrible berserker rage Zeus gifted Achilles with. The moment his emotions are overly aroused – be they good or bad – it possesses him and then there is no reasoning with him.' Hera lowered her voice conspiratorially. 'I hear that women are so terrified of him that he hasn't even taken a lover in years.'

Venus snorted again. 'Achilles needs a good dose of a strong, independent woman from the modern world. That would fix him right up and cure him of that berserker nonsense. Then he could be reasoned with. I'm sure now that he's not a ridiculous adolescent he has some kind of sense and doesn't particularly want to die before his hair even begins to gray.' She paused to sip her ambrosia and noticed that Hera and Athena were staring at her. 'What?'

'I do believe the Goddess of Love may just have our solution,' Athena said.

'Yes, and if *she* brings the modern woman to Troy, Zeus certainly won't hold me responsible for anything that happens because of it,' Hera said.

'So glad to help with your marital issues,' Venus said sarcastically.

'Will you do it or not?' Athena asked, being her usual blunt self.

'Of course I'll help. I'm as sick as you two of the whole Trojan War issue – rumors and all.' Venus brushed back her hair and sipped her ambrosia as she considered her next move. 'I am very familiar with the city of Tulsa in the modern world. It would be a simple thing for me to point my oracle in that direction. Perhaps through some judicious eavesdropping I can discover the perfect woman for Achilles.' She smiled and shrugged nonchalantly. 'Once I find her I could simply zap her here. We can have a little chat with her about helping us reason with Achilles before I send her to the Greek camp. I suppose . . .' Venus paused and sipped her wine while the other two goddesses waited impatiently for her to continue.

'You suppose?' Hera prompted.

'I suppose we should offer the woman a lovely reward or whatnot for her services.'

'Reward? Should it not be reward enough that she was chosen by a goddess?' Athena said, frowning.

Venus rolled her eyes. 'Athena, darling, you need to get out more. Modern mortals, especially modern mortal women, don't bow down and simper and worship us like sycophants. It's actually very refreshing to walk amongst them.' Venus smiled, remembering her adventures in Tulsa and the eternal love she had won. 'Just trust me on this one.'

'A reward for the mortal sounds fine to me,' Hera said while

Athena glowered at Venus. 'Why not grant her one boon? A favor from the Goddess of Love should satisfy any mortal, modern or otherwise.'

'Excellent idea, Hera.' Venus smiled impishly at Athena.

'I think it sounds like a good plan,' Hera said.

'Yes, we are all in agreement,' Athena said, although a little reluctantly.

Hera raised her glass. 'To the modernizing of Achilles and the end of the wretched Trojan War.'

'And,' Venus added with a smile, 'to modern women.'

Chapter One

'The Iliad? Did I hear you right? You're reading that misogynistic mess?' Jacqueline said as she searched through the pantry's colorful collection of red wine for another Shiraz to open.

'Are you having trouble sleeping? When I was in college Homer was a surefire remedy for insomnia,' Kat said. 'Jacky, if you're looking for another bottle of the Coppola Shiraz, it's still in the bag I left by the door.'

'As usual you read my mind, Kat,' Jacqueline called over her shoulder as she headed for the foyer of the chic home, doing a little impromptu shimmy in the full-length vintage beveled mirror that hung by the front door.

Laughing, Kat called after her. 'Shake that thang, baby!'

Jacqueline snagged the bottle of Shiraz and shimmied back to the group.

'I do wish I could move like that,' Kat said.

'Kat, honey, I love you, but y'all white girls do not have enough junk in your trunk to move like me. I am *luscious*.' Jacqueline dragged the word out with a sexy purr as she ran her hands down her voluptuous body and made kissing noises at her best friend. Grinning, she disappeared into the kitchen to open the bottle and called, 'So what were we saying?'

'We were talking about poor dead Susie having to read the wretched *Iliad*.' Kat winked at 'poor dead Susie.' 'Remind us, just exactly *why* are you suffering through reading that thing?'

13

Susie, who owned the fabulous 1920's era home the group of friends met at twice a month for their girls' night in, gave a long-suffering sigh and threw her hands up in frustration. 'First, *Katrina*,' she used Kat's full name in a very you've-been-bad-young-lady tone, 'I'm not dead; I'm in college, so I only feel dead. Second, I'm reading the fucking *Iliad* because it is required reading by the asshole chauvinist professor in the third to last fucking class I have to finish before I am able to graduate and, finally, at the totally ridiculous age of forty-eight, get my damnable BA.'

'Okay, tell us all again why a woman who is so incredibly successful that the utterly fab boutique that she started as a tiny women's accessory store in a not-so-good part of Tulsa and is now located smack in the middle of totally posh Utica Square, as well as the Galleria in Dallas, the Magnificent Mile in Chicago, and delicious downtown Denver, feels like she has to get a piece of paper that says she's smart?' Kat said between sips from her tall, frosty champagne-filled flute.

'No shit.' Christy raised her red wine balloon glass. 'I second that.'

'I'll third it.' Heather raised her glass, then frowned at it. 'And may I just say one more time that I will be so incredibly, amazingly, inexorably glad when I can get off this bubbly grape juice stuff and back to an excellent chardonnay that I may just pee myself with pleasure – or, perhaps, treat all of us to a boozy party. Heavy on the boozy part.'

'Sounds good to me,' Kat said. 'The party part, not the peeing part.'

'It's just one more month. And you don't want to pickle that baby,' Christy said, reaching over and patting Heather's very pregnant belly.

'I know, but I'm dying for a glass of wine!'

'Focus guys! We were sympathizing with Susie about the horrid essay she has to write over the wretched *Iliad*,' Jacqueline reminded them.

'And I was saying that I don't think she needs a piece of paper to show she's "smart" when she's already amazingly successful,' Kat said.

'Easily said by a woman with a masters in psych,' Susie said and then hurried on before Kat could interrupt her. 'Actually, every last one of you has that *meaningless* piece of paper – or a couple of them. Right?' She pointed first at Jacqueline, 'Ms. ER Nurse, you have a bachelor of science.' Then at Heather, 'You have a masters in education, don't you?'

'Guilty,' Heather said.

'Christy, you have a BS in physical fitness, don't you?'

'Yep, but if you want honesty I'll tell you that I kick ass as a personal trainer because of my gym experience and not because my parents insisted I go to college way back when.'

'Okay, I get that, but can you guys not see the common theme here? College is part of your success. Christy could probably still be a trainer without her degree, but Kat and Jacqueline could definitely not do their jobs without those pieces of paper and the knowledge they gained getting them. Right?'

Kat and Jacky nodded reluctantly.

'And Heather, you couldn't teach without the BS that came before getting your masters. Right?'

Heather sighed and patted her pregnant belly. 'Right, but today not having to teach and not being on my swollen feet while I scream at high school students as my ankles continue to balloon would be a lovely thing.'

Jacqueline shuddered. 'God, teenagers. They're so nasty. I don't know how you stand all of their hormones.'

'You'll get no argument from me. They're disgusting creatures,' Heather said.

'You're just grumpy because your ankles look like tree trunks. You used to like teaching, remember? Way back in Pre-pregnancy Land,' Susie said.

'I can't remember back to a time when I wasn't pregnant. I've always been this big and hideous.'

'Honey, have a chocolate.' Jacqueline passed the tray of truffles to her.

'It'll be better in a month or so,' Kat said.

Heather gave Kat a tired smile and popped the truffle in her mouth. Around the orb of dissolving chocolate she said, 'You know, Kat, it always amazes me how optimistic you are. What with all of those abusive asshole men you have to deal with in that clinic you run. I know if I had to deal with the jerks you've met I'd be a man-hating shrew, but you're not.' Heather peered at her like she was a science experiment. 'You actually like men, don't you?'

Kat's laughter was uninhibited and contagious. 'Yes, I definitely like men. And not all of the assholes I counsel are men – there are women jerks, too. Plus, they're not all abusive assholes. Many of them actually come to me *before* they've graduated to full abusive asshole status.'

'Just like me,' Susie proclaimed. 'I'm going to graduate some day.'

Jacqueline frowned. 'Uh, Susie. I don't think graduating to an abusive asshole is something to which you want to aspire.'

The older woman rolled her eyes. 'I'm talking about my BA and not about their asshole-ish-ness. When I get out of this awful lit class in a couple months it'll be way better. My final two classes are going to be a breeze. This is the last really horrid one

I have to take. As soon as I get this stupid paper on *The Iliad* written I'll feel lots better.'

'I know!' Kat said through the truffle melting on her tongue. 'How about you write your paper on how ridiculous it is that women got blamed for every damn thing in the Trojan War? I mean, I haven't read the thing in a zillion years.' She wrinkled her brow. 'Wait, I might never have actually read it and just faked my way through with the CliffsNotes, but what I do recall is that Helen took the fall for causing the war.'

'Hey, I remember that,' Jacqueline said. 'And wasn't there something about three goddesses starting the whole thing?'

'Yeah – Hera, Athena and Aphrodite,' Susie said. 'The goddess Discord was pissed about not getting invited to a wedding, so she threw a golden apple that read "for the fairest" into the group. None of the gods were stupid enough to judge that beauty contest, so a guy named Paris, who was the son of Priam, king of Troy, got stuck with the job. But he didn't actually choose which goddess was the prettiest. He chose which bribe he liked best. Aphrodite offered him the most beautiful mortal woman in the world as his own. He took that bribe. Helen was the most beautiful mortal woman, but she was already married to the Greek king, Menelaus. Paris stole her from Menelaus, with Aphrodite's blessing, and the Trojan War started.'

'Huh.' Jacqueline snorted. 'Sounds like bullshit to me. I mean, please. Why would goddesses give a shit about what some mortal guy thought?'

'That's true, Jacky,' Kat chimed in. 'You're not a goddess, but you rarely give a shit about men – mortal or otherwise!'

Jacqueline's perfectly shaped brows went up almost far enough to reach the hairline of her short, curly, Halle Berry-like hair. 'I'm not a goddess? Did you just say I'm not a goddess, Kat?'

Kat put her hands up in mock surrender. 'It must be this bottle of champagne talking.'

'How about that little "don't give a shit about men" comment?' Christy asked.

Jacky shrugged. 'Whatever. I like men okay. In theory.'

'See, that's why Jacky and I are such perfect BFFs,' Kat said. 'I am an eternal optimist and she's Ms. Pessimist. She reels me in when I get too far out there, and I remind her to give folks a chance – they're not all bad.'

'Folks aren't all bad – men are another matter,' Jacky grumbled.

'Down, killer!' Kat said.

Jacqueline fixed her dark chocolate eyes on her best friend. 'I do believe I'm going to cut you off from your second bottle of champagne.'

Kat grinned at her. 'No you're not! Remember our deal – I pay for our cab *and* I get to drink entirely too much champagne.'

'Uh, ladies, before you talk about calling cabs and such, could we please talk a little more about this paper I'm going to write for my jerk of a professor?' From somewhere Susie had produced a thick, college-ruled notebook and a well-sharpened number two pencil, which she held at the ready.

'Your jerk of a professor is not going to like a feminist paper,' Kat said.

'Hey, I said I wanted the BA. I didn't say I wanted straight As.' She grinned mischievously at her friends. 'To misquote the fabulous Bonnie Raitt, "Let's give him something to talk about."'

Venus laughed aloud. 'Darlings! This is exactly why my oracle found you.' She cooed and clapped her hands even though the group of modern mortal women could not hear the goddess and were oblivious that she observed them through her shining oracle, which acted like an infinitely long telescope from Olympus to Tulsa. Venus focused her vision on the woman with the infectious laugh, sparkling blue eyes and the adorable nickname of Kat.

'By Hermes' flamingly gay buttocks, she is absolutely perfect!' The goddess held up a manicured finger for each point she ticked off. 'She counsels men, so she should be able to handle Achilles and that silly berserker rage issue of his. She's optimistic and likes men.' The goddess's smile was sultry. 'Liking men is always a plus when seducing them. And she's astute enough to know intuitively the falseness of the ridiculous fiction about the Trojan War that has been repeated for . . .' – Venus paused and grimaced in annoyance – 'longer than I would have believed possible.' Venus focused her attention back on the little group of girlfriends and laughed along with them as she listened to them composing a very funny, very literate, very feminist essay for the professor they were calling Mr. Anus.

Venus liked all five of the women, which made her even surer that Kat was a suitable choice for the goddesses' mission. A woman's friends reflected who she was – and Venus definitely liked the reflection she was seeing from Tulsa. She especially liked the exotic-looking Jacqueline, who was obviously Kat's closest friend among the group. Jacky, as they called her, was sassy and saucy and compelling with her quick wit and her lovely caramel-colored skin. Venus considered for a moment whether she may be a better choice than Kat – and decided no, Jacqueline was wonderful, but Kat had more of the much-needed skills to conquer Achilles. Besides, Jacqueline's lovely dark skin would be too hard to explain among the golden Greeks. 'More's the pity for them,' Venus mumbled.

Venus narrowed her study down to Kat, concentrating with all of her vast powers. The Goddess of Love smiled in relief. No, Kat was not in love with any mortal man. Had she been, Venus, who was Love personified, would have sensed it. Actually, now that she was thinking about it, the goddess realized that out of the five of them, only the very pregnant Heather was committed to and in love with a man. 'Well . . .' Venus drummed her fingers on the side of the marble oracle. 'Perhaps when I've finished with this little Trojan War issue I'll return for some lovely matchmaking.' The thought made Venus hum happily. Finding a lover for the fabulous Jacqueline would be her first order of business.

'No!' Venus reined in her enthusiasm. 'First Achilles. Then I can dabble with matchmaking in the modern mortal world.' She grinned. 'Again.'

But first things first. She needed to bring Kat from the modern world to Olympus, which would not be particularly difficult. The goddess raised her hands and began summoning the power that as one of the Twelve Olympians would eternally be hers to command. The air between her palms started to shimmer with tiny specks of energy brilliant as miniature diamonds. As soon as Kat was alone, Venus could reach through the oracle and transport her to the portal from the modern world to Olympus that stood open, but invisible, in Tulsa. Then Venus would simply zap herself there and speak with Kat briefly. The goddess tapped her chin as she considered. She'd probably have to work some kind of obvious magic to prove to the mortal that she was truly Venus, Goddess of Love. But that shouldn't take long. She'd get that over with, and then return to Olympus with the mortal and call Hera and Athena here to her temple so that they could all explain in detail to the girl what was needed from her.

As her mortal friend, Pea Chamberlain, would say, easy-peasy.

Still building the power between her hands, Venus looked down through the oracle to see a giggling Kat and Jacqueline making their way more than a little unsteadily down the front steps of Susie's pretty home to a waiting car. Venus laughed. 'Good thing they aren't driving. Neither of them appears to be sober enough to handle one of those metal machines.' Nor were either of them – specifically Kat – sober enough to bring to Olympus that night. Well, that was probably for the best. She needed to get with Hera and Athena again and decide the best way to move Kat into Achilles' camp. Kat would need to have some kind of royal status ... or perhaps one of them could appear to Achilles and foretell the coming of a priestess who would need his protection ...

Venus sighed. This might be more complicated than she'd originally thought it would be. But no matter. She'd just use the oracle to follow Kat home – make note of where the mortal woman lived – and then pay her a little divine visit on the morrow.

Smiling, Venus turned her attention back to the oracle in time to see the huge Suburban run through the stop sign and crash into the little yellow car that held Kat and Jacqueline.

'No! Stop!' Venus screamed, instantly throwing the power she'd been generating through her oracle to protect and surround the car, freezing time temporarily so that the scene looked like a gruesome painting. But even as she gave the command she knew it was already too late. Venus drew a deep breath and waved her hands over the oracle. 'Let me see Katrina and Jacqueline,' she said solemnly.

The oracle's vision telescoped inside the crushed car. Venus's breath caught in a sob of sympathy. The women must have seen the accident coming. They'd thrown their arms around each other so that now they looked like broken dolls clinging to one another. Kat had a horrid gash on her head and her neck was turned in an unnatural angle. Jacqueline was closest to the spot of impact. Her chest had been completely crushed.

The two women were dead.

Venus felt a terrible sense of loss out of all proportion with how briefly she'd known the mortals. 'I should have been paying closer attention. I should have been able to stop it from happening,' she whispered in a tired, broken voice. 'They were so young – so vibrant. Their lives were cut off too soon.' As the goddess watched, two glowing golden orbs lifted from the broken bodies of the mortal women. Venus's eyes widened. 'Maybe there *is* something I can do!' Focusing her power she spoke the command through her oracle.

'Alight with life and love these spirits are – free to begin anew, to travel far. So Love herself commands of you – spirits, come to me to complete the task I would have you do!' Venus threw more power into the oracle and, like a flame drawing the mortals fluttering spirits, the souls of Katrina and Jacqueline lifted immediately to enter the stream of energy the goddess created until, with a sound like a champagne bottle being uncorked, they popped through the marble basin to hover in the air in front of the goddess.

When she glanced back through her portal she saw the yellow car burst into fierce flame.

Venus sighed. 'Well, darlings, now what are we going to do?'

Chapter Two

'You did what!' Athena sputtered (unattractively, Venus noted) as she stared wide-eyed at the glowing orbs that held the two mortal spirits.

'Well, I couldn't just let them die!' Venus said defensively, patting the orb that floated closest to her. 'It was just too awful and too soon. They're both so young.'

'Mortals die. Period. You shouldn't have interfered with what Fate decreed for them,' Athena said.

'Oh, please! These are modern mortals. They don't believe in Fate.'

Hera rushed into Venus's oracle chamber. 'What has happened? I came as soon as the satyr gave me the emergency message and I—' The goddess broke off as she caught sight of the floating orbs. Her smooth brow wrinkled. 'Are those mortal spirits?'

'They are indeed,' Athena said.

'Well, what ever are they doing here? Are they lost?'

'No. They are not lost. They are the spirits of two modern mortal women and Venus brought them here.'

Venus frowned at Athena. 'Are you having regular orgasms, Athena? If not, that could be why you're always so grumpy and judgmental.'

'Venus!' Hera's voice was sharp, reminding the Goddess of Love that she was in the presence of the Queen of Olympus. 'Why are the spirits of modern mortals in this chamber?'

'One of them' – Venus paused, studied the orbs and finally pointed at the one closest to her – 'this one, I think, is the spirit of the mortal woman I have chosen to help us out with our Achilles problem. The other is her best friend.'

'Which still doesn't explain why their souls are here in Olympus instead of in their bodies back in the modern mortal world where they belong,' Hera said.

'They can't be in their bodies because their bodies are dead,' Athena said. 'Actually, burned to nothing but ash.'

'Burned? Dead? But how could you choose a burned-up dead mortal for Achilles?' Hera rubbed her temple with one hand; the other she waved gracefully before her, plucking the goblet of ambrosia out of the air when it appeared and taking a long drink of it.

'It's all really very easy to explain,' Venus said, sending Athena a dark look.

'Then explain. Please,' Hera said.

'I chose the mortal woman for Achilles when she was alive. Then there was an accident while she and her friend were leaving a party and, well, they were killed. I simply could not stand it. They were so young and happy. And,' she added pointedly, 'Kat was so completely perfect for Achilles.'

'So you brought their bodiless spirits here?' Hera paused and sighed. 'Venus, I understand how easy it is to get attached to mortals, but you didn't do these women a favor. They should be on their way to the Afterlife that awaits them. There is nothing we can—' Abruptly Hera's voice broke off. A look of shock passed over her lovely face and the goblet of ambrosia slid through her hand to shatter on the marble floor.

'Hera! What is it?' Venus cried as she and Athena rushed to her side.

The goddess's face had gone horribly white. 'My priestesses! They are sobbing for me.'

'Here, sit. Breathe deeply and tell us what has happened.' Venus guided Hera over to a soft chaise as Athena conjured a fresh goblet of ambrosia, which she held to Hera's lips, but the goddess waved the drink away.

'It's the Greeks. They are sacking my temple that rests just outside the westernmost wall of Troy.' She passed a shaky hand over her eyes as if to wipe the image from her mind. Hera looked up at the two goddesses. 'I don't understand this. My temples do not get sacked. I am Goddess of the Home and Hearth, Goddess of Marriage and Family, Queen of Olympians. There is no reason to defile me.' Hera weaved a little like she was going to faint. 'I have to sit down.'

'You are sitting down,' Athena said.

'What do I do?' Sweat broke out over the goddess's too white face. 'My priestesses are beseeching me!'

'I don't know!' Venus sat heavily on the bench next to Hera, took the ambrosia goblet from Athena and drained it in one gulp. 'I'm Goddess of Love. People fornicate in my temples, which I don't consider defilement. Once in a while a bereft lover – a slightly crazy one at that – will hurl himself on his sword, but that really can't be helped.'

'I know what to do.'

Venus and Hera looked up to see Athena putting on the war helmet that had just materialized.

'Do I need to remind you that I am Goddess of War?'

Venus and Hera shook their heads in tandem.

'Then let us go. No one defiles one of our temples and gets away with it.' Athena's hard gray eyes narrowed. 'Or you two could stay here. Zeus will probably be angry that I've become involved.'

Slowly Hera stood. Her knees were clearly unsteady, but her voice was sharp as flint. 'Zeus and his orders to stay out of it be damned! No one who attacks my priestesses will go unpunished.'

Venus and Hera exchanged a glance. 'We're going with you,' said the Goddess of Love. 'If Zeus is going to be angry, let him be angry at all of us.'

'So be it,' Athena said. 'Stay close to me.'

Before the three goddesses disappeared Venus waved her hand in the direction of her oracle and a shimmering circle appeared around it, holding the two spirit orbs safely within its shell.

They materialized in the aftermath of destruction.

'Oh no!' Hera sobbed. Then she straightened her spine and pressed her lips tightly together. 'These are *my* women. I cannot fail them,' the goddess said grimly before beginning to move toward the first of the crumpled bodies.

'Stay with her. I'll deal with the butchers who are still here,' Athena told Venus before striding swiftly from the room toward the distant shrieks and muffled cries that were coming from the exterior of the temple.

Feeling sick to her stomach, Venus joined Hera as she bent over a woman's broken body. As were the rest of the women in this interior room of the temple, the dead mortal was wearing the sky blue linen robes of those who swear to the service of the Queen of Olympus. Venus thought that the fresh scarlet of her blood looked grotesque and a supreme defilement in this temple of Hera's that was usually filled with the soothing colors of pastels, the lovely scent of sweet incense and the music of women's laughing voices.

'She was one of my most elderly priestesses.' Hera's voice was thick with tears. 'She tended this temple for more than forty years.' The goddess touched the dead woman's head. 'Let your journey to the Elysian Fields be swift and peaceful,' she murmured, and the air around them stirred with the power of Hera's prayer. Hera looked at Venus. 'We must bless all of them.'

'Of course.' Venus squeezed her friend and queen's hand, and then the two of them began to make their way from body to body, bestowing on each fallen priestess an eternal blessing for peace and happiness.

It was at the base of Hera's statue in the innermost sanctum that they found them – two young women who had died with their arms wrapped protectively around each other. The dark-haired woman had a ghastly head wound. The blonde who had joined her in death had been skewered through the chest by a sword.

'Sacrilege! Blasphemy!' Hera hissed the words, her sorrow and horror at last being replaced by righteous anger. 'These two aren't even my priestesses. Clearly they were here beseeching my blessing.' The goddess pointed to the spilled goblet of wine and the broken jar of honey that lay discarded and ruined beside their bodies.

'She looks familiar.' Venus pointed to the dark-haired woman. 'Isn't that lovely purple and gold trim on her stola worn only by those of the royal house of Troy?'

'Hera!' Athena's shout interrupted them. The gray-eyed goddess burst into the inner room. She was spattered with blood and carrying a young, blue-robed woman in her arms. The woman groaned and, with a strangled cry, Hera rushed to her, helping Athena to lay her gently on the marble floor. The Queen of Olympus used her lap to pillow the fallen woman's head.

Venus peered down at the woman – and realized she was really only a girl, barely out of puberty. She had a terrible sword slash in her upper arm, which was flooding her and Hera in bright rivulets of fresh blood. Her eyes were closed, but she moaned again, proving she was definitely alive.

'Who did this?' Hera's voice was cold and hard.

'They were Agamemnon's men. This girl told me that most of them had already taken the priestesses of their choice and returned to the Greek camp. I made sure that the few who lingered will be camping in the darkened regions of the Underworld tonight,' she said fiercely.

'We must heal her.'

'Heal her?' Athena frowned.

'Yes, the three of us. We must heal her,' the Queen of Olympus repeated, looking beseechingly at her two friends.

'Did you want us to turn her into a graceful tree or perhaps an ever-flowing fountain to symbolize your weeping?' Athena asked.

'No, I want you to help me *heal* her. She stays as she is.'

'Very unusual,' Athena said. 'We usually save mortals by changing them into something else.'

Venus rolled her eyes. 'You really need to loosen up.' Resolutely she grasped Hera's hand, then held her other hand out for Athena. 'Yes, healing the child is exactly what we will do,' Venus said.

The Goddess of War frowned and muttered, 'This isn't usually how it's done,' but took the goddess's offered hand in hers, and then completed the divine circle by holding Hera's hand, too.

Venus was just composing a lovely healing rhyme in her mind when Hera's angry voice shot out.

'Hear me, Fate. With the power of this goddess circle I do erase this mortal child's wound and command that she survive this brutal attack!'

Venus and Athena gasped as they felt the immediate electric

drain of divine power course through their palms and slam into the girl priestess who still lay with her eyes closed in Hera's lap. The girl's back bowed as her body glowed, and then, just as suddenly as it had happened, the light and power were gone, and with a small cry, the girl sat up. Automatically her hand lifted to feel the ugly wound on her arm – then her eyes widened as she found nothing but healthy, newly healed skin there. Her gaze went immediately to Hera.

'My Goddess!' she cried in a soft, musical voice. 'It is you. I thought I was being granted a beautiful dream before my death.'

Hera smiled and touched the girl's cheek. 'You shall not die today, child. What is your name?'

'Eleithyia,' she said, bowing her head down so that it touched the floor beside Hera. 'Forgive me for not protecting your temple, Great Goddess!'

'Sweet daughter Eleithyia, this desecration is not your fault. I do not expect my priestesses to battle warriors! Arise, child, and have no fear that you have displeased me. I only wish I had known about this defilement sooner so that I could have saved the other priestesses.'

Slowly, the girl raised her head to stare with wide, adoring eyes at Hera. 'We had no warning. For all these years the Greeks have left the temples outside the city walls in peace. There was no reason to believe that they would attack so suddenly.' Eleithyia bit her lip to keep from crying.

'Eleithyia, you said Agamemnon's men stole Hera's priestesses?' Athena said.

The girl bowed her head respectfully to Athena before answering. 'That is what they said, Athena. First they came pretending to be nonviolent. Their leader, Talthybios, said that Agamemnon was angry. His war bride, Khryseis, had been returned to her father, and Achilles refused to part with his own war bride, Briseis, so they were looking for a fair young maiden to take her place and appease their king.'

Athena nodded her head. 'I heard Artemis speaking of this. Khryseis is daughter to one of Apollo's favorite priests. Artemis was so angered by this that she rained darkness and death over the Greek camp until they returned the girl.'

'Artemis and Apollo do get very upset when either has been insulted,' Venus said. 'It's that whole twin mentality.'

'Yes, we all know how touchy the two of them can be,' Hera said impatiently. 'But did you note that the trouble always harkens back to Achilles?' The other two goddesses nodded, in complete agreement once again with their queen. 'Go on, Eleithyia. You were saying that the Greeks came to the temple after Khryseis had been returned to her father,' Hera prompted.

Eleithyia ran a shaky hand over her brow. 'Yes, they were so charming and handsome that, at first, we thought they only jested about coming to take us away, and we laughed with them. Of course we explained to them that those of us sworn to the service of the Great Goddess could not become war-prize brides. They seemed to understand. Then they saw Leis.' She paused. Shuddering she drew a deep breath before she could continue. 'Leis is a great beauty and only recently sworn to your service, Goddess.'

Hera nodded. 'I do, indeed, remember the fair Leis taking her vows.' A shadow crossed the goddess's lovely face. 'But I do not remember seeing her body amongst the dead. Is she here?'

Eleithyia shook her head, tears leaking down her cheeks. 'No. The Greeks took her. We tried to stop them, and the men became outraged that we would reject them. They cut down any of us who got in their way.' The girl's shoulders shook but she forced herself to talk through her sobs. 'They even defiled your inner-most sanctuary, Great Goddess. They found the princess there, and murdered her at the base of your statue.'

'That's why she looked familiar to me. They've killed King Priam's youngest daughter, Polyxena!' Venus said.

Eleithyia nodded. 'The princess's handmaiden, Melia, comes here often to pray for your aid in ending the war so that her mistress's marriage with the young king of Sardis can finally take place. Today Polyxena accompanied Melia to pour libations and burn incense.' Tears flooding her face, Eleithyia looked up at her goddess. 'The Greeks struck the princess with less remorse than they would have cut down one of their horses.'

'What a terrible waste,' Hera said. 'She was so young – had so much of her life yet to live. It couldn't have been Fate's plan to have her leave the mortal realm so soon.'

Venus's sudden gasp had Hera looking questioningly up at her.

'That's it! That's our answer.'

'What ever are you babbling about?' Athena snapped.

'It's perfect, really.' Venus pointed to the inner sanctum. 'There are two bodies right in there. Two lovely, young, *soulless* bodies. And in my temple I just happen to be the proud possessor of two bodiless souls.'

'You're not implying we should—'

'Of course I'm not implying,' Venus interrupted Athena. 'I'm saying outright. We just fixed up Eleithyia's body with no prob-lem. The three of us can certainly do the same to Polyxena and Melia. Then I retrieve the modern mortal souls, place them in the new bodies, and Polyxena becomes Achilles' new war bride.'

'But, Goddess, Achilles already has Briseis for a war-prize bride,' Eleithyia said in her sweet, shy voice.

31

Venus smiled down at her. 'Not after your goddess pays a little visit to Agamemnon, he won't.'

'Me?' Hera said.

'Certainly. You're Goddess of Marriage. You'll simply appear to Agamemnon and tell him that his worries would be so much less if he had his war bride replaced, and you happen to know that Briseis would make the perfect little bride for him.'

'I don't even know the girl. And I certainly cannot stand that wretched Agamemnon and his overbearing arrogance,' Hera said.

'It may just work,' Athena said.

'Of course it will work.' Venus smiled approval at Athena. 'While Hera is appearing to Agamemnon you'll be paying the lovely Thetis a visit. Have her tell her son that she wants him to withdraw from the battle because of the disrespect Agamemnon has shown him in stealing his bride. Then mention as a little aside that she has arranged for a new war bride for him – a royal maiden who meets with her approval because she's not like the typical silly women he's used to. That should intrigue him.'

Athena narrowed her shrewd gray eyes at the Goddess of Love. 'In the meantime you will be readying our Polyxena for the role she will play in this.'

'Exactly. She needs to keep Achilles busy – too busy to consider rejoining the battle. She can also work on that nasty temper of his and perhaps love, or an earthy, lusty version of love, can reach the man inside the beast.' Venus grinned mischievously. 'Let's face it, Zeus prophesized Achilles' early end years ago, then he probably forgot all about it. You know how busy the King of Olympus is. If Achilles himself were to turn from his fated future, Zeus would, more than likely, allow his destiny to change.' Venus grinned at Hera. 'Especially if Zeus's wife were to exert some of her *influence*' – the Goddess of Love purred the word –'on her husband.'

Hera sighed. 'Your plan sounds convoluted, complex and open to errors.'

'Exactly why it is so perfect, darling,' Venus said.'Love is never simplistic, and Love is running this show.'

'May all the gods and goddesses help us,' Athena muttered.

Venus ignored her.'So, do we fix up those bodies for the two souls, or do we just stand here looking beautiful?'

'Let's get to work. I've had more than enough of the Trojan War,' Hera said.

'At least that is something with which all three of us agree,' Athena said.

'Absolutely,' Venus said.

The three goddesses strode into Hera's inner sanctum with the utterly confused Eleithyia trailing after them.

Chapter Three

'I don't know why we have to heal both bodies. The mortal woman you've chosen for Achilles is going to take Polyxena's body. Shouldn't we just send the other on her way to wherever it is dead modern mortals go?' Athena said.

Venus shook her head in disgust. 'Athena, you need more girl-friends. We're going to zap a modern mortal into an ancient princess's body and ask her to do our bidding. Oh, and, by the way, that little memory she has of an accident where she and her best friend are killed? Well, yes, that's unfortunate, but whatever. We needed her, so her best friend is toast. She should just go about our business and forget about her.'

'The problem with that is?' Athena said. 'And what does toast have to do with it?'

Venus rolled her lovely eyes. 'It's just an expression. A modern mortal expression that means done, over with.'

'And the problem with asking one mortal do so something for us without including her friend is that modern mortal women are different than ancient women,' Hera explained patiently. 'They're independent and smart and not used to bowing down and taking orders. Actually, now that I think about it, they're a lot like goddesses.'

'Exactly what I've been trying to tell her,' Venus said.

'I don't think I like that.' Athena frowned.

'I don't think you're going to like the lines that will start appearing on your face if you don't stop frowning so much,' Venus said.

'And I don't think you're going to like what happens if you rouse the anger of the Goddess of War,' Athena said.

'Enough!' Hera's voice shot out, ringing powerfully against the walls of her temple. Then she closed her eyes briefly and drew a deep breath. 'Your bickering is getting in the way of what we must do here. More importantly, it's giving me a headache.' The Queen of the Gods glanced at little Eleithyia, who was cowering in a corner. 'And you're scaring my priestess, who has already had enough stress for one day.'

Venus and Athena muttered apologies.

'Now, let us get this done.' Hera gave the two goddesses one more severe look before turning to Eleithyia. 'We'll need a cere-monial goblet filled with the temple's very best wine. Can you get that for me?'

'Of course, Goddess!' Recovering quickly now that she was given a familiar task, the young priestess scampered off, return-ing only moments later with a golden goblet filled with rich red wine.

'Very good.' Hera nodded her approval. Then she approached the bodies of Polyxena and her maidservant, motioning for Venus and Athena to join her. 'Bring the goblet here, Eleithyia, and stand before the bodies. When I begin the healing spell, raise the goblet so that the wine can be filled with our power. Do you understand?'

'Yes, Goddess.' The young priestess moved into place.

'Let us join in a circle of divine power.' The three goddesses solemnly clasped hands around the fallen princess of Troy and her servant. 'Concentrate on the wine in the goblet,' Hera told them. Then she cleared her throat and recited the spell:

> *'Joined together with a single mind,*
> *goddesses three our powers we do bind.'*

Eleithyia gasped as the wine in the goblet she had lifted above her head began to glow with such a brilliant light that it shined in reflection off the distant domed ceiling of the temple.

> *'Standing here bathed in conjured light,*
> *empower this wine with our combined might.*
> *The gift of healing is what we ask,*
> *fruit of the vine, accept this as your task.'*

'It is hot!' Eleithyia cried, but she didn't let loose her grip on the glowing goblet.

'It is the heat of the breath of life. Quickly, child, pour the wine within the lips of the princess and her servant,' Hera said.

Eleithyia immediately did as her goddess commanded. She bent and carefully poured half of the wine into Polyxena's slack and bloody lips, and the other half into the young maidservant's still mouth.

'I don't know if this is going to work.' Venus frowned as most of the wine ran down the pale cheeks of dead women. 'Maybe we should—'

Polyxena gasped and then drew a deep, almost painful sounding breath. Shortly after, Melia's chest began to rise and fall, too.

'Keep focused,' Hera reminded them before completing the spell.

> *'Wounds mend – health return*
> *the spark of mortal life within them burn!'*

As the goddesses and the priestess watched, the terrible gash on Polyxena's head faded, and then disappeared at the same time Melia's gaping chest wound shimmered and closed so that the two women lay perfectly healed, though the only movement in their eerily still bodies was their slow, steady breathing.

Eleithyia fell to her knees and bowed her head. 'It worked! You have healed them.'

Hera touched her priestess's cheeks softly. 'Only their bodies, child. Their souls are journeying to the Elysian Fields. They are but empty shells.'

'Well, it just so happens that I have two mortal souls in desperate need of shells,' Venus said. 'Shall I get them?'

'Yes, but Athena and I need to make our visits to Agamemnon and Thetis first.'

Athena frowned at the newly healed bodies. 'Shouldn't you do something about all that blood and such before you put the mortal souls in there? I'm no expert on modern mortals, but I do believe that any woman would be quite upset awakening to this mess.' The goddess made a general gesture at the blood-spattered temple.

'Ugh. As much as I hate to admit it, you're right.' Venus sighed. Then she fluttered her fingers absently at Athena and Hera. 'Go on, don't worry about this. I'll conjure some satyrs to take care of it.'

'Satyrs?' Hera said. 'Aren't they rather messy?'

'Of course – nothing makes a mess like a rutting satyr, which is why they're so good at clean-ups. They're used to it.'

Hera and Athena gave Venus twin looks of confusion.

'You don't think I clean up after all those orgies, do you?' Venus shook her head in disgust. 'I'm their goddess, not their mother.'

Athena snorted.

'Let's leave this to Love, shall we?' Hera guided Athena from the room before the goddesses could start bickering again. 'Have the little beasts clean quickly – this shouldn't take long,' she called back over her shoulder.

'Why is it that Love always gets stuck with the mess?' Venus muttered.

'Could it be because love can be so messy?' Eleithyia asked with a sweet, innocent smile.

'Darling, you're obviously new to this whole priestess thing, so I won't blast you into nonexistence for calling me messy.'

Eleithyia gasped and looked like she was going to burst into tears.

Venus sighed. 'Not to worry. That was just a little divine humor. Let's get the satyrs to work, shall we?' The goddess glanced down at the two bodies that awaited souls. 'And while I'm thinking about it I better come up with some new clothes for these two. All that blood will never come out.' She continued to mutter to herself as she conjured an entire herd of industrious satyrs and began putting the temple to order.

Hera materialized within the innermost chamber of Agamemnon's voluminous tents. Except for the young, hairless boy who was oiling the king's dark, perfectly curled hair, they were alone.

'The Goddess Hera!' The boy shrieked and dropped instantly to the ground, pressing his face to the richly carpeted floor. Agamemnon merely bowed – and not low enough for Hera's taste. She pointedly ignored the king and touched the back of the boy's blond head.

'Arise, child. I wish to speak with your king alone, but know that you go with my blessing.' Hera waited until the boy left the room before turning her attention to Agamemnon. She took her time studying him, knowing that it annoyed him to keep his head bowed before her. She noted how he'd swathed himself in gold and had to force herself not to grimace with distaste. Did the man think he was a god?

If so, he was vastly mistaken.

'Arise, Agamemnon. I come with glad news,' Hera finally said.

'Great Goddess, do you bring a message from the mighty Zeus?'

Hera's eyes flashed with anger and her voice sizzled with power so tangible it brushed, crackling, against the arrogant mortal's skin. 'I am not a messenger for my husband!'

This time Agamemnon's bow was low and obsequious and much more appropriate. 'Forgive me! I did not mean to offend the Queen of the Gods.'

Hera curled one lip delicately. 'More's the pity you don't mean offense because it comes so naturally to you. Heed my warning, Greek king, your arrogance will be your doom.' Happily, she saw him pale. 'But, no matter.' She waved her hand graciously, motioning for him to rise. 'The news I bring has to do with your empty bed.' Although Hera remembered the slender, hairless boy and wondered just how empty the king's bed had been.

'Indeed, Goddess, my war prize was returned to appease the golden twins. Though I meant no disrespect by claiming Khryseis, it seems her father disapproved.'

'Khryseis was no good for you. A king should have a worthy prize. Only Briseis is beautiful enough for one such as you.' Silently Hera promised herself that she would look up poor Briseis after this whole debacle was finished and grant the girl a boon to make up for sharing this blustering fool's bed.

'Briseis! She is lovely, but she belongs to Achilles.' The king's expression turned sly. 'Although I hear all that beauty is wasted on him. Achilles frightens maidens.'

Ah, Hera thought, *then the rumors about Achilles are true.* 'Exactly why Briseis would do better with you.'

Agamemnon stroked his thick beard contemplatively. 'True . . . true . . . but still, Achilles—'

'Does Achilles or Agamemnon rule here?' Hera interrupted.

'I rule the Greeks!'

'Then claim the war prize that most suits you,' Hera said.

Agamemnon met the goddess's gaze. 'May I do so with your blessing?'

'Of course. And to help soothe Achilles' well-known rage, I shall arrange for a bedmate to be sent to him. This new war bride will be unlike other women. You should know that she has my very special blessing.'

'I bow to your will, Great Goddess,' Agamemnon said.

'Excellent. Then send your men for Briseis immediately.' While Agamemnon bowed, Hera clapped her hands and disappeared in a rush of glittering blue smoke.

Thetis curtseyed respectfully to Athena. Then, hastily conjuring ambrosia and cushioned chairs made of mother of pearl, she motioned for the gray-eyed goddess to sit.

'Rest yourself, Athena. To what do I owe this—' Her words broke when she realized that the goddess was blood-spattered and hard-eyed. 'By Poseidon's trident! What has happened?'

Athena waved a dismissive hand at the bloodstains, which instantly disappeared. 'It is all because of the tedium of the Trojan War. We have decided it must end.'

Thetis's beautiful face drained of its alluring peach color. 'My son is fated to die in the Trojan War. If it is coming to an end, then so is his life.'

'That is what I'm here to speak with you about. We have an idea that may prove mutually beneficial to all of us. We believe the Trojan War can be ended without your son's death.'

'Anything, Goddess. I will do anything to save my son,' Thetis said, recovering some of her color. Then she added, 'Who is we?'

'Hera, Venus and me.'

Thetis's blue eyes widened. 'Three such powerful goddesses joined with one purpose!'

'Well, it isn't always an easy alliance, but we three do have one thing very much in common – we are well and truly sick of this war.'

'Four,' Thetis said firmly. 'We *four* are allied by this purpose, if there is some way my son can be spared.'

'Tell me, Thetis, is your son still pleased with the choice he made to end his life too soon?' Athena asked.

Thetis chewed her full bottom lip while she considered. 'Achilles won't speak of it directly, but I know him well. Over the past years he has become increasingly unhappy. Did you know he hasn't taken a lover in almost a decade?'

Athena's eyes widened. 'Truly?'

Thetis nodded. 'It's the berserker rage that overtakes him – women are frightened of him because of it. My son would never force himself on a woman, so he lives out the short time that remains to him alone except for his Myrmidons, and even they are becoming leery of him. I can feel my son's sorrow and I believe he keeps moving toward his fate only because the life he's living brings him nothing but loneliness.'

'So this war-prize bride who lives in his tent, she is not his lover?'

'Briseis is a beautiful young woman who is as frightened of my son as all of the rest of them have been, even though he has only treated her with kindness,' Thetis said.

Athena's smooth brow wrinkled in thought. 'But if he's kind to her, you would think that she would eventually accept him.'

'You have never seen the berserker rage possess him, have you?' Thetis asked quietly.

'No.'

Thetis shuddered. 'It is a thing terrible to behold. He is no longer my Achilles when it comes upon him. He becomes a monster, a beast, a physical manifestation of pure rage set only on violence.'

'But the bedroom is not the battlefield.'

'Any strong emotion can bring on the berserker,' Thetis said. She shook her head sadly. 'There is no mortal woman who would be willing to look beyond the rage and see the man, especially now that he has become so battle scarred.'

'Battle scarred?' Athena tried to think when was the last time she had actually seen Achilles, and decided it hadn't been since he was a boy on this very beach. 'But he was beautiful.'

'He used to be, but his victories in battle after battle have come with a price. He is not invulnerable, you know,' Thetis said defensively. 'He is mortal. It is only when his rage is awakened that the berserker claims him.' The sea goddess wiped away a tear that had slipped down her cheek. 'Sometimes it takes a lot for his rage to be awakened, and his body shows the remnants of a young life filled with blood and death.' Thetis dropped to her knees before Athena. 'I beseech you, Athena, as I did the day this horror was placed upon him, help my son break free of his terrible fate.'

Athena took Thetis's hand, pulling her gently to her feet. 'I may be able to finally answer that prayer. Can you get Achilles to withdraw from the fighting, even for just a little while?'

'Without a reason?'

Athena considered for a moment, then asked, 'Achilles is less impetuous than he was as a boy, but is he still as proud?'

'Sadly, I believe he is.'

Athena smiled one of her rare smiles. 'Then I can give you a reason for Achilles to withdraw. Listen carefully . . .'

Chapter Four

'I like the lovely wine color of these robes, don't you? They comple-ment her dark hair well.' Venus arranged the silken drape of the stola that swathed Polyxena's unnaturally still body.

'Anything that brings you pleasure brings me pleasure, Goddess,' said a nearby satyr.

'Yes, darling, I know. That's why I wasn't asking you. Now run along and finish wiping the last of that blood off the floor.' Venus patted the creature's cheek to take the sting from her words. 'Eleithyia, I was asking you.'

'Oh, yes, Goddess. I think the color is beautiful.'

'Then why are you frowning?'

'Well, it's quite, um, unusual that you've arrayed the maidserv-ant in such finery, too.'

Venus smoothed the creamy silk tunic so that the maidserv-ant's blush colored stola wasn't wrinkled. Then she frowned at the little priestess. 'Child, it is true that this is a servant's body, but the soul that is going to reside there is definitely *not* a serv-ant. It's going to be a big enough shock for poor Jacqueline to wake up in a strange body and find out she has to play the part of maid to her best friend.'

'You are, of course, the Goddess. I bow to your intelligence and wisdom and—'

Venus waved away her compliments. 'Bow later. Right now just tell me that the fabric is perfect.'

'The fabric is perfect.'

'Oh, Venus, the satyrs have done a wonderful job setting my temple aright!' Hera bustled in beaming at the randy woodland creatures and making them wriggle with glee.

'I told you they were marvelous,' Venus said, blowing kisses at the beasts closest to her.

'I am surprised that they did such a good job getting out all the blood and gore,' Athena said, materializing not far from Hera.

'And *them*.' Venus gestured grandly in the direction of the two newly cleaned and clothed bodies. 'Don't you think they look lovely, too?'

'The mortals look beautiful, as does my temple. Thank you, Venus, for a job well done,' Hera said.

'They are beautiful, though little but empty shells without souls,' Athena said.

Venus ignored the Goddess of War. 'All went well with Agamemnon?' she asked Hera.

The Queen of the Gods curled her lip in distaste. 'My opinion of that insufferable man hasn't changed one bit. I do feel terribly sorry for poor Briseis.'

'Which means he's going to take her from Achilles?' Athena said.

'Yes.'

'Good. Thetis will take care of nudging her son into withdrawing from the battle. She'll make it a point of pride. Apparently Achilles has matured from the impulsive teenager who chose glory and battle and he is not thrilled with the fate he chose for himself, but he's still typically prideful. Thetis assured me there will be no problem getting him to withdraw, at least for a short time,' Athena said. 'Now all that's left is for your mortal to work her magic and continue to keep Achilles out of the fray long enough for the Trojans to claim victory and then this whole mess will be ended.'

'Don't worry about my mortal. She'll do just fine.'

'Really? Does she speak ancient Greek?' Athena asked pointedly. Venus hesitated only briefly and said, 'She will after I do a little . . .' The Goddess of Love waggled her fingers, causing glitter to form in the air.

Athena snorted.

'Venus, perhaps you could put the souls into the bodies and we could get this business underway?' Hera said.

'Oh, yes! Of course. Satyrs.' Venus clapped her hands commandingly together. 'Return to Olympus. I'll send some Nyseideian nymphs to thank you for aiding me.' The hoofed creatures cheered as they disappeared. 'All right. Stand back. Give me room to work.' The Goddess of Love smoothed her long blonde hair and then raised her hands, palms up. 'I call the mortal spirits I recently made free – Katrina and Jacqueline, I command you come to me!'

Two glowing orbs popped into the air and floated to rest on Venus's open palms.

'First I gift you with the language you must know, so that as soon as you're here you'll be ready to go. So now is the time to begin the task I ask of you – ensoul these bodies that you may complete the job Love would have you do!'

Venus threw the glowing orbs at the bodies like she was a major league pitcher.

Kat gasped and choked. She sat up coughing and rubbing a hand across her forehead. Jacky moaned and pressed her hands to her chest in the exact place her wound had been.

'Oh, god, I feel like utter crap,' Kat said. 'How much champagne did I drink, anyway?' She cleared her throat and blinked her eyes. 'What's wrong with my voice and where the hell—' Her words broke off as her vision cleared. She stared, wide-eyed, at three gorgeous women who where watching her like she was a new species of flower that had just bloomed.

'Kat, I think I'm having a heart attack.' Jacky moaned again. 'Since when do hangovers feel like heart attacks?'

Kat pulled her vision from the three ridiculously attractive women and turned to look at the person who lay beside her and who was talking like Jacky, but didn't sound anything like her and . . .

'Holy fucking shit! Jacqueline? Is that you?'

The beautiful blonde blinked several times, trying to clear her vision, and continued to rub her chest. 'Who else would it be, the goddamn Easter Bunny? Why do you sound wrong? God, am I going deaf, too?'

'Have no fear, Jacqueline and Katrina. You are safe and well and under our protection,' said the woman who was standing closest to them, and was probably the most stunning of the three.

Kat closed her eyes and took several deep breaths. 'Drunken hysterical dream. I'll never drink that much champagne again. Promise. Time to wake up now and deal with my horrendous hangover.' She opened her eyes.

'You are not dreaming, mortal woman,' said the regal looking woman in flowing white robes trimmed in sky blue.

Then the statuesque woman with the unusual gray eyes stepped forward and spoke. 'We have altered your fate. Instead of allowing you to perish in the modern world we have plucked your souls from your shattered bodies and brought you to the ancient world. You may thank us.'

The woman who had spoken first frowned severely at the gray-eyed woman. 'Give it a rest, Athena. They don't need to thank us. It's not like they asked for this. And besides that, the whole abasing yourself before the gods thing doesn't work in the modern mortal world.'

'This isn't the modern mortal world,' snapped the gray-eyed woman.

'Really? I hadn't noticed. I thought—'

'Okay, what the fuck?' Jacqueline said, sitting up.

'Jacky?' Kat ignored the bickering women and turned to face her friend.

'Kat? Is that you in there?'

'Yeah, it is.'

'But you're not you. I mean, you're *nothing like* you. And what the hell are you wearing?' Jacky reached out to touch a drape of the burgundy-colored robe and her eyes became riveted on her hand. 'Katrina Marie Campbell, what is going on? Why. Is. This. My. Hand!'

'We can explain everything,' said the regal woman. She nodded to the most gorgeous one. 'Go ahead, Venus; explain everything.'

'Well, it's really quite simple. You two got in a horrid accident after you left your girlfriend party. I'd been watching you through my oracle.' She paused and smiled. 'I am Venus, Goddess of Sensual Love, Beauty and the Erotic Arts.' She pointed to the gray-eyed woman. 'This is Athena, Goddess of War, blah, blah.' Then she gestured to the regal woman. 'And this is Hera, Queen of Olympus. Anyway, as I was saying, I'd been watching you through my oracle and I witnessed your accident. I just couldn't let you die like that, so I snatched up your souls. Not long after that, Hera's temple was defiled and Polyxena, Princess of Troy, and her, uh, maidservant, Melia, were killed. So we did some

48

quick thinking, quick healing, and quick re-ensouling. And here you are – yourselves, but in different bodies. See, I told you it was really quite simple.'

'I–I–I—' Kat sputtered.

'I'm *white*!' Jacqueline sprang to her feet, staring down at her new body. 'Oh, Jesus god-fucking-bless America! Jesus! Jesus! I feel faint. My heart! Kat! I'm dying!' She reached out blindly and Kat hurried to her side, gripping her hand.

'You're not dying. We're dreaming. That's all.'

'Why in the goddamn hell would I dream I'm white?' Jacky cried as she clutched Kat with one hand and fanned herself with the other. 'My heart, lord, my heart. The pain!'

'Darlings, I told you that you're not dreaming,' Venus said.

'What is wrong with being white?' Athena asked.

'It's a drunken nightmare,' Kat said, trying to stay calm and use her best counselor's voice. 'We'll wake up in a second and find out that we passed out in your living room, again. Remember last New Year's?'

Venus stepped up to Kat and Jacky. She sighed heavily. 'I didn't want to do this, but you need to accept what has happened.' She waggled her slender fingers until the air began to glow with diamond dust and then she flicked the dust at them saying, 'Remember . . .'

Kat breathed in the sparkling dust with Jacky, sneezed, and was suddenly taken back to the aftermath of Susie's party. As if watching a macabre play, she saw the two of them stumble, laugh, and hold onto each other as she and Jacky got into the cab. The cab drove down Reservoir Hill to the four-way stop. Horrified, Kat saw an SUV run the stop sign and smash into them. There was a soundless pause, then with an awful whooshing the cab burst into flames.

'Oh, god! We're dead!' Kat said.

'We're dead and I'm white!' Jacky said. 'This just can't be right. I was sure I was going to heaven.'

'Well, me, too. I'm supposed to be going to heaven, too.'

'I dunno 'bout that, Kat. Remember your sorority girl days? The TU quarterback on the fifty-yard line? That kind of behavior adds up. That's all I'm sayin'.'

Kat's mouth dropped open. 'Take that back! I cannot believe you think I'm going to hell because of a few college indiscreetnesses.'

'Indiscreetnesses? Is that even a word? And you're not just goin' to hell – you sucked me down here with you.'

'Jacqueline, did it ever occur to you that *you* may have gotten *me* sucked down to hell? What about all those times you returned shoes? You said you never wore them but you really paid way more than you could afford and then wore them a few times and *then* returned them. Huh? How about that?'

'Oh, please. You know shoes are never a sin. And besides, I haven't done that in years.'

'Years?'

'Okay, months.'

Kat snorted and put her hands on her hips. 'And what about *your cursing?*' she said decisively.

'I don't curse. I use expletives.'

'You use what? That is such a load of—'

'Ladies!' Venus stepped between them. 'No one is in hell. You're dead, but you're not dead.' The goddess frowned and shook her head as if she needed to clear it. 'No, it's not as confusing as that. Your bodies are dead. Your souls live on. They're eternal. They're the essence that is really *you*. All I did was to zap them into bodies that are now working.'

'*Now* working? Where are the eternal souls that *were* in these bodies?' Kat said.

Venus looked uncomfortable and in the silence Hera stepped in. 'You, Katrina, are now dwelling in the body that did belong to Princess Polyxena of Troy. You, Jacqueline, are now dwelling in the body that did belong to Melia, her maidservant.'

'I'm a fucking maid! A white maid! Jesus lord, it just keeps getting worse and worse.' She looked blearily at Kat. 'I really did get sucked into hell with you.'

'I am *not* in hell,' Kat said.

'Neither of you are in hell,' Venus said quickly.

'Where are the souls that were in these bodies?' Kat asked her again.

Hera answered before Venus could. 'They are enjoying eternal happiness in the Elysian Fields of the ancient Greek Underworld.'

'Oh, lord, let me sit down. I'm in a dead white servant girl's body.' Jacky sat heavily on the steps of the altar, fanning herself again.

Kat was staring down at her body in horror. 'But I don't see any wounds. What did she die of?'

'Oh, lord! An awful plague? Kat, we're plague-some.'

'No, no, no,' Venus hastily reassured them. 'They didn't die of any illness. They were killed by Greek warriors.'

'Then where are the wounds?' Kat looked inside her robes, turning this way and that trying to see all of her body.

'We healed them before we re-ensouled the bodies with you,' Venus said.

'Now that's the first good news I've heard,' Jacky said, recovering enough to stop fanning herself. 'So just heal our old bodies and send us back. We'll forget any of this ever happened.'

'I'm sorry. I can't do that. Your bodies were completely burned.

51

I took your souls only because I'd already decided to ask you, Kat, to do a small favor for me.'

'Okay, let's see if I have this right,' Kat said. 'You were somehow spying on me—'

'And me,' Jacky inserted.

'And Jacky,' Kat continued, 'because you wanted me to do something for you, but then we died and you grabbed us? This makes no sense whatsoever.'

'Of course it does darling,' Venus said. 'Although I certainly don't think of my oracle as spying. Hera, Athena and I decided we needed the aid of a modern mortal woman. I was given the task of finding her. You seemed perfect. Then the tragic accident happened, but you still seemed perfect. At the same time Hera's temple was being sacked – two bodies became available – a little zapping here, a little healing there, and here you are, decidedly *not* dead and still perfect for the little task I need you to perform. And darlings' – Venus included the scowling Jacky in her brilliant smile – 'I'm going to grant you each a boon for aiding me.'

'The only boon we're interested in is being put back into our old bodies,' Jacky said firmly. 'And that doesn't mean nasty old burned-up dead bodies. We want to be put back into cleaned-up healed bodies.' She glanced down. 'Like these, only ours.'

'Ditto,' Kat said.

'It is simply not possible,' Venus said. 'Your bodies are beyond even our powers to heal. I'm sorry, but—' Venus began but Hera interrupted her.

'You may not have your old bodies back, but between the three of us we can find comparable vessels in your old world,' Hera said.

'Can comparable mean younger and better looking?' Kat asked.

'*And* we want final approval,' Jacky added.

'As you wish. If you perform the little task we ask of you, and it is your wish, we will return you to the modern world in mortal bodies of your choice.'

Jacky and Kat exchanged glances, turned their backs on the goddesses and put their heads together. 'Wonder how Queen Latifah's feelin'? Maybe she has some kind a terrible wasting disease the goddesses could hurry up,' Jacky whispered hopefully.

'I was just wondering the same thing about Catherine Zeta-Jones,' Kat said, keeping her voice low. 'So we'll go for it?'

'Yep,' Jacky said.

They faced the goddesses again. 'Okay, fine. All we need to do is this thing for you guys, and you'll put us back where we belong in the bodies of our choice. Right?' Kat said.

'Yes,' the three goddesses said.

'So what is this thing you need us to do?' Jacky asked.

'Simple. We want you to end the Trojan War,' Venus said.

'Jesus lord! You did take me with you to hell, Kat.'

Chapter Five

'Jacky, I think you may be right,' Kat said, plopping down next to her on the altar step. 'You know, we were just talking about *The Iliad* at Susie's house. Clearly our tragic deaths have happened and we've been thrown into some kind of literary hell. The next thing you know we'll be sucked into a fucking Thomas Hardy book.'

'Thomas Hardy? My god! The pain!' Jacky fanned herself furiously.

'Shit, I'm sorry I got you into this. Shtuping the TU quarterback definitely wasn't worth it.'

'Well, I knew having a white best friend would cause me some shit eventually.' Jacky held her very slender, very white arm out despondently. 'I just didn't know it would be this bad.'

'Again I would like to ask, what is so terrible about being white?' Athena said.

'Nothing, if you are white,' Jacky said. 'But I'm not.' She sighed. 'Or at least I wasn't before I went to hell.'

'By Zeus's beard they are exceedingly stubborn,' Athena said to Venus. 'You didn't tell us about that.'

'I told you they're different than ancient mortals. This is just part of it.'

'Hello! Right here – in hell – with you,' Kat said. Then she turned to Jacky. 'I wonder what they did to get sent to hell?'

'They're gorgeous. Women that gorgeous are always pissing someone off,' Jacky said.

'Oh, yeah, you're right. Forgot about that.'

'Are they saying that we've angered people? We're goddesses. We don't anger people; they anger us,' Athena said. She gave Venus a severe look. 'Tell them.'

'Uh, we can hear you,' Jacky said.

'Jacqueline! Katrina! You are *not* in hell. Stop this nonsense at once. And ending the Trojan War won't be that difficult. We already have a plan of action figured out for you,' Venus said.

'Hey, aren't these the three goddesses who caused the whole Helen/Paris thing?' Jacky said. 'You know, the wedding, the apple, the giving already-married Helen to Paris and whatnot.'

'Huh. I think you're right,' Kat said.

'Do you see how long that ridiculous rumor has lasted?' Venus told Hera. Then she turned back to the two mortals. 'That is exactly why we've had enough of the Trojan War. *We*' – she gestured at Athena and Hera – 'did not start this war, and we're sick and tired of being blamed for it.'

'So typical for that wretched Agamemnon to blame others,' Hera muttered.

'What Venus, Hera and I have decided is that this war has gone on far too long. We want it stopped. Now,' Athena said.

'And why do ya think Kat and I could help you with that?' Jacky asked.

'Yeah, sounds like you need to zap some scientists here so they could whip up a lovely weapon or two of mass destruction—'

'As if those can actually ever be found,' Jacky input.

'As if,' Kat agreed. 'But if you're thinking we can do something like that you've definitely got us mixed up with someone else.'

'Hey, and bringing modern weapons to the ancient world sounds like it'd be messin' with the Prime Directive or somethin',' Jacky said.

'God, you are such a dork,' Kat said. 'This is hell, not *Star Trek*. Although the two do have some odd similarities.'

'See, it's blasphemy like that that got you in this situation.'

'Achilles!' Venus blurted. Both mortals turned questioning looks on her. 'Achilles is the key to the war going on and on. If he and his Myrmidons withdraw from the battlefield the Greeks won't be able to sustain the siege of Troy. They'll lose heart and go home where they belong.'

'Again, not understanding what this has to do with us,' Kat said.

'Actually, it has to do with *you*, Katrina,' Hera said, though she gave Jacky an apologetic look. 'Your friend is here because Venus didn't think the two of you would want to be separated.'

'I told you so!' Jacky said.

'Shit,' Kat said. 'I need a drink.'

'Excellent idea.' Venus looked around the chamber until she spied Eleithyia where she was sitting wide-eyed in a dark alcove. 'Darling, would you get us all some wine. It is a rather long story.' The little priestess darted from the room and Venus drew a deep breath. 'Now, let me explain everything to you . . .'

'No way is that plan gonna work,' Jacky said.

'Of course it will work,' Venus said.

'Come on, get serious. Who ever heard of a therapist saving the world? That didn't even happen in *Buffy*,' Jacky said.

'What is a buffy?' Athena asked.

'I'm starting to believe this might not be hell,' Kat said. 'You know they know who Buffy is in hell.'

'You have a point,' Jacky said. 'By the by, may I just mention that your Buffy comment is every bit as dorky as my love for *Star Trek*.'

56

'No, you up dork me because you're into both of them.'

'I wasn't until Spike got all delicious with that nasty sex. God, I'd really like to make him pop like a champagne cork,' Jacky said.

'What is a buffy?' Athena asked Venus again.

Venus shrugged. 'You can't expect me to know *everything* about modern mortals.' The goddess took a long, fortifying drink of wine before continuing. 'Kat, will you help us with our plan?'

Katrina chewed her bottom lip. 'Basically you want me to do a super-duper counseling session with Achilles to help him control his rage while I keep him from fighting.'

'Sounds like they want you to do a super-duper shtuping session with him, too,' Jacky said.

Venus ignored her. 'As I explained, Thetis, the mother of Achilles, has already put into motion his withdrawal from the battlefield.'

'Because his woman, uh Briseis, was taken away from him. And you want me to take her place.'

'Yes,' Venus said.

'Whose place am I taking?' Jacky asked.

'No one's, darling,' Venus said. 'You are simply Polyxena's maidservant.'

'Oh, Jesus fucking everlasting god. I almost forgot. Where is that little wine girl? I definitely need a refill.'

Eleithyia hurried to top off Jacky's goblet.

'Answer me this, Goddess of Love,' Kat said while Jacky drank. 'Achilles' woman just got taken away from him. If that pissed him off enough that he was willing to stop fighting why in the world would you believe that he'd be interested in moving on to another woman? I mean, it sounds like he had a thing for the old one.'

'It wasn't a love relationship,' Venus said. 'Achilles' pride was hurt by Briseis being taken, not his heart.'

'How can you be so sure?' Jacky asked.

'Agamemnon told me that Briseis's beauty was wasted on Achilles,' Hera said.

'Great. Kat, he's gay,' Jacky said.

'Gay?' Athena looked utterly confused.

'Achilles is not gay,' Venus said.

'Gay?' Athena repeated, tapping her foot in annoyance.

'It means he only shtups other men,' Jacky explained.

'Shtups means fu—'

'I understand what *that* means,' Athena said. 'And I agree with Venus. Achilles is not gay. But he hasn't taken a lover in many years, so Briseis was definitely not his lover.'

'How do you know that?' Venus said.

'His mother told me,' Athena said.

'Why no lover?' Kat asked.

'Oh, that's easy to explain,' Athena said. 'He frightens maidens.'

'Why?' Jacky asked, looking more than a little alarmed.

'The berserker rage scares them. Apparently it comes upon him when a passionate emotion is aroused – be it lust or anger,' Athena said.

'Yes, and maidens from the ancient world are not equipped to handle such a man, but I know that modern mortal women are different – stronger, smarter, more independent. Also, I heard you say that you counsel men as part of your living. That's why I chose you.' Venus finished with a big smile for Kat.

'Well, it's not just men I counsel. Actually it's mostly couples whose marriages are in trouble.'

Venus waved her hands dismissively. 'It's all the same. I also heard you described as very optimistic. And you said that you like men. See, you're perfect for this job.'

'And she says she wasn't spying on you,' Jacky said.

Athena suddenly added, 'Thetis mentioned something about Achilles' horribly scarred visage frightening maidens, too.'

'I didn't know Achilles was scarred,' Venus said.

'Neither did I,' Hera said.

Athena shrugged. 'Apparently they're battle scars. Thetis said the berserker rage hasn't always come upon him easily.'

'Well, that could be a good thing. It shows that he needs a trigger to make it happen. If I can get him to identify the trigger, then maybe he can disarm it,' Kat said. 'Sounds like Anger Management 101.'

'Interesting . . . You do not seem troubled by the fact that he is scarred,' Athena said.

Jacky answered before Kat could. 'As Venus keeps tellin' you, modern women are different. It takes more than a few scars to put us off.'

'I'd like to think that I have the ability to see beyond the physical,' Kat said.

'Ditto,' Jacky said. Then she pointed down at her body. 'Present company excepted. God, do I have to be wearing pink? I hate pink.'

'It looks good on you, though. You really are very pretty, Jacky,' Kat said.

'Pretty white,' Jacky muttered.

'No, really. Is there a mirror around here?' she asked Venus.

'Eleithyia, darling, could you bring us a lovely looking glass?'

The priestess hurried off and returned quickly with a medium-sized round mirror, framed in bronze. Kat took it from her and held it so Jacky could look at herself.

'See?'

Jacky's eyes got huge. Her hands went up to her hair. 'My dear sweet baby Jesus, I have *tresses*. Long, flowing, curling, blonde *tresses*.'

'They're pretty,' Kat said.

'They're fucking overwhelming. You know I have not one clue how to take care of white girl hair. Especially not this much white girl hair.'

'Oh, darling, don't worry yourself about that. I can help you. I'm an expert.' Venus shook back her head, causing her own amazing tresses to bounce and shimmer.

'I'm not in hell. I'm trapped in a romance novel,' Jacky said. Then she leaned closer to the mirror. 'And my eyes are absolutely sky blue.'

'Well, look at it like this,' Kat said. 'If we're trapped in a romance novel that means we're going to be having sex. Probably lots of sex.'

'Think so?' Jacky said hopefully. 'It'd be nice if it was an erotica novel.'

'One can only hope,' Kat said. Then she took a deep breath and turned the mirror so she could look at herself. 'Oh!' Slowly, she touched her face. 'Holy shit, how old am I? I look like a teenager.'

'And you, too, have some tresses,' Jacky said. 'Although they're black, and not as stunning as mine.'

'I thought black was good,' Athena said.

'I'll never understand them,' Hera whispered.

'Seriously, how old was Polyxena?' Kat asked, still staring at herself.

'I believe she was approaching eighteen summers,' Hera said. 'Prime marrying age, which is why she was here petitioning my aid. She wanted to be betrothed to the King of Sardis.'

'Good god, eighteen! That's way too young,' Kat said.

'You are unmarried, are you not, Katrina?' Hera asked politely.

'Totally unmarried,' Kat said.

'Me too,' Jacky said.

'And how old were the two of you?' Hera said.

'I'm thirty-six,' Kat said. 'Or at least I was.'

'You're such a baby, Kat. I'm thirty-eight,' Jacky told Hera. Then she frowned and stuck her face close to Kat's so she could look at her reflection again. 'Huh. I look young, too. No way are we even twenty.'

'Spinsters?' Hera said, clearly appalled. 'You chose spinsters?'

'As I have said more times than I should have had to: Modern mortal women are *different*,' Venus said.

Reflected in the mirror, Jacky's and Kat's gazes met.

'Unattractive old spinster,' Kat said.

'Dried up old hag,' Jacky said.

And both women burst into gales of laughter.

Chapter Six

'Oh, god, we are funny,' Kat said, leaning against Jacky, who was still giggling and wiping her eyes.

'Will you help us?' Venus asked.

Kat looked up at the goddess. 'What if I do my best, it doesn't work with Achilles, and he goes back to fighting? My mythology is shaky, but everyone knows he was a famous warrior who was killed because an arrow pierced his heel, the only place he wasn't invulnerable. He lived to fight and he died fighting.'

Venus rolled her eyes. 'His heel is the only place he's vulnerable?'

'Rumors,' Hera said, shaking her head. 'More incredibly annoying rumors.'

'So the heel thing isn't true?' Jacky said.

'It makes no sense whatsoever,' Athena said. 'How could piercing his heel kill him, or anyone? Modern mortals will believe anything.'

'Hello! It was written by people back in *your* day – not by us. The tendon that runs behind the heel was even named after him. A long time ago,' Kat said.

'Hey, what about that Trojan horse thing?' Jacky asked. The goddesses turned blank looks to her. 'The stupid war was won when, uh . . .'

'When the Greeks snuck inside the walls of Troy hiding

inside a humongous hollow horse,' Kat finished for her. 'Or something like that.'

Venus shook her head. 'First we started the war. Then Achilles can only be killed though his ankle. Now there's a huge horse that wins the war? It just gets more and more ridiculous. No,' she said firmly. 'None of that is true.'

'Okay, so basically even the meager details Jacky and I can remember from our waste-of-time humanities classes are bullshit.'

'Sounds like it,' Venus said.

'All right. So what is the truth? Achilles is not invulnerable, but he is a warrior. That part is right. Right?'

'Achilles isn't immortal, but the berserker rage makes him extraordinarily difficult to kill. And, yes, he has been a warrior his entire short life.'

'Oh, god, tell me he isn't a teenager, too,' Kat said.

'No, he isn't quite thirty. It was prophesied by Zeus that if Achilles chose a life of glory and battle he would not live to see thirty summers, but he would be remembered for thousands of years.'

'What? *Achilles* chose this? Then I don't know what you expect me to do,' Kat said.

'He made the choice when he was a boy. He has grown and changed since then. Thetis says Achilles tires of his childish decision and longs for peace, but his fate seems set and he has lost hope of changing the path he is on,' Athena said.

'Okay,' Kat said slowly. 'I'll try to help Achilles. But only on the condition that, win or lose, help or not, Jacky and I are sent back to *our* world.'

'In the kick ass bodies of our choice,' Jacky added.

'If you succeed in ending the Trojan War, you will each be granted one boon.'

'Hera.' Kat faced the Queen of Olympus. 'It really isn't fair of you to expect me to swoop in and fix a guy I've never met before in a situation that is more than a little outside my normal realm of expertise.'

'Nevertheless, that is the deal we offer,' Hera said. 'And keep this in mind – the more days that pass since your unfortunate accident, the more difficult it will be for us to seamlessly weave you back into your old lives.'

'So you can't even guarantee what you say you're guaranteeing?'

'I can guarantee that we will use all of our vast powers to attempt to do so,' Hera said.

Kat looked from the Queen of Gods to Venus. The Goddess of Love was decidedly unhappy about Hera's 'deal,' but she shrugged and shook her head sadly, making it obvious she couldn't do anything about changing her queen's mind.

'Fine,' Jacky spoke up. 'Kat will take care of business, and she'll do it quickly, no problem. You, Miss High and Mighty, just keep your end of the deal.'

'I always keep my word,' Hera said.

'Then we're set,' Kat said.

'Not entirely,' Venus said. 'I think it needs to be made clear that they are under divine protection.'

'Agreed,' Hera said.

'I, too, agree,' Athena said.

'Good. It's your protection they're going to be under,' Venus said to Athena.

'Why mine?'

'Well, it can't be me because, according to Greek rumors, I caused the whole Paris/Helen problem. It can't be Hera because she just told Agamemnon to take Briseis from Achilles. You're

64

the only one left. Plus, you have a history with Odysseus, as well as Thetis, who will have told her son that *you* assured her his war-prize bride would be replaced. So Polyxena has to be under your protection,' Venus said.

'Yes, well, I suppose you're correct,' Athena said reluctantly.

'You know, I'm not sure that I like the sound of "war-prize bride." I'm no prude, but I choose who I sleep with. And besides that, I'm no one's property,' Kat said.

'Ditto,' Jacky said.

'Thetis assured me that her son will not force himself on a woman,' Athena said.

'Okay, well, that still leaves the issue of me being his property.'

Athena's smooth brow furrowed in confusion. 'You are a woman and a war prize. You *are* his property.'

Kat's hands went to her hips. 'I am no one's property.'

'Being Achilles' property will help to keep you safe, and keep you with Achilles,' Venus said.

'Hey, whose property am I?' Jacky asked.

'Polyxena's,' Venus said.

'Shit,' Jacky said.

'There will have to be an explanation to cover their oddness,' Hera said, giving Jacky a stern look.

'You are right, of course,' Athena said, studying Jacky and Kat as she spoke. 'Their strange ways will be noticed.'

'You could say that Kat is your instrument, that you have imbued her with sacred knowledge,' Hera said.

'That's it! Imply that she's an oracle; they're always behaving oddly,' Venus said.

'That explains Katrina, but what about her?' Hera pointed her chin at Jacky.

'Sweet baby Jesus I'm right here! God, it's annoying when you talk about me like I've gone all deaf and dumb,' Jacky said. 'Besides, I do not behave oddly.'

No one said anything for several breaths, then Kat sighed. 'How about this – I'm a bizarre oracle, so it's really not a stretch that my serv—' She caught the killer look in Jacky's eyes and corrected hastily, 'That my circle of friends would be bizarre, too.'

'That is not entirely believable,' Athena said slowly.

'But all we have,' Venus said. 'All right,' she told Kat, 'just make it work.'

'Hang on. I thought we were going to be under Athena's protection. So why do we have to explain anything?' Jacky said.

'You will be under my protection, but I cannot stay with you.'

'Then how the hell will you protect us?' Jacky said.

'You will beseech my aid,' Athena said.

'Or mine,' Venus said.

'Or mine,' Hera said, even though she was still frowning at Jacky.

'Sounds weak to me,' Jacky said.

'But it's all you have,' Venus said.

Jacky snorted and opened her mouth to comment, but men's voices coming from outside the temple interrupted her. Athena waved one hand quickly in the air and it was as if a secret view screen opened, showing half a dozen warriors entering the temple.

Kat only caught a brief glimpse of a golden man who walked in the lead before Athena closed the view.

'It's Achilles.' Eleithyia sounded a little short of breath. 'I've only seen him from a distance, but his golden armor is unmistakable.'

Kat's stomach instantly knotted. Jacky took her hand and squeezed.

'It's gonna be okay. You're one hell of a therapist. And, might I add, currently one very hot young chippie.'

'Versus the very hot old chippie I used to be?'

'Exactly, but you still got the old chippie up there.' Jacky pointed to Kat's head. 'And there.' She pointed from her head to her heart. 'Berserker boy doesn't stand a chance.'

'Okay, let's do this,' Kat told Venus.

Venus smiled warmly at her. 'Remember, the Goddess of Love believes you are perfect. You and your delightful friend.' Then she turned to Hera. 'We must leave. Athena should face the warriors and establish her protection. Our presence would only confuse things.'

Athena nodded. 'I shall meet with you in Venus's temple momentarily.'

'Go with my blessing, odd modern mortals,' Hera told Kat and Jacky, then she kissed Eleithyia gently on her forehead. 'You, my little priestess, have pleased me greatly today.'

As Eleithyia curtseyed deeply, Hera and Venus disappeared in a shower of glitter.

'It's really kinda cool that they can do that,' Jacky said. 'And you know what? I'm starting to believe them. We might not be in hell.'

'I like your erotica novel theory better anyway,' Kat said.

'Gird yourselves, mortals, and follow me,' Athena commanded before striding regally from the chamber.

Kat and Jacky rolled their eyes at each other and then, waving their good-byes to Eleithyia, they followed the goddess.

The warriors had just reached the center of the outer chamber of Hera's temple, which had no real walls but was ringed by graceful marble columns and open to the sky. Kat was distracted from the men by the world that surrounded them. It was an amazingly beautiful day – clear and warm. The air smelled of the sea and sweet incense.

'If this is hell, it's gorgeous,' Jacky whispered, gripping Kat's hand even tighter.

The men caught sight of them, or more specifically, Athena, and Kat didn't have any more time for the scenery.

'The Goddess! It is the Goddess, Hera!' One warrior cried and the half dozen or so men all fell to their knees.

Actually, Kat noted that all of the men, except two, were kneeling. The taller of the two had his back to the sun and the slant of the afternoon rays made it difficult for Kat to see him well. She just got an impression of lots of hair and muscles and height. The other man was closer to the goddess and Kat was able to get a good look at him. The guy was fairly ordinary looking – average height, brown hair, nice body (which could be easily seen in the short leather tunic thing he was wearing). There was nothing remarkable about him at all until he spoke, and then Kat was instantly attracted to his cultured, intelligent voice and his eyes that sparkled with wit. He walked to within just a couple feet of the goddess before he sank to one knee, but he didn't bow his head in supplication as were the rest of the kneeling men. Instead he pressed his right fist over his heart and smiled with obvious affection up at Athena. His first words were spoken so softly that had Kat not been standing beside the goddess she would not have heard him.

'Hail Athena, my Goddess. It has been long since you have appeared to me and I have missed you dearly.'

'It is right that you miss me, Odysseus. The price of being

beloved of a goddess is that you are subject to her whims, not she to yours as with a mortal woman.'

Athena's voice was sharp, but Kat was shocked to see how amazingly tender the goddess's expression had become as she gazed down at him.

'Foolish Myrmidons!' The tall man barked in a deep, gruff voice at the other warriors. 'How could you mistake Athena, Goddess of War, for Hera?' He stepped forward to kneel beside Odysseus and bowed his head respectfully. 'Hail Athena! Forgive my men. Their brains have been addled by Trojan sea and sun. They meant no disrespect.'

'I forgive them, Achilles. You and Odysseus may rise.'

Achilles! His name shivered against Kat's skin. Then he stood and lifted his face.

Her first thought was that she understood why he scared maidens. Her second was that she wondered how, in this ancient world without penicillin and blood transfusions, he had ever lived through so many wounds. Kat kept her expression carefully neutral. She heard Jacky's muffled *'huh'* from beside her, but knew the ER nurse's reaction wasn't shock or fear, but that she also had to be wondering how the hell he'd survived such horrible injuries.

Kat needn't have worried about fixing the expression on her face. Achilles didn't have so much as a glance for anyone except Athena.

'By your presence here I assume Thetis has spoken to you,' Athena said.

'She has, Goddess,' Achilles said.

'Agamemnon has taken your war prize.'

Even though Athena didn't frame the words as a question Achilles gave a tight nod and said a clipped, 'He has.'

Kat noticed that the men behind him scowled at this and stirred restlessly.

'Then I shall replace that which you lost. I bring to you Polyxena, Princess of Troy, Daughter of Priam!'

Athena made a grand gesture and stepped aside. Achilles' gaze turned to her and Kat thought her feet had grown roots and sunk into the marble floor of the temple. *He had the most incredibly blue eyes!*

Jacky coughed, and as she covered her mouth managed to push Kat forward.

'Princess Polyxena, greet Achilles, Leader of the Myrmidons,' Athena prompted.

Thankfully, Kat managed to put on her therapist face. She smiled politely and, in a perfectly modulated, perfectly calm, perfectly fake voice said, 'Hello, Achilles. It's nice to meet you. I've heard a lot about you.' Then she walked purposefully forward and, still smiling, held her hand out to him.

Achilles hesitated. He looked from her hand to her face and then back down at her hand again. Kat kept the smile plastered on and the hand hanging out there in the breeze. Finally he took it, gingerly, and bowed quickly over it as if he would kiss her, but stopped well before his lips touched her skin. Then he dropped her hand and took a quick half step back.

'I greet you, Princess,' he said, but his gaze had already shifted back to Athena.

'I must return to Olympus. Achilles and Odysseus, let me make it clear that Polyxena is unique. She will never be a normal war prize – she is much more. I have decided to imbue her with sacred knowledge. Think of her as you would my beloved oracle. She and her maidservant are under my protection. Anyone who would dare harm them shall invoke my eternal wrath.' Athena raised her voice so that the power in it brushed physically against the kneeling men.

'We understand, Goddess,' Achilles said.

'Be sure you keep her safe,' Athena said. 'Odysseus, a word.'

The goddess motioned for Odysseus to follow her out of hearing range, leaving Kat and Achilles standing awkwardly together. Kat wanted to stare at him. Of course staring was what all women probably did when they first met him. Or they wouldn't look at him at all. Just like she wasn't looking at him at all. God, she was acting like an idiot. Resolutely Kat looked at Achilles to find him staring over her shoulder at nothing with his jaw clenched.

He must hate first meetings like this, she thought.

Kat cleared her throat and, almost reluctantly it seemed, Achilles' gaze met hers.

'Achilles, I'd like to introduce you to my servant,' Kat stumbled just a little over the word. 'This is, uh, Melia,' she blurted, almost forgetting her best friend's new name.

Jacky stuck her chin in the air and made a weird little half-curtsey, half-bow. 'Pleased,' she said.

Ignoring Jacky completely, Achilles said, 'You would *introduce* me to your slave?'

'Well, yes,' Kat said.

'Jesus god, it's like I'm not here again,' Jacky muttered.

'Highborn!' Athena's commanding voice made all of them jump. The goddess walked briskly back to them. 'Melia was highborn – a princess in her own land before she was abducted and sold to Troy. Polyxena has chosen not to break her spirit. As I told you, the princess is unique.' Athena turned her back to the warriors so that she could give Kat and Jacky severe looks. 'I depart now.' She faced the men again and raised her arm majestically. 'Be forewarned that I will be watching, and one never knows when I shall return.' The goddess disappeared in a glittering cloud of gray smoke.

'Such a drama queen . . .' Jacky whispered to Kat.

'Come, Princess. I will show you to your new home.' Without waiting to see if she followed him, Achilles marched away, leaving his soldiers to form a column around the women and follow behind him.

Chapter Seven

'Sweet Jesus on a cracker, will you look at that,' Jacky whispered to Kat.

They stood on the edge of an enormous trench, dug between the grassy plain that sloped down from the plateau on which Troy had been built, and a wide, white sand beach kissed by a turquoise sea so clear and blue it almost hurt Kat's eyes. But it wasn't the bizarre trench or the beauty of the sea that had made Jacky whisper and stare. To their left, as far as they could see, the beach was crowded with brightly colored tents and men. Just offshore the sweetly rounded harbor was filled with ancient wooden ships.

'This way, Princess,' Odysseus said, breaking the spell the sight had cast.

Blinking, Kat looked up at him. They had fallen behind the warriors, who had turned to the right and followed the shoreline after they had climbed down and then out of the trench.

'Achilles and his Myrmidons do not camp with the rest of us,' Odysseus said, with a rueful twitch of his lips.

'Even before Agamemnon took Briseis?' Kat asked.

Odysseus nodded. 'Even before.' He motioned for the two women to walk with him. 'The dislike Achilles and King Agamemnon feel for one another is common knowledge. Though it is only recently that the dislike has turned to outright hatred.'

'It doesn't sound smart to hate your king outright,' Jacky said.

Odysseus glanced with mild surprise at Jacky before answering her, and Kat breathed a silent sigh of relief. Maybe their oracle-and-her-weird-highborn-servant masquerade would actually work.

'Achilles is Greece's greatest warrior. Perhaps the question should be why a king would alienate himself from his champion.'

Kat laughed sarcastically. 'How about because of arrogance, vanity and lust? Aren't kings prone to those things?' She was silently singing a rousing chorus of 'God Bless America' when she thought about current American politics and the song skidded to a metaphoric halt.

Odysseus's gaze was shrewd. 'And yet they say your father has none of those characteristics. Instead it is rumored that he is wise and honorable and much beloved by his people.'

'He's not the only king I know,' Kat said quickly, hoping that she wasn't putting her foot directly in her flapping mouth, and wishing desperately college hadn't been so many years ago and that she'd actually paid attention during world lit class.

'They say you were to be betrothed to the son of the King of Sardis,' Odysseus said.

Holy shit! She was almost engaged? And to a king, no less. Huh. Kat swallowed hard. Venus should have given them a damn briefing. 'Uh, I'd really rather not talk about, you know, my life *before*.'

Odysseus bowed his head in silent acknowledgement of what Kat guessed must be her ruined life.

'So, what kind of a girl was Briseis?' Kat asked, neatly changing the subject.

Odysseus's brows went up at the question. 'She was a war prize – beautiful and compliant.'

Jacky snorted, which made the famous hero smile.

74

'How did she get along with Achilles?' Kat asked.

Odysseus's tone turned enigmatic. 'As all women get along with him.' He hesitated and added, 'Achilles is a great warrior.'

'There's more to life than war,' Kat said.

'Not since Paris took Helen, there hasn't been,' he said. 'In my world or in yours.'

'Maybe it's time that changed,' Kat said.

Odysseus's gaze speared her. 'Has Athena sent you here to grant us victory over Troy?'

No, actually, I'm here so that Achilles stays out of the war and, as quickly as possible, the Trojans win, she thought, but when Kat spoke she only said, 'As Athena said, I'm here for Achilles.'

'Of course you are,' Odysseus said, making it clear that was the last thing he believed.

The seashore had gone from being flat and sandy to dune filled and grassy, and Kat was glad that she and Jacky had to fall back, scrambling single file behind Odysseus around the mini-hills, and making it impossible to talk. Then the dune gave way abruptly to a cove that was impressive in size, though smaller than the harbor where the Greek fleet docked. It was protected on either side by huge jutting teeth of dark coral. Between the teeth were more ships – all black sailed. Kat stopped counting at thirty something. The beach in front of the cove was filled with tents.

'Achilles is there, closest to the shore.' Odysseus slowed so that the two of them could walk around the sea side of the encampment with him as he made his way toward a huge tent that sat apart from the others. Its canvas had been dyed a yellow so bright it almost appeared gold, and on each side of it was painted a majestic eagle.

Kat could see that Achilles was outside the tent and had

joined a little circle of men standing around someone seated in the middle of them.

'Nice of him to wait for us,' Jacky muttered. 'Mr. All That needs some etiquette lessons.'

Kat sighed, silently agreeing with Jacky.

They had just caught up with Achilles, who paid them no attention. Clearly he was totally involved with whatever was going on with the guy in the middle of the circle, and Kat was wondering if she should ask him where she was staying, or if she should just go on inside the tent and check things out, when she realized what everyone was staring at. A guy was sitting on a bench, and he was bleeding pretty badly from a nasty cut down the outside of his left bicep. An old, short guy was rummaging around in a raggedy straw basket. With a grunt of victory, he pulled from the basket a large needle that looked almost as sharp as it was dirty. It was already threaded with a long length of something that reminded Kat of black fishing line. The old man looked at the bleeding guy on the bench and, with a wicked smile, said, 'Well, my boy, this will hurt.' He bent over the arm, and started pressing the edges of the flapping flesh together, clearly getting ready to sew.

'Oh, no you do not!' Jacky exploded from Kat's side, snatching the needle from the old man who stood openmouthed staring at her. 'This' – she held up the needle – 'is disgusting. If you stick it in that' – she pointed at the gaping wound – 'his arm is gonna fester and rot.'

'How dare this woman—' the old guy began and Kat shoved herself to Achilles' side.

'She's a healer,' Kat told Achilles.

'I am a healer!' the old man sputtered in outrage.

'No, you're a quack. And one with dirty hands,' Jacky said.

Kat ignored both of them and focused on Achilles. 'She's been given special knowledge by Athena.'

The old man rounded on Kat. 'And who are you?'

'Athena's oracle and Achilles' war-prize bride,' Kat said smoothly.

'Athena's oracle is a war prize! Bah! What game is this? Do you think Kalchas, soothsayer and prophet of the Achaians, would not know of the arrival of a divine oracle?'

Odysseus cleared his throat. 'Kalchas, my old friend, we've just returned from the Goddess's presence. Athena did, indeed, gift Achilles with Polyxena, who she has proclaimed her oracle.'

Kalchas narrowed his rheumy eyes. 'You say you saw Athena yourself?'

'That is what I say.'

'And I say you have always been a better prophet than healer, Kalchas,' Achilles' deep voice silenced everyone. 'Polyxena's servant will heal Patroklos. That is if my cousin has no argument with it.'

The bleeding guy's voice was good humored. The sound of it made Kat glance over at Patroklos and she saw that he was cute, young and very, very blond. 'I bow to your will, cousin,' he said, and then he flashed white teeth at Jacky, adding, 'And, of course, to the will of the gods and my beautiful healer.'

'Good. I'll need this mess' – Jacky held up the filthy needle – 'boiled. I'll also need—' She paused and Kat was sure she was discarding words like 'disinfectant' and 'penicillin.' 'I'll need the strongest alcohol you have.'

The men blinked at Jacky, faces question marks.

Kat turned to Achilles and touched his arm, noting but not reacting to the fact that his body twitched under her hand like a skittish horse. 'She means the strongest drink you have. Something that gets men drunk easily.'

Achilles looked at Odysseus. 'Didn't you say that vile drink Idomeneus brought with him from Crete would take the hair off a hound?'

Odysseus smiled. 'I did indeed. Idomeneus owes me a favor.' He turned his smile on Jacky. 'Rest assured, I'll get you your strong drink, little Melia.' He jogged off in the direction of the rest of the Greek camp.

'What else does she need?' Achilles asked Kat.

'I need thin, *clean* linen strips,' Jacky said as if he had been speaking to her. Kat noticed that Achilles' wide mouth twitched up at one edge in just the hint of a smile, and he addressed his next question directly to Jacky.

'Anything else, little Melia?'

'Something to numb the pain,' Jacky said, barely glancing over her shoulder at Achilles as she continued her examination of the nasty wound. 'Like, uh, the juice of the poppy, maybe.'

'I thought that was what the strong drink was for,' Patroklos said through gritted teeth, clearly trying to pretend like her poking and prodding wasn't causing him excruciating pain.

'No, and hold still. The drink is to clean this out. By the by, what cut you?'

'*Who* cut me is the better question. Ajax did,' Patroklos said, and then couldn't help wincing as she prodded the wound too deeply.

Achilles snorted. 'You're lucky you didn't get your arm and your fool head cut off sparring with Ajax.'

Patroklos started to shrug, caught Jacky's severe look, and obviously thought better of it. 'He's bigger than me, but he's not as fast.'

'Looks like he was fast enough,' Jacky said. Then she glanced over her shoulder at Achilles again. 'Is someone going to get me that stuff, or are we just going to let him bleed to death?'

'Get the healer everything she asks for,' Achilles commanded, and several men took off.

It didn't take but a few minutes for everything to be assembled. Soon, much too soon for Kat's stomach, the needle and thread had been boiled, and Patroklos had been dosed with something that looked and smelled like cough syrup. He'd also taken several gulps of the 'vile drink' Odysseus had fetched, so he was bleary eyed and happy, and Jacky was currently giving her *the look* – the one Kat had dreaded – and motioning her to 'come here.'

Kat sighed and walked over to her.

'Yes, you have to help me,' Jacky told her.

'You know I'm crappy at this blood stuff. Can't you get the old guy to help you?'

'No, he scuttled off when I started boiling the needle. I think he's allergic to clean. You're it.' Jacky handed her a wad of clean linen. 'Just blot the blood while I sew. It's easy.'

'It's disgusting, and I may puke.'

'You're a shrink. That's kinda like a doctor. I don't know how you can get queasy at the sight of blood.'

'Hello – I treat people with *emotional* wounds. The only blood a shrink deals with is metaphoric.'

'You two have an odd type of speech,' Patroklos slurred at them.

'Blondie, my patients don't talk unless I ask them somethin',' Jacky told him sternly, giving him a little smack on the head to punctuate her words, which made him chuckle drunkenly. She looked back at the growing circle of men who were watching them and raised her voice commandingly. 'Someone should hold him. It'll mess up the tasteful yet manly scar I'm plannin' for him if he jerks around.'

Achilles strode over to them. He sat on the bench facing his cousin and grabbed him firmly by the forearms. 'Go on,' he told Jacky. 'He won't move.'

Kat decided that there was no sound grosser than that of a needle skewering human flesh, and was reminded all over again why she had opted for shrink school versus standard medical school (thereby never fulfilling her mother's dreams of having a 'real doctor' as a daughter). So instead of focusing on the seeping blood that she was dabbing for Jacky, and then puking up her guts, Kat kept stealing glances at Achilles, who was talking in low tones to Patroklos about some kind of race he'd won back in Greece, which was making the guy laugh, even though Jacky kept telling him to hold still and be quiet. Both men ignored her, which gave Kat the perfect opportunity to gawk at Achilles.

He was definitely a big guy. He had to top six-four with broad shoulders and a deep chest to match. He had excellent hair – long and thick and tawny. It was pulled back in a low ponytail with a leather thong, but a bunch of it had escaped and it reminded her of a lion's mane. His hair was his second most striking feature after his incredible blue eyes. Well, actually, no. If she was going to be honest with herself the most striking thing about Achilles were the scars that crisscrossed his body. The longest one on his face ran from just above his left eye, through his brow, somehow missing the eye it continued down his left cheek. His nose was crooked, obviously having been broken multiple times. His strong right cheekbone was zigzagged with a puckered scar that looked like it had been made by a rusty butter knife. Another scar wrapped around his neck like his throat had literally been slit, and she wondered, again, how the hell he'd lived through such horrible injuries.

His bare arms were heavily muscled and burnished a pretty golden brown. Back in the real world Kat knew women who would have killed for that shade of spray-on tan. But there, too, the perfection of his skin was marred by thick scars that ranged in color from old, white lines to one or two that were still angry and pink. From her vantage point she couldn't see his legs very well, but Kat was sure they'd be the same as the rest of him – riddled with lines and welts.

Her eyes snuck back to his face. He had an excellent mouth. That was for sure. None of those too-thin lips and weak chins for Achilles. Actually the truth was that if you ignored his scars he was a damn handsome man. If you didn't ignore his scars he was a damn scary looking man.

'Uh, do you mind *not* gawking and really assisting me?' Jacky said, loud enough to have Achilles glancing up in surprise at them.

'You know if I stare at the blood I'm going to puke. Or pass out. Or both,' Kat said.

'Fine. Then just dab the blood occasionally and hold these god-damned fucking tresses back out of my way. I do not believe what a pain in the ass Barbie locks are.' Between stitches Jacky glanced at her and smiled sweetly. 'That is unless you're too busy gazing at those blue eyes.'

Kat's cheeks burned and she could feel said 'blue eyes' boring into her. She looked down at him and, sure enough, he was staring at her with an obviously guarded expression on his face. Their eyes met. *He thinks I keep looking at him because of his scars*, Kat realized. So, still meeting his gaze Kat said clearly and deliberately, 'Can I help it if the man has gorgeous blue eyes?'

Patroklos chuckled drunkenly. 'The princess thinks you have pretty eyes, cousin.'

'She also thinks she needs to borrow this,' Kat said, and reached out to pull the leather tie from Achilles' hair.

Achilles jerked back as if she had a hot iron in her hand and she was trying to press it against his cheek.

'Hey! Hold. Him. Still.' Jacky glared at Achilles.

'Sorry, that was my fault,' Kat said. Then to Achilles, 'I just wanted to use your leather tie to get her hair out of her face.'

'Yes. Of course. Go ahead,' Achilles said in clipped words.

Kat pulled the leather tie from his hair, liking the feel of its thickness for the short time it brushed against her fingers. Then she pulled back Kat's blonde waves and knotted the tie securely. 'Here, that should help.'

'Thanks. Keep blotting the blood. Just don't look at it too long 'cause I am not in the mood to be picking you up off the sand, and I sure don't want to clean up puke.'

'I'll do my best not to inconvenience you,' Kat muttered, and went back to sneaking peeks at Achilles. Only now more often than not the warrior caught her looking at him because *he* was not looking at *her*, too.

'All right. That'll do,' Jacky said. Kat yanked her attention from Achilles back to the now less bloody and newly sewed up ungaping wound. 'Hand me that strip of linen.' Kat handed her the bandage and watched as Jacky expertly tied it around the guy's arm. 'Keep this clean and dry. I'll check on you tomorrow,' Jacky said to Patroklos. 'He should rest now,' she told Achilles.

Achilles nodded and helped the decidedly groggy Patroklos to his feet. Patroklos promptly pulled away from his cousin to address Jacky, who was fastidiously reboiling the needle and what was left of the suturing material.

'Thank you for saving my life,' he slurred and swayed. Kat bit her lip to keep from giggling at him. He looked like a drunken frat boy. Actually a tall, cute, drunken frat boy.

'You weren't going to die of that scratch, idiot,' Achilles growled at him, though Kat could see that he, too, was stifling a smile.

'No. No.' Patroklos lifted his finger in the air like a great statesman making a point. 'I insist that little Melia saved me, and I owe her a life. Mine. So I announce from here on she is under my protection.' Then he paused, frowned and blinked blearily at Kat. 'That is if her princess will allow it.'

'Oh, please. Whatever,' Jacky said. 'Just sober up and get well.'

Patroklos looked confused by Jacky's strange words, but seemed undaunted. 'My pledge is honorable. Princess, if you deem it so, the lovely Melia shall be formally under my protection.' He hiccupped and swayed again, this time precariously close to losing his balance, but kept his expression drunkenly serious.

Kat thought he was absolutely adorable. It would probably do Jacky good to have blondie following her around like a lab puppy, licking her lily white ankles. Kat giggled at the visual image she'd just conjured. 'Hey, it's all right by me.'

'Then it's official. Melia is servant no more, but is now war-prize bride to me. Patroklos.' He thumped his well-muscled chest and then cringed at the pain he'd caused himself.

'Huh?' Jacky sputtered.

Patroklos grinned at her as if she was a big, red-bowed present and it was Christmas morning. 'And I proclaim your skill for healing, my lady, is almost as great as your beauty.' Then he bowed, and promptly fell flat on his face in the sand at Jacky's feet.

'Oh, sweet weeping baby Jesus,' Jacky said, completely disgusted. 'Grab him. He's gonna mess up my stitches.'

The three of them were pulling Patroklos to his feet (again) when old Kalchas hobbled up to them.

'Agamemnon commands the presence of Achilles in his tent, and orders him to bring Princess Polyxena, the so-called oracle, with him.'

Chapter Eight

Kat felt like a fish riding a bicycle as she trudged through the sand behind the silent and glowering Achilles and wished for about the kazillionth time that she had realized what the hell cute and totally messed-up Patroklos had been asking when she'd, stupidly, been all 'all right by me' to his protecting Jacky. Who knew that meant Jacky would be whisked away to his tent and she'd be left best friendless to flounder along after Tall, Blond and Grumpy?

It was seriously a pain in the ass. They were almost to the Greek camp. The sun had set a little while ago and the scene on the beach in front of her was amazing, what with all the tents and torches and campfires. But the soft leather slippers on her feet were full of sand. The long dress/robe/toga thing she was wearing, while a great color and very flattering to her new young body, was also annoying as hell to keep lifted up so that she didn't stomp on the bottom of it and fall on her face. Her hair was long and thick and, yes, quite lovely she was sure, but the breeze from the ocean had picked up and, as Jacky would say, was blowing her goddamn tresses across her face. Plus, she was hungry. And tired. All she wanted was some carry-out, a bottle of wine and a *Top Chef* marathon on Bravo TV.

When a bur worked its way inside her slipper, Kat decided that she'd had it. She stopped and cleared her throat. Achilles didn't even pause in his trudge.

'Hey! You left me way behind,' she yelled after him.

He did stop then. She was pretty sure she saw his shoulders heave with what was probably a monstrous sigh before he turned around to look back at her.

She looked at him.

He looked at her.

'There is a bur in my shoe,' she called across the stretch of sand that separated them. 'And I am tired of scrambling around back here trying to keep up with you.' When he made no response she rolled her eyes. 'Your legs are longer than mine.' He still didn't say anything. 'What? Are you a caveman? A little help here would be nice.' She threw up her hands, completely exasperated.

Achilles walked slowly back to her. 'You talk a lot,' he said.

'Yeah, well, you don't talk enough,' she told him, and when he was close enough, she reached out and grabbed his arm so she could balance to take off her slipper and dump out about a gallon of sand.

Kat could feel his eyes on her as she peered into her shoe trying to find the bur, and she let him look. Finally she found it, plucked it carefully out of her shoe and then matter-of-factly grabbed him with her other hand so she could repeat the procedure on her other shoe.

'You do not fear me?' His voice was deep and somber, though he sounded absolutely perplexed.

Still using him as a balance, Kat slid on her other shoe as she looked up at Achilles. 'Should I be afraid of you?'

'Women *are* afraid of me, whether or not they should be,' he said.

Shoes free of sand and burs, Kat stood up straight and breathed a relieved sigh before brushing her hair out of her face and saying, 'You didn't answer my question.'

His lips twitched. 'As you did n

'You haven't given me any reason
mean, I'd appreciate it if you'd slow do
help me wade through this sand, but sl
translate into fear in my mind.'

He stared silently down at her and she recog
struggle reflected in the depths of his sea-colored e
offered her his arm.

'Thank you.' Kat smiled and slid her hand around
and they resumed their trek to the Greek camp, this tim
Achilles not acting like he was leading a death march.

'Melia seems to be a remarkable healer,' Achilles said.

'She is,' Kat said, not sure what else to say. *Yeah, she's a great ER nurse* was definitely inappropriate. Then a thought struck her and she decided to go with it. 'What kind of man is Patroklos? What I mean is, will he be good to her? And, uh, is he a patient guy, because Melia is a rather unusual woman.'

'That I have already discovered,' Achilles said. 'And, yes, Patroklos is a man of honor.' He glanced down at her and added, 'He is also kind.'

'And he's not married already or anything?'

'No.'

'So, how about you?'

'Me?'

'Are you married? Or anything?' Kat asked, even though she already knew the answer.

'No. I have no wife. Or anything.'

The silence stretched between them. Before it could become any more uncomfortable, Kat said, 'I'm hungry. Do you think Agamemnon will feed us?'

'No,' he said. 'We will not break bread with Agamemnon. He

s my presence only to

s your king.'

ing.'

t my stomach growl‐
him.'

much as it did Kat,
head and smiling.
long enough for

ould smile more.

t answer mine.'
o, so no, I don't fear you. I
wn, lend me an arm and
ght rudeness doesn't
ized an internal
es. Finally he
is bicep
with

the little jolt that passed
her words and she wondered how long it'd
been since the guy had been complimented by a woman. Then
she remembered what the goddesses had said about him – that
he'd taken no lover in years because women feared him, and she
felt an unexpected little jolt of her own sizzle through her. *This
ancient hero and warrior – the man whose physical prowess people
knew about thousands of years after his death – hadn't had sex in
years.* Talk about starving . . .

'Rest assured, Princess, I will see that you are well fed when
we return to my tent.'

Kat met Achilles' gaze and the little jolt that had sizzled
through her crackled and flared until she felt a lovely rush of
heat begin deep inside her.

'I'll count on it,' Kat told him softly.

Then they were both jolted out of their moment of intimacy
by a shout of 'Hail Achilles!' as a warrior in full armor saluted
formally and then pulled aside the flap of an enormous tent for
them.

Holding tight to Achilles' arm, Kat stepped into a cacophony of exotic sights and sounds and scents. Right away Kat decided gold must be Agamemnon's thing. The walls of the tent were scarlet, but practically everything else was gold gold gold. The thick woven carpets were gold. The chairs, most of which were filled with gray-bearded men wearing flowing robes and a bizarre amount of jewelry, were gold. The columns that held up the tent were gold. The goblets people were slurping wine from – gold. The three-tiered dais that was placed majestically at the rear of the tent, as if it were at the end of a catwalk – gold. And the pièce de résistance wasn't the huge gilded throne that sat on top of that dais, but the old guy that perched on top of the throne.

He was big, Kat had to give him that, and he was wearing an enormous gold tunic-toga thing that looked like the mutant love child that would have been born if an Elizabeth Taylor Cleopatra costume and a classic Liberace cape had been allowed to mate. Plus, he was wearing enough jewelry to make the other grandpas clustered around him look like cheap relations. Not to mention his (gold, of course) crown, which glistened in the torchlight.

But what Kat kept staring at wasn't the gold or the jewels. What freaked her out more than any of the opulence was his hair. It was long – as in down to his chest. And it was obviously dyed a dark, very fake-looking brown. It was also curled into Shirley Temple ringlets that somehow joined his long, totally dyed beard that was also ringletted. His eyes were lined in black, setting off his drag queen appearance perfectly. Actually she was finding it difficult not to giggle at the ridiculous pomp and circumstance until he spoke and she felt Achilles' arm turn from warm man to hard-edged steel under her hand.

'So good of you to answer our summons, Achilles. Though you are, as usual, late.'

Agamemnon's voice was powerful and contemptuous, as if he were addressing an annoying child. Its effect on the gathering was instantaneous. The talking stopped as everyone's attention shifted to Achilles. Kat couldn't help but notice how many of the men's eyes widened in shock as they took in the fact that her arm was wrapped through his. Automatically she lifted her chin and glared back at them. Hell, no, she wasn't like *other* women, those shrinking violets who peed themselves over a few scars and some grumpiness. She'd be grumpy, too, if she hadn't had sex in years. Crap. Now that she thought about it, she *hadn't* had sex in years. At least not decent sex. And not with someone besides the Magic Tickler.

Then Kat realized that as she'd been babbling to herself no one else had been talking. At all. Achilles just stood there like a statue of himself. Agamemnon's look was darkening and Kat braced herself for a kingly storm, when his expression suddenly relaxed and turned bizarrely jovial.

'Ah, we see why you've been struck dumb. You're unused to escorting beautiful women. Imagine that the Trojans have been battling the mighty Achilles for nine years. Luckily for us they didn't know it only took the touch of a woman to slay him.' Agamemnon chuckled cruelly and reached a hand out to stroke the young girl who sat in a scantily clad pool of gold silk on the floor beside his throne. The girl, who Kat assumed must be Briseis, was glaring at her hostilely, but she didn't so much as glance at Achilles.

Kat could not believe what an asshole this guy was. And he was their king? Jerk. Bully. She seriously hated bullies. Well, as she knew from years of experience, when one was dealing with a bully it was best for one to show no weakness and to confront the asshole directly. Kat glanced around the room until she found the face she was looking for, and was relieved that he was one of the few men present who wasn't laughing like a good little sycophant along with Agamemnon.

'Odysseus,' Kat said, raising her voice so that it carried over the laughter. 'I was confused earlier today when you remarked on my father's reputation for being wise and honorable and beloved by his people, as if that was unusual. Now I understand. They are traits that appear to be in short supply in your Greek rulers.'

'Impudent harlot!' Old Kalchas screeched as he popped out from behind the king's throne. 'She should be beaten for her disrespect!'

Several of the other men started shouting for her blood, too, but Odysseus's raised hand stilled them.

'Have a care, Kalchas. Athena has proclaimed Polyxena not just under her protection, but her oracle,' he said. 'Remember, I witnessed Athena gifting her to Achilles, and there was no mistaking the Goddess's will.'

'The princess is also under my protection.' Achilles' voice cut through the angry muttering that had begun in response to Odysseus's proclamation. 'I have no wish to quarrel with any of you,' he continued, but Kat saw that it was obvious that he didn't look at the king, purposefully excluding him in the 'no wish to quarrel' statement, 'but if you so much as touch her, I will kill you.'

Kat's eyes went to Achilles' face. He said it so calmly, so matter-of-factly, but his expression was implacable, and Kat had no doubt that he meant exactly what he said.

Agamemnon's patronizing laughter cut through the silence Achilles' words had caused.

'Oh, come now, Achilles. Save your death threats for the Trojans. Well, all the Trojans except this small, soft-looking one.

After all, we're not threatening your new war prize. It is good that you found a replacement so quickly, and such a lovely one at that.' Agamemnon smiled at her and Kat's smarm meter went to high. 'You'll need your strength on the morrow. I was visited by Hera today, and I believe that was a sign that our victory is close at hand. Tomorrow will be a great day for Greece!'

Kat had to work not to have her mouth flop open in surprise. Hera's visit was a sign that the Greeks were going to win the war? She could only imagine the goddess's reaction to that news. Kat had never heard such utter bullshit. No wonder this place had given birth to the mother of all rumors.

But the men bought every word of it and shouted in testosterone-filled response. Achilles waited until the tumult had died down and then he said a single word that appeared to shock the gold-loving king to his marrow.

'No.'

Agamemnon recovered his façade of patronizing indifference quickly. 'No?' He said with a sarcastic smile. 'Is there a problem with the Myrmidons, Achilles? Some new sickness? I returned Khryseis, as you insisted. That stopped the darkness that had settled over our camp. Now what sacrifice do you ask of me?'

'I ask no sacrifice of you, Agamemnon. I simply ask you to fight your own battles.' Achilles pulled his arm gently from her hand and walked forward, addressing not the richly dressed old men in gilded chairs, but the young warriors who stood behind them. 'Why is it that wars are talked about by old men, but fought only by young men? If I want a woman, I fight for her. If I want riches, I fight for them. If I want glory, I fight for it. I have never taken something for which others have fought and died.'

Along with everyone else in the room, Kat was mesmerized by Achilles. He wasn't just a mindless killing machine bent on glory and fortune. Achilles was a leader of men, a king in his own right. He moved through the room until finally he was standing before Agamemnon's dais.

'Perhaps it is time you fought for that which you would claim as yours, great king.' Unlike Agamemnon, Achilles' voice wasn't thick with sarcasm. It was firm and deep and honest. He held the king's gaze easily using the truth, not demeaning tricks.'And perhaps it is time I rested. There is more to life than war.' He turned and looked back at Kat. 'Today I have been reminded that Athena is Goddess of Wisdom as well as Goddess of War.'

'You cannot withdraw from battle!' Agamemnon exploded to his feet, all pretense of control gone.'I am your king and I command you to fight!'

Achilles turned slowly so that he was, once more, facing Agamemnon.'You are not my king. I have never sworn loyalty to you. I am the son of a king and I lead my own men. I am only here because of a youthful mistake.'

'Do you really believe you can run from your fate?' Agamemnon sneered.

'I have no intention of running, but I can tell you that I will fight again only when there is something worth dying for,' Achilles answered and then strode back to Kat.

'Stop him!' Agamemnon shrieked.

Achilles reacted instantly. He pushed Kat toward the tent flap, backing protectively in front of her while he unsheathed his sword and held it ready before him. Kat saw the warriors hesitate. That they didn't want to fight Achilles was abundantly clear.

Suddenly there was a wild flapping of wings and a huge owl, white as untouched snow, burst into the tent. The men gasped as it landed in front of Achilles and stared at them, as if daring anyone to move.

Odysseus was the first person to break the silence. He took two strides forward and kneeled before the owl. 'As you wish, my Goddess,' he said. Then he stood and confronted the room. 'Athena's will is clear. Achilles and the princess are not to be harmed. Should any of you wish to go against the will of my Goddess, you shall also have to go against me.'

That was the last Kat heard, because Achilles had backed their way out of the tent. Grasping her arm firmly, he steered her through the Greek camp, heading across the beach to Myrmidon territory.

She didn't see the warrior, Talthybios, whisper into Agamemnon's ear a story about a temple he had sacked earlier that day, and a princess who should have been very, very dead.

Chapter Nine

Kat didn't take Achilles' arm on the return trip – he took hers, practically keeping her feet from touching the sand as he propelled her through the Greek camp and then across the stretch of beach and dunes that separated them from his Myrmidons. Even had she not needed all of her breath to stay upright, Kat wouldn't have barraged him with the zillions of questions she had. In just a few minutes, Achilles had turned from a scarred, almost shy man to an imposing warrior king, and Kat needed a little time to process the change in him.

For the first time she began to wonder about this berserker rage that overtook him. Kat thought he was still himself. He wasn't foaming at the mouth or violently out of control as he would be with what the historians called a berserker rage. She glanced sideways at his stony face. His entire body seemed to be alert. No damn way could anything or anyone sneak up on him. His sword was unsheathed and it glittered dangerously in the moonlight reflected off the sea. But Achilles' sword wasn't the most deadly thing about him. It was Achilles himself that was a weapon – and the scars on his body now truly made sense. He'd used himself as a tool – as a machine. A killing machine.

Finally they reached the Myrmidon camp and Achilles slowed, and then released her arm.

'Automedon!' he shouted. 'To me!'

A short, muscular man whose leather chest plate had the image of a chariot carved into it ran up to Achilles.

'Agamemnon has deluded himself into believing he can command me. He may try to press the point. Double the watch.'

'Yes, my lord!' Automedon saluted and jogged off.

Achilles continued walking through his camp and with each step he took Kat could see the tension release from him. By the time they reached his tent, the stony look that had overtaken his face had relaxed and he had sheathed his sword.

'Are you still hungry?' he asked, speaking to her for the first time since they'd left Agamemnon's tent.

'I am.'

'The dinner meal is served there.' Achilles pointed to a camp-fire situated between his tent and the rest of the camp. 'Come, the food is simpler here than in Agamemnon's tent, but much less bitter.'

They walked over to the campfire where delicious scents wafted from a huge iron caldron that was simmering over it. About a dozen men were seated on large rocks and driftwood that had been pulled in a circle around the fire. They were being served by a couple women who were pretty enough, but wearing plain linen robes. Jacky was, unfortunately, nowhere to be seen.

The men greeted Achilles familiarly, speaking to him with obvious respect, though there was no bowing or scraping. Immediately a woman handed him a bowl filled with aromatic stew and a hunk of fresh bread. Kat noticed she avoided look-ing directly at Achilles. He motioned to Kat, and the same woman hurriedly filled another bowl and brought it and bread to her. As her eyes met Kat's there was an obvious shock of recognition. Almost imperceptibly she bowed her head and murmured, 'Princess.'

Kat was eating the excellent fish stew and thinking that it would probably be best if she avoided the other women as much as possible for the short while she'd be here. It only made sense that many of the war prizes were Trojan and they would know her, or at the very least recognize her as their princess. Or, more accurately, recognize the young body she now temporarily inhabited as their princess.

'How goes it with Agamemnon?' an older warrior asked Achilles.

'He's much the same – arrogant and rude and under the mistaken impression that he can rule me.'

'You set him aright, didn't you my lord?'

Achilles' lip twitched in what Kat was beginning to recognize as his version of a smile. 'I did, which is why the guard will be doubled tonight, and every night hereafter.'

The men grunted wordless agreement.

'I have formally withdrawn from the battle against the Trojans.' Achilles dropped that bomb nonchalantly between bites of his stew. Kat watched the men's faces carefully, and saw expressions that ranged from shock to disbelief and even to anger, though it was only the older warrior who spoke.

'For how long, my lord?'

Achilles shrugged. 'Until I feel the need to fight for another man's glory.'

'But, my lord, we have been fighting for the glory of Achilles,' blurted one of the younger men. 'So that your name will be sung for centuries.'

Achilles nodded and looked from man to man. 'And you have all fought bravely in this war for almost ten years because of a fate not of your own choosing. It may be time for each of us to reevaluate our fates.'

'Do you ask that we fight on without you, my lord?' the younger man said.

'I ask only that each of you follow his own conscience, as I will follow mine.'

No one spoke for several minutes, and then the old warrior yawned and stretched and said, 'I believe these old bones deserve a rest from battle. I will stand down with Achilles.'

'And I,' said the younger man.

'I as well.'

'I.'

All of the Myrmidons present chimed in, siding with their leader. Kat studied Achilles as his men chose him over battle and glory. He stared sightlessly into his bowl of unfinished stew and made little response to any of them.

When he finally spoke again, it was to her and not to the men who had resumed their casual conversation around him.

'My tent is now your home. Anything Briseis left within is yours. If you lack anything, these women will bring you whatever you need.' Then he tossed his bowl down by the fire, grabbed a wineskin that lay nearby, and without another word strode off toward the shore.

Kat didn't have a clue what she should do. The men ignored her. The women, who were sitting a little way off from the men, kept shooting her furtive, yet curious looks. The only thing she knew for certain was that Achilles had just annoyed the crap out of her. Hadn't they been getting along okay? It had seemed like it. Then that business with Agamemnon had screwed up everything. With a sigh she got up and approached the woman who had given her the stew.

'Hi. Uh, I was wondering if you knew where my, um, servant, Melia, is,' Kat said.

'No, Princess. We have not seen your maidservant.' The woman fidgeted nervously. 'How may I serve you? Are you well, Princess? You have not been harmed, have you?'

'No, I'm fine. Perfectly fine,' Kat assured her.

The woman stepped closer to Kat and whispered, 'Princess, I am Aetnia, a kitchen maid from your father's palace. I was captured with a group of servants who were buying fish outside the city more than two years ago. It will be difficult, but we can help you escape. Once you are within sight of the walls, Hector will surely come to rescue you.'

Kat blinked in surprise, taken aback by the earnestness of this woman who wanted to help her. 'Oh, no, I don't need anything else tonight,' she answered loudly enough for the men to hear. Then she lowered her voice and whispered, 'Thank you, but I don't want to escape. At least not right now.' Raising her voice again, she continued, 'I think I'll turn in. It's been an exhausting day.' And she retreated quickly to Achilles' empty tent.

Okay, it wasn't exactly empty. It was just Achilles-less. The tent itself was filled with beautiful things. Kat gave a low, appreciative whistle. No way was the man who had collected all of these treasures a mindless killing machine bent only on war and destruction. The tent was huge, though not as large as Agamemnon's. It was softly lit by scented oil lamps suspended from ceiling supports. Under her feet was a thick crimson carpet with birds and wild flowers woven throughout it. Hanging on the tent walls were tapestries of exquisite detail. Most of them showed sea scenes, though a few depicted a lovely temple-filled city on a hill that overlooked the sea. Except for his helmet, a few spears, and a golden shield that bore the figure of an eagle on it, there was no evidence that the tent belonged to a soldier at all. In the rear of the tent Kat could see a bed, thick with linens and canopied with gauzy curtains. She was studying it nervously and thinking that it might seem big at the moment – minus Achilles laying on it – but she was sure that with him present there was no way she could sleep all chastely without brushing against his skin and touching him and his battle-hardened muscles and . . .

Then she noticed the thick pallet of comforters and pillows that made an opulent nest situated way on the other side of the tent – literally as far away from the bed as was physically possible for it to be and still be inside the tent.

'That's where the war prize must sleep,' she said aloud to herself. And, hell yes, regardless of how stank and trifling it made her, Kat was disappointed. 'Yep. I'll admit it. Out loud. It would have been *interesting* to sleep next to him and try to keep my hands off him. Ur, I mean try to keep his hands off me.' She laughed at herself. 'Katrina, honey, it has been too damn long since you've had sex. With a partner.'

She continued looking around the room and, with a happy little cry, found a pitcher filled with red wine sitting alluringly next to a couple empty goblets. 'Well,' she said as she poured herself a generous cup full. 'He did say the stuff in here is my stuff, so I'm definitely commandeering the wine.'

There was a chair beside the table she'd found the wine on, and Kat sat while she sipped.

Okay, well, today hadn't really gone so terribly. Besides the whole she-and-Jacky-dying part, that is. Plus, that was just temporary. Hera was definitely going to owe them, and soon. It almost didn't seem fair. Achilles was doing her work for her. It was obvious that he was sick of fighting and pissed at Agamemnon, which Kat could totally understand. So the little tiff about Briseis was the proverbial straw on the camel's back. All that was left for Kat to do was just encourage him in the direction he was already going. She could actually relax and pretend like this was an unexpected vacation. She looked down at her new body, stuck her leg out, letting the drapey, togalike robe fall to the side to reveal the young, tight, well-formed limb.

'So does what happens in the ancient world stay in the ancient world?' she said absently, peeking inside her outfit to check out her perky young boobs.

Kat wondered where Jacky was and what she was up to. 'Probably nursemaiding that blond cutie.' And she should take a lesson from Jacky. She should learn to loosen up and have a good time – make the best of this situation. 'In other words, if I want to shtup Achilles, I shtup him. Hell, it'd be good for both of us. I'm always telling my clients to be sexually empowered. Okay. Shrink, heal thyself.' Kat refilled the wine goblet and left the tent, walking purposefully toward the shore.

It wasn't hard to find Achilles. The moon was high and full in the sky. Reflecting off the calm sea it was like a giant nightlight. Plus, Achilles was a big guy who was making no attempt to hide. He was sitting on a rock facing the water. He'd taken off the breastplate of his armor, as well as the metal things that covered his shins and he was wearing a loose thin tunic that opened at the chest and left his arms and legs bare. Kat thought he looked like a Greek statue sitting there, illuminated by the night and bathed in ancient mysticism.

'It is dangerous to walk alone at night.' He spoke without looking at her.

'I'm not alone – I'm with you.'

Achilles turned his head and looked at her. 'Is there something you require, Princess?' The question was cordial, but his tone was remote, almost cold.

'Yes, company,' Kat said honestly, and was pleased by the surprise she saw in his eyes. 'It's my first night here. It's not what I'm used to and I'm a little homesick,' she said honestly.

'You must hate me for stealing you away from your family – your kingdom.'

'You didn't steal me; Athena did.'

'And do you hate the goddess?'

'No.' Kat shook her head. 'She was just doing what she felt like she had to do. Plus, you're not so bad.'

He made a sound that seemed part laugh, part snort. 'You are so odd, Polyxena of Troy. Are all the princesses of your city like you?'

'Absolutely not,' she said with complete certainty.

Then he did laugh – really laugh, and Kat thought what a great sound his laughter made echoing musically with the lapping of the surf.

'Got any more wine in that floppy thing?' she asked, moving closer to him and holding out her empty goblet. He filled it up and the two of them sipped wine and gazed out at the sea. The silence between them was companionable, and Kat thought how weird it was that a man who supposedly scared the crap out of women could be so easy to be around. Which reminded her . . .

'That was a good thing you did today in Agamemnon's tent,' she told him.

He glanced at her and raised his brows. 'So says a Princess of Troy. Of course you would believe my being absent from the battle against your people a good thing.' He said it as a simple statement without sounding angry or resentful.

'I suppose you're right, but I wasn't thinking about that just now. I was thinking that I wouldn't want to fight for a man like Agamemnon, either.'

happening to him. She'd tripped some kind of trigger, and Achilles was fighting to control what the goddesses had described as his berserker rage. Okay. Fine. This she could handle.

'Achilles, you should get in the water,' she said in a calm, clinical voice.

He looked up at her then and Kat had to quell a surge of fear within her as she saw that his face, his entire body, literally seemed to be changing, growing bigger, stronger. His eyes flashed in the darkness with an eerie scarlet fire that reminded her of old blood.

'What are you saying—' He struggled to speak between heaving breaths.

Kat forced herself to continue sounding calm. 'You have to break the cycle of what's happening inside you – confuse the reaction that's trying to take place in your body. Get in the water,' she repeated. 'That might do it.'

He started backing toward the waves with lurching, almost painful-looking steps. Just before he threw himself into the sea he yelled a single word to Kat.

'Run!'

Chapter Ten

Even though it was decidedly unprofessional, Kat ran. What in the hell had started to happen to Achilles? She'd seen men struggle with fits of rage before – she'd even seen men literally mad with out-of-control anger. None of those men had changed physically, yet she was sure Achilles' body had become bigger, stronger, scarier and—

'Oof!' Kat ran directly into Odysseus.

'Easy, Princess, easy,' he said, grabbing her elbow to keep her from falling on her butt. Then his eyes narrowed as he took in her white face and generally disheveled appearance. 'Achilles.'

'Yes,' Kat said, gasping for breath.

Odysseus moved her defensively behind him as he peered back toward the shore. 'I don't hear him coming. Was it one of Agamemnon's men who attacked him?' He spoke while he continued to keep watch behind them.

'No.'

'The men attacked *you*?' He took her elbow again and began leading her to the campfire. 'The Myrmidons will never stand for this. I must tell them of—'

'Odysseus, wait. No one attacked me. Ur, well, I mean no one sent by Agamemnon attacked me.'

Odysseus slowed and gave her a considering look. Then his eyes widened in understanding. 'Ah, I see. The berserker took him while he was alone with you.'

'Yes.'

Odysseus looked seaward again. 'It seems he has controlled it. He did not follow you.'

'I told him to get into the sea,' Kat blurted. 'He did, and told me to run.'

'You ordered the great warrior Achilles to get into the sea as his rage was coming upon him!' Odysseus laughed. 'I would have given much to have seen that.'

Kat frowned at him. 'It's not funny. He . . . he *changes*.'

Odysseus's look sobered. 'He does. It is the price he pays for the choice he made long ago. Or rather, one of the prices he pays.'

'I don't understand. I thought – well, I thought when I heard the, uh, rumors about him that he just had an anger problem. But what was starting to happen to him was way more than that.'

They'd come to Achilles' tent and Odysseus motioned for her to sit on the bench just outside it. The warriors who had been eating were gone – the fire was neatly banked. Kat could feel that the camp was still awake and watchful, but there was no one within hearing range of their conversation. She met Odysseus's intelligent gaze.

'I'd like to ask you to explain to me what happens to Achilles.'

'Princess, I am not certain if I should—'

'Athena wants me to help him,' Kat broke into his denial. As she expected, evoking the name of the famous warrior's patron goddess had an instant effect on him.

'What is it you wish to know?'

'I saw him start to change. Physically. What happens to him?'

'I've witnessed it many times, and each time it is newly terrifying and awe inspiring,' Odysseus said. 'When Achilles is roused enough – whether by pain or fear or even passion – the berserker rage Zeus gifted him with comes upon him. It is as if Achilles becomes possessed by a rage-filled god.'

'Is it still him? I mean, does he know what he is doing?'

'Achilles remembers his actions when the berserker leaves him, but when it is upon him he is fully under the control of it.'

'How does it go away?'

'The rage eventually burns itself out, leaving Achilles drained, but himself once more,' Odysseus said.

'That's why women fear him. Because it's not really him. I mean, he literally changes.'

'And now will you fear him, too?' Odysseus asked her.

Kat met his eyes. 'No. I'm not like the other women around here.'

'Like other women or not, under the possession of the berserker Achilles is dangerous. I would advise you to have care when you're alone with him.' Odysseus seemed about to say more, but instead, jaw set and face unusually sober, he stared back in the direction of the sea.

'I'll be careful. Plus,' she added with a grim smile, 'I'm under the protection of a goddess, remember?'

His expression softened and he smiled at her. 'I would not forget my goddess, Princess.' Odysseus hesitated, then added. 'Yet even under Athena's protection, you ran from him.'

Kat sighed. 'Yeah, well, it seemed like the smartest thing to do. What was happening to him surprised me. I was caught off guard, which won't happen again. So you say that strong emotions trigger the change.'

'They do.'

'Then why didn't he change in Agamemnon's tent? Achilles hates the king, right?'

Odysseus nodded, 'Yes.'

'Hatred is a strong emotion, and I know he was mightily pissed by what happened in there.'

Odysseus gave her a puzzled look.

'Pissed equates to angry,' she explained quickly.

'Oh, yes. Agamemnon usually makes Achilles very angry.'

'Okay, again, then why didn't he change?'

Odysseus shrugged. 'Achilles was calm, his anger was controlled and—'

'Wait! Answer me this,' Kat interrupted. 'Achilles has to train to maintain his fighting edge, right? So he practices with the sword, or whatever, and he probably runs or works out or both. Right?'

Odysseus's brow furrowed. 'Achilles trains often. He is also an excellent runner.'

'Does the berserker come on him when he's training?'

'No. I have never seen the berserker claim him as he trains.'

'But he gets all hot and sweaty and worn out?' Kat asked, getting visibly excited.

'Yes, of course.'

'That's it!' Kat said. 'If he stays *physically* calm it doesn't matter how mad he gets. The change doesn't happen. And it works the other way, too. As long as he keeps his *emotional* response under control, it doesn't matter how intense he works physically, he'll stay himself. That's why he has so many scars. I'll bet his heart rate and his breathing have to elevate *along with* a major emotional spike for the change to begin. So he has to let someone beat the shit out of him to get his heart rate up, *and* get pissed about it.' A little thrill went through her as she realized what that meant about the kisses they'd been sharing. 'I suppose that makes sense, if any of this does,' she said more to herself than to Odysseus. 'The change is physiological as well as emotional, so it must take a trigger that is based on both.'

Odysseus was studying her intently. 'You are a most unusual woman, Princess.'

Kat opened her mouth to make a quip about 'that's all a part of being an oracle and whatnot' when Achilles' deep voice sounded from somewhere close behind them.

'To what do I owe the pleasure of your company, Odysseus?'

Odysseus smiled smoothly and stood, grasping Achilles' forearm in greeting as he joined them. 'Can an old friend not visit for no particular reason?'

Kat saw that Achilles' hair and tunic were soaking wet and he was carrying his breastplate, as well as the empty goblet she didn't remember dropping. There were dark circles under his eyes she would have sworn hadn't been there before they'd had their interrupted make-out session, but other than that he looked perfectly normal again.

'So Agamemnon sent you,' Achilles was saying.

Odysseus's smile widened. 'Of course.'

Achilles' lip twitched. 'And you will have to report to him that I was, indeed, serious, that I will not join the battle tomorrow.'

'And your Myrmidons?'

Achilles shrugged his broad shoulders. 'My men are my companions, not my slaves. They shall do as they wish.'

'Which means they stand down with you,' Odysseus said.

'Apparently.'

'I bid you good night then, and return to my tent. After reporting this sad news to our king,' Odysseus said.

'He is your king, not mine,' Achilles said.

Odysseus lifted one shoulder. 'As you have said many times

before. Good night, my friend.' He bowed his head to Kat. 'I wish you good night, too, Princess.'

'Good night, Odysseus,' Kat said.

Just before he walked away, Achilles said, 'Odysseus, I thank you for seeing that the princess returned to my tent unharmed.'

Odysseus's smile turned sad. 'Old friend, I do not believe the princess was in any real danger. I simply kept her entertained while we awaited your return.'

'Good night, my friend,' Achilles called after him.

It was only after Odysseus was gone that Achilles looked at her. Kat met his gaze and forced herself not to fidget nervously. She wished he would say something, but he just continued to look at her, his expression inscrutable.

Finally she decided to say the most neutral thing that came to her mind. 'You look tired.'

He gave a slight nod. 'As do you.'

'I suppose I am.'

Achilles cleared his throat. 'You have no reason to trust my word, but I swear that you need not fear sleeping in my tent. I will not touch you. I will not harm you. What happened on the beach will not—'

'I believe you,' Kat interrupted him, realizing suddenly that she didn't want to hear him tell her that what happened between them on the beach was a mistake he wouldn't repeat. 'And I'm not afraid of you.'

The disbelief on his face was easy to read.

'Okay, I'm not afraid of who you are right now,' Kat corrected. 'And I'm not afraid that you're going to spontaneously change into something else without, well, let's just say extreme provocation.'

Achilles grunted, though he didn't look convinced by her little speech, and gestured to the tent flap. 'Then you should go to your bed. You do look tired.'

Kat stood and walked the short distance to the opening of Achilles' tent. When she saw that he wasn't following her she said, 'Aren't you coming?'

'I thought I'd give you time to . . .' He hunched his shoulders and his words trailed off.

'How long are we going to be sharing a tent?'

He blinked in surprise at her question. 'I do not know.'

'Probably more than a night or two, right?'

'Yes. Probably.'

'Then we might as well get over being all awkward around each other,' Kat said matter-of-factly, neatly avoiding mentioning that the reason they were behaving so awkwardly around one another was because they'd just made out causing him to almost turn into a raging monster. 'So come on in here with me, okay?'

He grunted again, but this time he nodded and when she ducked under the flap he followed her.

Once inside, Achilles ignored her completely. He went directly over to the huge bed, stepped inside the gauzy curtain, and with his back to her, proceeded to strip off his tunic and dry himself with a linen robe.

Kat sat on her nest of a bed, took off her shoes and wiped sand from her feet. Then she unwrapped herself from the silky, ruby-colored robe that was the top layer off what she was wearing, leaving her dressed only in a thin cream-colored tunic that somehow fit loosely while still being flattering to her young body. And the entire time Kat busied herself semiundressing she tried unsuccessfully not to sneak glances at Achilles.

When he emerged from behind his bed curtain to dim the

lanterns, she saw he was naked except for a short linen towel-like thing that was wrapped low around his hips. Kat stared, disbelieving at the scars that riddled his muscular chest. As if feeling her gaze, his eyes flicked to hers.

'You have more scars than I've ever seen on one person,' Kat blurted.

His jaw tightened. 'I know I look like a monster.'

'No, you don't,' she said quickly, relieved that they were talking again. 'You just look like a man who has used his body as a weapon.'

He stared at her and then he gave a brusque nod. 'Exactly.' He turned down the last of the lanterns, leaving the tent lit only in a dreamlike light. Then he went back through the gauzy curtain and got into bed.

Kat wanted to give up for the night – to roll over and close her eyes and pretend that she was really passed out on Jacky's couch and would wake up with nothing more than a wicked hangover. But she couldn't – not if she wanted to get back to her body and her life. Hera had said she had to work fast, so she didn't have time for self-delusion and procrastination. And there was more to it than that. Achilles' touch had sealed the attraction she'd already felt for him. Kat wanted to help him. She also was self-aware enough to admit that she wanted him to touch her again. Yes, what had started to happen to him had scared her. It had also excited her. *He* excited her, as did the knowledge that Achilles had not been with a woman in a very long time.

'Achilles,' she spoke softly, not wanting to wake him if he had fallen asleep.

'You have nothing to fear, Princess.'

'You're not asleep,' she said, then rolled her eyes at herself. She was an educated, intelligent woman and that was the best she could come up with?

'I do not sleep,' he said flatly.

'Ever?'

'Rarely.'

She smiled, even though he couldn't see her. 'Now *that* I know I can help you with.'

There was a pause and then he said, 'How?'

'Well, I have to come closer to you. If that's okay.'

'You may come,' he said, but Kat thought his tone was decidedly unthrilled.

She parted the bed curtains to find him sitting stiffly up, his back leaning against the carved oak headboard. Kat gestured at the edge of the bed. 'Mind if I sit there?'

'No, I don't mind.'

She sat down – actually, she perched on the edge of the bed. Still he changed position so that there was no way his legs were in any danger of touching any part of her body. His blue eyes were watching her warily.

'You said you can help me sleep.'

'I can,' she said.

'How?' But before she could answer he added, 'I won't drink a potion or smoke a vile-tasting weed.'

'Fine with me.'

'Then how?'

Kat thought for a moment, trying to figure out the best way to describe hypnotism to a warrior from the ancient world. Finally she settled for, 'It's a spell I can do with Athena's power. An oracle thing.'

He nodded and looked serious. 'The goddess does have vast powers. What must you do?'

'Actually, it's more something that you do and I help you with. Hang on.' Kat went through the curtains and lifted a dimmed lantern from its hook, bringing it back to sit on Achilles' bedside table. She turned the wick down even lower, so that there was only a small flickering flame. Satisfied, she returned to her precarious perch on the bed. 'To start with, you have to relax,' Kat told him.

He looked skeptical.

She smiled. 'Just trust me. I'm the oracle.'

'Well, oracle, were I able to relax I would be able to sleep. So there, you see, is the problem.'

'All right, let's just talk. Maybe I can sneak the spell in.'

'Talk?'

'Yeah, a lot like we're doing right now. And a lot like we were doing earlier tonight.'

He looked away from her. 'I owe you an apology, Princess. I should not have touched you as I did.'

'If I remember correctly, I touched you first.'

'I should not have allowed it. It was dangerous.'

'Odysseus told me about the rage that overtakes you,' Kat said slowly.

'That is why I shouldn't have allowed it,' he said.

'Does it happen every time you, uh, kiss a woman?'

His eyes met hers again. 'It happens when I become aroused.'

'Every time?' Kat asked softly.

'I – I do not know.'

'What does that mean? How can't you know?'

His blue eyes met hers. 'Simple.' Achilles moved so fast she had no warning. One moment he was sitting there. The next he'd lunged forward and grabbed her wrists, pulling her forward so that her face was just inches from his.

'I cannot know because I do not usually allow myself to desire a woman. To touch a woman. Not as I am desiring and touching you now.'

Oh, shit, Kat thought. *It would have been easier if I'd been sent to hell.*

Chapter Eleven

'Really?' Kat kept her voice carefully neutral. 'So you didn't manhandle and then proceed to scare the living shit out of Briseis?'

Her words had the desired effect on him. The rusty light that was beginning to tinge his eyes faded and he let loose her wrists as if she'd burned him.

'No,' he said shortly. 'I never touched the maiden Briseis.'

Kat quelled the urge to rub at the marks he was sure to have left on her wrists. 'You didn't touch her, but she was scared of you anyway, wasn't she?'

'She was.'

'Okay, this is something you need to understand once and for all. I. Am. Not. Like. Briseis. Actually I'm not like any of the women you've ever known. If you and I are going to get along – and I think we are – you're just going to have to accept that and quit judging me like you would other women.' She looked around and breathed a sigh of relief when she saw another goblet sitting on the bedside table. 'God, I need a drink.' Kat got up, grabbed the goblet and headed for the pitcher of wine she'd already started to empty. She glanced through the gauze curtain back at Achilles. 'Mind if I have a glass of wine?'

He looked perplexed. Again. 'Of course not.'

'Good.' She poured a full goblet and then, carrying the pitcher with her, went back to his bed. She set the pitcher on the bedside table next to the lantern, then this time Kat didn't perch nervously on the edge of the bed like she was a demented pigeon scared of a statue (a.k.a. Achilles) who had suddenly come alive. She plopped down on the bed, curling her legs under her comfortably, sitting closer to Achilles, and took a long drink of the excellent red wine before she spoke. 'Okay, here's the deal. I think I can help you. Not just with your nonsleeping issue, but also with your, well, nontouching-of-a-woman-you're-attracted-to issue, too.' She gave him a nervous little smile. 'That's assuming that you really are attracted to me.'

His mouth twitched in his little almost-smile. 'I am.'

'But if you touch me too much, which, and again I'm assuming, includes stuff like the make-out session we had on the beach earlier, you're going to have a problem with turning from you' – Kat pointed to him and then off into the distance, kind of like he was part of a PowerPoint presentation – 'to that other you I almost met this evening.'

'Then you don't see me as him.'

The tension in Achilles' voice was beyond obvious, and Kat reached out slowly to rest her fingers lightly against a puckered scar that ran the length of his left bicep.

'No, I don't. How could I? Odysseus explained what happens to you, and I witnessed the beginnings of it. What you were turning into is definitely not what you are now.'

For a moment Achilles bowed his head, as if such an enormous weight had just been lifted from him that he had to bend to bear the absence of it. Then slowly, meticulously, his shoulders straightened and his head lifted. Achilles met her eyes.

'You are the only woman I have ever known who has understood that. It is not me. It is something that possesses me. I cannot control it. I can rarely stop it. I cannot even summon it at will.' He made a derisive sound deep in his throat. 'If I could I would not have had to make myself hideous with these scars.'

'They don't make you hideous,' Kat said. Her fingers still rested on the ridge of the old scar on his bicep. 'They're a part of you. In my mind they're just the physical evidence of how hard you've had to work.' She smiled at him. 'There's bound to be a price for everyone knowing your name.'

'You've said it correctly. It is my *price*. My penalty. My burden and, ironically, my choice.' He looked down at where her fingers lay gently against his arm. 'When I was a boy I was given the choice of my fate. I was asked to choose happiness and love and a life that would be full, but forgotten, or a warrior's life of battle and death too soon, but eternal glory. I chose glory. I wanted my name to be sung for untold generations.' Achilles' deep voice was bitter with self-loathing. 'Do you know that I will meet my death here, before the walls of Troy?'

'I've, uh, heard the rumor that you would.' Of course Kat had heard about it. She remembered that much mythology. Achilles, the warrior who was invulnerable except for his heel, was killed by an arrow through said heel, near the end of the Trojan War. Kat felt a jolt of panic. Why the hell hadn't she thought more about that?

'How long have you been here fighting the Trojans?'

'Almost a full decade,' he said.

'Well, shit!' Kat grabbed his hand. 'I don't want you to fight anymore.'

His brow lifted. 'Did I not just proclaim to Agamemnon that I have withdrawn from the fighting?'

Kat felt a ridiculous surge of relief that was extraordinarily short lived. Wait . . . in Homer's incredibly boring *Iliad* hadn't Achilles withdrawn from the battle, too? But then he'd rejoined it and ended up being speared through the heel. But why? What had made him fight again?

'Goddamnit!' Kat cursed, turning to refill the goblet again. 'I so should have paid better attention in school.'

'School?'

She shook her head, brushing off his question while her mind raced. Okay, it was logical to believe the reason he rejoined the war, and was eventually killed, had something to do with his berserker rage. Fine. So she'd work on helping him break the triggers for the rage and then, voila! He wouldn't be uncontrollable. He'd actually stay out of the fighting and wouldn't be killed.

'Okay, yes. I've heard you're supposed to die in the Trojan War. But I've been sent here by Athena to make sure that doesn't happen,' she said boldly, shrugging internally. Athena and the other two goddesses didn't want him fighting. Him not fighting and him not dying were practically the same thing.

He was watching her with an intent expression in his compelling blue eyes that she thought might be the beginnings of hope.

'I am fated to die before the gates of Troy after the death of your brother, Hector.'

Kat felt a terrible clutching in her stomach. That's right – she remembered something about Achilles killing the King of Troy's son, who just happened to be the brother of the body she was temporarily inhabiting.

'Well, then we will just have to be sure you don't kill Hector, won't we?'

'You believe a god-ordained fate can be changed?'

'I know a goddess who believes it. Actually I know several goddesses who believe it, and I've found that women are usually more reasonable about subjects like war and violent death than men. So let's go with the goddesses' version on changing fate, shall we?'

Achilles' expression was absolutely serious. 'There is little I wouldn't give to change my fate, Princess.'

'Good. Then let's get started.' Kat smiled and held the goblet out to him. 'Have a drink with me. I'm going to talk to you about relaxation.'

An hour and two goblets of wine (mostly drank by Achilles) later Kat had the urge to grab his wide shoulders and give him a massive shake. And she would have, if she thought it would have done any good. Achilles was lying flat on his back, staring up at the ceiling. His body was rigid and he was definitely not relaxed.

'Look, you're never going to relax if you don't believe you can.'

'I don't allow myself to relax,' he said gruffly.

'Well, you're going to have to learn how. All right. Try this. Think about each area of your muscles like they're parts of you that need to be trained – individually. The training you're giving them is to relax completely. So you're really just ordering parts of your body to do something. It's no different than ordering your arms to pick up a sword and then swing it to protect yourself.'

He turned disbelieving blue eyes on her. Kat sighed.

'When you sleep do you lay flat on your back like that?'

He thought for a moment, then said, 'No.'

'How do you lay? What position makes you comfortable?'

He hesitated, then lifted his left arm over his head and cocked his left knee up. His right arm he rested loosely over his waist. Achilles tilted his head a little, looking marginally more comfortable.

'That's better,' she said, thinking how utterly sexy he looked lying there with no shirt on, his thick mane hanging around his shoulders, his gorgeous blue eyes trained on her and all of that lovely, toned muscle with those dangerous scars muted by the flickering lantern light.

'It is difficult to relax while you stare at me like that.'

Shit! She jumped guiltily. 'Try harder. Ignore me.' Then she remembered that the wife of one of the couples she'd counseled used to hold her husband's hand all during their sessions. No, she hadn't just held his hand. The woman used to rub it gently and her husband, who was ridiculously nervous about going to a counselor, always relaxed under her ministrations (they had actually stayed married – they'd just needed some communications help). 'Okay, give me one of your hands,' she said suddenly.

Achilles frowned at her. 'What do you want with one of my hands?'

'I'm not going to hurt you,' Kat said with an ironic lift of one brow. 'You don't need to be scared of me.'

'I am *not* afraid of you.'

'Then give me your hand.' She held out her own in invitation.

The frown turned into a scowl, but he gave her the hand that had been resting behind his head. Kat held it in both of hers, and slowly began to firmly massage it, working on the callused pad. She glanced up at him. He was watching her with hooded blue eyes. The scowl had been replaced with a carefully expressionless mask.

'Tell me about your favorite place,' she said.

'What is it you wish to know about it?' he said after a moment's hesitation.

'Describe it. Close your eyes and pretend like you're taking me there.'

He watched her for a few more breaths, and then – to her surprise – he actually closed his eyes.

'There is a hidden cove off the coast of Phthia.' He paused and opened his eyes. 'Phthia is my birthplace.'

Kat nodded and kept rubbing his hand. He looked down at it, then back up at her. 'Go on,' she prompted when he didn't continue. 'Tell me what the cove looks like.'

'The water there is calm and clear,' he said.

'Close your eyes and take me there,' she said.

He frowned again, but closed his eyes. 'The sand of the beach is white. The rocks that jut from it are dark. The water is a distinctive blue.' *Probably just like your eyes*, Kat thought, but kept the notion to herself. 'It is a shallow cove, and there is a hoof-print shaped ridge of coral in the middle of it.' At first he spoke self-consciously, in short, halting sentences, but soon he seemed to forget she was there, and as he painted a picture of his favorite place while she rubbed first one hand, and then the other, Kat could see his wide shoulders relax and his breathing deepen. 'My mother, the sea goddess Thetis, comes there often. Oysters that grow black pearls live there, beneath the coral, and I have often retrieved them for her. The fish there are fat and lazy, like the sea birds that perch on the black rocks . . .'

He paused, and Kat spoke in the calm, steady voice she used to help induce a hypnotic state in her clients. 'Think about being there, Achilles. Let my voice take you back to your cove. You're laying on the beach . . . the sand warm against your body . . . the gentle waves are kissing the shore . . . rhythmically. Listen to me . . . let my voice take you there. You're totally at peace . . . completely relaxed. Your feet are relaxed, warm in the soft sand. There is no anger in your cove . . . no war. It is warm and protected. Your legs are completely relaxed . . .' Kat went on, methodically taking Achilles through the relaxation exercise as she gently released his hand and watched him closely as his warrior's body finally let loose and his breathing became deep and regular.

With no change in her tone Kat asked, 'Are you there, Achilles?'

He paused, and then said, 'Yes.' His deep voice was slightly slurred.

'Good. I want you to know that no anger can reach your cove, or you while you are there. Your mind is at peace. Your body is relaxed. Do you understand?'

'Yes.'

'Good. You're in your cove tonight, which means you are going to sleep deeply. As I count I want you to become more and more relaxed. Your body is heavy ... ten ... you need to rest it ... nine ... the sand is warm ... eight ... inviting your weight ... seven ... you are safe ... six ... completely relaxed ... free of rage ... five ... it cannot find you there ... four ... tonight you will sleep in your cove ... three ... and not awaken until past dawn ... two ... until then your heavy body will rest peacefully ... one ... safely.'

Kat let her voice trail off. If she were any judge, and she definitely was, Achilles was extremely susceptible to hypnosis. Which, she decided, made sense. This berserker thing that possessed him had to screw with his state of consciousness, and once that was messed with it left his subconscious open to suggestion. She smiled, totally self-satisfied. He was definitely hypnotized, which actually meant he was in what amounted to a trance state. He would awaken from the state, presumably after dawn, as she had suggested, feeling completely refreshed.

Kat studied his face. He looked different so relaxed. Usually he carried himself with a rigidity that made it apparent, at least to her, that he was constantly worried about what would happen if he let loose. And she could hardly blame him after getting a firsthand glimpse of the berserker that waited to possess him. But right now Achilles thought he was on his special beach, safe and warm and relaxed. His face had lost that hard edge to it. His lips had softened, and were parted just a little bit, reminding her of how they'd felt against her mouth. What Achilles lacked in kissing experience he certainly made up for in enthusiasm and in strength.

Her gaze glided across his naked chest. She usually wasn't a fool for muscles, but Achilles didn't have the stupid steroid-pumped body of a preening gym 'warrior.' His body was his tool. He used it well and he used it hard. And it bore the marks of such use.

Almost without her realizing it, her hand sneaked out so that her fingers could, once again, rest lightly on the old puckered scar on his bicep. She ran her fingers lightly up the scar, feeling its ridge. And then her fingers were straying to another scar that had once been a nasty slash along the top of his shoulder. This one was flat and thin. *It must have healed cleaner than the other,* she thought.

There were several scars on his chest. The worst was a jagged pink line that didn't look very old. It went from above his left breast all the way down, crisscrossing his ribs and then disappearing under the light sheet he'd pulled haphazardly to his waist. Kat let her fingers follow the scar down his breast and over his ribs. Her fingers were moving lower when Achilles moaned.

Kat froze, her eyes immediately on his face. His eyes were closed and he still looked completely under. 'You are deeply relaxed. Still in your cove.' Then she bit her lip. She probably shouldn't ask . . . she definitely shouldn't. *Well, why the hell not? He's not one of my married patients. God knows it'd be good for him.*

Kat cleared her throat and then asked softly, as her fingers continued to follow the path of his scars, 'What do you feel, Achilles?'

'Your touch,' he said immediately.

'Do you like it?'

'Yes.'

'It is your cove, Achilles. Your special place.' Kat's heartbeat started to increase as she spoke, but her voice stayed hypnotically soft and calm. 'You can have whatever you wish in your cove. So, tell me Achilles, what is it you wish?'

'I wish you would not stop touching me.'

Chapter Twelve

Deep in Kat's body Achilles' words caused heat to spread like she'd just downed a shot of twentysomething-year-old single malt. She felt the slick need between her legs and subdued the urge to press her thighs together to seek relief. It wouldn't do any good anyway, that was not the kind of relief she needed. Kat's eyes drifted lower to the bulge that was becoming more and more obvious beneath the sheet.

Could she do it? Could she make love to him and keep him hypnotized?

Unethical skank! Her inner editor shrieked at her. Thankfully Kat was excellent at gagging her inner editor. Plus the real question she needed to ask herself wasn't if she could keep him hypnotized, but whether she could keep him calm enough that the berserker wouldn't possess him. And she was far from sure she could keep him calm and make crazy, sweaty love to him.

Well . . . maybe they wouldn't make crazy, sweaty love. Seriously there were just so many levels between celibacy and crazy lovemaking – or even sweaty lovemaking. Perhaps she could find a level that would work.

Again Kat reached out to touch Achilles. This time she let her hand caress a path over his chest and down to his hard abdomen. Her fingers dipped under the sheet. She didn't actually touch his cock, but Achilles' skin trembled beneath her fingers and he drew in a deep breath, which he let out in a moan.

'You're still in your cove . . . relaxed . . . warm . . . safe,' she murmured, being careful to keep her voice hypnotic, which was damn difficult because her breathing had definitely picked up. 'What else do you see there besides sea and coral and sand?'

'You,' he said. His deep voice was, thankfully, still relaxed and he sounded dreamy and exquisitely sexy.

'Yes,' Kat said before she could change her mind and turn back into a boring professional (sadly *not* practicing the oldest profession). 'I'm there. What am I doing?'

'Lying beside me,' he said, and then before she could prompt him with another question he added, 'There is no fear in you, and you are touching me.'

'Achilles, there is no fear where you are – no anger – no pain.' Suddenly she had the urge to cry. How long had it been since he'd been touched without fear or anger? Following her impulse, she lay down, facing him. Her head rested on his shoulder, her hand on his chest. 'You are becoming more deeply relaxed,' she murmured softly. 'My touch is your anchor. Your desire is guiding it. What do you desire, Achilles?'

'You.'

And that was it. That single word was her undoing. 'Then you'll have me,' she said, sliding her hand down slowly . . . slowly . . . until she grasped his hard shaft. Achilles moaned as she stroked the long, thick length of him. 'Remember, this is a dream . . . only a dream . . .'

He moaned again and his hips lifted to meet her strokes. Kat slid her legs under the sheet and moved closer to him, and with a rush of liquid excitement she realized that he was completely naked. The loose linen wrap that had been covering him had come free, so there was nothing except the thin silk of her underdress between them.

To hell with this! Kat thought, tugging the flimsy silk up so

back in bed with him and snuggled up against that incredibly hard body, but what would happen in the morning when he woke up? Would she be greeted by a surprised Achilles or by a blood-thirsty berserker? Not willing to take the chance, Kat curled up in her thick pallet of downy linens, and was almost immediately asleep.

Kat didn't wake up until the kerfuffle coming from outside the entrance to the tent crept into her dream, turning the gorgeous Italian pool boy/man who was massaging her shoulders into a shrieking fishwife. Jolted out of her fantasy Kat sat up in time to see Jacky bursting into her tent. The small, deceptively sweet-looking blonde stalked over to stand in front of her. She put one hand on her very slim hips. The other Jacky pointed straight down at her vagina.

'My va-jay-jay is covered with *blonde* hair! Can you fucking believe that? I've never seen such a thing,' Jacky said.

Automatically Kat shot a glance at the curtained bed in the rear of the tent and was relieved, and a little disappointed, to see it was empty. She rubbed her eyes and smoothed her hair back out of her face.

'Well?' Jacky said, tapping her foot impatiently against the thick carpet.

'Well what, Jacky? You're a natural blonde. What did you expect?'

Jacky plopped down on the edge of her pallet. 'I don't know. I mean, I didn't even look last night when I peed. And anyway, it was dark. Then this morning I was washin' up, and there it was. It was a shock, I tell you.'

Kat stretched luxuriously. 'I love you, Jacky, but you're kind of a moron.'

Jacky narrowed eyes at her that were unfamiliar in their color, but completely familiar in their expression. 'I am not a moron. I'm just white.' She lifted blonde brows. 'Of course, some people might say that's the same thing.'

Completely unbothered, Kat grinned and stretched again. 'You know, you just need to relax and go with it. We're not going to be here long and—'

'Sweet baby Jesus, you've had sex!'

Kat frowned at her BFF. 'How can you tell that? And I didn't really have sex. At least not technically.'

'First, easy. You're all rumpled and glowy. And you haven't been this relaxed in' – Jacky paused, obviously mentally counting – 'in about three and a half years. Which is how long it's been since you've had sex. Second, what do you mean not technically? And please recall that we decided several years ago that oral sex is definitely sex.'

Kat fidgeted. 'It hasn't been three and a half years. It's been three years and four months.'

Jacky snorted.

'And I didn't have oral sex.'

'*But* . . .' Jacky prompted.

'But I had sex – kind of.'

'Explain Katrina Marie.'

Kat sucked a deep breath and then said in an enormously fast rush, 'I-hypnotized-Achilles-and-while-he-was-under-I-had-a-heavy-make-out-session-with-him-and-we-both-came.'

'Christ on a cracker. You raped Achilles.'

'I did not! He said yes.'

'You want to try sayin' that again. This time with the truth stuck in there.'

'You're really crabby now that you're white,' Kat procrastinated.

'I've always been crabby, as you know very well. Stop stalling, Katrina.'

Kat sighed. 'Okay, well, he *kind of* said yes.'

'You know shtuping the TU quarterback on the fifty-yard line is nothing compared to raping an unconscious guy.'

'Jacqueline, I did *not* rape Achilles.'

'Katrina. Was he in control of all of his faculties?'

Kat's grin was slow and satisfied. 'It certainly felt like he was.'

'Fresh! You are so fresh! And that is not what I meant. I mean was he conscious or under your diabolical influence when you shtuped him?'

Kat chewed her lip, hesitated, and then gave up. She always told Jacky everything – she might as well get it over with. 'Look, earlier last night I met him out on the beach after Agamemnon's bullshit. And, well, we'd been getting along at the king's tent, even though I did piss off the king. God, he's as annoying as Hera said. Anyway, what I said was nothing compared to Achilles announcing that he and all his men who had a mind to follow him would be withdrawing from the battle.'

'Bet that went over with Agamemnon like hot turds.'

'Yeah, and Achilles told him off and we almost had to fight our way out of there. And may I take this opportunity to mention that Briseis doesn't seem like a very nice girl.'

'You met her?'

'Not really. She was lounging against Agamemnon's royal knee throwing me dirty looks.'

'What kind of looks did she throw at Achilles?' Jacky asked.

'She didn't. The bitch didn't glace at him one time. It wasn't like she wanted him, but more like she just didn't want me to have him. I ignored her and held on tight to Achilles' arm. That really freaked her out.'

'Holding onto his arm freaked her out? What is she, some kind of weird virgin?'

'No, my guess is she's like most of the women from this time. They're freaked out by anyone touching Achilles on purpose.'

'Why?' Jacky asked. 'Is it just that berserker thing? Hell, remember my brief but unfortunate thug phase and Rashod a.k.a. X? He was mean as a snake, but he watched himself and showed some damn sense during the short time I dated him. Yes, I do admit that he is now doing time for accidentally killing his neighbor, LaShawn Johnson, but clearly when we stopped dating he also stopped using good sense.'

'Jacky, Rashod a.k.a. X, pulled out a nine millimeter gun and in broad daylight shot LaShawn and his dog – dead. Five times each, if I remember correctly,' Kat said. 'I do not think you can call that an accident.'

'Rashod a.k.a. X, only meant to shoot LaShawn's pain in the ass yappin' dog. LaShawn lost his damn mind and got out there all between the bullets and the dog. Which, in my professional medical opinion, is not very bright.'

'Why were we talking about Rashod a.k.a. X?' Kat asked, utterly confused.

'Because I'm just sayin' if that little Briseis and all the rest of the milquetoast white chippies around here are oh so scared of your boy, I think they could use a little fieldtrip to North Tulsa to chat with some of the brothers to straighten them right up. Truly, Kat, how scary could Achilles be?'

'It's not Achilles,' Kat said slowly. 'He's not scary. He's sexy and kind of sad and lonely. It's the berserker they're afraid of, and they should be. I got a glimpse of him, Jacky. He hadn't even fully possessed Achilles, and it was awful.'

'Katrina Marie, did he hurt you?' Jacky moved instantly into the persona Kat liked to think of as Super Nurse.

'No. I, uh, ran.'

Jacky's blonde brows met the hairline of her flowing tresses. '*You* ran. As in away from him, across the beach, with your bosoms floppin'?'

Kat looked down at her young chest. 'I don't think these bosoms flopped much. They're almost unnaturally perky. But, yes.'

'So you raped him as some kind of twisted revenge scheme? It's borderline brilliant, but still very stank of you.'

'Look. I did not rape him. The whole thing was really an accident.'

'Oh, yeah, like Rashod a.k.a. X's unfortunate murder one accident.'

'No, not like that. I was trying to relax him. Apparently Achilles doesn't sleep, or at least not much.'

'So you, what, gave him a relaxing blow job and *that* made you come? You're seriously more desperate than I thought.'

'Again, no. I didn't give him a blow job nor am I desperate, Jacqueline. I hypnotized him.'

'And then came the blow job?'

'No! I didn't blow him. I jerked him off. But not before I'd taken my pleasure from him,' Kat said with a satisfied smile.

'You sat on his face while he was hypnotized? Guys can do that when they're under?'

'I didn't sit on his face! God, you're nasty beyond belief.'

'Oh, please. I'm not nasty; I'm a nurse. This is all clinical to me. Pretend like you're at the doctor's office. What happened?'

'I, uh, rubbed myself against his, uh, pee pee,' Kat said, feeling her cheeks get hot.

Jacky fell back against the cushions and burst into gales of giggles. 'Oh, god, you said *pee pee*!'

'Would you stop!' Kat shoved her friend's shoulder. 'Look, I really didn't mean for it to happen, but there he was all naked and muscular and angsty, and then I touched his scars, and then his, uh, *penis*' – she enunciated the word carefully, glaring at Jacky who unsuccessfully tried to stifle a giggle – 'got all hard and he said he wanted me to keep touching him and I did. And I did not shtup him because I was worried that the berserker would show up. Plus, if you want to get all technical about it, he wasn't exactly one-hundred percent himself.'

'As in not exactly conscious?'

'Whatever. So that's what happened. The end. Could we please change the subject?'

'You know, this whole hypnotize-'em-and-make-'em-service-you thing is really an excellent idea. Think you could teach me how to do it?'

'Absolutely no way in hell.'

'Well, there is a rumor going around that we might be in hell, so you want to rethink that answer?'

'No. And now to officially change the subject – how's Patroklos and what did *you* do last night?'

'I, not being as stank as you, slept. And my white boy is fine, thank you. At least I'm assuming he is. He was gone when I woke up this morning.' Jacky's lineless brow furrowed. 'I suppose I should find him and be sure he hasn't gotten those stitches dirty or whatnot.'

'In other words, Patroklos stayed passed out all night.'

'Totally.'

'That "totally" sounded kinda wistful.'

'Kat, you are displacing your stankish-ness on me. I'm not interested in the white boy like that.'

'Oh, that's right. He's all tall and young and muscular and handsome. Icky. Who would be interested in that?'

'He's white. White boys think I have too much ass and attitude.'

'Uh, Jacky, *you're* currently a skinny white girl, remember? So all you have is too much attitude.'

'Please. I'm in denial. What say we get something to eat and I work on filling out this skinny ass?'

'Good idea. I'm starving.'

'Rampant stankness will do that to you.'

'Jacqueline, your blonde and flowing tresses are looking rather disheveled this morning. If you're not good I won't tell you how to deal with them.'

'Fresh,' Jacky muttered as Kat dressed. 'So damn fresh . . .'

Chapter Thirteen

Kat and Jacky were munching cheese and olives and some kind of fried swine, and as a side dish arguing about the ethics of hypnotism, when Aetnia, the maid who had recognized her the night before as princess, went rushing by, and then paused when she saw Kat.

'What is it, Aetnia? Where's everyone going?' Kat asked.

'The men are drilling by the beach, Princess. I'm – I'm sure Achilles would wish for you to come, too.' Then she scampered away.

'Last night he certainly seemed like he wished for me to come, too,' Kat said smugly.

'Really? You mean when he was conscious or afterward?'

'Both,' Kat lied.

'Well, then, let's go check him out. Unless you're scared to face him whilst he's actually walking and talking.' Jacky jumped up and started quickly after the disappearing maidservant.

'He was talking last night,' Kat muttered and pulled a face, but followed Jacky anyway.

'I mean, I for one would love to see if he's still under your diabolical spell.'

Three women who were headed in the same direction as them gave Kat fearful looks and began whispering amongst themselves as they overheard Jacky's words.

'There is no spell, you dork,' Kat said loud enough for the

huddling women to overhear. Then she lowered her voice for Jacky only. 'The hypnosis ended when he woke up this morning – refreshed, and hopefully, good as new.'

'And just exactly what is he going to remember about last night?'

Kat grinned. 'Only as much as he wants to.'

'Okay, *that's* diabolical,' Jacky said.

'No *that's* ingenious,' Kat countered.

Jacky gave her a dubious look, but they were both too busy climbing over dunes to bicker with any enthusiasm. Then the sandy, grassy mini-hills gave way to a smooth, wide beach that was filled with—

'Seminaked men!' Jacky trilled.

'With swords,' Kat purred. 'It *is* a romance novel!'

'Hey, there's your boy.'

Jacky's pointing finger called Kat's attention to the largest group of men. In the center of the group was Achilles, stripped to the waist and circled by four men. They were in full armor, even though Achilles was practically naked, holding only his shield and a weird-looking short sword.

'Damn, he has muscles on his muscles,' Jacky said. 'And I don't know how the hell he survived those wounds. No wonder they say he's immortal.'

'Is that what they say?' Kat whispered as they joined the other women who were sitting on driftwood watching the men.

Jacky shrugged. 'I overheard some stuff last night. The Myrmidons talk about him like he's a god.'

'He's not. He's just a man,' Kat said firmly, and then tried not to wince as two of the four men lunged at Achilles. She needn't have worried about him. His reactions were so fast he seemed to belie her words. He dodged aside, spun and smacked both men smartly on their asses with the flat part of his sword. The watching Myrmidons broke into loud guffaws, complete with crude comments. Achilles' answering grin was surprisingly good-humored and he gestured for the other two warriors to *come on*. They lunged. Achilles moved to the side and easily parried with his eagle-crested shield. The warriors backed off and Kat realized why his sword looked weird – it was wooden.

'He's not even using a real sword!' Kat told Jacky.

As if he heard her, Achilles' startlingly blue eyes looked up from the circling warriors directly to her. Kat saw the surprise that widened his eyes, and then felt the electric snap of attraction that sizzled between them. At that moment one of the warriors struck and Achilles was late in his reaction. The warrior's sword blade skimmed lightly down Achilles' chest, leaving a thin ribbon of scarlet, before he slapped it aside with the nonlethal wooden sword. With a growl, Achilles dropped into a crouch. Kat noticed the change in the surrounding warriors at once. The circle backed off and the men who were sparring with Achilles seemed to hold their breath. She watched Achilles take deep gulps of air as he obviously fought against the onrush of the berserker.

Then there was a flash of silver-blond and a tall figure detached himself from the retreating circle. Completely unarmed, Patroklos walked purposefully up to Achilles, making a surreptitious motion to the other two warriors to back off. His smile was clearly reflected in his voice and he spoke nonchalantly, as if he had no idea Achilles was struggling with becoming a monster.

'They say, cousin, that none can beat you in a wrestling match. I say that's because they do not have the inside knowledge of a kinsman.'

Slowly Achilles' body straightened out of the feral crouch. Kat saw his lips twitch up slightly. 'And what inside knowledge would that be, kinsman?'

'That you are like a great snapping turtle. Dangerous and unpredictable, but helpless when you've been pushed on your back.'

As Achilles laughed, Patroklos launched himself at the older man and, just like that, the shadow of the berserker was gone and the men were cheering again as the cousins grappled in the sand.

'If that damn stupid white boy rips open my stitches I'm gonna strangle him.' Jacky stood up, obviously preparing to march into the group of men and pull Achilles and Patroklos apart.

Kat snagged her wrist and pulled her back down beside her. 'You are so not going down there to yell at Patroklos in the middle of all of that testosterone and me-Tarzan, you-Jane mentality.'

Jacky stayed seated but grumbled, 'I'm gonna be pissed if he messes up those stitches.'

'Oh, relax. Achilles will make sure he doesn't hurt himself,' Kat said automatically, and then as she continued to watch she realized how right she'd been. They were putting on a good show. The two men were tossing each other around and being highly entertaining, but Kat could tell that Achilles was definitely avoiding Patroklos's injured shoulder.

'Okay, I'll just admit it,' Jacky said. 'There is something completely sexy about all this warrior machoness. I mean, look at them. They're all bare chested and muscular and sweaty and oh, so "I'm gonna bang my chest and kill the dragon for you" that it makes me want to let him ravish me.'

'Him?' Kat asked with a waggle of her brows. 'Who him?'

'Patroklos, of course. Don't get fresh.'

'And did you say *ravish*? Since when could anyone ravish *you*?'

'Since I turned white.'

Kat was laughing when Aetnia and two other servants approached her. All of them gave a little curtsey/bow.

'Excuse me, Princess.' Aetnia spoke in a low, whispery voice while throwing furtive looks over her shoulder at the group of men. 'You should know that we are willing to do your bidding at any time. Simply say the word and we will aid you in escaping.'

'Escaping?' Jacky frowned at them. 'We're not escapin''

The women looked at Jacky as if she had sprouted wings. One of them began to rub something that looked like a penis amulet that hung from a braided hemp rope around her neck as she quickly backed a couple steps away.

'That's really nice of you, but like I said last night, I'm fine,' Kat said. Before Jacky's feathers could ruffle she amended, 'We're fine. Honestly. I'll let you know if we need anything.'

'Princess, I—' Aetnia began.

'You're being all annoyin'? Is that what you were gettin' ready to say?' Jacky interrupted with a saccharine smile. ' 'Cause you definitely are.'

The woman who was still clutching the penis amulet suddenly said, 'Melia, you were not a healer in the palace. You were only the princess's servant.'

'I've changed,' Jacky said in her take-no-prisoners voice.

'Melia has always had many talents,' Kat said, elbowing Jacky. A stirring in the group of men caught the edge of Kat's vision. 'Speaking of, it looks like the wrestling match is over and Melia had better check out Patroklos's stitches. So I'll see you later, ladies.' She grabbed Jacky's arm and hauled her away from the women. 'Jacky, those women know you,' Kat whispered to her.

'Those women do not know me.'

'They know *you*.' Kat fluttered her hand at Jacky's new body.

'Oh. I forgot. So?'

'So we don't need the drama trauma of a bunch of war prizes freaking over the fact that you and I aren't who or what we appear to be.'

'What difference does it make? Like you said, we're not gonna be here very long. Plus, you're a princess. They're servants. They can't do shit to you.'

'That doesn't—'

'Little Melia! My savior! Just in time to wipe up my blood!'

Patroklos grabbed Jacky, lifted her in his arms and kissed her soundly. Kat stared, mouth flopping, as Jacky giggled, pushed half-heartedly against him and blushed a gorgeous shade of pink. 'Put me down before you mess up my stitches. And where the hell are you bleeding now?'

'It isn't me this time. It's him.' Patroklos jerked his chin at Achilles. 'But I still want you to mop the blood from me, my beautiful little war bride.' He put Jacky down, but not before kissing her again.

Jacky took a shaky step away from Patroklos, and still blushing, turned to Achilles. 'Let me look at that sword wound.'

'It is nothing.' Achilles made an abrupt gesture with his hand, cutting off Jacky's advance. 'Worry about his stitches. I'll mind my own wound.'

Jacky shrugged. 'Whatever.' She glanced at Kat as she turned back to examine the smiling Patroklos's stitches. 'You should probably make sure it's clean.'

'I do not—' Achilles began.

Kat squared her shoulders and finally looked at him. 'It needs to be cleaned out.' Their eyes met. Kat wished like hell that his

143

face was easier to read. At the moment all she saw was the guarded mask he liked to show the public.

'I thought you did not like the sight of blood,' Achilles said.

'All the more reason to clean it off,' Kat said, trying not to be too glad he remembered she didn't like blood.

'Very well,' Achilles said.

'It doesn't look deep,' Jacky said, peering around Patroklos's shoulder. 'Saltwater should work fine.'

'There's an ocean of that right there. Perhaps, cousin, you should take another swim?' Patroklos put his arm around Jacky as he grinned at Kat.

Kat looked from Patroklos to Achilles and wondered just exactly what he'd told his cousin about last night.

Jacky, who had neatly sidestepped Patroklos's grasping arm said, 'Do not start with me. You're covered with sweat and sand *and* his blood. You need a swim, too.'

'Then we all go!' Patroklos took Jacky's hand and started off down the beach. Kat looked at Achilles. He raised a brow at her.

'You're covered with sweat and sand and *your* blood,' she said.

'Very well,' Achilles repeated. 'We go with them.'

They followed Patroklos and Jacky. At first neither of them said anything. Kat glanced at him. 'Sorry about that cut,' she said.

He looked surprised. 'Why do you apologize for something that isn't your fault?'

'It was my fault. You were looking at me and not paying attention to the guy coming at you with the sword.'

He gave a little snort of laughter. 'The fault isn't yours. I shouldn't have allowed myself to be distracted.'

'Do you always make sure you're in perfect control?' She asked the question automatically, and almost instantly regretted it. The night before he had definitely not been in control – not on the beach, and not later alone with her in his tent.

His blue eyes seemed to darken as they met hers. Instead of answering her he said, 'I slept last night.'

'I'm glad,' she said, and then cursed softly as she tripped on the edge of her robe. Abruptly he put out his arm for her to take. She wrapped her hand around his thick bicep, not minding at all that it was slick with sweat. 'Thanks,' Kat said.

'You have trouble walking on your own in the sand,' he said.

'Only because I'm trying to keep up with you,' Kat said defensively.

'I wasn't complaining,' Achilles said softly.

'Oh.' She smiled up at him. 'That's nice.'

'Is it?' He asked, looking honestly perplexed by her.

'Yes, it is.' Kat cleared her throat. 'Uh, about last night . . .'

Achilles' full lips tilted up. 'Do you mean about the relaxation spell you placed on me?'

This time Kat could read the teasing glimmer in his eyes. 'Just exactly how much of the, uh, *spell* do you remember?'

The tilt of his lips lifted and became a full, heart-stopping smile. 'Enough.'

Chapter Fourteen

Kat was trying to figure out what 'enough' meant when they caught up with Patroklos and Jacky, and deciding okay, fine. She was a professional. She would just ask him. When Jacky turned to her and with a relieved expression said, 'Good. There you are. Tell him that we can't go swimmin' with them because we have nothin' to wear in the water.'

Kat looked at Patroklos, who was smiling at Jacky adoringly. 'She's right. This silk stuff' – she picked up a fold of her outer dress and swirled so that it flowed gracefully around her – 'is pretty, but not good for the water.'

'Then you should both do what we're going to do. Shouldn't they, cousin?' Patroklos said, with a mischievous glance at Achilles.

The corner of Achilles' lips lifted. 'They should, indeed. It would save the lovely fabric of their robes.'

'Shall we?' Patroklos asked.

'Yes, cousin,' Achilles said.

And while Kat and Jacky watched, the two warriors stripped off every bit of their clothes and leaped, shouting, into the turquoise waves.

'Holy shit,' Kat said.

'God. My god.' Jacky fanned herself vigorously. 'I owe you an apology, Kat. Even if there has been a mix-up about my skin color there is no damn way we're in hell. We have gone straight to heaven.'

'Have you ever in your life seen such a beautiful body?' Kat asked dreamily, staring at Achilles and wishing desperately that he would swim back to shallower water. And then stand up.

'Kat, tell the truth. Patroklos looks like Spike, doesn't he?'

Kat wrenched her eyes from ogling Achilles long enough to roll them at Jacky. 'You are such a dork. And your *Buffy* infatuation is truly pathetic.'

'He does look like Spike! Check out that lean yet muscley physique and that silver-blond hair. All he needs is a change in hairstyle and a long black leather coat. Sweet weeping baby Jesus he has a six-pack to beat all six-packs. I'm going to have to shtup him. I think it's only right. How can I let all of that deliciousness go to waste?'

'He's not Spike, fool. Patroklos is a nice guy. Spike was the Big Bad.'

Jacky gave her a look that telegraphed *you're a moron*. 'Spike from *Buffy* season seven, Kat. Please try to stay with me here.'

'Sorry, did you say something?' Kat's eyes followed Achilles' every muscular, naked movement.

'Kat, is Patroklos's penis *pink*?' Jacky asked, shielding her eyes with her hand to get a better look as she squinted against the sun reflecting off the waves.

'Jacky, do not even try to pretend like you haven't had sex with a white guy before.'

'Just Bradley and just those few times. Remember how unsuitable I decided he was, what with his weird addiction to chocolate-covered maraschino cherries? He used to bite the bottom off those wretchedly cheap candies and suck the grossness out. Vile – totally vile.' Jacky shivered dramatically. 'Anyway I didn't notice any overly pinkness with him.'

'Well, Patroklos is a very white guy. Hey, think about it like this. His pink penis matches your blonde va-jay-jay.'

'Oh, lord, I need to sit down. Being white is exhausting.'

Jacky was looking around for a log of driftwood when Patroklos ran out of the sea to grab her hand. 'Swim with me, my beauty.'

Kat tried to keep her eyes to herself, which was damn difficult with Patroklos standing there dripping wet, smooth skinned and totally nekked. While Jacky babbled about not having a thing to wear, Kat moved her gaze seaward (versus downward). Achilles was walking slowly toward her. The water was still just a little over his waist, with waves lapping to his wide chest, so she was able to watch every bit of him emerge. *He is like an ancient god, golden and powerful and seductively imperfect.* He made her body feel flushed and ultra-sensitive, and her mind kept flashing back to the night before like an erotic projector flipping on inside her head. Just as she was wondering how she could drop her clothes and wrap herself around him without the berserker showing up and ruining everything, Achilles' posture changed. He left the water, walking swiftly to his discarded clothes.

'A runner from the Greek camp comes,' he said to Patroklos, who instantly stopped the kidding tug-of-war he was playing with Jacky and pulled his clothes on, too.

Kat squinted back down the beach and, sure enough, a man carrying a long, thin spear and a shield and wearing the same kind of scarlet cloak she'd seen Odysseus wearing was running toward them. He arrived minutes later, winded but obviously being sure to show Achilles careful respect by saluting him and bowing his head slightly.

'My lord, Odysseus, has sent me.' The warrior began speaking before he'd completely caught his breath.

'Is Odysseus well?' Achilles asked.

'Yes, but not all of the Ithacans have been so lucky. Today's battle was hard fought.' The warrior's voice was not condemning and his voice held no hostility, but beside her she could feel the tension that radiated from Achilles. 'Odysseus sends me to ask if the healer, Melia, would be allowed to tend them.'

'Is Kalchas too busy sniffing around Agamemnon to bother to tend the wounded?' Achilles said in a cold, flat voice.

'Kalchas!' Jacky practically shrieked. 'You mean that filthy old fool who tried to be sure Patroklos's arm rotted off?'

'Yes, my beauty, that would be Kalchas,' Patroklos said, draping an arm around her shoulders.

'Well, then, let's go.' Jacky extracted herself from Patroklos's arm and made a shooing motion at the messenger.

The messenger looked from Jacky to Patroklos to Achilles. Jacky looked from the messenger to Patroklos to Achilles to Kat, and then back to Patroklos. Kat braced herself for trouble.

Jacky put her hands on her narrow hips, an action which was totally Jacky-like when she was pissed, and Kat thought how weird it was that just the way she was holding herself made her look like her body was more lush. But before she could tie into Patroklos or Achilles, Kat stepped forward.

'She should help Odysseus's men. You know we've been sent here by Athena, and Athena is Odysseus's patron goddess. She'd want Melia to tend his wounded men.'

'It does make sense,' Patroklos said.

'I do not like her going alone.' Achilles looked pointedly at me. 'And you do not like blood, so you will not be going with her.'

'My beauty will not be going alone,' Patroklos said, putting his arm back around her. 'She has me. I will escort her.'

Jacky gave him a look that was one part long suffering, one

part amusement and one part appreciation. 'And will you be sure the men do what I tell them to do, even if it means they have to boil and wash things?'

'I will do that for you, if you perform a favor for me later.' Patroklos's infectious smile was more than a little naughty.

'I might be interested in that, if it doesn't involve anything that will tear out those stitches.'

Achilles gave the runner an almost imperceptible nod, and then, with Patroklos laughing and whispering to Jacky, the three of them began moving off down the beach in the direction of the Greek camp.

'Ithacan! Leave your spear,' Achilles said abruptly. The runner paused, looking nervously back at the scarred warrior. Achilles' lips twitched up slightly. 'I have a taste for sea bass.' The warrior, with obvious reluctance, handed Achilles his spear. 'Cousin, be sure this is replaced with one of ours.' Patroklos smiled and nodded, and then he and Jacky hurried after the retreating warrior. 'Did the man really believe I was going to spear him with his own weapon for nothing more than asking to borrow a healer?' Achilles muttered, more to himself than to Kat.

'Sure looked like it.'

'And here you are, alone with such a fearsome warrior. Some people would call you mad.' His turquoise eyes studied her.

'And how often have you speared one of Odysseus's men?'

'Never.'

'Well, then it sounds like I'm the sane one and the men like Odysseus's messenger are the ones who need a reality check.'

'No.' His deep voice had gone flat and cold. 'They are right to fear me. You should not ever forget that there is a monster waiting to possess me, body and soul.'

Kat met his gaze. 'I'll remember, but I prefer to focus on the man, not the monster.'

She saw surprise flash through his eyes. 'Have you always been so contrary?'

'Definitely.'

He snorted a half laugh. Then, still studying her carefully, he said, 'I'm going to spear some sea bass. You may come with me or return to camp. The decision is yours.'

'I like sea bass. A lot, actually. I'll come with you.'

He gave a short nod and they started walking side by side down the beach, away from the disengaged camps of the Greeks and the Myrmidons. He didn't offer Kat his arm, but he did walk slowly. They were so near the lapping water that Kat took off her slippers so that she could dig her toes into the wet sand. She did touch him then, using his arm to balance as she had the night before. He felt warm and strong under her hand, and she thought how weird it was that his presence could be so reassuring when the truth was there was a dangerous warrior and a monster lurking not far under his skin. She didn't look up at him, but she could feel his eyes on her, just as she could feel them on her as she walked closer to the waves, holding her robes up so that the warm water could play around her feet.

'Do you miss your home?'

His question surprised her into answering with complete honesty. 'Yes, I do. I'm homesick for normal things.'

'Such as?'

Kat realized she'd answered herself into a corner and thought quickly, discarding answers like the Internet and hot running water. When she finally answered, it was, again, with an honesty that surprised her. 'I miss my freedom. I'm used to being able to do what I want to do and not worry about asking permission. I like being responsible for myself.'

Achilles snorted. 'I heard old Priam was too lenient with his children.'

'My father is not too lenient!' Kat said automatically, thinking about her dad back in Oklahoma who raised her to have a backbone and to value herself, but who didn't tolerate any crap from her, especially when she had been an obnoxious teenager.

'Then explain to me why he would allow Paris to abduct the king of Sparta's wife.'

Shit! Helen's husband was the king of Sparta? As in the Spartans that spawned the kick ass three hundred? Kat dug into the wet sand with her toe and wished, for the zillionth time, she'd paid more attention to mythology in college. Finally she shrugged and said what she figured was probably close to the truth based on the vague information she did have (that he was a middle child and that he'd stolen someone's wife). 'Paris has always made stupid decisions the rest of us get stuck cleaning up.' Before he could ask any more difficult-to-answer questions Kat asked one of her own. 'So did it bother you today not to join the battle?'

Instead of answering her, Achilles pointed to a half circle of coral that was just a few feet off the shoreline. 'Bass like to rest in the shady spot there.' This time he didn't strip but waded, thick-soled leather shoes and all, out to the coral. He climbed up on a bench-like ledge and crouched so that he could look down into the water.

Kat sighed and picked up a smooth, round seashell, trying to think of something she could ask him he might actually answer.

'It did not bother me not to join the battle today.'

She glanced up from the shell to him.

'It does bother me that my absence might have caused the death of even one Greek.'

'But it's wrong to have you and your men keep fighting for someone who treats you like Agamemnon does.'

'Is it more wrong than to cause men's deaths?'

Kat wanted to tell him that his absence would cause the war to end sooner, and *that* would save lives, but Kat knew she couldn't. He was on the side of the Greeks. No matter how badly Agamemnon had used him and then pissed him off, he still couldn't want to hear that his people would be defeated. So instead she said the only thing she could: 'I don't know.'

In the silence that followed, Achilles suddenly moved with blurring swiftness and hurled the spear into the sea beneath him. When he pulled it up it had neatly impaled a large, writhing bass. He pulled it off the spear and tossed it up on the beach entirely too close to Kat's feet and she skittered several steps away from the flopping thing.

'You said you liked sea bass.'

'I do. Cleaned and cooked. By someone else.'

Achilles crouched back on the coral outcropping and returned to staring down into the clear water. 'Then I'll have to have one of the maidservants who like to whisper escape schemes to you take care of the preparation.'

Kat realized she shouldn't be surprised that he knew what was being whispered about in his own camp. 'And were you told my answer to those escape schemes?'

He looked up from the water to her. 'What was your answer?'

'I said no.'

'Why? Because you fear what I would do to you if I caught you trying to escape?'

Kat made sure her voice sounded as haughty as a princess. 'No. Because a goddess sent me here. I'll leave when *she* tells me to.'

'So you wish to leave me already?' His voice was neutral, verging on uncaring, but Kat recognized the loneliness in his eyes – she'd seen it the night before.

'No. I don't want to leave you.' As she said the words she knew they were true. She didn't want to leave him – not yet. Not until she had helped him to control the berserker and change his fate.

He didn't comment. He simply turned his attention back to the water. In no time there were two more huge fish added to the flopping pile on the beach. When he speared a fourth, he waded back to her and rammed the point of the spear through all four fish. Then, while Achilles carried them over his shoulder like a bizarre knapsack, they headed back to camp.

They walked awhile in silence, which, at least to Kat, didn't feel uncomfortable. But as they got closer to camp, and thereby closer to Achilles' tent and the inevitability of them spending another night together, her pile of unanswered questions became too heavy.

'I saw you fight off the berserker when you were drilling with your men today,' she said.

He glanced at her and then looked away. 'There really wasn't any danger of the berserker overtaking me. I was simply surprised, that and the pain from the sword scratch were enough to make the men leery of me. But neither the pain nor the surprise was great enough to cause the monster to possess me.'

'It didn't seem like Patroklos was very leery of you.'

Achilles smiled one of his rare full smiles. 'My foolish cousin believes I would never harm him and he often acts much too rashly.'

'But you wouldn't hurt him,' Kat said.

'I wouldn't. He is the closest thing I have to a brother or a son, and I would give my life to protect his. The berserker has no such loyalties.'

154

Kat thought about that and wondered just how true that statement was. Odysseus had said that the berserker had been possessing Achilles since he was about sixteen. The berserker was a being of anger and hatred and passion and killing. But did that mean he had no ability to develop a relationship with anyone in Achilles' life?

'Where did the berserker come from before he cursed your life?'

'Zeus,' Achilles said. 'He sent the berserker when I made my choice. First he offered a long, happy life filled with the love of a fine woman and the respect of my family and friends. I would die of old age and my fame would mean naught but to my family.'

'That sounds like an amazing future. Many people would give almost anything to know that their lives would be fulfilled by love and family,' Kat said.

'I took the second choice. I chose a short, but glorious life of constant battle. I will die on the battlefield before the great walls of Troy shortly after the death of your noble brother, Hector. My life will be bereft of love. No children will carry the burden of my blood in their veins. But even without those things, my name will be remembered in all parts of the civilized world for thousands of years to come.'

Kat didn't say anything. What could she say? *You made a crappy, immature decision.* She didn't need to say anything like that. It was already more than obvious that the mature Achilles – the man he'd grown into – knew deep in his soul that the childlike version of him had made a serious mistake.

'Which one would you have chosen, Princess?'

Chapter Fifteen

Achilles' question threw her off guard. Kat wasn't used to being asked the 'if you could change your life decisions would you' questions. She was the shrink. She did the asking. She glanced up at the scarred warrior walking beside her. He was waiting attentively for her answer, as if it truly mattered to him.

'It's different for girls,' she said, trying to reason through her answer and be as honest with him as possible. 'If someone had given my teenage self the choice you were given it wouldn't have been any choice at all. I didn't want to be a great warrior.' She smiled at him. 'I still don't. But had I been given the choice between ... say ...' Kat paused, considering. 'Well, between your first choice, which was basically to have a happy life fulfilled by all the normal things: marriage, family, home, blah, blah, or to have something heart-stopping, breathtaking and utterly ridiculously romantic. Like maybe a torrid, passionate love affair with someone who was completely taboo but whose love would flame forever in my soul even if it burned me out when I was still young.' Kat clutched her hands over her bosom dramatically and gave an exaggerated sigh, which made Achilles chuckle. 'I probably would have taken the ridiculous romantic choice, and then regretted it when I grew the hell up.'

'You would regret love?'

'Fire-hot passion with someone because he's off-limits isn't love; it's a little girl's fairy tale idea of love. Plus now that I'm a grown woman I know that it's possible to have both if you choose wisely.'

'Both?'

'Yeah, you can have a fiery passion for someone that can actually last, and he doesn't have to be the bad boy Mommy wouldn't let you date. It has to be the kind of fire that is fed with reality – as in communication and respect and such – versus the fantasy of . . .' She hesitated, wanting to refer to Romeo and Juliet, and finally finished with, 'the fantasy of love, or rather *lust*, at first sight.' She looked up at him to see if she'd totally lost her audience, but he was still watching her with an intent, curious expression on his scarred face. 'It's a little like the fact that you could have had both, too.'

'Explain.'

His abrupt tone said Kat might have pushed too far, but she figured there was no going back now.

'You're an amazing warrior and a great leader without the berserker. In just the couple of days I've been here I've seen you stand up to the king of an entire nation, lead your men, who follow you with complete loyalty, and beat four warriors at the same time. You did all of that without the berserker.'

Achilles didn't speak for several moments, and when he did his voice was hollow with regret. 'It is not possible to turn back the wheel of time.'

'Yeah, guess not . . .' Kat said as a vision of the queen of Olympus played through her mind.

Kat quickly decided missing running water and the Internet was nothing compared to not having grocery stores. True to his word, Achilles had tossed the bass at the feet of Aetnia and barked an order at her to cook it before he muttered something about 'seeing to Odysseus' and striding away, leaving Kat frowning at his broad back and trying to ignore the dead fish eyes.

Aetnia, of course, instantly jumped to, grabbing the fish and hurrying off to do whatever it is one did to real fish to get them filleted and ready for the deli case and eventually the skillet.

'I need a drink,' Kat said. And before she could so much as enter Achilles' tent in hopes that the pitcher of wine had been refilled, another maidservant seemed to magically materialize at her side, offering a goblet full of a lovely red. 'Oh, thanks!' Kat smiled at her.

The young woman blushed and bobbled a sweet curtsey. 'Anything for you, Princess!' Then she retreated back across the little clearing that separated Achilles' tent from the others and joined a group of women who were sitting together mending what looked from the distance like articles of clothing while they threw her curious glances and whispered among themselves.

Kat sighed and sat on the bench beside Achilles' tent. Well, she was playing princess. That probably meant that she shouldn't go over to the group of women and try to make friends. She wasn't a mythology expert, but that didn't mean she was utterly a moron about ancient history. Nobility didn't mix with servants. Period. That was already more than obvious by the way the women were reacting to Jacky's new, outspoken persona. Clearly Polyxena was the only noble war-prize bride in the Myrmidon camp. Logically if there were others, they would have shown up to commiserate. The smartest thing to do would be to keep as low a profile as possible and stay away from the other women, avoiding unanswerable questions as well as escape plots.

But by the time Aetnia got back with the filleted fish, Kat was completely bored just sitting there by herself. Plus she really hated the subservient way Aetnia scurried around like she was really worried about offending The Princess. It made her wonder how awful Polyxena had been.

'Here, I'll help.'

'Oh, no, Princess! This isn't work for—'

'Aetnia, really. I'll help. I want to.' Kat reached for a long wooden spatula-looking thing that was sitting on the cooking table beside the campfire. There was what seemed to be a perpetually simmering pot of stew hanging from poles over the fire, so Aetnia had placed the huge hunks of fish in two heavy iron skillets directly on the rocks that were interspersed with the glowing coals. 'I'll poke these two. You take those two.' Kat situated herself near the skillet she'd commandeered, enjoying the delicious smell of garlic, olive oil and fresh fish frying.

'As you wish, Princess.'

'So whose war-prize bride are you?' Kat asked to fill up the extremely dead air.

'I belong to Diomedes, Princess,' Aetnia said.

'I haven't met him yet. Do you like him?'

'Like him?' She looked confused. 'He does not beat me,' Aetnia said, as if that answered Kat's question. 'He is the warrior who wounded Achilles yesterday.'

Kat thought back, vaguely remembering a young, muscular guy who definitely had a big sword. She wished Jacky was there so they could make nasty puns about it, but she settled for smiling at shy Aetnia and saying, 'He seemed to know what he was doing with a sword.'

'I–I hope he didn't anger Lord Achilles,' she said in a little burst of breath.

'No, not at all.'

Aetnia looked so relieved Kat thought for a second that she was going to faint.

'Thank you, Princess!' she gushed.

'Aetnia, why were you so worried about Achilles being mad at Diomedes?'

The young woman's eyes grew huge and she lowered her voice fearfully. 'The berserker, Princess. It overtakes him and he becomes a monster. He can kill anyone when the creature possesses him.'

'Have you ever seen Achilles in his berserker rage?'

'Only watching from the walls of our beautiful city.' She shivered. 'That was terrible enough.'

'But you've been in his camp for, what, more than two years?'

'Yes, Princess.'

'And you've never seen the berserker take control of him here?'

'No, my lady.'

'You know, maybe you should consider that Achilles isn't as out of control and scary as everyone says he is.'

Aetnia gaped at Kat. 'My lady, you, too, have watched him from the walls of Troy. You've seen him on the battlefield cutting a swath through our men. I do not understand how you can say even one kind word about him.'

'Aetnia, Diomedes is in need of you. Return to his tent.' Achilles' deep voice coming from behind them made both of them jump, but Kat thought Aetnia looked like she was going to pass out.

'Y-yes, my lord!' She bobbed several jerky curtseys and literally ran off.

Kat frowned up at the glowering Achilles and was getting ready to tell him to quit being such a bully, that they were already scared enough of him, when Jacky made her grand entrance, followed closely by an unusually pale Patroklos.

'Oh, sweet weeping baby Jesus, is that fried food that I smell?'

She grabbed a pottery bowl from the table and sat on the log closest to Kat. 'I am *starving*.' She looked at Kat appraisingly. 'Did I miss something? Did hell actually freeze over and you cooked?'

'Don't start,' Kat told her, spooning up some of the hot, flaky fish for her friend.

'I do not understand how you can eat,' Patroklos said. 'Not after the wounds you tended today.'

'Believe me, she can eat,' Kat said, gesturing at Jacky with the spatula. 'She could eat a huge dinner while she lanced a boil while simultaneously playing with a ball of tapeworms.'

Jacky rolled her eyes at Kat. 'Don't pay any attention to her. She exaggerates. I wouldn't play with the tapeworms – I don't like parasites. Plus like I've been telling you all afternoon. You've been in battle. I have no clue why the blood and guts after the fact should bother you so much.'

'Battle is one thing. Afterward is another,' Patroklos said. He gave Jacky an adoring look. 'My beauty is not like other women.'

'True for so many reasons.' Jacky smiled flirtatiously at him. 'One of them being I believe in cleanliness.' Her gaze went from flirty to incredulous when she turned it on Kat. 'You would not believe how nasty the infirmary was with—'

'Wine!' Achilles cut off Jacky's gross recounting, as he called over his shoulder to the women who were mending clothes in front of a nearby tent. Several of them scrambled to do Achilles' bidding, disappearing for only a moment and then reappearing with goblets for everyone, as well as four clay pitchers of wine.

Kat thought it was interesting how the women skirted around Achilles, giving him a wide berth. One girl, who must have drawn the short stick, was filling up his goblet and her hands were shaking so badly Kat was sure she was going to make a mess of it. 'Keep an eye on the fish,' she told Jacky, and hurried over to Achilles. 'I've got this. Go on back to your sewing.' Kat took the pitcher from her and gave her a friendly smile. The girl bowed and then bolted. With a hand that was decidedly steadier, Kat filled Achilles' goblet.

'You know, if you didn't bark commands at them, they might stop jumping out of their skin every time you're near,' Kat said softly as they walked the short distance to the campfire together.

'They fear me even though they have no reason to. Commanding them or not will not change that.'

Kat thought he sounded angry, and she guessed she couldn't really blame him. The women showed their fear of him so openly that it must grate on his nerves. Kat spooned up fish and garlic for all four of them, and even Patroklos ate at Jacky's insistence. Then she and Jacky sat comfortable on the bench and ate the utterly delicious fish with fresh bread and wine, while Patroklos and Achilles sat on the sandy beach on either side of them.

Kat noticed Patroklos leaned his back intimately against Jacky's knees. They ate and talked easily together. Kat decided she liked Jacky with Patroklos. That he was a good man was obvious, but he also had a fun sense of humor, and he seemed to appreciate her. And Jacky definitely liked him – despite her cynical nature.

Kat looked down at Achilles. He was sitting close to her, but his back was so ramrod straight that no part of his body touched hers.

She bent forward and whispered in his ear as she tugged on a long strand of his golden hair. 'Lean back against me. You look uncomfortable as hell sitting all perfect and straight like that.'

He looked up over his shoulder at her, grunted, and then leaned against her legs. He was still stiff, so Kat butted him with her knees. 'Relax,' she whispered into his ear, and after only a little hesitation, he did relax, leaning back more comfortably.

Pleased with herself, Kat looked around as she ate the tasty fish and saw that all of the women who had been mending clothes across the campfire from them were staring at her with looks ranging from shock to fear. Kat sighed.

'What have you done to make all of those women so scared of you?' She asked him quietly, not wanting to be overheard, but Patroklos answered.

'The women condemn Achilles no matter what he says or does. He has never harmed one of them. None of us have. We are not barbarians. The war prizes who come to our beds do so willingly.' Patroklos paused long enough to give Jacky a big grin.

'Finish your dinner. I'll check your stitches afterward.' Jacky spoke matter-of-factly, but Kat could see that she also stroked the side of Patroklos's thigh with her bare foot.

'Will you check them in our tent? Alone?' Patroklos's eyes gleamed with obviously naughty intent, and for a split second he did remind her of Buffy's Spike – not that she would ever admit that to Jacky.

'Yes.' Jacky made her voice all breathy, speaking in what Kat thought was a pretty darn good imitation of Marilyn Monroe. 'There are some examinations that are much better done in private.'

Kat could have sworn only five more minutes had passed when Patroklos was picking up one of the pitchers of wine and two goblets and following Jacky, who said, 'Good night,' to Kat with a wink, into their tent.

'So they've always been scared of you?' She took up the unfinished thread of their conversation after they were alone.

Achilles answered her, but it was clear the subject made him

163

uncomfortable. 'Women have feared me since the first time the berserker fully possessed me when I was with the maiden to whom I was betrothed.' His voice had gone from reluctant to cold. The more he spoke, the more dispassionate he sounded, but Kat could see the way his shoulders had tensed again and how he held himself too rigid so that he was no longer leaning relaxed against her. 'I was nineteen and she was sixteen. She was of Ithaca's royal house, a distant cousin of Odysseus. We thought to join our families. I'd known her since we were children. The night before our wedding we snuck away to be alone. She wanted me, and I her. I'd had no idea the berserker could possess me during such a time.' His voice raised then, sharp with anger. 'I wasn't on a battlefield. There should have been no reason—' He broke off and shook his head.

'What happened?'

'I killed her – raped her to death. I came back to myself with her bloody, lifeless body beneath mine. I have not taken a woman since that night.'

Abruptly he stood and, without so much as a backward glance at her, Achilles disappeared inside their tent.

'Well, hell. Where's some Xanax and a good, sturdy straight-jacket when you need them?' Kat tried to joke with herself – to lighten the sadness of the oppressive mood Achilles had cast over them. Of course it didn't work. What he'd told her was awful. He'd killed the girl he'd loved and was supposed to marry.

She stood up, not wanting to sit there and let the women stare at her. Or worse, one of them might come over to her and whisper another escape plot that Achilles could overhear. Kat looked at the closed tent flap. She wasn't ready to go in there yet, either. With a sigh, she pulled off her shoes, hiked up her voluminous silk skirts and started walking toward the nearby seashore. Maybe the moon shining off the waves would calm her.

Kat had just reached the water when a huge burst of glittering diamond dust erupted in front of her, out of which Venus suddenly appeared.

'Darling, you're not doing a bad job, but I thought that, perhaps, you could use a little advice from Love herself.'

Kat shrugged her shoulders. 'Well, it definitely couldn't hurt.'

Chapter Sixteen

'Yes, yes, you're quite right. You were doing very well together.' Venus had materialized in an almost obscenely short silk tunic that showcased her long, shapely legs as she stood at the edge of the surf, letting the soft sea waves flow over her bare feet and calves.'I particularly liked when you cast that little spell over him and brought both of you to orgasm. Well done you!'

Kat felt her face flame.'Let's make a deal. If my clothes come off, you stop peeping at me.'

'But, darling.' Venus smiled.'You didn't have your clothes off.'

'You know what I mean,' Kat ground out between her clenched teeth.

Venus sighed prettily. 'Yes, of course, I understand. Actually the reason I was watching was to be quite sure Achilles wouldn't change when he became aroused by you, as he almost had earlier on the beach.'

'And he didn't,' Kat said.

'No, not while he was under your spell.'

'Venus, it's not a spell. You must know that. It's just hypnotism – a trick that can be played with the subconscious mind. It's used to get conscious barriers out of the way. Suggestions can be implanted during hypnotism, too, like don't smoke. Or don't eat so much.'

'Or only remember what happened if you want to?'

'Yes, like that. And, again. *No more watching*. But speaking of

– did you happen to listen in when he told me about raping to death the girl he was going to marry?'

'Achilles did not do that. The berserker did. You know they are not one and the same,' Venus said.

'I understand that, but it doesn't change the girl's outcome, or mine if I happen to trigger a berserker possession.'

'Katrina, darling, I don't believe you will.' The goddess paused, studying Kat carefully. 'And I don't think you believe you will, either.'

'Actually I believe that he can learn to control what triggers the possession. I may have figured out what it is that has to happen to call the berserker to him, and it's not as simple as him being physically aroused or emotionally excited. It has to be a very specific combination of the two,' Kat said.

Venus nodded. 'So you simply need to make sure both don't happen at once.'

'Well, it's not so simple. And both are bound to happen at the same time eventually. What I think I can do is get him to control himself enough so that he's just on the edge of the berserker's possession, but he doesn't trip over into it.'

'And all of this will take time and keep him away from the battlefield so that a quick, decisive Trojan victory can be orchestrated. Excellent! I will report everything back to Hera and Athena.' Venus's smile was brilliant. 'I knew you were the right choice for this job.'

'Thanks. I think.' But she couldn't help smiling back at the beautiful goddess.

'Oh, and you should know that I would never allow Achilles' berserker to harm you. Had you awakened him last night, I would have protected you. So feel free to experiment with your lovely hypnotism spell.' The goddess raised her shapely arm, obviously getting ready to disappear.

'Wait! Okay, not that I'm unappreciative about you saying you'll be sure the berserker doesn't rape and pillage me, but can we work out some way you could know I need your help *without* you spying on me in way too intimate moments?'

'Darling, goddesses do not spy. We watch attentively and oversee our adoring subjects.'

'Fine, let's just have your watching be not so personal, and your overseeing be slightly less attentive. Can't I have like a panic button I could press or something?'

'What a lovely idea! And I saw the perfect thing on display at one of Tulsa's exquisite jewelry boutiques on Brookside called Nattie Blue. My mortal friend, Pea Chamberlain, and I have recently discovered the delicious Garlic Rose restaurant there. Their food is fit for a goddess.' Venus laughed. 'And, of course, I would know!'

'The panic button. Remember?'

'Oh, of course, darling.' Venus lifted her arm again and made a fluttering motion with her long, elegant fingers causing diamond glitter to form in the air around her. And then, with a *pop* a golden heart locket was suddenly dangling from her fingers. Venus held it up in front of her face and frowned. 'Well, it's more modern-mortal-world-looking then I remembered. But not a problem. I can fix that.' Venus closed her hand around the locket and then blew gently into her fist. When she reopened her hand Kat saw that the locket was the same basic shape and size, but the golden color had changed. Now it reminded her of the buttery color of the golden jewelry Agamemnon had draped himself in. 'Perfect!' The goddess motioned for Kat to turn so she could fasten it around her neck.

Kat looked down at the heart that rested between her breasts. 'Venus, it's pretty, but how does this help me?'

'Simple, darling. If you need me you open the heart and call my name. I've inserted an oracle within it. I will hear and come to you.'

'And you'll *only* hear me when I open the locket?'

'Yes, of course.'

Kat lifted the locket and studied the outside of it. 'And it won't let you watch me oh, so attentively?'

'You shouldn't be so cynical, Katrina. It really isn't attractive,' Venus said.

'You didn't answer the question.'

'No, it's not the seeing kind of oracle, only the hearing kind. And only when it's open. Now go back to your Achilles and remember, Love is on your side.' Venus snapped her fingers and disappeared in a puff of glittering smoke.

Kat walked slowly back to Achilles' tent. She'd meant what she'd said to Venus, she did think that she and Achilles had been doing well together. Kat actually liked spending time with him. Yes, he was very alpha male and completely testosteroney. He was also interesting and sexy. But now here they were, back where they'd started last night with her being warned off by him.

Kat paused outside the tent, drew a deep breath and straightened her spine. Well, last night hadn't been so bad. Tonight she had the backup of Love herself and maybe she could work on a rerun . . . maybe even one with a twist.

He'd already dimmed the lanterns when she entered the tent. Kat could see his shape in bed, and that he was sitting up and definitely not asleep.

'I thought you might not return.'

'Where else did you think I'd go?'

'If the servants helped you to escape, I wouldn't stop them,' he said.

'Nice to know you want me here so badly.' She made no attempt to hide the sarcasm in her voice.

'What I want is not the point.'

'Well maybe it should be.' Kat strode across the chamber and pushed aside the bed curtains. 'Today when Diomedes accidentally wounded you, did you *want* the berserker to possess you?'

'No, of course not.'

'And so he didn't.'

'It's not that simple.'

'Achilles, maybe it is that simple.'

He shook his head, clearly disgusted. 'I have carried this curse for thirteen years. If that were true do you think I wouldn't know?'

'How about considering this theory: You *are* older now, you *have* dealt with the berserker for more than a decade. You understand it better. Hell, Achilles, you understand yourself better. Maybe there's a way you can use your age and experience to fight what triggers the possession.'

'So tell me, Princess, how do I practice this theory of yours? On whom do I chance unleashing a monster?'

'What do you remember from last night?'

'Everything.'

She felt a shiver of excitement at how his voice had deepened and became intimate with just that one word. 'Then you also remember that the berserker didn't possess you.'

'No, but you did.'

Kat forced herself not to squirm. She didn't particularly like Achilles believing that she had used some magic spell on him, but how else could she describe it? Explaining her master's degree and the intricacies of hypnotism was simply not a possibility. Instead she cleared her throat, tried not to look too uncomfortable and said, 'Well, I was sent to you by a goddess.'

'An oracle of Athena in my bed . . .' His lips tilted up just slightly. 'It is an intriguing, alluring thought.'

'I didn't stay in your bed all night last night.' She couldn't look away from the brilliant blue in his eyes. God, he was so incredibly male and sexy, and so obviously like playing with a captivating fire.

'Perhaps you could remedy that tonight.' And then, as if catching himself in saying too much, he added, 'If you think it wise, Princess.'

'Wise is probably not the word I'd use.' Like he was pulling her to him by an invisible rope, Kat approached the bed. Without saying anything he moved over, though not far enough to keep their bodies from touching. Kat sat beside him as she had the night before. 'So since I didn't run screaming from you, would you like to try that spell again?'

'There are few things I would like more.'

'You'll have to relax,' she said.

'And you will have to help me with that,' he said.

'Then close those gorgeous blue eyes,' she said with a smile.

His brows lifted in surprise.

'Oh, come on,' she teased. 'You must have been told you have beautiful blue eyes.'

'Not for more than a decade I haven't.' He didn't say it in an oh-please-feel-sorry-for-me voice. He said it in a practical, no-nonsense, that's-just-the-way-it-is voice. Which made Kat's heart squeeze.

'Well, I'm telling you. Now close them.' Kat brushed a hand gently down his face and he closed his eyes obediently. 'And relax your body.' He shifted his posture a little, like he was settling in against the thick down mattress. 'I want you to focus on your breathing.' Kat's voice automatically changed, became softer, more soothing, as she began to take Achilles through the stages of relaxation that would induce hypnotism. He responded more quickly than he had the night before, and within just a few minutes Kat had him back on the beach in his special cove, completely and deeply hypnotized.

'Tell me what you see in the cove tonight, Achilles.'

'The sun is setting. It's hot, but the breeze is cool against my skin.'

'What are you doing?'

'Touching myself while I wait for you.'

Kat's body jerked in surprise and she almost bit her tongue. She looked down. No, his hand was not actually under the very thin sheet literally touching himself, but she could clearly see the hard bulge that was growing bigger by the instant. Achilles shifted his legs restlessly, and the sheet dropped down far enough to let her see the engorged head of his penis, already slick with a drop of moisture that had escaped the slit.

'What is it you want me to do?' she asked softly.

'Touch me, Princess. It has been so long since I've known a woman's touch.'

His breathing had deepened, but not alarmingly so. Kat leaned forward, resting her hands gently on his chest. She felt him shiver under her touch. 'Remember,' she whispered, 'you're calm and you're dreaming.' She let her hands roam down his taut abdomen all the way to his thighs, pushing aside the sheet. 'You are an incredibly beautiful man,' she said softly. To Kat the scars that criss-crossed his body extenuated his power. They were visible signs of his strength and of the battles he'd fought and won.

His penis was fully aroused and lay stretched up his abdomen. She stroked it gently, letting her hand trail down to cup his

Kalchas's thin lips twisted into the caricature of a smile. 'Yes, I believe he would, great King.'

'In theory, only,' Agamemnon said.

'Of course, my lord.' They walked silently for a few steps and then Kalchas asked, 'Shall I cut a fat black bull from the herd, great king?'

'Yes, I do believe you shall.'

Kalchas hesitated. 'My lord, forgive me, but I must remind you that Zeus has made it clear he favors Priam. Would you not be risking his wrath to, in theory only, instigate his daughter's death?'

Agamemnon smiled slyly. 'One would believe so, except that I happen to be under the protection of Hera herself. And even Zeus does not like to evoke the anger of the Queen of Olympus.'

'Excellent, my lord. I know just the bull.'

Kat woke slowly. She felt fabulous. She stretched languorously, thinking that it must be Saturday, which meant she didn't have to be in the office at all. Mimosas sounded good. She'd call Jacky and they could meet at the Stonehorse Café for the bottomless Saturday mimosa special – to hell with that stupid diet idea. She would love her thighs as they were, and a size ten just wasn't that big.

Then she rolled over, opened her eyes and glanced down at said size ten thighs, which were, at that instant, very bare, very young and very size two to fourish and reality crashed back.

She gave the pillow beside her what she hoped was a nonchalant look while she held her breath. His side of the bed was empty, and she breathed again. Then she blinked and squinted. No, his side of the bed wasn't *empty*. There was something on his pillow. Kat sat up. It was a long, thin lotus blossom the color of

179

moonlight. Smiling, she picked it up and inhaled its delicate scent.

Achilles, the famous warrior who had been written about for thousands of years, had given her a flower. It made her ridiculously, romantically happy.

'Yes, indeedy, Virginia, there is a Santa Claus.'

Humming softly to herself Kat got up and washed. Then, naked except for Venus's golden heart pendant, *that I hadn't needed*, she thought smugly, Kat searched around the bed, trying to find her discarded clothes. She was just starting to worry and consider wrapping the sheet around herself and going in search of Jacky when she noticed layers of new silken robes draped across the back of a chair. The undertunic was a buttery yellow, and the over-robe was the same heart-stopping blue as Achilles' eyes. The outfit was diaphanous and gorgeous and probably worth a small fortune.

Clearly it was good to be Achilles' girlfriend.

Her tuneless humming changed to the chorus of 'I Feel Pretty' as she got dressed and combed her hair, thoroughly appreciating Polyxena's long, thick locks. Then she ducked out of the tent, pausing to blink and adjust her eyes to the sunlight.

As the day before, there was food ready at the campfire. Stretching and thinking about how sex always made her hungry, Kat headed to the table – in time to see Jacky coming from the direction of the Myrmidon tents. She was stretching, too, and looking sweetly rumpled. The two friends met beside the campfire.

Jacky looked Kat over from head to toe.

'Well, shit. Now I'm worried,' Jacky said.

'About what?' Kat said around a piece of excellent goat cheese she'd snagged from a laden tray on the table and popped in her mouth.

'Natural disasters.'

'Jacky, what are you talking about?'

'What do you figure are the odds of both of us gettin' laid on the same night?'

Kat grinned. 'Today, I'd say pretty good.'

'Which is definitely abby-normal. So I'm just sayin' it makes me worry about lightning strikes and tsunamis and such.'

'Don't be such a cynic. Everything is going to be just fine. Actually everything is going to be great.'

'Lord, I'd forgotten how nauseatingly optimistic sex makes you.'

'It is a beautiful day, isn't it?' Kat said.

Jacky shook her head in disgust. 'You seriously have it bad.'

Kat bumped Jacky with her shoulder. 'So Patroklos wasn't any good in bed?'

'I did not say that.'

'You're kinda grumpy.'

'I'm not grumpy. I'm—' Jacky paused for effect. 'Sore. This little white girl body needs some breakin' in.'

'Oooh!' Kat laughed. 'No, what you are is stank. Okay, I want all the details.'

'You first. Clearly you fornicated with your boy. You're still in one piece so I'm assumin' he didn't turn into a monster. Details, please.'

Kat broke off a piece of bread and dipped it in a dish of spiced olive oil. 'No, he didn't turn into a monster. Yes, we fornicated. And, yes. It was soooo good.'

'He stayed under your diabolical slut sex spell the entire time?'

'I am not diabolical. And, yes, mostly. There was a moment of concern at the end, but everything turned out fine.'

'In other words, your magical va-jay-jay saved him.'

'That's certainly how I like to think of it.' Kat hesitated, then added. 'Jacqueline, I like him.'

'Ah oh.'

'Yeah.'

'Okay, so where is this going?'

'Huh?'

'I mean, it's perfectly acceptable that you like him, nice even. But what's the next step? Are we completing our mission?'

'Venus seems pleased and Achilles definitely isn't fighting. So I guess we are.'

'You saw Venus?'

Kat swallowed another piece of cheese. 'Yep. She gave me this.' She lifted the heart locket and let Jacky inspect it. 'It's a panic button.'

'No shit? How does it work?'

'Supposedly I open it, call for her and she turns into the cavalry. I don't think literally, though. But what do I know? I barely remember the humanities class that dealt with mythology.' Kat dropped the locket back down beneath her robes. 'I'm just hoping it keeps Venus from constantly Peeping Tom-ing. Do you know she *watches?*'

'Doesn't surprise me in the least. She is Goddess of Love – that job has to come with a certain degree of nastiness.' Jacky frowned at the plate of olives. 'And I still don't like olives. Pass me some of that bread, would ya?'

'All right, your turn,' Kat said, passing the bread. 'Give me all the gory details.'

'He's young and very energetic. It was good.'

'That's it? Young – energetic – good? You've got to be kidding.'

'All right, fine. It was *very* good.' Jacky fidgeted and nibbled at a piece of dried meat.

Kat gasped. 'You *like* him!'

'So? You *like* Achilles.'

'Patroklos is so damn white.' Kat giggled.

Jacky narrowed her eyes. 'Katrina Marie, you've been tellin' me for a decade that I need to expand my dating pool and go out with more white boys.'

'Yep, and may I just say a great big—' Kat hesitated dramatically.

'Go on ahead. Get it over with.' Jacky sighed.

'*I told you so!*' Kat sang.

'Happy now?'

'Delighted.' She popped one of the olives Jacky was ignoring into her mouth. 'I really wish I had some tea or something to drink. I don't think they have coffee yet. Do they?'

'I dunno,' Jacky mumbled around bread and cheese. 'I may just do like the natives and go straight for breakfast wine.'

'Princess? Did you say you would like some tea?'

Kat looked across the campfire to see Aetnia, who was curt-seying nervously to her. 'Yes, that would be great,' Kat said.

'Acalle always has tea brewing at her campfire. She is Ajax's war bride. It takes an entire campfire of his own to keep him fed, so he's on the outskirts of the Greek camp, not at all far from here. It will take just a moment to get you some tea.'

She hurried off and Kat found herself calling, 'Thanks,' to her back.

'Wonder how long she'd been sittin' there listening in?' Jacky said.

'We really need to pay better attention to stuff like that.'

'I say whatever,' Jacky shrugged. 'She's just a servant.'

'Jacky, they used to do really nasty things to people they thought were different, a.k.a., witchy. Like burn them. Or impale them. Or crucify them. None of those things are pleasant.'

'They didn't do unpleasant things to people they thought were oracles of the gods.' Jacky pointed a piece of bread at Kat. '*You* are an oracle. Remember?'

'Yeah, but *you* aren't.'

'Point taken.' They chewed for a while in silence. 'Do you think we'll ever get back?' Jacky finally whispered.

'I don't know,' Kat said slowly.

'You do still want to go back, don't you?'

Kat hesitated.

'Katrina?'

'I do, of course,' she said quickly. 'But I . . .'

'You want to fix him first.'

'Not exactly.' Kat sighed. 'I want to save him.' She met Jacky's eyes, finding the friend within the unfamiliar shape and color. 'I don't want him to die.'

Jacky opened her mouth to respond when Aetnia hurried up to them, a large kettle in one hand and a pottery mug in the other.

'Here you are, my lady. Rose hips and chamomile with a hint of lavender, sweetened with honey.'

'Oh, thank you, Aetnia.' Kat took the offered mug while the girl poured the aromatic mixture.

'No problem. I didn't want some,' Jacky said with some asperity.

'Don't worry, I'll share,' Kat said.

'Oh, nevermind. I should go check on the injured men. Then Patroklos and I are going for a swim. *Without* swimwear,' she said with a wink.

'Where are Patroklos and Achilles?' Kat asked.

'My man said something about going to the Greek camp to sharpen weapons. I don't have a clue where yours is.'

'Oh, so he's a man now?' Kat kidded under her breath, conscious of Aetnia's listening presence across the campfire.

'Freshness,' Jacky mouthed back. 'Anyway,' she raised her voice. 'Gotta go check on the men. No rest for the wicked, ya know.' With a flip of her blonde tresses, Jacky sauntered off.

'My lady? I know where you can find Achilles,' Aetnia said, moving closer to her now that Jacky had gone.

'Oh, good. Where?' Kat asked, not caring that she sounded like an eager schoolgirl.

'I heard that he was training down by the seashore.' Aetnia pointed in the direction of the sea, but well down the beach away from both camps.

'Thank you!' Kat grinned at her, grabbed a piece of bread and cheese to go, and then called over her shoulder, 'Oh, and the tea is great.'

'Anything for you, my lady,' Aetnia said.

Kat could feel Aetnia's eyes on her as she walked toward the beach, which actually made her a little uncomfortable. Aetnia seemed nice enough, but she was definitely obsessed with the princess/devotion thing. Not to mention she seemed to be giving off a weirdly nervous vibe. But then again, what did Kat know? She'd never been a princess before. She was probably misjudging Aetnia because she was using modern standards. Promising herself to be nicer to the young woman, Kat headed down the beach, looking for her lover.

'My lover . . .' she whispered, and then laughed at herself. Yes, she did have it bad.

Chapter Eighteen

The beach was gorgeous if, sadly, empty of Achilles, or any of the Myrmidons for that matter.

'Where the hell did all of those half naked men get to?' Kat muttered.

She probably should have double-checked about where he was and *then* gone to meet him. Kat shielded her eyes against the sun's glare off the water. It had to be at least lunch time. Why hadn't she brought something like a picnic lunch? And a blanket, for that matter. Maybe they could practice some daytime hypnotism.

Of course that was difficult to do without the patient – or the victim (she could almost hear Jacky adding).

Kat sighed. Aetnia had obviously heard wrong. Maybe they were practicing in the area of the beach between the two camps. Feeling hot and annoyed, Kat headed back, walking close enough to the waves that she had to take off her slippers and hold her robes out of the way. But the water felt good against her feet and calves and she was kicking at the spray when a movement not far offshore caught her attention. Kat stopped and peered out into the crystal water, blinking to clear her eyes. There seemed to be something just under the water. She thought she saw flashes of silver and white and red. Hiking up her dress even farther, Kat took a step out imagining the brightly colored salt-water fish in the tanks at the Jenks Aquarium.

Shapes undulated just below the surface. Lots and lots of

shapes. At first Kat was struck by their odd beauty. They were gelatinous and glowed a blue-white light that reminded her of frozen meat lockers and the storage units sci-fi movies used for cryogenic holding. Weird . . . she could swear the water lapping around her calves had cooled by several degrees. When she saw the eerie, milky eyes she changed her mind about aquarium viewing and began to step back. Then Kat felt something clammy and cold slither around her ankle. She lifted her foot, meaning to brush off what was probably just a piece of seaweed and the sharp pain of a sting jolted her, followed almost instantly by a dreadful numbing sensation in her ankle and foot. Kat looked down.

It wasn't seaweed. What was wrapped around her totally dead-feeling foot was a long, thin tentacle that looked like a rat's tail covered in a clear membrane.

With a shriek, Kat tried to finish stepping back, but her leg had become completely useless and she fell to her knees.

The deeper water in front of her writhed with tentacles and glowing, sightless bodies as they closed on her.

Another tentacle snaked out. Kat ducked and tried to lurch back, but the thing was still gripping her ankle, and it was pulling her slowly into deeper water toward the swarm.

'Oh, god! Help!' Kat screamed. 'Achilles!' Where was her fucking knight in shining armor? Where was her hero? She managed to drag herself back a few inches and another membrane-wrapped tentacle snagged her other ankle, zapping her with a painful sting that faded even faster than the first bite as the numbness took hold.

Holy shit! These disgusting things were going to drag her under the water and kill her! She was going to die in this ancient world just as surely as she'd died in the car accident when Venus had—

Venus! Sobbing in relief Kat grabbed the locket and wrenched it open. 'Venus! They're killing me! Help!'

Then a tentacle wrapped around her wrist. Kat screamed in pain. Numbness blossomed throughout her hand and up her arm. Kat dropped the still-open locket, dug her other hand into the sand behind her like a claw and tried to hold on. *Please Venus, please hurry . . .*

Achilles was, indeed, drilling with his men – on the opposite end of the beach from where Aetnia had sent Kat. He had just stopped to wipe the sweat from his brow when the goddess materialized from a glittering cloud of smoke. One of the youngest Myrmidons instantly fell to his knees in supplication.

'Venus! Great Goddess! You have heard my prayers.'

'Of course, darling. Try telling her how you feel instead of moping,' she said quickly, barley glancing at him. Instead she motioned to Achilles, opening her cloak. 'You must come with me.'

Achilles blinked in surprise. He'd had nothing to do with the Goddess of Love for his entire life. What could she possibly want with him?

'The princess is in danger. Hurry!' Venus snapped.

With no hesitation Achilles grabbed his sword and stepped over to the goddess. Venus wrapped her cloak around him and they disappeared.

They were pulling her under. There was nothing Kat could do. She couldn't feel her legs. Her whole left side was numb. And she was having trouble breathing. The things had quit stinging her, and now their cold tentacles were slithering all over her body, almost caressingly. They moved languorously with the waves in a horrible parody of beauty and grace, and all Kat could do was gasp for breath and keep struggling back toward the safety of the beach.

Her mind was working clearly – her panic had subsided. Kat understood that had something to do with the poison that was filling her system. Just the same, she was grateful for it. It had only been moments since she had screamed into the locket, but already it was probably too late. Even if Venus showed up the poison would more than likely kill her. Kat was just deciding to close her eyes and give in to the inevitable when the world exploded.

Achilles materialized from a cloud of diamond smoke. Utterly detached, she watched him leap into the water beside her and slice through the tentacles binding her numbed body.

'Ah, Goddess! Please no. Polyxena! Listen to me. Do not close your eyes!' Achilles seemed to be shouting at her from very far away, even though logically she knew he was touching her – pulling her from the water.

The lazy tempo of the creatures instantly changed. Five membranes snaked out and wrapped around Achilles' sword arm. She knew the moment they stung him. She saw the jolt of white hot pain enter his body. As his eyes began to glow he literally tossed her onto the beach and then, with a feral snarl, he waded back into the deadly water.

Achilles changed. She watched the whole thing, crumpled on the beach, gasping for breath. Unbelievably his body actually got bigger. When his face turned so she could glimpse it, Kat saw a stranger – and one who looked more demon than human. His eyes blazed red. His lips were pulled back, baring his teeth. The sounds he made were terrible, more like a furious animal than a man. Kat thought he looked like a surreal photograph in which one person's body had been superimposed over another.

He was inhumanly fast, slicing through the undulating mass of creatures that had swarmed him. Obviously he was immune to their poison. Kat managed a small scream when the hundreds of little tentacles were replaced by one huge, snaking arm, thick as Achilles' waist. The panic fluttered alive inside her as she realized that must have been what they had been trying to pull her out to. Achilles sliced through it as if it were made of jelly. There was an earsplitting, hissing scream and then all the tentacles withdrew in a seething mass of blood and foam.

Achilles lunged out after them, roaring a challenge, but they disappeared quickly into the depths. Then he turned toward her. His eyes were still glowing red – a red that was reflected in the blood and gore that covered his body.

'*Princess* . . .' His voice was utterly changed – lower, guttural and completely not Achilles. He started to walk from the water toward her, his lips twisted in a dangerous smile.

Kat wanted to talk to him – to try to reach her lover, who she knew was still inside the monster. But she couldn't speak – she couldn't move. All she could do was watch as the monster who had been a man approached her, engorged, enraged and deadly.

There was a flash of silver from the sea behind him, and then a sweet, calm voice drifted across the waves.

'Achilles, son, you need to come to me.'

The monster paused, breathing hard. He turned around slowly, as if fighting against himself. Kat could see that a lovely woman with silver-blonde hair had risen from the waves.

'*Thetis.*' He growled the word.

The sea goddess's voice hardened. 'Be gone berserker! My son has no more need of you today.' She flipped her fingers at him and a crystal wave crashed up over Achilles, covering his entire body. When it receded, it had taken with it the blood and gore that had spattered the warrior, as well as the monster who had possessed him.

Instantly Achilles rushed out of the water to her. Kat was glad his eyes weren't glowing red anymore, and he definitely looked like himself again – scarred and imperfect, but hers. She tried to smile at him. She tried to lift her hand to touch him. But everything was very far away and gray around the edges, and her body wouldn't obey her.

'Mother!' she heard him call. 'Please help her!'

Then the silver goddess was kneeling beside her son. Kat thought her smile was the most tender, loving expression she'd ever seen. 'Of course I'll help her, my golden one.' The goddess touched Kat's forehead and she felt a rush of warmth and love, and then everything went black.

Chapter Nineteen

Kat heard Jacky's muttering before she opened her eyes. She was saying something that had to do with 'Christ on a cracker' and 'no goddamn sense'. Kat smiled. If she'd died and gone to hell, at least Jacky had come with her. Again. She opened her eyes.

'Hey,' she croaked. 'I thought you watched your language when you were on duty.'

Immediately Jacky bent over her, simultaneously taking her pulse and wiping her face with a cool cloth.

'Katrina, honey, are you back with me?'

'If you're calling me honey it must be bad. Did I lose a leg or something?'

'Oh, thank the sweet weeping baby Jesus, it is you.' Jacky kissed her square on the lips. 'Don't you ever, ever scare me like that again.'

'Well, hell, Jacky. It's not like I *asked* those disgusting things to attack me.'

'Okay, I want you to count my fingers.' Jacky held up three fingers like a baseball umpire.

'You have three fingers, just like Yoda. By the by, if you don't get a manicure soon and trim those things you're going to resemble him even more closely.' Kat batted weakly at her friend's hand. 'Do I have to sleep with you to get something to drink?'

'Thankfully, no, because your breath is really nasty right now.'

Jacky turned to the side table and poured water from a pitcher into a cup, then helped Kat drink from it.

'No wonder. Man, I so feel like shit.'

'Well, for a woman who's been in a coma for four days, you're lookin' remarkably and surprisingly alive.'

'Four days!' She gasped between long gulps of water.

'Easy. It'll make you feel sick if you drink too much.'

'I already feel sick.'

'You'll feel worse. And you may puke.'

She took one more drink and then reluctantly gave Jacky the cup and lay back on her pillow. 'Four days, Jacky? Why? Achilles' mom healed me from the poison. Well, at least I thought she did.'

'She did. Or rather Thetis did what she could despite your "remarkably breakable human shell" as Athena put it. You had to do the rest of the recovery by yourself.'

'Athena was here?'

'Yep. All three of them have been. Well, four actually, if you count Achilles' mom, who was with him when he carried you – half dead and totally freaking me out – into camp four days ago.'

'Huh. I feel special.'

Jacky rolled her eyes. 'You are *special*,' Jacky used air quotes around the word. 'When we get home I'll send the short bus for you.'

'Hey wait. If all of the goddesses were here why didn't they just use their powers to zap me awake?'

'I did mention that. And perhaps not in the nicest of tones.'

'You? Being short and crabby with someone? I'm so shocked. Imagine that not going over well with goddesses.'

'Nevertheless, apparently the bogey monster that grabbed you had more than a touch of magic behind it. The goddesses couldn't negate all of it. Your humanity had to fight it off by your own damn self.'

'Bet that made you grumpy.' Kat grinned at her best friend.

'Perhaps a little.' She took Kat's hand and squeezed it. 'I am so glad you didn't die on me.'

'Me too.' Kat squeezed back. 'Sorry I scared you.'

'That's okay. I've decided you owe me shoes.'

'Shoes?'

'Remember your gorgeous pair of red patent leather stiletto pumps I've lusted after?'

'Yeah.'

'I'm through lusting.'

'Jeesh, you are a mean nurse.'

'Thank you. Now tell me what the hell bit you.'

'I have no clue. One second I was walking along the beach trying to find Achilles, the next I saw something in the water so I stopped to look. Then this tentacle thing grabbed me and stung me, which paralyzed my leg. Then I got grabbed and stung again and again, which is when I pushed the panic button and yelled for Venus.' Remembering, Kat touched the locket that still hung between her breasts and shivered. 'Those things were seriously gross. All undulating and rat-tail-like, and there were literally hundreds of them swarming me.'

Jacky's face looked like she'd just eaten a lemon. 'Jesus god! Rat-tail-like? That is so vile!'

'Yeah, and they were pulling me out into deep water to feed me to what looked like their gigantic mama when Achilles materialized, changed into the berserker and kicked ass. Then his mom touched me and I passed out. The end. But didn't Achilles tell you most of that already?'

'Uh, no. Achilles has been Mr Big and Broody since he

brought you back and has barely spoken two words to anyone. Even Patroklos can't talk to him. Actually Patroklos has had a lot on his mind and I think he's tired of tryin' to get Achilles to do more than grunt and growl.'

'Jacky, are you making the boy crazy?'

'No. Patroklos and I are fine. Better than fine. It's the battle he's not fighting and stuff like that getting to him. But as long as Achilles doesn't fight – Patroklos doesn't fight, so I'm not really worried about it.' Jacky made a dismissive gesture. 'Anyway, my woman's intuition, which is quite good, says Achilles is brooding because you saw him turn into the Big Bad and he thinks you're gonna run shriekin' from him now. Of course you don't have enough sense to do that, which I tried to explain to him, but he wasn't listenin'. Actually that night I think he might have been drinking heavily. But whatever.'

'Maybe you should go get him and I'll explain to him myself how little sense I have.'

'That's a good idea,' Jacky said. Then she added. 'Kat, he did change into that berserker thing completely, didn't he?'

'Yes,' Kat said softly. 'It was awful.'

Jacky didn't phrase it like a question, but Kat nodded her head. 'It was absolutely awful. It wasn't him anymore. Whatever it is that possesses him isn't even human. It can't be.'

'But he was himself when he brought you back to camp,' Jacky said.

'His mom called to him, and then did something with the water and it was like it washed the berserker away.'

'Which you're interpreting to mean that the thing can actually be controlled. Am I right?'

'Aren't you always right?'

Jacky snorted. 'I'll go get your grumpy-ass man.' Before she left the tent she looked back at Kat. 'Promise you'll be careful.'

'Promise.'

'You know I love you.'

'You know I love you, too, Jacky.'

Jacky managed to smile through her worry as she ducked out of the tent.

Kat was just thinking about how awful her hair must look and trying to run her fingers through it when Achilles' bulk filled the entrance of the tent. His gaze went straight to her. She smiled. 'I do believe I owe you a big thank you for saving my life. Actually you and your mom.' When he didn't say anything, but just continued to stare at her, she babbled on. 'Your mom's gorgeous, by the way. And she seems like a lovely person, ur, I mean, goddess. If she's still here I'd love to meet her. Formally. *After* I look decent.'

'You look beautiful,' he said.

'You must be having problems with your sight. You should have Ja—I mean Melia look at your eyes. Her bedside manner leaves something to be desired, but she's an excellent nurse.'

Achilles' lips twitched up just a little at the edges. 'Melia is fiercely loyal to you. And my mother has returned to the depths. She cannot bide on dry land for long.' He paused, grasped his hands behind his back, then let them fall to his sides, then, as if he didn't know what to do with them, ran one hand through his hair, before finally saying, 'You do not owe *me* your gratitude for saving your life. It was not me who fought the creatures.'

Kat kept her gaze meeting his. 'I know that, but it was you who showed up for the fight. Plus, I'll bet you could have beaten those nasty things without the berserker.'

'No.' He spoke slowly as if he wanted to be certain she

understood. 'I could not have defeated the creatures without the berserker. The poison that almost killed you would have taken me. The berserker is what made me invulnerable to it.'

'Well, then, I'm glad the berserker was there.'

'How can you say that? I became a monster – a monster who would have raped you and left you for dead.'

'But you didn't. You came back. You stopped the monster.'

'Because my mother, a sea goddess, intervened!'

'Maybe,' Kat said reasonably. 'But maybe you can learn to stop the monster.'

'I don't believe that is possible.'

'Did you ever believe you would make love to a woman without the berserker possessing you?' she asked.

'No.' He hesitated. 'No, I did not.'

'What happened between us wasn't a dream. You know that, don't you?'

'I do know that,' he admitted.

'Then doesn't what I'm saying make sense?'

'You are an oracle of the goddess Athena. You have powers other women do not. That is why you can touch me and I remain a man.'

Kat automatically opened her mouth to tell him what utter crap that was. Then she closed it. She couldn't tell him.

And it hit her – why not? None of the goddesses had told her she couldn't. No one had said she needed to keep her real identity from Achilles. It was just the general Greek camp she had to fool. For a second she wished she could talk to Jacky first, but then again, she didn't really need to ask her BFF. Jacky was nothing if she wasn't honest. She told the truth – even when she shouldn't. It was part of what Kat loved about her. Plus, it was just plain stupid to keep this from Achilles. If she didn't trust him enough to trust him with her identity, she shouldn't have had sex with him. Everyone's mother even knew that.

'Achilles, would you please come closer? I need to talk to you about this oracle-of-the-goddess thing.'

Achilles walked through the bed curtain with a mixture of hesitation and anticipation. It was obvious that he wanted to touch her, that he needed to touch her. It was just as obvious as the fact that he was afraid to get too close to her in case she rejected him. She held out her hand and smiled. 'Would you sit beside me?'

The only thing about his guarded expression that changed was the relief that showed in his eyes. He sat beside her gingerly, taking her hand as if it were a butterfly. Then he surprised her by kissing it.

He spoke still looking down at her hand, circling the place he'd kissed with his thumb. 'When the monster left me and I saw you lying there I thought you were lost to me.' Then he looked up and met her eyes and she was shocked by the depth of sadness within his. 'I do not think I could bear losing you, too.'

That was the moment Kat stopped lying to herself. This wasn't just a mission. He wasn't a project she'd taken on for someone else. Somehow, regardless of time and worlds and logic, Achilles was Kat's destiny. She was bound to him as she'd never come close to being bound to any man in her world. And she didn't want to leave him. The realization was as freeing as it was daunting. Jacky was definitely going to kill her.

Kat had to clear her throat before she could speak.

'I'm not who you think I am.'

'You aren't Polyxena? But the servants recognize you as their princess.'

'Okay, I want to ask you to listen to me. Just let me say this, and if you start to not believe me because you think it sounds crazy, keep in mind how crazy it sounds that you can be possessed by a monster.'

Achilles frowned at her but said, 'I'll keep it in mind.'

'Good. The truth is that *this*' – Kat gestured down at her body – 'is Polyxena, Princess of Troy's body. But *this*' – she closed her fist over her heart – 'the soul inside the body, doesn't belong to Polyxena. At least it hasn't since the day Odysseus came to Hera's temple.'

'I do not understand.'

'The day I came to you Polyxena and her maidservant, Melia, were killed by Agamemnon's men as they sacked Hera's temple. That same day, in another time and another world, I was also killed in an accident, along with my best friend. Venus was watching me, so she grabbed our souls and ended up putting them in Polyxena and Melia's bodies.' She hurried on before he could say anything. 'No, it doesn't make much sense to me, either. The part I understand the most is that the goddesses wanted me here.' She paused on the verge of admitting to him that she was supposed to keep him out of the war so that Troy could win. But how could she ever tell him that? Kat drew a deep breath. 'They wanted me here for you. Athena and Venus and Hera all believe that your fate should be changed, and they think I can help you change it.'

As she spoke, Achilles had become more and more still. He didn't pull his hand from hers and he didn't look away from her steady gaze.

'You come from another world?'

'I don't know if it's exactly another world, but it is another time. It's the future.' She managed a little smile. 'A really long way in the future – like a couple thousand years or so.'

'And in your future do they know my name?'

'Yes, they do.'

He dropped her hand and stood, turning his back to her. 'Then how can you or the goddesses believe my fate can be changed? It has already happened!'

Kat thought about it and found the answer easily. 'It's fiction.'

He turned back to her. 'Fiction? Explain.'

'The stories of you and your time are told as fiction in our time – mythology to be specific. Stories that aren't true – that either never happened, or happened and then were exaggerated over time. Okay, here's a prime example. In my time people believe that you could have been immortal, you were completely invulnerable, except in your heel. You were struck by an arrow in your heel, which was your downfall.'

'My heel?' He looked down at his very normal-looking foot.

'Your heel,' she repeated. 'You're so famous for it that the tendon that runs behind the ankle,' Kat pushed the bedclothes back from her leg and pointed at the tendon, 'is known as the Achilles tendon all over my world.'

'That doesn't make sense.'

'Exactly my point. Well, unless you tell me that the only way you can actually be killed is to be shot or stabbed or whatever through your heel.'

'The heel isn't even a vulnerable area of the body. Slice the tendon and a man can usually be defeated because he's fighting without the use of one leg, but the wound alone won't kill him.'

'So your heel isn't invulnerable.'

'No.'

'And you're not immortal.'

'Of course not.'

'Okay, and how about this – fiction has it that Troy is defeated by a gigantic, hollow horse filled with Greeks. They sneak into the city inside the belly of the fake horse.'

'You jest.'

'I'm serious as a heart attack.'

'But a giant hollow horse is silliness.'

'Again, do you see my point? You and the Trojan War are written about in history, but the *facts* of your life and the war are mixed up and amplified with myths, so what really happens to you could, in actuality, be much different than the fate written about you.'

'And what is that fate?'

Kat didn't look away from his piercing blue gaze. 'You die here at Troy in this, the last year of the Trojan War.'

Chapter Twenty

Kat thought he would ask more questions about his death, but instead he just nodded briefly and disinterestedly. The only thing he seemed really interested in was her. 'Will you tell me your real name?'

'Katrina Marie Campbell. My friends call me Kat.'

'And you are not a princess?'

Kat laughed. 'No way. I'm definitely not a princess. I'm a shrink.'

'You make things small?'

'Oh, god no. I'm sorry. Shrink is a slang term for my job. I'm a psychologist. That's someone who counsels people – helps them to be emotionally healthy. My specialty is couples counseling.'

'And this is the reason you know the spell needed to calm me?'

'Yeah, but it's not a spell. Actually it's not magical at all. You can even learn to do it for yourself. It's called hypnotism. It's just a way of being able to relax deeply and reach your subconscious mind.'

'Like the dreaming mind? That's why, at first, I believed I only dreamed that you touched me.'

Kat felt her cheeks get warm. 'Yes. Okay, I'm sorry about that. I really didn't mean to take advantage of you. It's just that you were so ... uh ... *male*, and when I started touching you, you didn't want me to stop and—'

Achilles' laughter was loud and long and uninhibited.

'What?' She frowned at him. Okay, she wanted him to laugh and smile more, but not *at* her.

He kissed her hand again. 'I have not been touched by a woman in a decade and you are apologizing to me for something I think of as a miracle. You are an odd, magical woman, Katrina Marie Campbell.'

'Call me Kat,' she said. 'And it really wasn't ethical what I did. I don't want you to think that's how I normally behave.'

His amused expression sobered. 'Are you truly sorry about what has passed between us?'

'No, I'm not sorry about what happened. I'm sorry that I didn't talk with you about it first.'

He smiled. 'And I would not have believed you, and quite probably sent you away for your own protection. No, Kat, you have nothing to be sorry for, unless you do not want my devotion and my protection and my love, because I wish to give you those three things, along with so very much more.'

Kat took both of his hands in hers and looked straight into his blue eyes. 'I do accept your devotion and protection and love, and I also want something else from you.'

'Name it and if it is in my power to give it to you, I will.'

'I want you to stay out of the fighting until we're sure you can control the berserker. And I specifically want you to stay away from Hector.'

'The prophecy said that I was destined to die after I killed him.'

Kat squeezed his hands. 'Then don't kill him! How much easier could that be?'

'At this moment I cannot imagine what could provoke me to fight Hector.' His snort was self-mocking. 'I hold no grudge against Hector. I know he is an honorable man, well loved by his family and the Trojan people. I don't enjoy cutting down honorable young men in the prime of their lives when they have done nothing to me.'

'Good. That's settled. So we stay here together and we work on your self-hypnotism abilities.'

Achilles gave her a horrified look. 'I can't bespell myself!'

'Achilles, how many times do I have to explain to you that it's not a spell? It's nothing more than breathing and concentration and relaxation.'

'You really believe I can learn to control the berserker?'

'I don't know if you can control him,' she said honestly. 'What I do believe is that I can teach you how to be sure he doesn't possess you, so that you won't have to control him.'

Achilles got up and paced back and forth beside the bed. 'If the berserker no longer possesses me . . .' His words trailed off.

'Then your whole life won't be about fighting,' Kat finished for him. 'Your fate would change. Is that what you want?' Her chest felt tight while she waited for him to answer.

He stopped and looked at her. 'I could return to my country, marry, raise children and know love and peace and forever put war and death and hatred behind me.'

'You could,' she said.

'It sounds like a dream. The kind of unbelievable dream I had for two nights with you.'

'But it wasn't a dream. It was real.'

'Then perhaps the future that I'd thought impossible can be real, too. Yes. It is what I want,' he said firmly.

'All right – let's make it real.'

Achilles moved back to her bedside. 'You say it like it can come true, like my fate can be changed. When you look at me like this, and speak thus, I almost believe you.'

'Believe me, and more importantly, believe in yourself,' Kat said.

Achilles bent and kissed her gently on the lips. She could feel his hesitation and knew that he was afraid to push the line of intimacy between them, which she completely understood. No way did they need a return of the berserker, especially not when Achilles' belief in himself and his ability to fight the monster off was so shaky.

Thankfully, at that instant, her stomach let out a huge, obvious growl. Kat laughed. 'I'm starving.'

'Again,' he said, with his slight smile. 'I'll have the maidservants bring—'

'Ugh, no!' she interrupted, already swinging her legs over the edge of the bed. 'I need to get up – walk around – take a bath.' He looked like he was going to argue with her, but she held her hand out to him. 'Could you help me with all three of those things?'

'Anything within my power,' Achilles said, taking her hand and wrapping it securely through his arm.

Kat thought she felt surprisingly good for a woman who'd been poisoned, almost eaten and in a coma for four days. By the time she'd reached the bench outside their tent, she was definitely steadier on her feet, even though she sat down and let Achilles call for food and drink. Jacky was over by the campfire with Patroklos (who Kat thought looked utterly love struck), and they both hurried over to her.

'How are you feeling? Having any dizziness? Shortness of breath? Blurred vision? Anything still feel paralyzed or sluggish?'

'Fine. No, no, no and no. Would you just relax? I'm definitely—'

But before she could finish the sentence, Aetnia rushed over to her and threw herself at Kat's feet, clutching her ankles and sobbing.

'Oh, my lady! Forgive me! Please forgive me! I had no idea I was sending you into danger.'

Kat exchanged shocked looks with Jacky as she tried to extract herself from Aetnia's fervent and wet embrace. 'Aetnia, it wasn't your fault. You were just trying to help me find Achilles. You couldn't have known about those sea creature things.'

'No! It was my fault. I shouldn't have listened to her. I am so sorry, Princess.' She sobbed brokenly.

Achilles grabbed the maidservant's arm and lifted her roughly to her feet. 'You should not have listened to whom?'

Aetnia shrieked and cringed away from Achilles, holding her hand out pleadingly to Kat. 'Princess! Don't let him kill me.'

'Don't be silly, Aetnia. He's not going to kill you.' Ignoring Achilles' dark look, Kat tugged on his arm so that he let the girl go while she took Aetnia's hand and guided her to the bench to sit between her and a scowling Jacky.

'I wouldn't be too free with the no-one's-killing-her promises until we find out exactly what she had to do with the attack against you,' Jacky said.

Aetnia made a mouselike squeaking sound and scooted closer to Kat. 'Don't let the witch bespell me, Princess!'

Jacky hissed at her. Aetnia screamed. Kat thought she heard Achilles growl.

'Okay! Enough! Everyone just settle down.' Kat clamped a hand on Aetnia's shoulder to keep her from literally crawling into her lap. She pointed at Jacky. 'She is not a witch.' Then at Achilles. 'And he is not a monster. Now, you are going to take three deep breaths and then explain, slowly and without hysterical crying, what you're talking about. Breathe with me.' Even though Kat would much rather shake the ridiculous woman, she led her in taking three cleansing breaths. 'You're fine. Now talk to me.' When the maidservant's eyes skittered nervously to Achilles and Jacky, Kat did shake her shoulder. 'No. Talk to *me*.'

Aetnia's gaze snapped back to Kat's. 'It – it was w-when I went to the Greek camp to get your tea.'

Kat nodded encouragement. 'Yes, I remember. It was nice of you to get the tea for me.' Kat also remembered that it was shortly after that Aetnia had sent her to the seashore where she was supposed to have found Achilles, but she carefully kept her expression and voice neutral. 'What happened when you were in the Greek camp?'

'I saw Briseis. She was talking with a group of war brides at Acalle's campsite. She – she was talking about you and –' Aetnia hesitated, glancing fearfully at Jacky, who curled her lip at her.

'Briseis was talking about Melia and me,' Kat said, squeezing the girl's shoulder and forcing her attention away from Jacky. 'What was she saying?'

'And why does that have anything to do with the princess being attacked?' Achilles added, in a voice he was obviously trying to keep reasonable.

Kat could feel Aetnia begin to tremble under her hand. 'Just talk to me. It'll be fine,' she said soothingly. 'What did Briseis say?'

'She called Melia a witch and said she has bespelled Patroklos and might even be trying to teach you spells, too.'

Kat heard Patroklos snort and Jacky had a minifit of coughing.

'Is that all Briseis said?'

'No. She heard me ask Acalle for some of her special tea for you, and she told me that if I wanted to save you from Melia's evil that I should be sure you go to the seashore so that Achilles' mother, the sea goddess Thetis, could gift you with immunity to witchery. That is why I told you Achilles was at the shore. I thought only to save you, my lady! Please believe me!' And she dissolved into sobs again.

'That bitch set you up,' Jacky said. She gave Aetnia a disdainful look. 'And I don't mean this bitch. I mean Briseis.' Then she waggled her brows at Patroklos, who was standing beside Achilles. 'And did you know I've bewitched you, Blondie Bear?'

Patroklos grinned. 'Completely, my beauty.'

Jacky made kissing noises at him.

Kat ignored them, looking instead at Achilles, whose expression had become masklike and unreadable. 'Wow. Briseis must really have a thing for you. She wants me out of the way big time.'

'She couldn't want me. She didn't. She was as all other women toward me,' Achilles said, then his expression softened for an instant. 'All other women except you, Princess.'

'Would you have known it if she wanted you?' Jacky said. 'Not to be insulting or anything, Achilles, but you don't exactly strike me as an expert on what women want.'

'Don't be mean,' Kat said.

'I'm not! I'm just tellin' the truth. Briseis might have had a major thing for Achilles and he was clueless about it. Didn't you say she gave you massively dirty looks in Agamemnon's tent?'

'She did,' Kat said.

'It's not Briseis. It's Agamemnon,' Achilles said.

'Huh?' Kat and Jacky said together.

'Go on. Go back to the campfire and prepare food for the princess,' Achilles told Aetnia before he continued. She shot out of her seat on the bench and ran, stumbling, to the campfire. 'Briseis didn't send you to the seashore and what she believed would be your death because of desire for me. She has no power to summon sea creatures to do her bidding.'

'Agamemnon does. He has before,' Patroklos said.

Achilles nodded. 'Briseis is nothing more than Agamemnon's mouthpiece – the tool he used to get the princess into a vulnerable position.'

'But why? What does he have against me?'

'It isn't you. It's me,' Achilles said. 'The king and I have long been enemies.'

'It's more than just that,' Patroklos said. 'Agamemnon is trying to force you to return to battle.'

'Why would he think killing me would make Achilles fight?'

'Haven't you heard? We've been bespelled by both of you.' Patroklos's smile was as boyish and engaging as always, but Kat was surprised by the dark circles she was just now noticing beneath his expressive eyes. And had he lost weight? His high cheekbones certainly looked more visible.

'So you get rid of us witches, and you two will, naturally, jump back in the battle,' Jacky said.

'Because, according to Agamemnon's reasoning, you have nothing to live for except battle,' Kat said, meeting Achilles' blue gaze.

'According to most people that is all I have to live for,' Achilles said.

'I'm not most people,' Kat said.

Achilles' lips lifted at the corners. 'And that is something of which I am becoming profoundly grateful.'

Chapter Twenty-one

'The problem is, Agamemnon's men are being killed,' Patroklos said abruptly. '*Greeks* are being killed.'

Achilles turned to his cousin. 'Agamemnon knew the possible cost to the Greek people when he left our shores to attack Troy under the guise of rescuing a faithless woman. *Many* men have been killed during the past nine years.'

'The fighting was even when we were in it.'

'Cousin, I am not keeping you from the battlefield. You, as well as all of my men, are free to fight with the Greeks.'

'No!' Jacky said, standing up and grabbing Patroklos's hand. 'You can't fight without Achilles, and Achilles has damn good reasons for not fighting. Agamemnon, the guy who's supposed to be a great king and leader, is a liar and a cheat. He just tried to have a princess killed to get his way. He's like a sneaky old harem bitch. Don't let him get to you.'

Kat watched Patroklos caress Jacky's cheek and was touched by the obvious adoration in the warrior's eyes as he smiled at her best friend. 'Don't fret, my beauty. Fighting without my cousin is not something I want to do.'

'It doesn't sound like Agamemnon knows you very well if he thinks the way to get you back on his side is to attack someone you care about,' Kat said.

'Agamemnon is a fool,' Achilles said. 'I know. I recognize a fool. I have been one for much of my life. The king fights for

'How'd he take it?'

Jacky smiled. 'With only a minor amount of freak-out. I did have to promise to draw a picture of a car for him, though.'

'A car?'

Jacky shrugged. 'You know how boys are. I was just mentioning stuff from the modern world . . . one thing led to another . . . and poof! He wants a car.'

'Makes sense in a *Twilight Zone* kind of way,' Kat said. 'You love him, don't you.'

'Sadly, I do believe I might. You love Achilles, don't you?'

'I think I might.'

'We are well and truly fucked, aren't we?' Jacky said.

'Yep,' Kat said.

'He's really getting upset about staying out of the battle,' Jacky said, her eyes following Patroklos to the campfire. 'I'd say I wished the Greeks would hurry and lose, but things are so different now. I just don't know what to wish for, let alone what to do.'

'I know what you mean. Before they were going to lose and we were going to be zapped home. But now I'm, well . . .' She faltered.

'I'm not sure if I ever want to go back,' Jacky finished for her.

'Exactly.'

Odysseus felt old. His shoulder pained him constantly. He'd been wounded earlier that day during the battle. Leading a wave against Troy's damnable walls he'd gotten within an archer's range. He'd been lucky. The arrow had only scraped the length of his outer thigh and not embedded itself in his body. Still, it was a painful nuisance, causing him to sit heavily on a gnarled old driftwood log. Absently he pressed a hand against the bloody linen that he'd hastily wrapped around the leg wound. At least he had this stretch of beach to himself. Odysseus stared out at the moon-soaked sea and raised the wineskin to his lips.

'You look tired.'

Odysseus closed his eyes and let her voice wash over him. When he opened them the goddess had materialized in front of him. She was wearing robes the color of a dove's wing, which matched her unusual eyes perfectly. She hadn't brought her war helmet and shield, nor did she carry any other symbolic image of her power. He thought she looked like an exquisite maiden in the bloom of beauty and youth. Odysseus bowed his head.

'Your presence rejuvenates me, great Goddess.'

Athena waved away his flattery. 'Aren't you sleeping well? I've told you before—' Noticing the bloody cloth on his thigh she broke off with a little gasp. Then, as was typical for the Goddess of War, she schooled her face back into a stern expression. 'Why didn't you tell me you've been wounded?'

'It's just an arrow scratch – it is nothing,' he said.

'I'm your goddess. I decide what is and isn't nothing.' She stepped forward and sank to her knees beside him. 'Let me see it.'

'Athena, no! You shouldn't be—' Odysseus began, grasping the goddess's elbow and trying to lift her to her feet.

Athena pressed her hand against his chest. 'It is my wish to see for myself how badly my warrior is wounded.'

Her touch made his chest contract. With a sigh he released her arm and sat back, stretching his leg out so that she could see the wound. When he started to unwrap the bloody bandage, her soft hands stopped him.

'I will do this. You just need to be still.'

Odysseus sat there, frozen, breathing in Athena's unique scent. She was so close that as she bent over his leg her long golden hair brushed his body, causing him to feel aroused and

'How'd he take it?'

Jacky smiled. 'With only a minor amount of freak-out. I did have to promise to draw a picture of a car for him, though.'

'A car?'

Jacky shrugged. 'You know how boys are. I was just mentioning stuff from the modern world . . . one thing led to another . . . and poof! He wants a car.'

'Makes sense in a *Twilight Zone* kind of way,' Kat said. 'You love him, don't you.'

'Sadly, I do believe I might. You love Achilles, don't you?'

'I think I might.'

'We are well and truly fucked, aren't we?' Jacky said.

'Yep,' Kat said.

'He's really getting upset about staying out of the battle,' Jacky said, her eyes following Patroklos to the campfire. 'I'd say I wished the Greeks would hurry and lose, but things are so different now. I just don't know what to wish for, let alone what to do.'

'I know what you mean. Before they were going to lose and we were going to be zapped home. But now I'm, well . . .' She faltered.

'I'm not sure if I ever want to go back,' Jacky finished for her.

'Exactly.'

Odysseus felt old. His shoulder pained him constantly. He'd been wounded earlier that day during the battle. Leading a wave against Troy's damnable walls he'd gotten within an archer's range. He'd been lucky. The arrow had only scraped the length of his outer thigh and not embedded itself in his body. Still, it was a painful nuisance, causing him to sit heavily on a gnarled old driftwood log. Absently he pressed a hand against the bloody linen that he'd hastily wrapped around the leg wound. At least he had this stretch of beach to himself. Odysseus stared out at the moon-soaked sea and raised the wineskin to his lips.

'You look tired.'

Odysseus closed his eyes and let her voice wash over him. When he opened them the goddess had materialized in front of him. She was wearing robes the color of a dove's wing, which matched her unusual eyes perfectly. She hadn't brought her war helmet and shield, nor did she carry any other symbolic image of her power. He thought she looked like an exquisite maiden in the bloom of beauty and youth. Odysseus bowed his head.

'Your presence rejuvenates me, great Goddess.'

Athena waved away his flattery. 'Aren't you sleeping well? I've told you before—' Noticing the bloody cloth on his thigh she broke off with a little gasp. Then, as was typical for the Goddess of War, she schooled her face back into a stern expression. 'Why didn't you tell me you've been wounded?'

'It's just an arrow scratch – it is nothing,' he said.

'I'm your goddess. I decide what is and isn't nothing.' She stepped forward and sank to her knees beside him. 'Let me see it.'

'Athena, no! You shouldn't be—' Odysseus began, grasping the goddess's elbow and trying to lift her to her feet.

Athena pressed her hand against his chest. 'It is my wish to see for myself how badly my warrior is wounded.'

Her touch made his chest contract. With a sigh he released her arm and sat back, stretching his leg out so that she could see the wound. When he started to unwrap the bloody bandage, her soft hands stopped him.

'I will do this. You just need to be still.'

Odysseus sat there, frozen, breathing in Athena's unique scent. She was so close that as she bent over his leg her long golden hair brushed his body, causing him to feel aroused and

214

breathless, yet afraid she would notice and disapprove. Did she realize how much he loved her? Of course she did. She was his goddess. She knew everything.

'This could fester. Why have you not cleaned and dressed it properly?' Athena looked up at him, a frown causing her smooth brow to wrinkle slightly.

He started to fabricate a story about being too busy to notice it, but the words that came from his lips were much different than those his mind had planned. They were, instead, from his heart. 'I was too weary to bother with it, Goddess. I almost wish it would fester and take me. Then, at least, I could rest.'

Her eyes narrowed in what an unknowing person would see as anger. But Odysseus understood Athena's every expression and what he saw was the shock that his words caused within her.

'You will not die. I forbid it.' The goddess placed her hand gently against his wound. She closed her eyes, obviously gathering her power. Then she whispered, 'Flesh obey your goddess's demand. Knit blood and skin, now, at my command.'

Athena's hand began to glow and Odysseus sucked in a sharp breath as her power surged into him. Her heat was a fire blazing in his blood, and he could feel his very flesh obeying her whispered command and healing itself. When she lifted her hand and opened her eyes, there was nothing but smooth flesh on his thigh and a small, pink scar.

'See,' he said softly, smiling into her gray eyes. 'I told you your presence would rejuvenate me.'

Athena smiled one of her rare smiles. 'Stubborn man. Will you always insist on flattering me?'

'As long as I am yours, my goddess.'

'Then I will be eternally flattered, for you will always belong to me, Odysseus.' Slowly, as if warring against herself, Athena pressed her hand against his thigh again. This time her touch was caressing instead of healing. Still kneeling beside him, the goddess stroked his skin. 'How long has it been since first I appeared to you?'

Odysseus didn't hesitate. 'Just over twenty-two years, Goddess. You first appeared to me before I could even grow a beard.'

'You were a delightful boy – already showing signs of wit and wisdom, and such a sweet, smooth face.' The goddess's usually sober expression softened into a smile of remembrance.

Odysseus thought his heart would break free from his chest at the sight of such loveliness. When his hand lifted to rub the stubble of his beard he hoped she didn't notice how it shook. 'Unlike now, my goddess. There is no sweet, smooth-faced boy here anymore.'

He expected her to agree with him, laugh and retreat back into what he thought of as her divine mask – the one that hid Athena's deepest feelings and kept the goddess from flaring with rage or passion. Instead she completely took him off guard by lifting her hand to stroke his cheek.

'I still see the boy,' she said in a voice so low that Odysseus had to strain to hear her above his rapidly beating heart.

Odysseus stared down at his goddess – the woman he'd loved since he was an untried boy. She'd appeared to him many times over his life. She'd chosen him as her warrior, as the mortal man to whom she bestowed her blessings above all others. But she'd rarely touched him, and she'd never come close to fulfilling his secret desire for her.

'What is it, Athena? What has happened?'

She took her hand from his face and stood, turning her back to him. 'Why must there be something wrong? May I not touch you for no other reason than because I wish it?'

He stood, too, and moved closer to her. 'Of course you may touch me, and for any reason you wish!' Odysseus raised his hands, longing to take her into his arms, but stopped himself. Athena was not a mortal woman. He could never forget that.

Still with her back to him she said, 'Did you know that even Achilles has found love?'

'He loves her, does he? I wondered if he would allow himself to.'

'You don't sound surprised,' Athena said, turning to face him.

Odysseus smiled and shrugged. 'It seems to me that love is rarely predictable.'

'Do you love Penelope?'

At the mention of his wife's name Odysseus's smile faltered. 'She is my wife and the mother of my son. I respect and honor her as such.'

Athena touched his face again. 'But do you love her?'

Almost without conscious thought Odysseus pressed his cheek into her hand. 'In my way, I do.'

'And what does that mean?'

'It means that I gave my heart to another just over twenty-two years ago. Since then there has been little left to give anyone else.'

'My Odysseus . . .' Athena whispered.

Before he could change his mind, Odysseus bent and pressed his lips gently against hers. When their mouths met a shock of desire sheared through his body with such intensity that it mixed pain with pleasure. Athena gasped, clearly feeling it, too, and her arms wrapped around his neck as she pulled him down to her and opened her mouth to deepen the kiss.

They stood there for what seemed like a very long time, their mouths exploring, their bodies pressed together. Suddenly Athena broke the kiss. She was breathing hard and her perfect mouth looked swollen, her cheeks pink where the roughness of his beard had scraped her. The goddess gazed up at him, gray eyes wide with several different emotions. Achilles prayed silently that desire and acceptance were chief among them.

'Venus was right,' Athena said softly. 'We should have become lovers years ago.' Without moving out of his arms, the goddess waved her hand over the beach around them, and a thick satin blanket materialized beneath them.

Very deliberately she stepped away from him, and then undid the ornate brooch that held her robes in place over her shoulder. The gray silk slid down her body to flutter at her feet and remind Odysseus, once again, of the delicate wings of a dove. She stepped out of the pool of cloth and gracefully lay down, creamy skin luminous and perfect in the moonlight as she reclined against the satin. Athena held her hand out to him.

'Come to me and prove the love you've had for me these past many years, my Odysseus,' she said.

Odysseus lay beside her, losing himself in his true love's body. He knew he could not possess her as his own. He knew this might be the only time he would ever know her intimate touch, but he gave his body to her without hesitation and with utter, joyous abandon, much as he had given her his heart all those years ago.

It would have to be enough . . . he thought afterward as Odysseus held Athena and their tears mingled. *Somehow it would have to be enough.*

Chapter Twenty-two

'I was wrong,' Venus said, bursting into Hera's private chamber.

'Was? I believe the correct word is "am," as in "I *am* wrong to disturb you in your chamber, my queen."'

'I know, I know. I wouldn't have bothered you except I do believe it's an emergency,' Venus said, conjuring ambrosia out of the air.

'What has happened? Do not tell me your little mortal who's in Polyxena's body has gotten herself almost killed again. By Zeus's beard! This Trojan War gets more and more annoying by the day.'

'No, Kat's fine. It's Athena.'

Hera had been reclining on a velvet and gold chaise, delicately nibbling sugarcoated, ambrosia-soaked grapes, but Venus's proclamation had her sitting straight up in concern. 'What is it? What has happened to Athena?'

'She has had sex with Odysseus.'

Hera blinked once, twice, then shook her head as if to clear it. 'I could not have heard you correctly. I thought you said Athena has had sex with Odysseus.'

'That is exactly what I just said.' Venus sat on the chaise next to Hera and conjured a glass of ambrosia for her queen. 'I was keeping an eye on the Greek camp. I mean, we certainly don't want another debacle like the attempt on Kat's life.'

'Of course – of course, you must be diligent. What did you see?'

'Sex. Between Odysseus and Athena. On the beach.' Venus spoke in shocked little bursts between sips of ambrosia. 'She conjured a satin blanket for them. It was actually very romantic, if slippery.'

'You watched after you knew who they were?'

'Of course not!' Venus drank her wine, not meeting Hera's eyes. 'Though I can tell you, from the little I saw, that Odysseus is very, um, *enthusiastic.*'

'Well, good for Athena. She has been far too serious for far too long.' Hera lifted one slim brow at Venus. 'And *this* is what you're saying you were wrong about? I'm surprised at you. How many times have I heard you rail at Athena that she needed to orgasm, she needed to loosen up, she needed this, that and the other. Now she's finally got some of the "other" and you think it's a problem? You, Goddess of Love, do not make sense.'

'I wanted her to do all of that with Odysseus *before* we decided to step into the Trojan War on the side of the Trojans. After what happened on the beach tonight do you think Athena is going to allow Odysseus and his men to be defeated?'

'Oh no.'

'That is my point. So we've gotten Achilles out of the way and set up events to bring about the end of the war. Now here comes the Goddess of War, firmly behind Odysseus's firm behind. Even if she only manipulates things without actually stepping into the battle, she will more than equal the absence of Achilles.'

'Perhaps you should have a little talk with your mortal. If we sent Achilles back into the fray along with Athena's influence, I imagine the war would end quickly. And that is what we wanted,' Hera said, sighing heavily. 'Though the thought of that wretched Agamemnon being victorious certainly rankles me.'

'I suppose I could . . .' Venus said.

'You suppose you could, but?'

'But I've also been watching Achilles and Katrina. They're in love,' Venus said.

'And this is important to me because?'

'Because if Kat loves him she won't be willing to send him to his death. Remember that little prophecy about Achilles being killed before the Trojan walls after he kills Hector?'

'Your modern mortal is but one player in this drama. I will not allow her to get in the way of what needs to be done,' Hera said.

'Hera, you have, of course, had dealings with modern mortals, and you do visit Tulsa to see your son from time to time, I know that. And I mean no disrespect when I say this, but for all your interaction with modern mortals, you really don't understand them. They don't revere or fear us as do the ancients.'

'They should!' Hera snapped. Then she drew a deep breath and controlled her temper. 'You know that I do not enjoy being cruel, so we'll wait a little longer and see what happens. But if Athena weighs in on the side of Greece, we will have no choice but to put our might behind the army and aid in their victory. I will not risk creating enmity with the Goddess of War.'

'There are those who would argue that love is stronger than war,' Venus said, with an unusual hardness in her voice.

Hera touched the goddess's arm softly. 'I did not mean to say that Athena is more important to me than are you. But would Love want to cause civil strife amongst the gods for the sake of one modern mortal?'

'Isn't that what I'm being accused of in the ancient world, only the strife I was supposed to have caused over one mortal woman is between the Greeks and the Trojans?'

'Yes, and how do you feel about that?' Hera asked shrewdly.

'I despise the fact that the war is being blamed on me,' Venus said.

'So I'm assuming you wouldn't want anything similar to happen on Mount Olympus.'

'No, I wouldn't.' Venus sighed. 'So we wait and see what happens.'

'And if Athena aids Odysseus?'

'Then Achilles will have to reenter the battle,' Venus said.

'Good. We've decided,' Hera said.

'Sadly, we have.'

Venus sipped her ambrosia and thought about how distraught Achilles had been the four days Kat had been unconscious. *Well, at least he has known love, no matter how brief.*

'Okay, all I said was I wanted a bath – as in being submerged in water versus splashing in a little bowl that smells like roses. You're kicking me out of your camp for that?' Kat asked teasingly.

'Did I not tell you that I would give you anything you wished, if it were within my power?' Achilles touched her arm briefly where it linked with his. She noticed he did that a lot lately – touched her with brief, gentle caresses. He didn't let his touch linger and he didn't kiss her. It was as if he was attempting to become used to her in stages – small stages that wouldn't arouse the berserker. She felt his eyes on her and looked up to see him watching her closely. 'Tell me if we've gone too far. I won't have you fatigued.'

They'd gone down the beach away from camp for a while, and then turned inland, following a little goat path. It hadn't been a short walk, but it hadn't turned into an exhausting hike, either. 'Like I told Jacky. I've slept enough for decades and I'm perfectly fine.' Kat made the statement firmly. Not that she hadn't been freaked out by how much last night's meal and discussion had exhausted her. She'd planned on another little hypnotism exercise with Achilles, but had been out the second her head had touched the pillow. And, worse, she'd slept all the way through to early afternoon. She felt good now, but the whole incident had scared her. She'd already killed off one body. What was the limit? What if this one went bad, too? Would Venus save her? And if she did, what kind of body would the next one be? She was actually getting attached to this one and wasn't sure if she wanted to even consider what might—

'You look troubled.' Achilles broke into her internal babble.

'I was just thinking about mortality,' she said.

'Mortality – that is a subject I have thought little about until lately,' Achilles said.

'Really? I would have thought that after you made the choice to die young, you would have been counting down the years and thinking about it all the time.'

He gave a self-deprecating snort. 'When I was young I rarely thought – and if I did it was only of the next battle and the next opportunity for glory.'

'Hey, twenty-nine is not old. You're still really young.'

'I haven't been young for more than a decade.'

Kat looked up at him, knowing that the deep scars that had prematurely aged his face had also taken a similar toll on his soul. 'Maybe some of that can be reversed,' she said.

Obviously noting the direction of her gaze his lips lifted and he said, 'Your friend is an excellent healer, but even she cannot reverse these.' Achilles pointed at his facial scars.

Kat grinned. 'Was that a *joke*? And the sky didn't fall in, nor did you get struck by lightning.'

'It's your bad influence on me.'

'Don't you mean the fact that I've bespelled you? Remember, Jacky's a witch – I'm a witch – everywhere a witch – witch.'

'I stand corrected. You have bespelled me.' Then he surprised her by pulling her, briefly, into his arms and hugging her hard. 'And we are here.' Achilles took her by the shoulders and turned Kat around.

'Achilles! It's beautiful!' Kat was facing an oasis. Willows ringed a basin formed by butter-colored limestone. A stream dumped into the basin, filled it and then gurgled out the other side. It was small, but definitely big enough for someone to bathe comfortably in. Overlooking the oasis was a small temple that reminded Kat of a gazebo, only this one was made of marble with graceful columns and a domed roof. In the middle of the temple a blanket had been spread out. Atop it sat a laden basket. 'What's all this?' Kat asked, walking around the pool to the temple.

'It's a shrine dedicated to Venus. I discovered it years ago. It's been abandoned because of the war. I've come here many times to think – to get away.'

Kat glanced back at him, surprised to see that he looked embarrassed. 'There's nothing wrong with that. Everyone needs time alone.'

'Ah, but Achilles, terror of maidens and battlefield berserker, is not everyone. If my men knew I found solace at a shrine dedicated to the Goddess of Love.' He laughed humorlessly and shook his head. 'They would probably begin to believe that I had finally gone mad.'

'But they seem to have accepted me being with you just fine. Haven't they?'

Achilles shrugged. 'Right now they are too preoccupied to even be shocked by you warming my bed.'

'They want to fight,' Kat said, her stomach clenching.

'They do.'

'And what do you want?'

'You already know my heart. I long for nothing as much as to return to Phthia and to find peace.' Achilles paused, meeting her gaze before he continued. 'And love.'

'You've already found love,' Kat said softly.

Achilles closed the distance between them, joining her in the middle of Venus's shrine. He took her hand. 'Have I found love? Even though we don't know that the berserker can be defeated?'

'Yes, you have. And the berserker can be defeated; I know it.' Slowly and deliberately, Kat rose on her tiptoes, while pulling him gently down to her. She kissed him softly. She didn't linger or deepen the kiss, but she also didn't make a frightened rush to get away. The kiss was her promise to him that the future he'd dreamed could be real. But she didn't push it – she didn't push him. Smiling, Kat looked down at the basket. 'If this shrine has been abandoned for years, how did this get here?'

'Your wish to bathe reminded me of this place. While you slept today I brought these things out here. I thought you might enjoy getting away together.' He said the words with his usual gruff confidence, but Kat could see the question in his eyes. One sign of fear or hesitation in her would undo him.

'You were absolutely right – it's a great idea.'

He smiled and bowed with exaggerated formality. 'Your bath awaits, Princess, and then we shall dine on whatever I frightened Aetnia into packing.'

Kat shook her head at him. 'It's probably a couple of arsenic sandwiches with a side dish of glass stew.' Then she glanced down at the clear pool of water and her throat suddenly felt dry. 'Have you checked it to be sure that there aren't any slimy things in there that might be waiting to eat me?'

'Would the word of a sea goddess reassure you?'

Surprised, Kat looked around the little tree-lined oasis. 'Is your mom here?'

'She came with me earlier today and made quite certain everything was safe for you.'

'I've got to quit sleeping so much. I miss everything.' Kat took a step closer to the water. It did look harmless and utterly inviting. And it would be so good to get completely clean.

Achilles cleared his throat. She met his eyes.

'I'll be here, with my back turned while you bathe. You need only call out to me and I can be by your side in an instant.'

'Wouldn't it be better if you kept an eye on me? What if something grabs me and I can't call out to you.' Kat watched the different emotions play across his face: desire and fear and need. When she realized fear was winning out, she said, 'Why is it that the berserker doesn't possess you when you argue with Agamemnon? Doesn't he make you terribly angry?'

He looked surprised at her question, but answered readily enough. 'Of course he does. The old bastard rarely fails to anger me.'

'Then why doesn't the berserker possess you?' she asked again.

Achilles shrugged. 'I suppose because I've grown accustomed to how he makes me feel. I tell myself it's just Agamemnon, and the king is not a battle I am allowed to fight.'

'Then why not tell yourself that I am just Katrina, the woman you desire. This is the way I make you feel, and I am not a battle you are allowed to fight.'

She saw hope flare and then die in his eyes. Achilles shook his head. 'No. It is not the same thing.'

'It could be if you believed it was.'

He kept shaking his head. 'No. I will not chance it.'

'Well, I will. Listen – you have warning before the berserker possesses you, don't you?'

'Some,' he said reluctantly.

'Okay. It's simple then. You sit down up there. Make yourself comfortable. There's wine in that basket, right?'

'Yes.'

'Drink it and relax. I'll bathe. You keep an eye on me to be sure nothing stings me senseless.' She held up her hand when he opened his mouth. 'Yes, I know. Jacky says I'm already lacking sense.' His lips twitched. 'You really shouldn't listen to her.'

'At this moment her observations seem very insightful,' Achilles said.

She frowned at him in mock severity. 'Whatever you do, don't ever tell her that. So, you sit up there. I'll bathe. Everything will be just fine.'

'And if it isn't?'

'If you start to look crazy I'll use my panic button.' She lifted the locket that still hung around her neck.

He looked doubtful. 'Venus might be busy.'

'Nah, she gave me her word. Plus she is one seriously nosy goddess. She'll be here, even if it's just to gather gossip.' Kat walked the few steps back to him and put her hand gently on his arm. 'Here's the deal. You need to believe in yourself and in your ability to keep me safe as much as I believe in you.'

'You believe I can keep you safe?'

Kat smiled into his scarred, life-battered face. 'Of course I do. You *have* kept me safe.' She kissed him softly on the cheek then started determinedly toward her waiting bath, crossing her fingers in front of her and sending up a silent prayer to Venus, *If you have to watch, maybe now would be a good time . . .*

Chapter Twenty-three

What in the holy hell had she been thinking? Kat tried not to hesitate too long while she frantically decided how best to take off her clothes without seeming too enticing, and yet also not seeming like she was scared shitless and bolting for the concealing water.

Concealing water? Kat squinted down at the clear little pool. Where were algae and a good dose of clouding pollution when you needed them? *Get it over with, Katrina*, she ordered herself. She pulled off the light green silk outer robe that had replaced the new blue one the gross sea things had ruined. Her under-robes were soft layers of eggshell silk. Kat let them fall around her feet. She hadn't really thought about the fact that neither panties nor a bra had come with any of her outfits – until then. *Just remind yourself that you're glad he's looking at this tight young little body, versus your pushing forty-year-old, needing to lose fifteen pounds and take your flabby butt to the gym body.*

Kat tried for regal looking as, naked, she stepped into the pool, bracing herself for what she expected to be freezing cold water. But at the first touch of the tepid pool she felt a shiver of delight and, with a happy sigh, submerged herself. Only then did she look up at Achilles. 'Hey! It's not cold.'

He had done as she'd instructed and was sitting, in a semi-relaxed manner, on the blanket, leaning against one of the marble pillars. He had an uncorked wineskin in his lap. She thought he looked a little tense, but other than that completely himself.

'It's too shallow to be cold, at least this time of the year. The sun warms it and the willows shade it, keeping the water a perfect temperature.' As he spoke she noticed he kept his eyes on hers, not allowing his gaze to travel down to her body, which the water did little to conceal. 'When I first discovered this shrine I thought the pool must have been why it was built and then dedicated to Venus.' Achilles smiled a little sheepishly. 'Seems a perfect place for a goddess to bathe.'

Kat grinned. 'Why, Achilles, I do believe you are a closet romantic.'

He snorted. 'I am no type of romantic.'

'Ha! You left a flower on my pillow. I would call that evidence exhibit number one of romanticism.'

He took a long drink of wine and then said, 'How do you know I left it?'

'Oh, that's right. It must have been Aetnia – or maybe Briseis. Both of them just love hanging out in your tent.'

He snorted again and tried, unsuccessfully, to cover his laughter.

'Exhibit number two is that picnic basket full of goodies for me.'

'This basket?' He pawed around inside it and pulled out a piece of cheese wrapped in flatbread. He took a big bite and around his full mouth said, 'This basket is for me, not you.'

'Sure it is,' she said, scrubbing the bottom of her foot with a handful of sand. 'Romantic evidence exhibit three is that blanket.'

'And why is that romantic?'

'Because you don't want me to get my delicate skin dirty.' She lifted her other foot, the bottom of which was still dirty, and waggled her toes at him.

His laughter was free and easy. She thought it was the

most wonderful sound she had ever heard. 'The blanket is for me, too.'

'Oh, yeah. Because I know how obsessed you are with comfort and relaxation.'

He exaggerated a long stretch, causing it to be her turn to laugh.

'Hey, speaking of comfort, I've been meaning to tell you how much I like the tapestries in your tent. Are they of a particular place or just random scenery?'

'They're all of Phthia. It gives me a sense of home to be surrounded by them.'

'Phthia must be very beautiful,' she said, scrubbing her hair and wishing she had her favorite shampoo and conditioner.

Achilles' faint smile was wistful. 'It is, indeed. Someday I would like to take you there.'

'I'd like that, too.' She paused and then decided she might as well ask him. 'Achilles, why don't you just take your Myrmidons and leave now? You've withdrawn from the fighting. You've broken with Agamemnon. Why stay?'

'I've thought of it. If it were just me, or even just you and me, I would. But my men are Greeks. Phthia is a part of Greece. It would go hard on them and their families should they return before the war is over.' He shook his head. 'No, we stay until the end – whether we fight or not.'

'What are you going to do if the Greeks lose?'

'Go home.'

'And if they win?'

His lips twitched. 'Go home.'

'So it doesn't really matter to you who wins or loses?'

'It does matter. I don't want Greeks to die. But Agamemnon and Menelaus are responsible for that. I am only responsible for the deaths of my own men. Hopefully I will not lose one more Myrmidon.' He paused before continuing. 'I should not have come to Troy. I only did so because I believed my fate could not be changed, and because Odysseus asked it of me.'

'And now you believe your fate can be changed.' She didn't phrase it like a question but he nodded.

'Now I believe many things I didn't just days ago.'

Kat smiled at him and then dunked her head completely under the water. When she surfaced, shaking water from her hair and sputtering, Achilles was looking relaxed and content.

She studied him carefully for a moment, and then decided it was time for her to get out of the water, and time for their relationship to move forward another step.

'Achilles, do you still desire me?'

He blinked, obviously surprised by her question. 'Yes. Of course.'

'But there you are, relaxed and chatting with me. And here I am, naked.'

His brows went up. 'That is true.'

'And, unless I'm wildly mistaken, there is no berserker possession going on – or even imminent.'

'That is not something easy to be mistaken about. No, there is no berserker here.'

'Or even close?'

'Not close, either.'

'So you think I can get out of this pool and come up there with you?'

Kat saw him swallow hard. 'Naked?' he asked.

She smiled. 'Actually I was planning on asking you for the blanket until I dry.'

'Oh. Yes, of course.' He looked embarrassed, which Kat

thought was a huge improvement over him looking stony faced and emotionless or scarlet eyed and completely crazy.

When he made no further move, she said, 'Could you bring me the blanket?'

She'd rarely seen him awkward. Even at rest he had a warrior's feral grace, but when he jumped up and gathered the blanket he definitely gave off a bull in the china shop vibe and Kat had to bite the side of her cheek to keep from laughing.

She stood up and walked out of the water. His gaze never left her eyes, even when he opened the blanket for her and she stepped, naked and dripping, into his arms. Kat felt a tremor go through his body as his arms closed around her. Kat stepped back and smiled at him as if he saw her naked every day. The struggle on his face was obvious. There were no signs of the berserker, but Achilles was no longer relaxed, and she understood if his relaxation level continued to decline and his stress level to rise, she was, quite literally, flirting with danger.

'Tell me a story,' she said.

His face was a question mark. 'A story?'

'Yeah.' The hand that wasn't clutching the blanket around her took his, and she pulled him up toward the shrine and the waiting picnic basket. 'Tell me a story about your childhood while we eat. Something back in Phthia.' She gave him a mischievous look over her shoulder. 'Something *not* flattering.'

His snort sounded amused. 'What if I was the perfect child and I did nothing that was not flattering.'

'Then I'll eat the basket instead of the lunch you bullied Aetnia into packing.' Kat sat beside the basket, arranging her blanket around her and wringing out her wet hair before checking out the food. 'Yum! Cheese, meat, olives and wine. All of my favorite food groups – fat and booze and salt.' Achilles had taken

233

his position next to her, leaning against the pillar again and making an obvious attempt to relax and not stare at her bare shoulders. She handed him some bread and meat. 'Good thing this body is so young. Less chance all this cheese will go to my butt – or at least not immediately.'

'Back in your time you aren't young?'

Kat looked up from the food to him. Achilles didn't look shocked or upset at the idea of her being old, just curious. She smiled. 'Back in my time I'm almost a decade older than you.'

He did look shocked then. 'You left your husband and children to come here?'

'Oh, god no. I've never been married and I definitely don't have any kids.'

'Did you take vows of chastity to a goddess?'

'You know, Hera and Athena were confused about this, too. In the modern mortal world women don't get married so young. Okay, well, not educated women with any sense and decent teeth. Actually some of us don't get married at all. Or have children. We don't have to.'

'Then what do you do with your lives?'

Kat's smile was long and slow. 'Exactly what we want.'

'You're like men!' Achilles proclaimed, as if he finally understood.

'I guess from your point of view that's true.' She raised one brow at him. 'And in case you're wondering. I have no intention of changing that about myself, even if I have changed worlds.'

He gave her a considering look. 'Does that mean you don't ever want to marry or have children?'

Kat ignored the little sizzle of excitement his question had her feeling. 'Not necessarily. What it means is that if I get married or have children it will be because that's what I want and not because it's what's expected of me.'

'Agreed,' he said.

'Good. Now I want to hear a story about you as a little boy.'

'An unflattering story.'

'Absolutely, they're the best kind.'

'All right.' He settled in against the pillar and crossed his legs at the ankle, occasionally taking a drink from the wineskin while he talked and she worked her way through the food in the picnic basket. 'When I was a boy I didn't believe I could drown.'

'Makes sense. Your mom being a sea goddess and all.'

'It would have made more sense if I had been an immortal, too. But I wasn't, even though I acted like I was.' He shook his head, remembering. 'I drove my nursemaids mad. And when I outgrew them, it was my tutors I drove mad. I took ridiculous chances – swimming too far out to sea, getting caught in undertows and barely escaping – silly, reckless things like that. It got so bad that my father was going to forbid me from going to the sea at all.'

'Bet your mom didn't like that idea.'

He laughed. 'No, not at all. But she also didn't like the idea of her only son being killed in a childhood accident caused by his own foolishness. So the two of them got together and planned a little lesson for me.'

'That doesn't sound good,' she said after motioning for him to pass her the wineskin.

'It wasn't. I must have been, oh, not quite twelve years old, which made Patroklos not even seven. He was forever shadowing me, which annoyed me to no end, but this particular day he told me that he'd discovered a boat abandoned in a cove and he would take me to it.'

235

'And since you thought you were a sea god, a boat was perfect for you,' Kat said.

'Clearly you're using the same reasoning my parents used. And, yes, I did insist Patroklos take me directly to *my* boat. On our way to the cove the weather changed quickly, as it often does in Phthia. A squall moved in. I actually saw fishermen returning to shore. I scoffed at them – cowards! And Patroklos and I set sail.'

'Patroklos was in on your parents' scheme?'

'No, they'd just used him as a pawn. My cousin went with me to sea because he would follow me anywhere.'

Kat watched his face soften when he spoke of Patroklos. 'You love him very much, don't you?'

'He is brother and son to me,' Achilles said simply. 'So we sailed into the storm. We were just far enough offshore to get ourselves in serious danger when a wave hit us and I was washed overboard. Patroklos was screaming for me and trying to throw me a line, but the storm-tossed waves were unusually violent.' His lips tilted up.

'Unusually? You mean as if a sea goddess had stirred them up?'

'That is exactly what I mean. I was foolish and reckless, but I wasn't stupid, and it didn't take me long to realize I was drowning. I remember trying to call for my mother, but the waves stifled my cries. I cannot tell you how much seawater I swallowed before the dolphins came, but it was enough to have me utterly panicked.'

'Wait, did you say dolphins?'

He chuckled and nodded. 'Dolphins. They butted and bobbed me around, keeping me on the surface as if I were a melon they were playing with, until they got me up on the beach.'

'So they saved you?'

'Oh, yes, they saved me. They brought me safely to the main dock of Phthia, which was filled with fishermen and fishwives, and my parents, along with most of the royal court who just happened to be taking a stroll down to the docks at that moment. They were all there in time to see me butted out of the water, half drowned and completely naked, by a school of dolphins.'

'Naked?' Kat started to giggle.

'Naked.' Achilles nodded again. 'Somehow while they were battering and butting me around they managed to pull off all of my clothes, even down to stripping me of my sandals.'

'You must have been quite the sight,' Kat said, while trying to control her fit of giggles.

'Apparently I was. They talked about it for years. You can still make some of the old servant women cackle hysterically if you bring it up.'

'Did it have the desired effect on you?'

'You mean did it scare some sense into my foolish young head?' He lifted a shoulder. 'Yes and no. I realized I could drown, and I suppose I was more careful after that – or at least more careful about my arrogant proclamations. The boy it really worked on was Patroklos. To this day he loathes boats and turns a sickly shade of green just thinking about sailing.' Achilles smiled and took the wineskin from her. 'And that, my lady, is my unflattering childhood story.'

Kat laughed and clapped while he took a long drink of wine. Then when he handed it back to her he leaned forward and kissed her, softly, on the lips. She closed her eyes and leaned into him. Not aggressively, just warm and inviting, letting him set the pace. When they finally parted both of them were breathing heavily, but she could see no sign of the berserker in his clear blue eyes.

'I can hypnotize you again,' she whispered.

'I know you can.' He touched her face and let his hand slide down to caress the slope of her bare shoulder. 'And I will allow you to if you feel you must.'

'But?' she asked.

'But I would like to make love to you without the spell. I want to experience all of it, and not just as a wonderful dream. Will you let me, Katrina?'

Chapter Twenty-four

Achilles studied Kat's expressive brown eyes while he waited for her to answer him. He could feel the increase of his breathing and heartbeat, but both were always elevated when he trained, and the berserker never possessed him then. *I don't need him then. I don't need him now,* he repeated silently to himself.

'Yes, Achilles, make love to me.'

Her words speared through him. 'You're not afraid?' he said.

'Of course not. As long as you're here, I'm safe.'

He pulled her into his arms and held her close against him, inhaling the clean, wet scent of her hair and feeling the slight dampness of her skin. By all the gods he would not let her trust in him be misplaced! He wasn't a callow boy anymore. This would not end as his first love had.

Achilles kissed her, reminding himself to move slowly, to stay in control. She opened her mouth and his tongue met hers in a sweet, exploratory dance. Her arms wrapped around his shoulders and she leaned into him, causing the blanket to fall free from her body.

She froze, midkiss. With steady, deliberate moves, Achilles leaned back so that he could see her naked body. He held very still while he looked at her, and then reached out and ran his hands in a long caress from her neck, down over her breasts, the curve of her waist, all the way over hips and thigh. Then his eyes met hers again.

'You are exquisite,' he said reverently.

Kat smiled then, and Achilles saw the future in her eyes – his future. The one he'd stopped dreaming about, stopped believing in. She had brought it back to him as a true possibility. He didn't know what wonderful thing he'd done to cause the goddesses to bless him with this woman who was such a miraculous gift, but he silently promised them that if they gave him a lifetime with her, he and his children, and his children's children would honor them always.

Achilles slid his hands around her waist and took her into his arms again, kissing her deeply and letting his hands smooth over the impossibly soft skin of her back, down to her lovely ass. He cupped it, pressing her more firmly against the erection that throbbed taut and heavy between his legs. Her hips moved in response and an enticing memory of their first encounter filled his mind and he remembered how her hot slickness had felt gliding up and down against his shaft.

A wave of desire crashed over Achilles, drowning in its intensity and he struggled to hold onto his control as he felt the searing, red hot intensity of the berserker lick against his lust-fevered skin.

'Open your eyes, Achilles. Look at me.'

Kat's sweet voice was cool relief against the fire in his mind. He opened his eyes and met her gaze. The berserker threatened. He knew she had to see his shadow lurking, ready to possess, to smother and repress all of his humanity. Yet she didn't show any fear. Her smile was confident. She didn't pull out of his arms and she didn't open the locket and call for her goddess's rescue.

'You're not going to leave me,' she said in that calm, beautiful voice. 'You're going to stay here with me. You're going to keep me safe.'

'Yes,' Achilles murmured, kissing her gently. 'I will keep you safe.' He reached within himself and found his inner core – that part of himself that was the seat of his spirit – and Achilles centered himself there. 'This passion is different than what I need for war.' He hadn't realized he'd spoken the thought aloud until she answered him.

'Yes! What you need to love me doesn't destroy.'

'Instead it builds,' he said.

Looking into her eyes he shifted her body so that she lay beneath him. Achilles lifted himself on one elbow so that he could continue to keep his gaze on hers as his hand cupped her breast, rubbing the hardening nipple against his callused palm. Her full lips parted as her breathing increased. When his hand moved down to the slick cleft between her legs, Kat moaned and arched her hips to meet him. She put her hand over his, guiding him, teaching him how to please her, and even when she shuddered in climax she still stared into his eyes.

Before the tremors of release had left her body he raised himself and slowly sheathed his throbbing cock within her tight heat.

'Stay with me, Achilles. Don't leave me,' she whispered.

'I won't ever leave you,' he said, his voice deep and rough with the effort it took to maintain control. He lifted his hips, gliding almost all of the way out of her and then he tunneled within her again, harder this time.

'Achilles.' Kat breathed his name.

He stroked himself within her.

'Achilles.' She moaned.

He thrust into her.

'Achilles . . .'

It was as if she surrounded him completely. His body. His

soul. Anchoring him, not just to her, but to sanity and to his humanity. When he finally found his release it was her name on his lips, and her face in his eyes. And his soul was his own.

Achilles and Kat got back to the Myrmidon camp as the sun was setting. Walking hand in hand and talking easily together, they reached the illumination of the campfire. Kat watched Aetnia's eyes widen when Achilles tossed the empty basket at her feet and said, 'Thank you. That was well packed.' Then, while everyone stared at them openmouthed, Achilles kissed her soundly and said, 'I'll be back after I've spoken with Patroklos.' And he walked off, looking incredibly pleased with himself.

'Excuse me? Did he just say thank you?' Jacky popped up from where she was lounging beside the fire.

'I don't know why good manners surprise you so much,' Kat said, plopping down beside her. 'Ah, crap. I need a goblet of—'

'Wine, my princess?'

Kat looked up, grinned at the girl, and took the goblet she offered. 'Aetnia, you're a mind reader.'

'And I'll take some more, too,' Jacky said. Aetnia hesitated, glanced at Kat, who nodded quickly, and then filled Jacky's goblet, even though her hand was shaking. 'Thank you ever so, Aetnia,' Jacky said with exaggerated kindness.

'Be nice,' Kat whispered.

'Oh, boo!' Jacky stomped at Aetnia, who scuttled around to the other side of the fire.

'Must you tease her?'

'For your information she is a hateful hag when you're gone. This whole 'my princess this' and 'my princess that' is a big act. When you're not here she slithers around committing major gossip with those women who give you weird looks all the time.

Somethin's up with that girl. I may have to kick her scrawny white ass.'

'Uh, Jacky. Please recall that at this moment your ass is also white and scrawny.'

'Yes, but I have been eating steadily and I'm determined to change that.'

'Well, go on about your business,' Kat said.

'To big asses,' Jacky said, raising her goblet.

'To *your* big future ass,' Kat said, clicking her goblet against Jacky's.

Jacky took a long drink then raised her brow at Kat. 'All right. Details.'

Kat scooted over closer to her and lowered her voice. 'We had sex.'

'Good god, you put the boy under again? And I mean that figuratively as well as literally.'

'No. He was perfectly in control of all of his faculties.'

'Not unconscious and thinkin' he was dreaming?'

'Absolutely not.'

'Are you tellin' me today you two had aware-we're-having-sex sex, versus the semiconscious-almost-rape sex you had those other two nights?'

'I did not rape him.'

'And I say whatever to your semantics. Just answer the question.'

'Yes. We had totally aware – totally-all-there-sex sex.'

'You are grinning like a fool, so it must have been good.'

'It was utterly delicious,' Kat said.

'And he controlled the berserker?'

'Well, actually, it was more like he controlled himself so the berserker didn't possess him.'

Jacky sipped her wine and stared into the fire.

'All right. What is it?' Kat said.

'I'm just a little concerned that he didn't control the berserker.'

'But what difference does it make? He controlled the thing not possessing him, isn't that the point?'

'Kinda. I imagine it makes a big difference if you're ever around him when he is possessed,' Jacky said.

'Maybe I won't be. When this war is over he's going home – to a *peaceful* life. If he's never in battle again, the berserker may never come on him again.'

'So, in other words, your theory is that you're gonna ignore it and hope it goes away.'

'No, not exactly.'

Jacky rolled her eyes.

Kat frowned at Jacky. 'Okay, maybe.'

'Well, let's hope your theory is more successful with berserker possession than it is with, oh, say, pregnancy.'

'Achilles will be fine,' Kat said firmly.

They both stared into the fire and sipped their wine.

'You're staying with him, aren't you?' Jacky finally asked.

'Yes.' She looked at her best friend. 'What are you going to do?'

Jacky sighed. 'Sadly, it appears that I'm going to spend the rest of my life white.'

Laughing, Kat put her arm around Jacky. 'Well, we can try to tan you up. Would that make it better?'

'Hell no! I am not one of those white girls who bakes her skin in the sun and then looks like fucking beef jerky when she hits forty. I have entirely too much sense for that. How many times have I yelled at you to keep your light ass out of the sun?'

'Too many to begin to count.'

'That's right. I have more damn sense than that,' she repeated. 'You know what white girls lying out in the sun remind me of?'

'Turkeys drowning in the rain 'cause they're too stupid to get in out of it or swallow,' Kat said promptly.

'How did you know that?'

'Jacky, you have called me a drowning turkey only about a gazillion times.'

'Well you should bring your white ass in out the sun.'

Kat stared at her. Hard.

'What?' Jacky said.

'Your cheeks are looking pink to me. As in *sunburn* pink.'

'Oh, bullshit! I just have a little healthy color. That's all.'

'And that's how the obsession begins,' Kat said smugly.

The two women looked at each other and then dissolved into laughter.

When her giggles were under control Kat wiped her face and looked around the campfire clearing, populated by the usual group of war-prize brides who were sitting as far away from Kat and Jacky as they could get.

'Wonder what's taking Achilles and Patroklos so long?'

'Let's hope he's talkin' some sense into Patroklos's thick skull.'

'What's going on?' Kat asked.

'Patroklos is acting very crazy about this nonfighting situation. Apparently today Odysseus was like Superman – no one could touch him and he led his men on one hell of a charge. Word is that they could win if this keeps up.'

'They, as in the Greek they?'

'Yep.'

'Huh. Well, that's good. I guess. The goddesses just wanted the war over. Odysseus all of a sudden being invincible makes the war over. So what's Patroklos's problem with it?'

'No problem 'cept he wants Achilles and the rest of the Myrmidons to join in. He says they could for sure win if that happens.'

'Oh,' Kat said softly.

'Yeah, oh.'

'Do you think I should get him to do it? Get him to fight?' Kat's stomach clenched as she waited for her friend's answer.

'Your boy might very well die if he keeps fighting, right?'

Kat nodded. 'I don't remember much of the stupid *Iliad*, but that fact is pretty hard to forget. Achilles dies in the Trojan War.'

'Then no,' Jacky said firmly. 'Don't let him fight. You just found him, and you had to go to a whole other world to be with him. It's too soon to lose him. I know it's too soon for me to lose Patroklos. I don't want the fool to fight.'

'Okay, then I stick with the original plan and do what I can to keep Achilles out of it.'

'Sounds good to me.'

'Let's drink on it.'

'That sounds good, too.' They clinked their goblets together again and settled in to wait for their men.

'By the shaggy testes of satyrs you were right!' Venus paced back and forth across the inner chamber of Hera's Mount Olympus Temple. The Queen of the Gods' oracle swirled with images of Odysseus leading the Greeks in charge after victorious charge against the Trojans. 'Athena gifted him with something more than her goddessly juices. The man is clearly invincible.'

'What did I tell you? She never takes lovers so she's completely enamored with her human plaything,' Hera said, frowning into her oracle.

'It just proves what I've been saying for eons. She's incredibly repressed and needs to loosen up. Athena should have been trysting with Odysseus on the beach for years, then this wouldn't have been such an emotional experience for her.' Venus sighed dramatically. 'And you know this means there will be absolutely no reasoning with her.'

'So we were both right. What are we going to do about it? This war needs to end. Now.'

'I really hate to say it, but I think we may as well back the Greeks. Let's just get this thing over with,' Venus said, frowning into the oracle.

'So you're going to command your little modern mortal to persuade Achilles to lead his Myrmidons back into battle?'

Venus hesitated, obviously not wanting to answer her queen.

'Venus! We are in agreement. You simply must be sure Achilles leads his Myrmidons into the battle.'

'I suppose you're right,' Venus said reluctantly.

'Of course I'm right. We've already established that. Now let's just be sure all of this happens very quickly, *before* Zeus gets wind of anything. He's supposed to be staying neutral, which is why we're supposed to be staying out of it, too,' Hera said.

'But we all know his weakness for the Trojans, especially for old Priam,' Venus said.

'I know, I know, Zeus started the whole thing by supporting Laomedon against Poseidon all those years ago, though he should have never backed a mortal against the Sea God, but those two are always arguing about something and Zeus is terrible about holding a grudge. I really wish he would—'

'*Hera! Wife! Where are you?*' Zeus's voice thundered throughout Olympus.

Hera jumped guiltily.

Venus rolled her eyes. 'He's so demanding. And it's really rude of him to bellow across Olympus for you.'

'You think I don't know that?' Hera hurried to her oracle and waved a hand over it to clear the scene from Troy. 'When *I* want *him* do you think he's ever to be found? Of course not. But let him have even the smallest need for me and his great blustering voice doesn't hesitate to search me out.'

'Perhaps I should have a word with him,' Venus offered helpfully. 'You know Love has rights other immortals do not. Not even the King of Olympus is above a little marital advice.'

'No, no, no, thank you, but no. Our marriage is just fine.'

Venus looked doubtful. 'Well, darling, I can tell you that you need to keep him occupied while I work my magic down there.' She made a little gesture at the now blank oracle.

'*Hera!*' This time Zeus's voice was much closer.

'Yes, of course! Go. I'll take care of things here,' Hera said.

'This will help.' Venus flicked her fingers at Hera, showering the Queen of Olympus in diamond dust that soaked into her skin.

'Wh—' Hera began, then gasped as her body flushed and her nipples instantly hardened.

'Just a little lustful present from Love to her queen.' Venus winked and then disappeared.

Body tingling, Hera rushed out of her inner chamber and ran into her husband's imposing body.

'Zeus! Whatever are you doing sneaking up on me like that?'

'Sneaking! The Supreme Ruler of the Gods does not sneak! And why are you running about guiltily?' he asked, peering over her shoulder into the inner chamber she'd just left.

'I am not running, and I am certainly guilty of nothing. I was simply answering your summons in a timely manner, as any considerate wife would.'

Zeus snorted.

'Why are you bellowing for me and disturbing all of Olympus?' she countered.

'I could not find you. You weren't in our throne room. Nor were you in the gardens where you usually walk at this time of day. So I called for you. I did not bellow,' he said petulantly.

'Of course you didn't bellow,' Hera assured him, shifting her mood smoothly and smiling as she waved away the comment. 'What is it you desire, my lord?'

'I've seen so little of you lately I thought you might enjoy accompanying me on a visit to the ancient world.'

Hera made a mental note to be much more visible to him – at least until this silly war was over. 'As usual, you are so right, my love,' she said sweetly. 'I have been far too busy lately with my divine duties.'

He gave a pleased little grunt. 'Good. It is decided. You will accompany me to Troy. I hear rumblings that the Greeks have made sudden headway in the war – so sudden that there are rumors of divine interference, even though I have forbidden the Olympians to take an active role in the battle. So.' He held out his arm for her. 'Let us visit Troy. Perhaps you and I can have an intimate lunch on the beach after I make quite certain no one has been disobeying me.'

Hera's stomach fluttered with panic that she quickly squelched. Drawing on the dusting of lust Venus had sprinkled into her skin, she took his arm and smiled coquettishly up at Zeus, leaning her full breast and its erect nipple against his muscular arm. 'I thought you called for *me*, my lord?'

'I did,' he said, obviously trying not to be moved by his wife's unusually pliant attitude. 'I thought we should go to Troy together – form a combined front.'

'Oh.' Hera pouted prettily, pursing her full pink lips and giving him a meaningful, sideways glance. 'I thought you desired me for something more intimate than travel and official duties.'

'Well, I do, of course. As I said . . .' he began, and then stopped speaking as his wife lifted his hand and took his forefinger within the warm pink nest of her mouth and suckled it deeply, flicking the tip of it with her cunning tongue. 'Ah, wife.' He moaned as her other hand found the hardening thunderbolt between his legs. 'I have missed you, and you do please me.'

'I have just begun to please you, my lord.'

His need to travel to Troy replaced by a more immediate need, Zeus pulled his wife into his arms, and with a masterful motion transported them instantly to their bedchamber, where she did indeed please him, over and over and over . . .

Chapter Twenty-five

'Patroklos, why can't you understand?' Achilles said. He'd met his cousin returning from the Greek camp and the two of them were walking side by side down the beach as they argued. 'I may have a chance to change my fate, and I intend to take the chance.'

'I do understand.' Patroklos stopped and faced Achilles. 'I, too, want your fate to change. But that doesn't mean you can't lead our men in battle. It simply means you need to stay away from Hector. It's only after you kill him that you're fated to die.'

Achilles shook his head. 'Battle is as *simple* as chaos. Saying I simply need to stay away from one of the Trojan warriors is well and good when I'm not possessed by the berserker in the middle of the smoke and blood and confusion of battle.'

'I'll help you. All the Myrmidons will help you. We'll be sure Hector gets nowhere near you.'

Achilles smiled and cuffed Patroklos playfully. 'If you intend to nursemaid me, how am I supposed to lead anyone in battle?'

Patroklos moved away and said sharply, 'This is not a jesting matter.'

'Do you think I jest about my fate?'

'No.' Patroklos sighed and ran his hand through his hair in frustration. 'Nor do I take the prophesy lightly. The last thing I want is your death, cousin.'

'But you've grown accustomed to it.' Patroklos began to protest, but Achilles cut him off. 'I'd become accustomed to it, too. I was to die before I saw thirty summers, at the gates of Troy, after I killed Hector, but my name was to live on for centuries. It was the choice I made, and when I was young, glory and the immortality of my name were all I thought of. Then I grew older and understood the nature of what I'd chosen and I knew regret, but my fate was a boulder rolling down a mountainside. I could only travel with it. Then *she* came and everything began to change.'

'Yes! That is exactly my point. Everything is changed now. The goddesses plucked Katrina and Jacqueline's souls from another world, another time, and brought them here to change everything. How could they then allow your death?'

'Perhaps because I'd been foolish enough to ignore all that they sent me and blundered heedlessly back into battle?'

'Achilles, you said that today you kept the berserker from possessing you. That had to be a gift from the goddesses. Couldn't they mean for you to use it in battle? To have the ability to fight and lead us without losing yourself to the berserker?'

'My gift is Katrina. She has enabled me to withstand the berserker. And she will not be going into battle with me. Ever.' He put his hand on his cousin's shoulder. 'I love her. I want to spend the rest of my life with her, and I want that to be more than a short span of days.'

Exasperated, Patroklos shouted, 'I love Jacqueline! But that doesn't mean I don't want to fight for the glory of Greece.'

'You would not be fighting for the glory of Greece. You would be fighting for the glory of Agamemnon.'

'That's not how history will remember this war,' Patroklos said.

'History be damned! I've had enough of living for what will or won't be said of me in the future.'

'The men need your help, Achilles. You could save lives.'

'I have saved lives,' Achilles said between gritted teeth as he stared out at the moonlit ocean. 'Over and over again Agamemnon has used me to fight his battles. For once I choose to save my own life. For once I have a chance at a future I've only dreamed of. I will not throw that away – not for Agamemnon and his greed.'

'That isn't how I see it,' Patroklos said. 'I wouldn't be fighting for Agamemnon. I'd be fighting for Greece.'

'If you're foolish enough to take a chance with your life and throw away the goddess-given love with which you've been gifted, then fight! I'm not stopping you.' Achilles turned and began walking away down the beach.

'The men won't follow my lead!' Patroklos shouted at his back. 'They'll only follow you. I am not Achilles!'

'Would that you were!' Achilles called over his shoulder. 'Then I would gladly live your long, fruitful life, and you could charge onto the battlefield with your hard head to your vainglorious death!'

Patroklos watched his cousin stride away and then he picked up a conch shell and, with a cry of frustration, hurled it into the sea. 'And he calls me hardheaded,' he muttered to himself as he paced back and forth at the edge of the surf. 'I don't know why he's ever bothered to wear that golden helmet. As damnably thick-skulled as he is no sword could possibly harm him.' The young warrior wanted to howl with anger. Why wouldn't Achilles see reason? Leading the Greeks one more time into battle – the final battle of the Trojan War – wouldn't cause his death. The goddesses had changed things. They certainly wouldn't allow all their efforts to be wasted. And Patroklos was truly grateful. Not only did he believe his cousin would live, but he had found the woman of his dreams. He wasn't throwing Jacqueline away by wanting to fight. He was embracing his honor. And anyway, she'd be there waiting for him. Afterward she'd bandage his wounds, and take him into her soft body and heal him.

But there would be no honorable last battle. If Achilles wasn't there to lead the Myrmidons, they wouldn't fight, and even with Odysseus's sudden brilliance on the battlefield the war would continue to drag on and on. 'I do wish I was Achilles – just for one day,' Patroklos said.

'You know, darling, that's not a half-bad idea,' Venus said, as she materialized in a cloud of glittering smoke beside him.

'Goddess!' Patroklos gasped and dropped to one knee, bowing his head to her.

'Arise, Patroklos, and let me look at you.'

'Goddess?' Patroklos asked, obviously confused, but rising to his feet as she'd commanded.

'Hmm . . . ' Venus walked a slow circle around the stunned warrior. 'You're almost the same height and build, clearly you're related. His body is thicker, of course, and you're much blonder than he, but under armor that won't be so noticeable. Plus, I'll add a little magical this and that. Put on his helmet and the rest of this armor and no one will be able to tell the difference, especially in the heat of battle.'

'Goddess, I don't understand.' But even as he said the words, Patroklos knew what the Goddess of Love was planning, and his heart beat hard and fast with anticipation.

'Don't you, darling? You said you'd like to be Achilles so that you could lead the final charge of the Greeks against the Trojans.

I believe I can give you your wish. If it is truly what you wish. Is it young Patroklos?'

Patroklos wanted to shout with triumph and instantly accept the goddess's offer, but the golden Olympians were often capricious and their whims could be dangerous and deadly. 'Why do you wish to aid me, Aphrodite?'

The goddess frowned and the air around them heated, whipping fitfully against Patroklos's skin in response to her irritation. 'Can you Greeks not remember that I prefer to be called Venus?'

Patroklos bowed his head. 'I beg your pardon, Great Goddess. I meant no disrespect.'

Venus drew a deep breath and the breeze died, returning to pleasant coolness of the seaside night. 'Of course you didn't, darling. I shouldn't be so touchy. I've just been under terrible stress lately. This war is wearing on my nerves, which brings me back to the reason for my little visit and your question. I wish to aid you because the war has gone on long enough. We want it to end. You can help that happen.'

'We? So the gods are truly becoming involved?'

'Actually the goddesses are.'

Patroklos's eyes widened in understanding. 'Athena is aiding Odysseus.'

'Among other things,' Venus mumbled, then cleared her throat delicately. 'Yes, and I am aiding you.'

'I'm honored, Great Goddess. But why me? I have never been your supplicant.' He smiled a little shyly. 'The truth is until lately I knew very little of love.'

Venus touched his cheek and he felt a warm flush of love and happiness rush though his body. 'But you have found love, haven't you?'

Unable to speak, he nodded.

'That is why I've chosen you. Newfound love is a powerful emotion. It holds a very special magic. I've seen it stave off death, heal souls and thwart fate. I'm going to use the magic of newfound love and your physical resemblance with your cousin. Coupled and blessed by me, those things will allow you to impersonate Achilles just long enough to lead the Myrmidons and the Greek army against the Trojans. You'll head the charge when the great walls are breached.'

Excitement shivered over Patroklos and his eyes blazed. 'I'll do it, Goddess! I'll do it for Greece and for you.'

Venus inclined her head slightly in acknowledgement of his pledge. 'I am pleased. Now all you need is Achilles' famous armor and my blessing just after dawn.'

'My cousin keeps his armor in his tent. How do I—'

'Leave that to me. Love will keep Achilles occupied,' Venus said.

'But the Myrmidons, how do I rally them without alerting Achilles?'

'Simply pass the word amongst the tents tonight that Achilles has called a special training session for the morning. They are to meet here.' Venus gestured around them at where they stood on the beach, halfway between the Greek and Myrmidon camps. 'Shortly after dawn. Imply that he has become restless. The men are already surprised at his choice to withdraw from the fighting. It will take little to convince them he has returned to his old ways.'

Patroklos nodded slowly, considering. 'True, and if Love is keeping Achilles busy in his tent, he won't hear of the early *training* session he was supposed to have called.' He grinned. 'My cousin will be truly angered when he finds out he's been duped.'

Venus's smile was blinding in its beauty. 'And by that time the war will be over and the Greeks victorious. Achilles will be too busy rejoicing and making plans to return to Phthia to be too angry with you.'

'You, my lady, are brilliant,' Patroklos said with a gentlemanly flourish and bow.

The goddess batted her long-lashed eyes coquettishly. 'Of course I am, darling.'

'And the Greeks – will they be told Achilles is going to lead the charge?'

Venus raised a slim brow. 'I do believe Odysseus can aid us with spreading word of that.'

'Then it is decided.'

'It is. At dawn I will await you behind your tent.' Venus paused, as another thought came to her. 'You'll need to get Jacqueline out of the way. She's a modern woman, and she'd never sit idly by while you led the Greeks into battle.'

Patroklos nodded and chuckled softly. 'Jacqueline would not sit idly by ever. She has the body of a sweet maiden and the heart of a brave warrior. She is a most unusual woman.'

'Well, she is, but you don't know many modern mortals. Still it causes a problem for us in the morning. She is truly besotted with you and she won't . . .' Venus's words trailed off as she began to smile.

'Goddess?'

'She is so besotted with you that she wishes very much to please you. Before dawn awaken her.' The goddess smiled suggestively. 'Awake her *thoroughly*, and then tell her that second only to her you desire the young, tender clams that the sea exposes at low tide.'

'Low tide?' he said, obviously not understanding.

Venus sighed. 'Low tide will be at dawn. Ask her to dig clams for you while you train with the men. She'll leave your tent at dawn and be out of the way.'

'Are you sure she'll do that for me?'

'Fulfill her first. Pledge your love to her. Then she'll dig clams for you. Modern mortals are logical. You did something nice for her – she'll want to do something nice for you.'

Patroklos smiled. 'It's really that simple?'

'Well, it will be after a sprinkle or two of my magic. Now go to her brave Patroklos, and on the morrow be prepared for glory!' Venus clapped her hands together and disappeared in a poof of glittering smoke.

Patroklos, grinning broadly, kicked into a swift jog, determined to take Jacqueline into his tent and spend the remainder of the night worshipping love.

It wasn't difficult to find Athena and Odysseus. It didn't take the divine magic of being love incarnate to recognize the moans and murmured sighs of the passion they were sharing. Out of consideration, Venus materialized around the curve of the beach inside a grove of slender trees. Quietly she approached the lovers. Athena was lying back on a satin blanket, wearing only a transparent silver robe. Odysseus, completely naked, and, Venus noted with appreciation, much more powerfully endowed than she had imagined, was kissing the arch of the goddess's foot. Venus hoped Athena had bothered to have the forest nymphs give her a thorough pedicure, and made a mental note to speak with her later about such things.

Venus cleared her throat.

Odysseus grabbed his sword and in one quick motion whirled around, crouching defensively in front of Athena.

Venus raised a brow. 'How deliciously protective you are, darling.'

Athena was on her feet in an instant, stepping between Odysseus and Venus. 'How dare you interrupt me! You have no right to—'

'Oh, blah.' Venus rolled her eyes. 'Save your bluster for the mortals. And I'm not interrupting for long. I just have a quick message for Odysseus.'

Athena's eyes narrowed. 'What do you want with him?'

Venus's smile was slow and knowing. 'Jealousy? How very amusing. Ridiculous, but amusing. But, no, I have no intention of ravishing your lover. Odysseus, darling?' Venus looked around Athena, who continued to glare at her. Odysseus stepped to his goddess's side, giving Venus a delightful look at his full frontal glory. 'Good, there you are. And may I say you are looking quite well.'

'The message!' Athena snapped.

Venus sighed. 'Oh all right. It's just this – Achilles will be leading the Myrmidons into the battle tomorrow morning shortly after dawn.'

Odysseus's fists clenched and his smile was fierce. 'I knew he would relent!' Then he turned to Athena and dropped to one knee. 'Tomorrow my goddess, my love, the Greeks will give you victory over the Trojans.'

'Yes, isn't that interesting?' Athena answered, but her eyes never left Venus. 'And why would that be happening?'

'Well, if you hadn't been so *preoccupied* lately you'd know why.' Venus made a motion for Athena to follow her a few paces away. 'If I could have a word with you in private?'

Still frowning sternly at the Goddess of Love, Athena told Odysseus, 'I'll be just a moment.' And she followed Venus down the beach. 'Explain yourself,' she said when they were beyond his hearing.

'First of all, I must say I told you so. You should have taken him as a lover ages ago.'

'My love life is not open for discussion.'

'Darling, I'm not discussing your love life, just your previous lack of one. Anyway this whole thing is rather simple. You've been aiding Odysseus, which has basically nullified Achilles' absence from the battlefield.'

Athena drew a deep breath, obviously readying herself to launch into an excuse. Venus's upraised hand silenced her. 'Oh, save it. I say good for you.' She glanced over Athena's shoulder where Odysseus waited for his goddess. 'Actually I say *very* good for you. But you did mess up our little plan.'

'I realize that,' Athena said shortly.

'So, Hera and I have altered it. The Greeks might as well win. I mean, it's not like we actually care. We just want the war to end.'

'I care,' Athena said.

'I can see that – so this works out doubly well for you. The Greeks win. Your lover is a Greek. All will be happily ever after. Hey, maybe you can manipulate it so that it takes Odysseus another decade to get home. That way you can have him all to yourself for a lovely long affair.'

Athena's gray eyes narrowed again. 'We are *not* discussing my love life.'

'By Poseidon's wet buttocks, you're boring!' Then remembering where she was, Venus glanced nervously out to sea. 'Sorry darling, you know I said it with love.'

'Would you please stay focused? What about Achilles and his fate? Does this mean he dies tomorrow?' Athena said.

'Oh, don't worry about that. Achilles will be sleeping safely in his bed. It'll be Patroklos, plus a little of my magic, who is actually leading the Greeks. But do not share that information with your boyfriend.'

'He is not—' Athena blustered.

'Oh, whatever. Just don't tell him. I'll see you tomorrow after this whole thing is finally over. Unless you're otherwise occupied.' Venus blew a kiss at Odysseus, and then she disappeared.

Chapter Twenty-six

Agamemnon's voluminous tents were filled with celebration. Of course most of the revelers were Agamemnon's contemporaries – men either too old or too highly placed to be involved in the actual fighting – but one would never know from their toasts and their boasts that they hadn't been in the thick of the battle. And there were women aplenty. Young, supple war prizes who, if not exactly eager to please, were willing to pretend they were for the advantage such a night might gain them.

Briseis hated them – every old, shrunken-testicled, rutting goat. Though even as she hated them she shot surreptitious smiles to those she found the least repulsive. Agamemnon could tire of her at any time, and if he did, only one of these soon-to-be corpses would be all that stood between her and whatever peasant warrior managed to fight off his comrades for her.

What she wouldn't give to belong to someone as virile as golden Achilles. His scars had never bothered her, and the thought of the berserker had always excited more than frightened her. But when she had belonged to him, he had never so much as glanced at her unless he'd wanted her to fetch wine or food for him. Since he'd allowed Agamemnon to take her, Briseis had cursed herself for not being bolder when she'd had a chance at him. She should have gone to his bed uninvited. She should have thought of bespelling him as Polyxena had.

'Briseis! More wine!' Agamemnon ordered, reaching down

from where he sat on his golden throne to cup her breast and tweak her nipple for the benefit of the watching generals.

Briseis wanted to curl her lip and hiss at him like a viper. Instead she arched her back erotically and said huskily, 'Anything you wish, my lord.' Then she picked up the large empty wine jug and took her time walking past the other men, stroking the smooth side of the pottery suggestively and allowing them ample opportunity to gaze at her aroused young nipples and fantasize about anything they might wish.

As soon as she left the tent, Briseis's sensuous walk disappeared and she moved with the catlike silence she'd perfected when she was just a child. Naturally the bovine warriors who huddled around the wine casks didn't hear her approach. When she heard his name, she froze in the shadows.

'Achilles! Truly? Are you certain?' One short coarse-looking man said.

'I heard from Odysseus himself. It must be truth,' came the reply from a taller, pockmarked soldier.

'With Achilles and his Myrmidons leading the charge, victory will be ours tomorrow, brothers!'

'I didn't believe he would fight again. I heard that the Trojan princess had cast a spell over him,' said another man.

'She only cast a spell here,' the short man said, grabbing his genitals and thrusting his hips up, 'and not here.' With his other hand he lifted his sword and swung it in a singing arch around his head. All the men laughed.

Briseis stepped out of the shadows. 'Agamemnon wishes more wine. Fill this for me,' she said coldly and held out the jug.

The short man took it and said, 'I'll fill it for you.' His lingering gaze said that he would love to fill her as he did the jug, but Briseis knew that as long as she was Agamemnon's war prize none of the men would speak openly of their lust. Agamemnon could do anything he wished to her, his men could not.

He handed her back the jug, eyes staring at her erect nipples plainly visible through her transparent robes. 'What is your name?' she asked him.

He smiled, showing rotting teeth. 'Aentoclus, my lady.'

'Aentoclus, if you ever so much as look my way again, I will tell Agamemnon that you tried to rape me, and I will ask my lover, your king, to bring me your testicles in retribution.' While the warrior blanched a sickly pale color, Briseis smiled and walked away, holding the jug carefully so that it didn't splash wine on her clothing.

She quickly went back to Agamemnon's side, this time ignoring the appreciative looks of the generals. She refilled his goblet and leaned into the king's side, whispering to him, 'I have news of Achilles.'

Agamemnon's shrewd gaze darted briefly to meet hers and what he saw there made him clap his hands together and command, 'More music and dancing!' The music flared as pubescent girls clothed only in gold chains undulated through the tent, pulling the attention of the men from their king.

'What have you heard?' he asked quietly.

'Achilles and the Myrmidons are leading the charge tomorrow,' she whispered, nuzzling his ear.

She felt the jolt of shock that went through his body. 'You are quite sure about this?'

'Odysseus himself is passing the news.'

'If this is true . . .' His arm tightened around her. 'You are a jewel of rare price, my dear.'

'I am your jewel, my lord. Always your jewel.' Briseis smiled smugly and snuggled into his side, sneaking one soft hand down to stroke the inside of his thigh. No, he would not tire of her. It didn't matter what she had to do, she would remain Agamemnon's war prize, even when they returned to Greece.

'Kalchas!' Agamemnon lifted his voice over the sensuous beat of drums.

'Here, my lord.' The old prophet seemed to materialize out of the air itself.

Just like a poisonous mist, Briseis thought, although she always kept her disgust for the revolting old man carefully hidden. He was a favorite of Agamemnon's and Briseis was far too cunning to make an enemy of him.

'Fetch Ajax to me.'

'Ajax, my lord?'

Briseis noted the generals overhearing Agamemnon's command looked similarly confused, as they should. Ajax was brilliant on the field of battle. Off the field of battle he could hardly put together a complete thought. The man was literally as big and strong and stupid as an ox.

'Yes, Ajax. I had a dream last night that he was key to a great victory tomorrow. I wish to tell him of the dream and of the reward I plan to gift him with for his heroic actions.'

'Yes, my lord.' Kalchas bowed and scuttled from the tent.

The generals who had overheard smiled and nodded at their king. Dreams were sent by the gods, and seeing their king acting on one of his was something of which they all approved.

Of course Briseis knew Agamemnon was lying. The only thing he'd dreamed of the night before had been her open thighs. He'd told her so that morning as, upon waking, he'd put his face between them.

She nuzzled his ear again and whispered, 'What are you up to, my lord?'

In one swift motion Agamemnon pulled her onto his lap so that she straddled him and his erection pushed intimately between her spread legs. She leaned into him and, veiled by her hair, he spoke, 'If tomorrow Achilles fights the Trojans, it will be his last battle, as well as the day we are finally victorious. I have waited almost ten summers for the damned prophesy of his death to come true, and I will wait no more.'

'But I hear from my sources in the Myrmidon camp that they believe Polyxena is thwarting the prophesy. Perhaps that is true – you know even Poseidon's minions could not kill her.'

Agamemnon bit her neck and whispered, 'All Achilles need do is to kill Hector and his death will follow. Zeus has proclaimed it. Not even an oracle protected by a goddess can change that. Polyxena has been keeping him from the battlefield, and thus away from Hector. Perhaps Achilles' arrogance has led him to believe his little oracle can somehow protect him on the battle-field. I'm simply going to be sure Hector's path to Achilles is clear and then let fate take over.'

Briseis laughed huskily. 'My lord, you are brilliant!' Then she moaned and rocked against his hardness, closing her eyes and pretending she straddled the strong young body of a warrior.

'The spell couldn't be that simple,' Achilles said.

'I keep telling you – it isn't a spell, it's self-hypnotism, and it is that simple. And that complex. The mind is amazing. It alone can make a person believe he's sick, or better yet, believe he is perfectly well when he should be sick. I've seen some miraculous things in the ten-plus years I've been in practice.'

'And this *self-hypnotism*, which is not a spell but seems very much like a spell, can actually help me keep the berserker at bay,' he said, taking a thick strand of Kat's hair, wrapping it around his finger, and then bringing it to his lips. 'It's like a sable's pelt. I'll never tire of touching it.'

'I got lucky,' Kat said, tilting her head so that he could touch her hair more easily. 'Polyxena had a seriously nice head of hair.'

Achilles smiled. 'I forget that this body has not always been yours. What color was your hair before?'

'Blonde. It wasn't long like this, but it was pretty good hair, too.'

'You would be beautiful in any form to me,' he said, and kissed her lips gently.

'That is a very sweet thing to say. But you're not going to get me off subject so easily. Yes, self-hypnotism, which is *not* like a spell at all, can help you learn to control your body and your emotions so that you can keep both relaxed enough, no matter what is going on with you, to avoid the triggers that cause the berserker to possess you.'

'Ah, and then our son will not accidentally trigger me to be possessed by the berserker when he believes he cannot possibly drown because he is the grandson of a sea goddess,' Achilles said, looking into her eyes.

Trapped in the blue depths of his soul, Kat saw a future where she lived and loved at this amazing man's side and she knew she would want his babies – she'd want them, and their grandchildren, and whatever was the ancient and magical Greek world's equivalent of the traditional family and the picket fence. Hell, she even wanted the damn dog. She wanted it all. 'And what if he is a she?'

Achilles blinked, obviously not having considered this as a possibility. Then he snorted and his lips twitched up in his little almost smile. 'I suppose I will have to double my practice of self-hypnotism then – or perhaps not practice it at all. Would becoming a berserker be a good or bad thing when suitors try to woo my daughter from me?'

Kat grinned. 'I think control is still the key here. If he shows up sagging or wearing emo pants and eyeliner, we let the berserker loose. If he looks like a good kid, you just growl and scare him a little.' Achilles' brow knitted together in confusion. Kat laughed. 'How about this – you only eat the suitors we don't like.'

He frowned at her. 'Not even the berserker actually eats people.'

She lifted her brow.

'Well, not usually he doesn't,' Achilles amended.

Kat was just trying to decide if she really wanted to question Achilles further about the whole 'usually he doesn't eat people' thing when a woman's shriek carried clearly into their tent. Achilles had just leapt to his feet when the shriek was followed by gales of giggles. He'd taken one hesitant step toward the tent flap when Kat grabbed his hand and pulled him back to bed.

'As embarrassing as it is to admit, that is Jacqueline. And, no, she doesn't need rescuing.'

Achilles sat back down on the bed beside her. 'Is she always that loud?'

'No. That's her "oh, baby, I think I just won the lottery shriek and giggle." Which means that I can tell you with one-hundred-percent accuracy Patroklos is not still pissed off at you. He is out there giving Jacky the time of her life.'

'Huh.' Achilles grunted. 'The boy is certainly causing a ruckus. He and Jacqueline should be quieter – more reserved.'

Kat's brows shot up. 'Achilles, *you* are a stodgy old spinster. My god, listen to you – you sound about a hundred years old.'

'I am not a spinster.'

'And to think Hera and Athena accused Jacky and me of being spinsters just because we're, well, old. You, Mr. Hero Warrior, are actually an old fuddy-dud, without being old.' More giggles drifted through the tent to them, this time punctuated by a deeply sensuous and insistent male voice. 'And he,' Kat jerked her chin in the direction of the tent flap, 'is definitely no "boy."'

'Are you lusting after my young cousin?' Achilles asked, blue eyes sparkling.

'How about I answer that question after I get all the details from Jacky tomorrow?'

'You are a tease,' Achilles said and, growling playfully, he pulled her back on the bed with him.

'Yep, and you are a spinster,' Kat said, pretending to struggle.

'Would a spinster do this?' Achilles bent and covered her mouth with his. The kiss was not wild and out of control. He remembered to pace himself – to monitor his breathing and be sure that lust didn't overwhelm him and bring on the berserker. But that didn't mean the kiss wasn't deep and passionate and an intimate promise of more to come.

When he finally lifted his mouth from hers, Kat was breathless. 'If I take back the whole spinster thing, will that mean you're going to stop kissing me like that?'

'Never,' Achilles whispered.

'Glad to hear it, because I don't want you to ever stop.'

'I won't my Katrina, my princess . . .'

And Achilles made love to her. Slowly, languorously, letting her body serve as his blueprint he built her pleasure, one touch at a time, until they both found completion.

As Kat drifted to sleep in his arms she thought that having a man who loved her slowly and carefully was the most erotic experience of her life.

Venus materialized inside the dim tent after the lovers were deeply asleep. Moving silently as a shade, she brushed the bed curtain aside and smiled down at Achilles and Katrina. *True love*, she thought happily. *I knew this woman was meant for something special the first instant I saw her — and Love is never wrong.* Then she raised her hands over the couple and whispered the spell:

> *Achilles, hero and warrior, I want you to sleep*
> *Well into the morning, soundless, replete.*
> *Wake when the sun is high in the sky.*
> *What Love commands, you cannot deny.*

From her raised hand a waterfall of diamond dust sprinkled over Achilles' body. The warrior smiled and drifted deeply into Love's magical embrace.

Sighing with self-satisfaction, Venus left their bedside, easily finding the place where Achilles' famous armor lay discarded in the corner of the tent. With a slight flick of her wrist, she and the armor disappeared. Venus had one more stop to make to sprinkle a little conciliatory magic on stubborn Jacqueline, and then she had only to wait till dawn when she would meet Patroklos, clothe him in Achilles' borrowed armor and a touch of her power and then this whole war issue would be dealt with. Venus sighed again. It was always work, work, work. When this was over she definitely would treat herself to a much deserved vacation.

Chapter Twenty-seven

Jacky came awake slowly. She was having the most deliciously erotic dream. Spike (from season six of *Buffy*, so he was still the Big Bad) had his glorious cheekbones between her caffe latte thighs and he was putting that beautiful mouth to excellent use. She'd always believed there was a whole other world in that mouth.

She jolted awake.

There was, indeed, a beautiful blond man's face between her legs, but her thighs were young, too damn skinny and too, too damn white. Not that that little fact really mattered much to her at that moment.

'Patroklos . . .' she murmured. He looked up at her and paused briefly in his work.

'Yes, my beauty. Are you awake?'

'Almost,' she said sleepily, considerately spreading her legs so that he fitted more comfortably between them. 'Why don't you see if you can bring me the rest of the way *awake*?' As he got back to business, Jacky thought it was like he'd been blessed by the Goddess of Love herself, which, she realized, might truly be possible and made a mental note to thank Venus. Then Jacky found that she was having trouble thinking at all.

'Psst! Kat! Wake the hell up.'

Kat's eyelids fluttered. God, was she having an awful dream? She could swear Jacky was bending over her, shaking her with one hand while she carried a wooden bucket (bucket?) in the other.

'Go away,' she rasped to what she hoped was a dream apparition. 'I'm calling in sick – crazy people be damned. Let them counsel themselves today.'

'Get up, fool. You're not dreaming. I got somethin' to do and you're comin' with me.' Jacky snapped back the bed sheets, exposing all of Kat's naked body. 'Damn, you're young,' she said, studying her friend.

Kat rolled out of bed and snatched up her underrobe. 'Do you mind? You do not need to see all my business.'

'Please. I *know* all your business. By the by, your thighs are much thinner in this life than they had gotten in the last one.'

'Jacqueline. Your ass is narrow.'

Jacky sucked air and got ready to launch into an all out assault when a deep snore made both of them turn to statues. Kat looked slowly back at the mound of bedclothes and the naked man. Jacky tiptoed and peeked over her shoulder.

Achilles lay on his side, his torso and one scarred but distinctly muscled thigh poking nakedly from the crisp linen sheets. Kat turned back to Jacky and put her finger against her lips. 'Shh!' She snatched up the rest of her clothes and grabbed Jacky's hand, hauling her from the tent. Outside Kat looked incredulously up at a sky that was just beginning to show a hint of rosy dawn's fingertips. 'What in the holy hell are you doing: one – awake at this insane hour, and two – waking me up, too?'

Jacky glanced at the sky and then back at her BFF. Then she fidgeted.

'Oh no, no, no. You woke me up for a really, *really* stupid reason,' Kat said.

'Maybe,' Jacky said.

'Why are you holding a bucket?'

'We have to get somethin'.'

'Something?'

'Yes, somethin' for Patroklos,' Jacky mumbled.

'*Pardon moi?*'

Jacky cleared her throat. 'Somethin' for Patroklos,' she repeated, this time so that Kat could hear her.

'You want to get something for *Blondie Bear*. So explain why my sleep is being disturbed.'

'Don't call him Blondie Bear. I've decided I adore him for himself, and not for his fortuitous resemblance to Spike. And you have to come with me because you're my best friend and you love me.'

'Oh, it's that embarrassing?'

'Absolutely.'

'Can we drink this early?'

'In my professional nursing opinion in the ancient world it's healthier to drink wine than water.'

'Which means yes?'

'Definitely. I'll grab a wineskin on our way out the camp,' Jacky said.

'Are there any fried swine sandwiches ready, too?'

'Already thought of that.' She pointed to a cheesecloth-wrapped packet nestled inside the bucket.

'All right. I'll go with your silly ass.' Then Kat hesitated and glanced back at Achilles' quiet tent. 'But how long are—'

'Oh, please. Your boy is sleepin' like a drugged old woman in a rest home. He'll be out for hours.'

'Okay, fine. I'm coming.' Kat followed Jacky as she grabbed a wineskin from the table by the banked campfire. There was no one around except a sleeping maidservant, and she didn't move when the two of them trudged from camp. 'And for your information, the simile is supposed to be sleeping like a baby, not like a drugged old woman.'

'Kat, you need to spend more time in a hospital setting. Babies sleep like shit. Drugged old women sleep for days. Get a clue.'

'And now you're being fresh. Maybe I should just go back—' Kat began but Jacky grabbed her hand.

'Sorry – sorry. Ignore me. I haven't had coffee since I've been white. It's made me a little cranky.'

'Jacqueline, where are we going?'

'To dig clams.'

'Huh? It sounded like you said something about digging.'

'Yes, I did. Don't steamers sound good to you? Lots of butter?'

Kat stared at Jacky and almost tripped over a tuft of sea grass. 'Wait. Are you telling me you're digging clams for Patroklos? To eat?'

'We. We are digging clams for Patroklos to eat.'

Kat's giggle started in little bursts, but every time she looked at Jacky the bursts got bigger and bigger until Jacky glared at her while she wiped her eyes and gasped for air.

'What!' Jacky said.

'You – are – cooking – for – a – man,' Kat said between fits of laughter.

'Am not. This is almost exactly like going to the grocery to buy the stuff so that someone else can cook for my man whilst he and I sit back and enjoy dinner.'

'Oh, poor deluded girl,' Kat said, only semisuccessfully controlling her hilarity. 'Let Dr. Kat help you. Honey,' she said slowly, like she was talking to a second grader. 'You are actually hunting and gathering, and coming precariously close to being domesticated.'

'You know, I just saw you naked. You are scrawny. I do believe I could kick your ass.'

Kat burst into giggles again.

'And,' Jacky added, 'you need a good bikini wax.'

'Really?' Kat asked innocently. 'Are you sure? Could you take a closer look for me?' she said as she pretended to hike up her robes. 'This body is new and I really don't know what's what with it.'

'Oh, Jesus wept, do not lift your goddamn skirt!'

'No, really, nurse. I think I feel a burning sensation. Can you check it out for me, please?'

'You are the nastiest thing I know,' Jacky said, trying not to laugh.

'Which is why you lurve lurve lurve me!' Kat said hoisting up her skirts and dancing around like a cancan girl.

'Would you stop messing around? My man wants some steamers and that, along with the best sex he's ever known in his virile young life, is just what I'm going to give him.'

'Hey Miss Smartie, do you even know how to dig for clams?'

'How can you even ask me that question? My people grew up near the water.'

'But you grew up with me near the center of the country in Tulsa. Hello. No ocean there.'

Jacky drew herself up to her full, yet miniscule height, and Kat thought how funny it was that she could be plunked into a body the direct opposite of hers, and still retain so much of her innate gestures and expressions and just plain physical stubbornness.

'I Googled clam digging for that last vacation we were going to take. You know the one – before we died?'

'Yes, I do have a vague memory.' She frowned. 'But in the

Cayman Islands I didn't remember anything saying we had to dig for our own food. Hell, we weren't even supposed to have to get up to get our own drinks.'

'Nevertheless, I did some research. Follow my lead and all will be well.'

'Hey, what's Patroklos doing right now?' Kat asked.

'Sleeping.' Jacky's smile was slow and totally nasty. 'Did you know there's a whole other world waiting to be discovered – by me – in that man's mouth?'

'Do tell!'

'This mornin' he woke me up with his face between my legs. I thought I'd died, again, and this time there was no question about whether or not I was in heaven.'

'And to imagine that I may have been likewise awakened had you not messed that up for me,' Kat said.

'Relax. Your boy did not look like he was up to any calisthenics this morning. Let him recover, hussy. Anyway this shouldn't take long. When we get back you can slip into bed beside him and see if you get lucky. By the way, I did notice Achilles has a nice, long length of thigh.'

Kat waggled her eyebrows. 'That's not the only long length he has.'

Jacky laughed, then she caught Kat's gaze. 'We're completely in love with them, aren't we?'

'Completely,' Kat said.

'It's very odd,' Jacky said.

'Yep,' Kat said. 'You know, I think I'm going to miss champagne almost as much as hot running water.'

'Well, you could squander your wish on a lifetime supply of champagne,' Jacky said.

'My wish?'

'You know, as soon as the war's over the goddesses owe us each a wish.'

Kat blinked. 'Well, shit. I forgot all about that.' Then she raised a brow at her friend. 'You want me to squander my wish on champagne so you can drink it, too, without having to wish for it.'

'That makes me sound very shallow, Katrina.'

'But I'm right, aren't I?'

'Yes, definitely.' They'd reached the receded shoreline and Jacky started tying up her skirts, motioning for Kat to do the same. 'Okay, this is easy. We just feel around with our toes out there where the low tide has exposed all that naked sand to find the clams. Then we dump them in the bucket and take them to a menial to cook.'

'All right, but if something tries to eat me . . .'

'Yeah, yeah, I know. I'll press your panic button or scream for Achilles. But don't worry about it. His mama said she'd make sure nothin' from the sea attacks you again. Hey, now that I think about it, it'll probably be very cool having a goddess for a mother-in-law.'

'You're right. Sadly for you, I hear Patroklos's mom is a Harpy.'

'Jesus wept! Are you kidding me?'

Kat grinned at her and started digging around in the smooshy wet sand. 'Would I do that?'

Jacky had been right. The clams practically leapt into their bucket, which made them wonder if Achilles' sea goddess mom might be lending them a little unseen hand. So it was barely a couple hours past dawn when the two of them, well fortified by swine sandwiches and an abundance of wine, started to meander slowly back to camp.

And then the day exploded.

'Wonder what's up with him?' Kat asked, pointing to a warrior who was coming in a flat run down the beach.

Jacky shaded her eyes and squinted to get a better look. She shrugged. 'Patroklos mentioned something about the men training early today. Maybe they're starting a new sprint-down-the-beach drill.'

'Training early? Really? Weird that Achilles didn't say anything.'

'Perhaps his mouth was too busy with other things last night,' Jacky said.

Kat opened her own mouth to agree totally, with some juicy girlfriend details added in, when the runner caught sight of them and instantly changed direction to head straight for them.

'This doesn't feel right,' Jacky said.

'Crap,' Kat said in agreement.

The warrior reached them. Kat recognized him as Diomedes, Aetnia's man. He was gasping for breath, but his words were still sickeningly clear. 'Princess, you and Melia must come. It's Patroklos. He is dying.'

Jacky grabbed Kat's hand. 'Take me to him. Now,' Jacky said.

The warrior reversed his path, slowing his pace so that he wouldn't outdistance the two women. Kat wanted to ask what had happened, but she didn't have any breath to waste on words. Obviously neither did the silent and stone-faced woman who ran beside her. It seemed to take forever, but they finally got back to the Myrmidon camp and Patroklos's tent. Kat looked at the somber, blood-spattered men surrounding the tent and her heart sank.

She and Jacky entered the tent to find Patroklos lying on the wide bed, drenched in fresh blood, with Kalchas hovering over him like a carrion bird.

'Get away from him,' Jacky snapped, shoving the skinny old man aside. 'Oh, god, no.' Was all Kat heard Jacky say, and then her friend was all business. She glanced up at the two warriors standing bedside. 'Help me get him out of this armor.' They obeyed her automatically, pulling off armor that had turned from gold to a damp scarlet.

Kat felt a rush of sickness as she got a clearer view of Patroklos's nasty neck wound. He was bleeding from several lacerations on other parts of his body, but it was his neck that looked particularly terrible. Jacky bent over him, prodding and poking. Without looking up, Jacky spoke to her. 'You have to find me something like a straw. It can't collapse, but it can't be too much bigger than a straw. Hurry, Kat.'

'I'll find something.' Kat paused only long enough to squeeze her friend's arm and then she ran from the tent.

When she saw Odysseus approaching she could have cried with relief.

'Is he dead?'

'Not yet, but I'm afraid he will be unless you help me with something,' Kat said.

'Anything.'

'I need a reed, or anything about this long and hollowed out like this.' Kat showed him with her hands. 'It can't be flimsy or too flexible – it can't collapse. Do you understand?'

'Yes. This way.' He turned on his heel and Kat scrambled to keep up with him as he hurried toward the dunes. 'Lucky it's mid-summer. They're too weak during the spring, and too brittle during the winter, but this time of year they may work.' Odysseus seemed to be talking more to himself than to her as he searched through the grasses. 'We thought it was him, you know.'

'Him?' Kat was barely listening. She just wished she knew what the reed looked like so she could help him.

'Achilles. We thought Patroklos was Achilles – even I believed it. That's what Athena had told me.'

Kat looked carefully at his face. Odysseus appeared uncharacteristically angry – almost like he was pissed at his goddess. She touched his arm and his attention went from the reeds he was pawing through to her. 'You didn't know about this ruse, did you?'

'I have no idea what you're talking about,' Kat said.

'Where's Achilles?'

That took her aback. 'He should be around here with you, or at least with his men. I got up before he did this morning, but I thought he'd be with the Myrmidons.'

Odysseus stared at her for a long minute, before finally saying, 'It's true. You had nothing to do with it. You don't know what Patroklos did.'

'Odysseus! Enough of this – what happened!'

The famous warrior faced her, locking her in his intelligent gaze. 'This morning Patroklos donned the armor of Achilles. He had to have had a goddess's touch, because the boy *was* Achilles. We followed him onto the battlefield – we all followed him.'

Chapter Twenty-eight

'No!' Kat gasped. What the hell was he thinking? He wasn't supposed to fight without Achilles.

'He got tired of waiting.'

'And so he put on Achilles' armor and pretended to be him?'

'It was more than that. Patroklos was Achilles. He looked like him – moved like him – fought like him. He sounded like him. Even after he was cut down, I believed he was Achilles.'

Kat's body felt numb and tingly at the same time. 'And Patroklos managed it all on his own? They're cousins, but they don't look *that* much alike. We've been goddess-dupped.'

'Athena lied to me.'

The depth of betrayal in his voice shocked Kat. 'My guess is that there was more than one goddess in on this scheme.' And then another, more terrible thought slammed into her. 'Odysseus, who cut down Patroklos?'

She knew the answer before he spoke it.

'It was your brother, Hector.'

Kat's knees went to water and she sat straight down on the dune. 'Oh, god.'

'Hector is still alive, Princess,' Odysseus said kindly.

'How could this have happened?' she said, putting her face in her hands.

'Ajax. It was as if he was possessed. He bellowed a challenge to Hector saying that Achilles had finally come for him, and then he cleared a path between the two warriors. Hector killed him just before he and Patroklos began to battle.'

'This doesn't make any sense. Achilles wasn't going to fight Hector – he wasn't going to fight anyone.'

'He's going to fight Hector now,' Odysseus said grimly.

'What?'

'If Patroklos dies, Achilles will exact vengeance for his death.'

Kat stared at Odysseus, almost uncomprehending, and then a terrible shiver skittered through her body. 'Patroklos can't die. Find the reed and get it back to Jacky.'

'Jacky?'

Kat shook her head, as if trying to clear it. 'Melia – I meant Melia. Get the reed to her.' She stood up, forcing her legs to work. 'I'm going to find Achilles.'

Odysseus touched her arm. 'Be careful, Princess. Achilles is not the berserker, and the berserker is not human. He will kill you – never doubt that fact.'

Kat nodded tightly and started to turn away, but his words stopped her.

'I know you and Melia are not what you seem, but unless you are immortal do not think you can defeat the berserker.'

She met his gaze for another moment before sprinting off. Her mind was totally focused on one thing – Achilles. She knew where he was. The weird way he'd slept through Jacky's wake-up call made sense now.

Kat burst through the tent flap. The inside was cool and dimly lit – and Achilles hadn't moved since she'd left with Jacky. She hesitated, looking down at his sleeping face. He was so peaceful, utterly relaxed and sprawled across the bed. His golden hair had fallen over part of his face, obscuring his scars and making him look so young that for a second she couldn't breathe. She knew

282

everything would change after she woke him, and she didn't want to shatter things – she didn't want to shatter him. Kat smoothed the hair away from his face and he didn't stir. She kissed his cheek and his lips tilted briefly up. Then she shook his shoulder.

'Achilles, you have to wake up.'

She had to shake him hard before he rolled over groggily and blinked up at her.

He smiled. 'Katrina, I was dreaming of you.'

The sweet look on his face made her stomach hurt. She braced herself and kept her voice calm and steady. 'You have to come with me. There's been an accident and Patroklos has been hurt.'

She watched him shake off the last of whatever had kept him asleep all morning.

'How bad is it?' he asked as he pulled on his clothes and started for the door.

'Achilles.' She caught his arm and he paused to look down at her. 'It's bad. You need to ready yourself. Patroklos is going to need you, and not the berserker. There is no battle here to fight,' she said slowly and distinctly.

'Yes, yes, I understand,' he said a little impatiently. 'Where is he?'

'In his tent. Remember,' she added in a low voice as she hurried outside with him, 'Jacky is a nurse – a very talented healer. So it's going to look bad, but . . .'

Her voice faltered and she was unable to speak the lie. She couldn't tell Achilles that Jacky could save Patroklos. Then she realized that she needn't have been worried about what she said or didn't say to him. Achilles hadn't heard her. He was striding to Patroklos's tent and she had to jog to keep up with him. When he saw the blood-spattered Myrmidons standing in full armor around the tent, silent and grim faced, Kat felt the shock that went through his body as if it were her own. He paused before he ducked inside the tent, bowing his head and taking several long, deep breaths. She touched his arm and his gaze met hers.

'No battle here to fight,' he said softly.

'No battle here to fight,' she repeated, as if the words held power.

They entered the tent. Achilles took two steps toward the bed and then the wet, awful sound of breath gurgling through blood hit both of them and he stopped as if he'd walked into an invisible wall.

Jacky glanced up. Her eyes went quickly from Achilles to Kat. 'Did you bring it?'

'Odysseus is getting a reed,' Kat assured her. 'He should be here any second.'

'I need it yesterday,' Jacky said.

'It's a sword wound. He – they've been in battle,' Achilles said as he lurched forward to the side of the bed, inadvertently kicking a section of the discarded bloody armor. He glanced down. Kat saw the question cross his face, and then his eyes widened in recognition. 'He was wearing my armor.'

To Kat Achilles' voice sounded dead, but it somehow reached Patroklos. He opened his eyes and his gaze went immediately to Achilles.

'By the gods, what have you done?' Achilles said, reaching for his cousin's hand.

Patroklos couldn't speak. All he could do was struggle to breathe. His bloody lips formed the words *Forgive me*, and then his eyes rolled to show their whites before they fluttered closed.

'He wore my armor and led them into battle,' Achilles said in his dead voice as he watched the unconscious Patroklos try to breathe.

'We thought he was you, my lord,' Diomedes said from a shadowy corner of the tent.

Kat saw his eyes flash up at the warrior, and Diomedes moved his shoulders restlessly. 'Everyone thought he was you. Even Hector thought he was battling you until he knocked off his helmet. Then he stopped and—'

'Hector!'

Kat had never heard anything like the coldness in Achilles' voice. It chilled her through to her soul.

'Yes, my lord. It was Hector,' Diomedes said.

'So Hector has killed him,' Achilles said in the same, emotionless tone.

'Not yet he hasn't,' Jacky snapped. 'Don't say that kind of crap. He might be able to hear you.' She didn't spare a glance for Achilles, but looked at Kat instead. 'I need the reed. Now. If Odysseus has it you have to go get him.'

Kat nodded and started back toward the tent flap, almost as reluctant to leave Achilles as she was freaked out by what would happen if she didn't get Odysseus and the reed.

'Go. Find him,' said Achilles' strange, cold voice. 'Get what she needs.'

Kat had just turned when Odysseus entered the tent. Breathing hard he rushed to Jacky and handed her several long, hollow reeds of slightly differing, strawlike sizes.

'Will these do?'

'They'll have to,' Jacky said.

And Patroklos stopped breathing.

'Patroklos! Cousin!' Achilles shouted, and began shaking his shoulder, much as Kat had done to awaken him moments before.

'Enough!' Jacky commanded. 'Odysseus, get Achilles out of here.'

'I will not—' Achilles began to roar.

Kat moved to his side and touched his arm. 'You're not helping him like this.'

Achilles looked wildly down at her.

Kat kept her voice calm. 'There is no battle here, Achilles.' She glanced quickly at Odysseus. 'Take him out of here.'

Odysseus nodded, approaching Achilles carefully. 'My friend, you must—'

'I need this room cleared, now!' Jacky's no-nonsense voice broke in. 'Everyone out except the princess.'

Kat saw that Achilles was set to argue, and she stepped between him and the bed. 'There's no time for this, and no way we'd be able to deal with the berserker in here. If there's a chance of her saving him, you need to get out of here and keep yourself under control.'

Kat held her breath as she watched Achilles' jaw tighten and his turquoise eyes darken in anger, but he gave a stiff nod and, followed by Odysseus and Diomedes, left the tent.

Kat turned back to the bed in time to catch a wad of clean linens Jacky had tossed at her.

'Climb up on the bed beside him. Try to keep the blood wiped up and out of my way,' Jacky said as she hastily inspected the reeds Odysseus had given her. Choosing one, she bent over Patroklos, a small sharp knife closing on his throat.

Kat clenched her teeth against rush after rush of nausea while she assisted Jacky in the tracheotomy. It seemed to take days, but logic told Kat that only minutes had passed when Patroklos's chest began to rise and fall gently again. Kat drew a deep, relieved breath – then she looked at Jacky who was still pale and grim lipped.

'He's breathing now. Isn't he going to be okay?'

'It's temporary. His neck's sustained a lot of damage. This is a Band-Aid on a dam. It's not going to last.'

'What do we have to do?'

'Get him to a hospital. With real doctors, and real medicine, and real surgery.' Jacky wiped her wet brow with her sleeve. Kat noticed her hands were shaking. 'He's gonna die, Kat. There's nothin' I can do to stop it. Not here – not now.' She pressed the back of her hand against her mouth to try to stifle a sob.

'No. No, hell, no. He is not going to die, not because of some meddling, goddess-be-damned scheme.' Kat opened the heart locket that dangled from the chain around her neck and shouted into it, 'Venus! It's an emergency. I need you now!' Kat held her breath, praying silently, *Please, oh please show up*.

In the center of the room a cloud of diamond dust exploded, and Venus stepped from the fading glitter. 'Darling, what is it? I was sure Thetis said there wouldn't be any more nasty sea surprises.' The goddess's gaze traveled up and down Kat's decidedly uninjured form. 'But you look perfectly healthy. Katrina, you know I adore you, but you really shouldn't waste—'

'It's not me. It's Patroklos,' Kat interrupted, pointing at the bed behind Venus.

The goddess turned and then gasped. 'No! This wasn't supposed to happen.'

Kat stepped up beside her. 'You knew he was taking Achilles' place,' she said.

Venus's beautiful eyes filled with tears. 'It was a good idea. Patroklos leads the Greeks to victory pretending to be your Achilles. The war is over, and Achilles lives.' The goddess shook her head sadly at Jacky. 'I didn't mean for him to get hurt.'

'Save him,' Jacky said in a low, strained voice.

'Please,' Kat said. 'If you didn't mean for him to get hurt then you should save him.'

Venus approached Patroklos's battered body. She pressed her hand on his forehead and closed her eyes. A shudder passed through her and she made a small, painful sound. 'He's going to die. This is beyond my powers to heal. It's fate.'

'No!' Jacky yelled. 'You changed fate before. Kat and I died, but you snatched our souls – you altered our fate. Do it again.'

'I cannot. There are some things beyond even Love.'

'No there aren't,' Kat said firmly. 'Love is stronger than anything – it has to be. You can save him, Venus. All you need to do is mix magic with the modern world, and you've definitely done that before.'

'What's your idea, Katrina?' Venus asked, obviously intrigued.

'Give him a little of your goddess magic. Not enough to change fate, just enough to lend him some extra strength, and then send him to Tulsa. Let modern medicine change fate. They do it all the time.'

'My magic and your modern world . . . You may be right.'

'Saint John's emergency room would be best. You know Tulsa – you could do it,' Kat said.

'It might work,' Venus said.

'Nothing will work unless you hurry,' Jacky said, lifting Patroklos's slack wrist.

'Do you love him?' Venus asked her suddenly.

Jacky met her eyes. 'Yes.'

'Then I simply must help you.' Venus smiled, kissed her palm and blew the kiss onto Patroklos, who shimmered briefly as if he'd been dipped in glitter. 'Now, go with him and be sure you are the first face he sees when he awakens.' The goddess clapped her

288

hands together and Patroklos and Jacky disappeared in a poof of glowing smoke.

Neither Kat nor the goddess saw Agamemnon, who at that moment backed out of the tent. They also hadn't noticed when the Greek king had slipped within the tent, silently prepared to pretend regret at the death that should have been Achilles. Kalchas had brought him the bitter news of the masquerade after Agamemnon had already entered the Myrmidon camp, coming as soon as he'd heard that 'Achilles' had fallen under Hector's hand. By that time too many warriors had seen him. Had he turned back then *he* might have been blamed for the charade that had caused Patroklos his life.

But his irritation and frustration had vanished with the little scene he'd witnessed between the goddess and the two women pretending to be Polyxena and her servant. So the gods were actively orchestrating the war. He'd known it all along! Hera herself had probably whispered into his ear to hurry to the Myrmidon camp. Yes, he was sure he'd heard the goddess's soft voice. And now he knew exactly what to do. Silently he left the tent and turned to face the Myrmidons who were keeping watch.

'Patroklos is gone,' he said solemnly, loving the irony in the truth he was only partially revealing. 'Where is Achilles? He must be told.'

Diomedes stepped forward. 'He has gone to the shore with Odysseus. We were to send word to him there.'

'Ah.' Agamemnon nodded. 'He was trying to hold off the berserker in case Patroklos needed him. Well, that is of no consequence now. Your lord should be told.' Diomedes glanced over the king's shoulder at the tent. 'The women will be preparing his body. It is a house of death now, and no place for warriors.'

'But who will tell Achilles?'

'I am his king. I will tell him.'

Diomedes hesitated. 'But, my lord, perhaps—'

'Perhaps,' Agamemnon cut in, 'you should gather your men at the edge of the battlefield. What do you believe Achilles will do when he learns of his cousin's death?'

'Sire.' This time it was Automedon who spoke. 'Should we not prepare for the funeral games of Patroklos? Will he not be honored for his bravery?'

Agamemnon widened his eyes in exaggerated surprise. 'Of course *I* would say he should be thus honored, but what do you believe Achilles will say? Or rather, what do you believe the *berserker* will say?'

The men muttered and Agamemnon smiled to himself.

'We will gather the men and prepare to return to battle,' Automedon said. Diomedes nodded in agreement.

'And I will give Achilles this grim news,' said Agamemnon.

Chapter Twenty-nine

'I really did think it was a good idea,' Venus said with a long-suffering sigh after Patroklos and Jacky had disappeared. 'I mean, how was I to know he'd run into Hector? Hector and Achilles have avoided each other for an entire war. It just doesn't make sense.'

'It does if you factor in divine interference,' Kat said.

'What? Me? I didn't do anything to Hector. I barely did anything to Patroklos except to maybe nudge along an idea he'd already been playing with and sprinkle a simple glamour over him.'

'I don't mean you. But we all know that there are several goddesses playing in this sandbox.'

'And gods,' Venus said, considering. 'Hera did have to keep Zeus busy. He was showing far too much interest in Troy, and she said he said he'd heard the Olympians were interfering in the war.'

'Ya think?'

Venus frowned at Kat. 'I am not talking about Hera, Athena and me. Well, at least not about Hera and me. Athena has lost her head a little, but it was bound to happen some time. By Apollo's hard shaft she's just so repressed! Nevertheless, what the three of us have done is really inconsequential. We shouldn't have attracted Zeus's attention.'

'I think you're underestimating the effect the three of you

have on mortals, but whatever. Here's the point – this war needs to end before anyone else dies.'

'Exactly our point, darling.'

'Fine. Let's get it done.' Kat glanced nervously at the tent door flap. 'First, what in the hell am I going to tell them about where Patroklos and Jacky went?'

'Don't tell the Myrmidons anything except that your maid-servant, a healer gifted by the gods, must be alone with him to pray and fast and heal him. They'll assume divine intervention, but they'll stay fairly quiet about it unless they see Patroklos, healed and healthy, walking about.'

'And I'll tell Achilles the truth.'

'If you must, although you know there are some things Love even keeps to herself.'

'He knows.'

'Pardon, darling?'

'I told Achilles the truth about us. Patroklos knows, too.'

'Oh, of course they do.'

'You don't seem surprised,' Kat said.

'Darling, you and your delightful friend are many things; unobtrusive is not one of them.'

'Okay, well. As long as you know. Now, how are we going to stop this war?'

'If you will remember, this is the point at which I brought the two of you – you in particular – into this mess,' Venus said. 'If we'd known a quicker way to stop the war, we would have done it ourselves, but short of starting a war in Olympus – *another* war in Olympus, which none of us are willing to do, we settled for you.'

'I keep coming back to the horse.'

'Darling, what horse?'

'The Trojan horse. The one written about in the stupid *Iliad*,' Kat said.

'You mean the enormous horse that carried the Greek army inside it within the walls of Troy? Like Achilles can be killed if you kick his ankle? That horse?'

'Okay, yes. Clearly there was fictional license taken by whatever his name was, but maybe there's a sprinkle of truth to it. I did see some of the war brides wearing pendants that looked like horse heads.'

'And some of them also wear pendants that look like erect phalluses, but that doesn't mean we're going to build a giant penis, fill it with warriors and roll it into Troy. If that would work I would have thought of it years ago. I am rather a penis specialist.'

Kat rubbed her head. She felt terrible – all hot and sandy and salty and bloody. And Venus was giving her a headache. And she needed to tell Achilles that everything was going to be okay with Patroklos. At least, she hoped everything was going to be okay with him. 'I have to go talk to Achilles,' she told Venus. 'Patroklos is really in Tulsa, right?'

'Absolutely.'

Then Kat's stomach flipped. 'Venus, you are going to bring them back, aren't you? Jacky and Patroklos? You can't just leave them over there, what with Jacky being in the wrong body and all.' *And in a different world than me*, her panicky mind voice added.

'Of course they will return. Both of them. If he lives. If he doesn't I'm not certain that Jacky would want . . .' The goddess paused, noticing Kat's wide-eyed look, and then shook her head. 'No, he simply must live. And, yes, I will bring them back. In the meantime I'll just do a little zapping here and there, quickly,

293

before word leaves this tent that they've, well, left. Actually . . .' Venus raised her hand. 'Darling, you should go now. I'm going to seal the tent.'

'But what if someone notices? Or tries to get in?'

Venus smiled. 'It's the ancient world, Katrina. If they can't open the tent they'll believe it's cursed – or blessed. It all depends upon point of view.' The goddess fluttered her fingers at Kat. 'Go on.'

'Okay, I'll take care of Achilles. You keep thinking about ways to end this war,' Kat said.

'Yes, yes, of course. Call if you need me,' Venus said.

'Count on it,' Kat muttered, and ducked out of the tent, feeling a weird slam and lock as the flap closed behind her.

She blinked, adjusting her eyes to the bright, midmorning sunlight. She couldn't believe it was barely noon. It seemed like years had past. Where the hell was everybody? Not one warrior was in sight. 'Achilles?' Kat called, walking around the side of the tent. 'Odysseus?'

No one. Not a warrior or a war-prize bride stirred. 'This is giving me a bad feeling,' she said to herself, as she hurried to Achilles' tent.

The first thing she noticed was Aetnia, sitting slumped over on the bench by the campfire. She looked up at Kat, cheeks washed with tears.

'Aetnia? Are you okay?'

'Oh, my lady! It is so terrible! He's going to kill Prince Hector – I know he will!'

'What, slow down. Who is going to kill Hector?'

'Achilles, of course! That terrible brute! Agamemnon is bringing him the news of Patroklos. The berserker will take over then, and our poor prince will be doomed.' The maidservant clasped

294

Kat's hands suddenly. 'Perhaps you can warn him, my lady! We'll go now. Agamemnon might not have reached Achilles yet. The day is young. Hector is probably still on the battlefield. You could be within the walls of Troy in no time.' She pulled at Kat's hands as if she would drag her into Troy.

'Stop it, Aetnia. I don't have time for this.' The girl let go of her hands, face filled with shock and confusion. 'Tell me where I can find Achilles.'

Aetnia's head began to shake back and forth slowly. 'What has happened to you, Princess? Has Melia truly bespelled you?'

'Aetnia, that spell stuff is utter bullshit. Why in the hell are you, and all the other women here, so willing to believe that when a woman acts against the norm she has to be under a spell, or wrong in the head, or something else bizarre? How about this – how about considering that maybe I've made my own mind up about Achilles and about this stupid war, and it might not be what the . . .' She paused, almost saying government, and then amended it with what would make more sense to Aetnia. 'It might not be what the rulers of this place want us to think.'

Aetnia's mouth opened and closed, reminding Kat of a carp.

'I've gotten to know Achilles and some of these other men. You've been with Diomedes for how long now? Two years? Maybe this war is wrong on both sides, and maybe it just needs to be over. Oh, and by the by, Achilles is not a monster,' she added for good measure. 'Now, where is he?'

Aetnia pointed to the sea behind Kat. 'He and Odysseus went to the shore. Agamemnon followed them there not long ago.'

'Thanks,' she said quickly and started off. Then called back over her shoulder, 'And you might want to consider thinking for yourself.'

* * *

Agamemnon had seen the berserker before, many times actually. Although it was usually from a distance as Achilles defeated the champion of this or that tribe and saved the Greek army a nasty battle. All of those times the king had never been frightened of the creature that possessed the warrior. Not so this time. What Agamemnon witnessed this time petrified him.

He'd caught up to Achilles and Odysseus at the seashore, where the scarred warrior paced back and forth at the edge of the waves, obviously attempting to control his roiling emotions. Odysseus had been speaking to his friend in a low, calming voice when he noticed Agamemnon approaching, and both men went silent and still as the Greek king joined them.

'Tell me,' Achilles said.

'He is gone. Patroklos is no longer of this world,' Agamemnon said with perfect honesty. 'I honor his memory by telling you myself.'

'Honor?' Achilles snarled. 'There is no honor is this world or justice or hope. My cousin died pretending to be me, that isn't *honorable*.'

'I disagree, Achilles,' Agamemnon said, carefully controlling his sense of glee as he watched the rigid control with which Achilles usually held himself crumble like the support column of an acropolis. 'His sense of Greek honor is what made him create the pretense. It was Fate who put Hector in his path.'

'Fate! I curse Fate and all of her minions in Olympus! This world has no honor or justice or hope, but it does have *vengeance*.' The word came out as a growl.

'Achilles, my friend. Let us go back to camp and plan your cousin's funeral games,' Odysseus said, stepping between the king and the warrior.

'Listen to Odysseus, Achilles. I will even agree that no Greek will go to battle for a full ten days of gaming to honor him,' Agamemnon said with exaggerated concern. 'Though we will have to wait until the fighting is over for the day. Many of the Myrmidons are still battling Hector. He has been fighting like a man possessed since he cut down Patroklos,' Agamemnon finished, loving the irony he evoked by using the word possessed.

Odysseus grabbed the king's arm. 'Enough, Agamemnon. You know the Myrmidons followed—'

Agamemnon wrenched his arm from Odysseus's grasp. 'You dare too much, Ithaca!' Then the king's eyes widened and he stumbled back several paces.

Odysseus whirled around, shouting, 'Achilles, no!'

It was too late. Achilles' eyes were already beginning to glow a rusty, bloody scarlet. 'Tell her the dream has ended. She should return to her home. Ask her to forgive me.' His voice was already beginning to deepen into the guttural snarl of something decidedly not human. Then he lifted his arms to the heavens and let loose a deafening roar as, with a rush, rage cascaded into his body.

Agamemnon continued to back away from what used to be Achilles. This possession was different. His body grew and twisted with obscenely exaggerated muscles. His scars, always grotesque, overtook the rest of his skin so that he appeared to be pieced together by wounds – defined by pain. His face retained only the bare structure of the man, but built on that structure was the visage of a beast, monstrous, inhumane, a creature who knew nothing but anger and pain and the lust for blood. Agamemnon realized what had happened and, even in his fear, had to repress a shout of victory. Until that moment Achilles had always battled the berserker. He'd fought to retain a vestige of humanity so that he could find his way back to himself.

This time Achilles had no intention of returning.

What Agamemnon was witnessing was the utter destruction of the man – the fragmenting of his soul. Though Achilles might still be somewhere within the twisted shell, he had given up and finally completely accepted his fate.

With another frightening roar, the thing that had been Achilles sprinted off toward the walls of Troy.

Agamemnon drew a long, relieved breath. Then he felt Odysseus's eyes on him. He gave the Ithacan king a bland look. 'I did him a favor. He's done fighting it now, and, doubtless, his name will be remembered for ages for what he's about to do.' *That piece of the puzzle*, Agamemnon added silently to himself, *was annoying, but unavoidable.*

'You bated him on purpose.'

'He chose glory long ago. I was simply giving him his wish.'

Odysseus's sharp gaze studied the aging king. 'You lied.'

Agamemnon lifted one golden clad shoulder. 'No. Patroklos is no longer in this world and the Myrmidons are on the battle-field, as, I'm quite sure, is Hector.'

Odysseus was shaking his head and looking at the Greek king with pure disgust when Kat stumbled over a dune and rushed up to them.

'Achilles!' She gasped, trying to catch her breath. 'Where is he?'

'Embracing Fate instead of you, *Princess*,' Agamemnon said with a sarcastic sneer.

'What have you done, you old shithead?' she said.

'Don't you dare speak to me in such a manner, woman!'

'Oh, fuck off!' Kat yelled, stepping forward into his face, which shocked him so badly that he actually took a step backward. She gave him a disdainful look and turned her back on him, speaking instead to Odysseus. 'What's happened?'

'Achilles knows Patroklos is dead. The berserker has utterly possessed him and he's gone to kill Hector,' Odysseus said.

Kat felt the world tilt. Over a bizarre humming in her ears she said, 'No . . . no, he's not dead.'

'He will be shortly. There is no stopping it. The monster has already defeated the man,' Odysseus said.

'Not Achilles, Patroklos,' Kat said, fighting not to sob in despair.

Odysseus rounded on Agamemnon. 'You said Patroklos was dead.'

'I said he'd left this world, and he has.'

Kat gasped, reading the truth in Agamemnon's smug eyes. 'You knew Patroklos wasn't dead. You saw them disappear.'

'What I saw was proof that you are not a princess of Troy.'

She curled her lip at Agamemnon. 'You're finally right about something. No, I'm not an ancient woman you can bully.'

'Really? You look soft and weak to me.' Agamemnon made a threatening move toward her, but Odysseus stepped swiftly between them.

'You won't touch her,' he said.

Agamemnon hesitated, and then chuckled mockingly. 'I suppose it's only right that you have her now that your friend is finished with her. But you should know that she's been lying to you, too. She's not Athena's oracle. She's in league with the Goddess of Love. I saw them together.'

'Perhaps you should return to your camp, great king.' Odysseus's voice was flint. 'Your battle is about to be won for you, and you should be there to seize the glory.'

Agamemnon narrowed his eyes at Odysseus. 'She's only a woman. Will you stand with her against your king?'

'God, you're such an asswipe!' Kat blurted before Odysseus could speak. 'You think I'm just this?' She pointed down at her body. 'This is just a shell – it's temporary. It's the spirit inside that lasts and really counts.'

'Oh, I believe you, *Princess*,' Agamemnon said, voice rich with sarcasm. 'Which makes what has happened to Achilles even more tragic. What was inside of him is gone. But don't despair. His name will certainly last forever.'

Kat felt rage build within her. Acting purely on instinct, she wrapped her hand around Venus's pendant and with the other pointed a condemning finger at him. 'Today is your lucky day. You were right twice. I am not an ancient princess, and I am in league with the Goddess of Love. So it's with Venus's power that I say love will betray you, like you betrayed my love. Love will be your death and your curse.'

Agamemnon shuddered, but recovered himself quickly. 'You can't curse me, witch creature. I have the protection of the Queen of Gods herself.'

Kat's laugh completely lacked humor. 'Really? Last time Hera and I chatted about you she said you were an arrogant fool.'

'You lie!'

'If I'm lying, then let the sea monsters Hera helped save me from come up here and grab me.' Kat took a couple resolute steps to the edge of the water. The waves washed over her shoes as she waited, looking seaward, and then when the placid water didn't so much as stir, she slowly turned her gaze back to Agamemnon. 'You're screwed.'

Agamemnon stared at her and what he saw in her eyes made his face drain of color. 'Stay away from me, witch!' he cried. The king began to hurry back down the beach toward the Greek camp, golden robes flapping behind him like he was an over-sized, gilded gull.

Kat stared after him and prayed with every fiber of her being that curses really did work in this world.

Chapter Thirty

'You have to take me to Achilles,' Kat said.

'That will only get you killed, or worse. You've gotten close to Achilles. The berserker could easily target you. If that happens killing you would be the best possible outcome.'

'Bullshit! Getting Achilles back would be the best possible outcome. Now take me to him.'

'The battlefield is this way.' Odysseus gestured up past the dunes that eventually gave way to a field of wheat, a grove of lovely olive trees, and various temples that used to be quite busy, and then, beyond the temples, the massive walls of Troy. As they hurried toward the great city, Kat thought she recognized Hera's temple where she and Jacky had first been zapped into this world.

'I'll lead you as close as I can, but you'll need to stay clear of the battlefield. It is no place for a woman,' Odysseus said.

'Odysseus, I'm not going to lie to you. I have no intention of staying clear of the battlefield. I'm going where Achilles is, and that's all there is to it.'

'You aren't Athena's oracle, are you?'

Odysseus pulled her attention from focusing on not stepping on her skirts as she practically jogged to keep up with his long stride. 'No,' she said. 'I'm not Athena's oracle.'

'Are you immortal?'

'I wish. Which means hell no. I'm just a woman.'

'Not even one of Athena's priestesses?'

Something in his voice made her look up at him, and she saw a terrible depth of sadness in his eyes and remembered how he had looked at Athena. Then she also remembered how stark his expression had been when he'd said the goddess had lied to him. What had Athena done to him? *He loves her*, Kat realized. 'Well, not exactly. I work for three goddesses. I guess you could say I'm closest to Venus.' She didn't mean to sound oh-so-divine, but it was damn difficult to explain. 'Look, there's a bunch of stuff going on here, and it can definitely be confusing.'

'The goddess didn't take me into her confidence. I thought she . . .' He looked away, clearly too hurt to continue.

Kat felt terrible for him. She didn't know much about Odysseus or about Athena, but she recognized heartache and betrayal. She also recognized a decent man when she saw one, and she definitely liked Odysseus.

'Venus is the goddess who cooked up the whole thing with Patroklos to impersonate Achilles. Athena didn't have anything to do with it. She probably didn't even know about it.'

'I hope that is true. I hope she hasn't been using me,' Odysseus said haltingly, and Kat could see what it was costing him to show such vulnerability. She'd seen it many times before in her office, and always when a man had found himself truly, deeply in love. Kat hoped Athena deserved him.

Kat decided to tell him as much of the truth as she knew. 'I've seen you and Athena together and I can tell you that there is a bond between you, one she doesn't appear to take lightly.'

Odysseus stared at her for a long while. 'It is a difficult thing to love a goddess. I have a wife, you know. She's been waiting almost ten years for me to return to our kingdom.'

'And do you love her?'

'Athena asked me that question recently. My answer was the same then as it is now. I honor Penelope as my wife and respect her as the mother of my son. But my love?' He shook his head. 'That hasn't been mine to give away since I was a youth.'

'What happened then?' Kat asked the question, but she was pretty sure she already knew his answer.

'I met Athena, and pledged my life and my love to her service.'

'You didn't realize the seriousness of your choice then?' Kat asked.

'Oh, I realized it – I embraced it. I've belonged to Athena since the first moment I saw her. I have never regretted my love for her, even when it seemed I was no more than a slight favorite among many. I didn't even mind being used as a pawn – I was her pawn, and that was enough. Until now. Today, for the first time, I find myself wishing I did not love the goddess.'

He sounded utterly destroyed, and even in the midst of the turmoil with Achilles and Jacky and Patroklos, Kat wanted to help him. 'You and Athena have become lovers.'

Odysseus nodded, giving a little self-mocking laugh. 'Yes, despite knowing that doing so is unwise, I have fallen gladly, joyously, into her arms. Remember this, Princess, or whoever you really are, when mortals love the gods there is a price to pay, and it's usually the mortal who pays it. Achilles is the product of such love, and I have watched his mortality, his humanity, suffer for as long as I have known him.'

'I'll remember, but it seems what you're saying is that Achilles has been a victim, too.'

'He isn't Achilles anymore. You'll soon see.'

There didn't seem to be anything left to say, and Kat concentrated on keeping up with Odysseus as she wondered just what the hell she thought she was going to do when she finally found Achilles. In the middle of battle. Totally berserked out. She could hear Jacky's voice calling her a damn fool.

And then she realized that it wasn't Jacky's voice that was crowding into her mind, but the voices of many men and horses, swords and pain. They struggled up the side of an olive-lined ridge, Odysseus taking her elbow to help her, and Kat stumbled to a shocked halt.

'Oh, holy shit!' she blurted.

The walls of Troy stretched before her, thick and tall and impossibly magnificent. They were made of butter-colored limestone, and the midday sunlight made them shine a soft, compelling yellow. She could see some of the city built up inside the walls, the centerpiece of which was a graceful, pillared palace that stretched all along the inside of the city walls to the left of the huge front gates. Beautiful arched windows led to ivy-hung and flowered balconies that afforded excellent views of what should be the placid and prosperous comings and goings of merchants, farmers and the people of Troy. Now the empty balconies looked out onto chaos.

'So many men,' Kat said, staring at the melee of warriors who shouted and screamed, fought and died in front of the city walls. *How will I ever find him?* But before she could voice the question, a terrible roar sounded from the center of the battlefield, so powerful that it had no trouble carrying over the two armies. 'Achilles,' she said softly.

'Not Achilles,' Odysseus said. 'You're not dealing with the man. You're dealing with the monster.'

'The man is still inside the monster,' she said stubbornly.

'Perhaps, but I saw no evidence of that when he gave himself over to it.' Odysseus paused, and rested his hand gently on her shoulder. Kat looked up at him questioningly. 'As the berserker was possessing him he asked me to give you a message. Achilles said that the dream was over, and that you should go home. It was his final wish, along with asking that you forgive him. Reconsider, Princess. Imagine what it would do to him if he knew that he had again destroyed the woman he loved.'

Kat's throat burned with unshed tears. She remembered all too well the story Achilles had told her about the berserker raping and killing his young fiancée, who had also been Odysseus's cousin.

'I know you're making sense,' she said. 'And I know it must seem to you like I'm behaving recklessly and being ridiculously stubborn, but here's the truth, Odysseus. I'm not from your time. I'm not even from your world. I'm a different kind of woman than what you know here, and I have the power of generations of independent thinkers and educated mothers and sisters, daughters and girlfriends, all within me. I believe in myself, and what the power of one woman can bring about. That gives me a different kind of strength, a strength that Venus and Hera and Athena knew would be needed here. I can change what's happening. All I have to do is trust myself and believe that Achilles will trust me, too.'

Odysseus had listened to her carefully, studying her intently while she spoke. 'You make me hope you are right, Princess,' he finally said.

'Katrina, that's my real name. My friends call me Kat.'

He smiled. 'Well, Kat, shall I lead you into chaos?'

She bobbed a little curtsey. 'There are few men I'd rather go there with, kind sir.'

The battlefield was like nothing Kat could have ever imagined. The smells alone were horrendous, the sights and sounds utterly frightening. As soon as they'd reached the outskirts of the fighting, Odysseus sent a Greek runner to gather as many of the Myrmidons as he could find. Kat waited impatiently behind the battle lines, wishing for modern communications and transportation, and all the while the roar of the berserker sounded over and over again, filling the air with a bestial violence that made the men fighting and dying mere yards from her seem tame.

The Myrmidons responded to Odysseus's call much more quickly than Kat would have anticipated, and soon she was looking at the surprised, blood-spattered faces of familiar men who nodded to her in respectful greeting.

'We're taking her to Achilles,' Odysseus announced.

The Myrmidons' faces were utterly confused.

'But he is Achilles no more,' Automedon said.

As if to punctuate the warrior's words, another roar shook the battlefield and Achilles' own men shuddered.

'I know about the berserker, but I think I can reach Achilles,' Kat said, looking from man to man. 'Patroklos is not dead. All I have to do is get to a small part of Achilles and make him understand that.'

'Patroklos lives!' Automedon said, as the men nearest them took up the cry and let it ripple through the group. Then the smiling warrior turned back to her. 'Bring Patroklos to the battlefield, Princess. Even overtaken by the berserker, Achilles must recognize his cousin. When he sees that he is alive, all will be well again.'

'Yes!' said another warrior whose name Kat couldn't remember. 'We may even get to Achilles before he has killed Hector and called the prophesy to him.'

Everyone was looking expectantly at Kat, even Odysseus. Kat wished like hell she could produce a living, walking, talking

Patroklos, but of course that was impossible. Even if the warrior was actually alive, he was probably in surgery. Pulling him out of the modern world would kill him as surely as Hector's sword.

'Patroklos can't be brought out here on the battlefield. It would kill him. He's alive, but he's badly hurt. No, I'm all you have. You have to take me to Achilles.'

'Achilles will not see you, my lady,' Automedon said sadly. 'It will only be the berserker, and we cannot save you from him if the creature decides to destroy you.'

'I know that. You won't have to save me. I'll save myself.'

Every single man looked at her as if she had just said she was going to sprout a red cape and fly faster than a speeding bullet.

'Just take me to him,' she said with a sigh. 'I'll take care of the rest of it. No, I won't hold you responsible for my deadness if things don't work out. And once you get me to him, all you guys back off. I don't want any of you getting hurt.'

She saw the incredulous looks and heard a muttered, *'She doesn't want us getting hurt?'* which she ignored. They were definitely not helping her confidence level.

'All right. Let's get her to Achilles,' Odysseus said.

The men snapped to like the experienced, disciplined warriors they were. They created a phalanx, putting her safely in the middle of them. Then they began to move onto the battlefield, fighting slowly, as one man, moving inexorably forward, drawing ever nearer the animalistic cries that came from the creature who used to be Achilles.

Afterward Kat couldn't decide if the nightmare trip across the battlefield had taken a very short or a very long time. It had seemed she had entered a place where time had no meaning, a *Twilight Zone* landscape of death and blood and violence that her eyes took in, but her soul refused, at least temporarily, to see.

Later the memories came to her, mostly in black-and-white snapshots of horror, but at that moment she had marveled what the human mind could deny to survive.

Then the pace of the group changed, picked up, before coming to a stop. Odysseus was beside her, breathing hard. 'There is only one more layer of men between us and the berserker. We should push easily through.'

'Okay, good. Just get me close to him.'

'You may not have long before he's upon you,' Odysseus said.

'Let me worry about that.'

Odysseus nodded and called the men surrounding them to order. 'Push through the line then open the column for the princess!'

Kat was sick and scared. As she moved forward again with the men she thought she might puke and was gritting her teeth together against it when the dark shields in front of her parted to let in daylight and madness.

He was standing in a clearing of dead men. Blood had turned the dirt to rusty clay. His back was to her, giving Kat a bizarrely peaceful moment in which to study him. Odysseus and the other men had been right – this creature was not Achilles. His body had grown to such huge, misshapen proportions that the tunic she had last seen him wearing had split, leaving him naked except for a short linen wrap knotted around his waist. She must have made an involuntary noise because he suddenly whirled to face her. Kat felt the men tense. She glanced at Odysseus and told him 'Go!' before walking away from their protection.

The creature growled. Kat took a few more steps, distancing herself from the other men, then she stopped and met his burning red gaze. Blood and gore covered his scarred body. It ran in dirty rivulets from his matted hair. His face was not his own.

Like his body, it was misshapen, as if there was something under his skin trying to stretch its way free.

'Achilles, it's me, Katrina.' She made sure her voice was steady and calm, as if he were a client who had just told her that he was thinking about suicide. And wasn't that just what Achilles was doing? He believed he'd caused his cousin's death, so now he was planning on paying for that with his own. 'Achilles,' she repeated his name. 'Patroklos is not dead.'

Achilles curled his lip, baring his teeth. He began to move toward her, slowly but with a deadly, almost seductive grace. She thought he reminded her of a huge poisonous snake. Kat wanted to turn and run for all she was worth back into the sea of warriors behind her. Instead she drew a deep breath, sent a silent, pleading prayer asking Venus for help, and held her ground.

'Achilles,' she said sternly. 'You have to listen to me. Patroklos is not dead. He's alive and he's going to be fine.'

As he circled her he made a noise that sent chills skittering across her skin – she realized the creature was laughing.

'Achilles,' she said again, turning her body so that she could continue to meet his gaze. 'I know you're there somewhere. I know you can hear me. Patroklos is not dead.'

'I will taste you.' His voice was so awful, so utterly *not* human, *not* Achilles that she had to clench her hands into fists so that their trembling wouldn't be obvious.

'No, I don't think you will.' Kat kept her voice as well as all of her mannerisms carefully neutral, as placid as possible. 'Achilles loves me, and he won't let you hurt me.'

His laughter was terrible, mocking and monstrous. 'Foolish woman, I am not Achilles.' Almost within touching distance he stopped circling her. She could smell him – blood and sweat and something feral and male.

'Well, that's obvious.' She lifted her chin, pretending with every skill she'd learned in her clinical experience to be calm and unaffected by him. 'Achilles—' she began, but he cut her off.

'No! Achilles is no more!'

As he lunged toward her, Kat stumbled back, her composure crumbling. 'Achilles!' she cried. 'You have to come back to me!'

She saw recognition flicker through his eyes, cooling the scarlet and causing the monster to pause awkwardly. 'Yes! Achilles!' Kat smiled, dizzy with relief, but before she could say more or move toward him, her arm was being yanked roughly back and up, and she was pulled out of the clearing and off her feet.

'Ah, gods, we thought you were dead!' said the handsome, kind-eyed man who had lifted her onto the back of a quivering black stallion and into his arms. 'Polyxena! Sister!'

Kat looked into Hector's eyes as the berserker roared his challenge and charged.

Chapter Thirty-one

Keeping one arm around her, Hector kneed the stallion so that it sprang to the side, narrowly avoiding Achilles' charge. With a fluid motion, the big horse spun while Hector grabbed a spear from the saddle quiver and hurled it at Achilles. Kat screamed, but with the berserker's inhuman reflexes Achilles knocked the spear aside as if it had only been a toothpick.

'Hector! No!' Thinking frantically she pulled on the stranger's arm. 'Leave him. Let's get back inside the city walls.'

Hector glanced down at her, trying to maneuver the stallion to avoid Achilles' next rush.

'You cannot have her!' the creature snarled.

'By the gods! It is you he's after.' His arm squeezed her protectively.

'Get me out of here Hector!' Kat yelled above the noise of battle.

'Trojans! To me! Protect your Princess!'

For a second Kat thought it would work and they would leave Achilles to roar impotently at the walls of Troy, giving her time to figure out what the hell to do next. Hector had begun backing the stallion from the clearing and a line of Trojan warriors was rushing to meet them. Then the creature that had been her lover gave a terrifying cry and hurled himself at Hector's stallion. As Achilles flew past them his bloody sword tore down the horse's flank. The stallion screamed, stumbled and lost his rear footing on the slick, bloody clay. Kat automatically threw herself forward, clutching the stallion's wide neck. She felt Hector's grip on her release at the same instant Achilles snagged his shoulder, ripping him from the saddle.

Then everything happened with blinding swiftness.

Hector regained his footing. He ran to the stallion, pulling his sword and shield free. His eyes met Kat's. She saw his love for Polyxena there, and knew that he would do anything to keep his sister safe.

'Get inside the walls. I'll hold him off for as long as I can.' Hector raised his hand and brought it down on the horse's rump, sending him galloping across Trojan lines.

Achilles followed the horse, roaring with fury. Hector ran, jumped and put himself directly in the berserker's path, cutting him off from Katrina. The Trojan warriors encircled Kat and the wounded stallion, but she had an excellent view of the battlefield as they fought off the Myrmidons, now rallied by Odysseus, and began moving her toward the city gates. Her eyes were locked on Achilles and Hector, and she watched everything as if in slow motion. Hector fought bravely, but he wasn't battling a human. The creature was utterly uncontrollable, but Hector stood his ground, until Achilles sliced through the muscles of his thighs, and even then the brave man fought from his knees, keeping the monster engaged as the massive gates groaned open enough for Kat, the stallion and Hector's guard to slip within. As they closed Kat heard a wail of despair begin from atop the Trojan walls and she knew that Hector, Prince of Troy, was dead.

The soldiers took her directly to the king. Priam's arms enfolded Kat, and she wept with him while he held her.

'A miracle from the gods . . . a miracle from the gods . . .' he kept repeating over and over. Finally he steadied himself and called for wine for both of them. Only then did Kat get a good look at him, and her heart squeezed. He was an older, shorter version of Hector – a handsome man with kind brown eyes and thick silver and black hair. With a little jolt Kat realized that his eyes weren't familiar just because Hector had had them. They were familiar because since she'd been transported to the ancient world and plunked into this body, those same expressive brown eyes had been looking out from her face, too.

Priam collapsed into a high-backed wooden chair exquisitely carved with plunging stallions. His hands shook as he drank deeply of the offered wine. Feeling lightheaded, Kat sipped her own wine, and then handed the goblet back to a servant who had been crying silently but openly. She heard a choked noise, and more arms were suddenly around her. An older, elegant woman who was too thin and a delicate, beautiful twenty something cried while they embraced her. Overwhelmed, Kat could only stand there and wish this had all been different – that she'd managed to make things right.

'It is true. Hector is dead. Achilles has killed him.'

Kat looked up with the women who had been holding her to see who had spoken. A slender man stood in the arched door to the spacious chamber. He was probably not much older than Polyxena, and he, too, had kind, expressive eyes. A blonde woman stood behind him in the shadow of the doorway, her beauty undiminished by the tears that washed her cheeks. She stared with adoration at the young man who had just spoken. Kat thought she'd never seen anyone so gorgeous – she easily rivaled even Venus's beauty. *Paris and Helen – it has to be.*

Then his awful words registered on the group and the woman who must be Priam's wife, the mother of Hector and Paris and

Polyxena, threw herself onto the floor at the king's feet while she tore her hair and wailed. The other woman who had been embracing her didn't make a sound, but crumpled to the floor, unconscious.

'Get Astyanax. Holding Hector's son will help her survive this,' ordered the young man as he came into the room.

'Yes, Lord Paris.' A crying servant hurried to do his bidding.

Paris rushed to the fallen woman, whose eyelids were beginning to flutter weakly. He lifted her and carried her to a chaise not far from Priam's throne. Then Kat was in the young man's arms. She hugged him hard and she could feel the tremors that went through his body. 'You are alive . . . You are alive,' he whispered over and over, his warm breath mixing with the tears that dampened her hair.

Kat couldn't do any more than nod. Her mind was in tumult. Her heart felt as if it was shattering over and over.

There was a sobbing gasp from behind them, and Paris released his sister reluctantly, moving back to the chaise. 'Andromache, I've sent for your son,' Paris spoke softly to the reviving woman. 'Astyanax is being brought to you.' He touched her cheek and then he drew himself up and slowly, almost painfully, he turned to his father.

The king was stroking his wife's hair. Her face was buried in his knees and her wails had become broken sobs. Priam's face was absolutely expressionless.

'Father,' Paris said brokenly, wiping the back of his sleeve across his face. 'He's dead, Father.'

The old monarch's eyes rested briefly on his youngest son. His blank expression did not change, but he focused his gaze over Paris's shoulder as if he was looking into the past.

'You should take your sister to her chamber. I cannot see you when I am mourning my son.' Priam's voice wasn't cruel, but it, like his face, was devoid of expression, which made it all the more terrible.

Paris seemed to crumple in on himself. 'Father, I am your son, too.'

'Yes, that is something the gods will never let me forget,' Priam said. 'Go now. Return to my presence only when I call for you.' He paused, and then added, 'Take your woman with you.'

'Come, sister.' Paris held out his hand for hers and, not knowing what else to do, Kat took it and let him lead her from Priam's throne room. As they passed Helen, she fell into step on Paris's other side. Kat saw that she kept her head bowed, as if she was trying to obscure her face with her shining hair.

They walked silently through a marble-floored hallway, past several lovely, airy rooms. It was as if despair walked with them. All around them sounds of women crying echoed in the magnificent palace. Finally they came to a silver-inlayed door and Paris stopped.

'I will send maidservants to see to you,' Paris said. His cheeks were still wet and his voice was rough with emotion. 'I'm so glad they didn't kill you, little Xena.'

And as it had been for the brief time she'd been with Hector, she could tell that Paris had loved Polyxena, too. Impulsively she hugged him. 'Thank you,' Kat whispered.

Paris clung to her. 'It's my fault,' he said brokenly. 'I caused his death. I caused all of their deaths.'

Kat pitied him. He was really not much more than a teenager – he must only have been thirteen or fourteen when he'd taken Helen from the Greeks. These two kids had started a war that had gone on for almost a decade? It hadn't taken meeting Agamemnon and his cronies for Kat to know what utter bullshit that was. She shook her head at the sad young man. 'No, Paris, it's gone way beyond being your fault.'

'Come, love. Polyxena needs to bathe and rest. Come with me, sweetest one,' Helen coaxed in a voice like poured honey.

Still sobbing, Paris nodded and stumbled away mostly supported by Helen's arm around his waist.

Kat entered the chamber untouched by its splendor and stood numbly while she waited for the maidservants to come to her. They were there in minutes, grim-faced women who treated her reverently, but who kept breaking into sobs. Kat let them bathe, anoint and dress her in a simple silk robe. They left her wine and food and then, amid whispers and sobs, seemed to melt away.

Feeling detached and unfocused, Kat walked across the room to a huge, arched open window. Gauzy gold curtains picked up what was obviously the light from a fading sun, and shimmered evening colors of rust and orange and yellow. Sounds of fighting men drifted with the warm breeze and Kat stepped out onto a balcony that perched above the front walls of Troy, commanding an amazing view of the battlefield. She didn't let her eyes look at it, though, just like she didn't let her ears acknowledge that the one voice she could hear above all the other cries and clashing of two armies was the one that had possessed her Achilles. Instead she gazed beyond everything to the distant, watery horizon and the sun that was dying into the sea. She stared at it until the tears that blurred her vision filled her eyes, spilled over and ran down her cheeks.

Then through grief and noise and confusion Kat heard another sound. Her mind picked it up as it washed over her like clear, cool water over smooth river stones. Something about it reached her, soothed her and brought her subconscious the answer before her thinking mind understood it.

There was a clanking followed by many *click-click-clicks*, and then a familiar groan she'd heard only once before, when she'd ridden Hector's wounded stallion through the opening gates of Troy.

Kat stepped out to the edge of the balcony. Following the clicking noise, she looked down and to her immediate left. Built inside the thick walls was an indention, a niche large enough for a man to stand comfortably within, a single arrow-slitted window gave an abbreviated view of the battlefield. Beside the man was an enormous chain, the links of which were half the size of his body. Kat watched the links slither down in a hole at the man's feet like a waterfall of iron. There was a system of large iron levers in front of the man. His hands were on the levers, which were all pushed in a downward direction.

'Close the gates!' On the platform outside the niche a warrior suddenly called an abrupt command and lowered a scarlet flag he had been holding over his head. The man in the niche immediately tripped all of the levers, pushing each of them up. The chain stopped its slithering motion.

Leaning farther out over her balcony Kat peered down at the front gates of Troy as more than two dozen warriors rushed to close the gates while archers held off the bedraggled looking Greek army. The gates had been opened far enough for all of the Trojan warriors to retreat within the city, so it took a considerable amount of time to get them closed, but finally, with another eerie groan, the city was sealed.

Kat's gaze went back to the man in the niche. He and the soldier holding the flag saluted each other and then relaxed into a stance that resembled parade rest.

So it took a couple dozen men or so to close the gates of the city, but only one to pull down some levers and open them?

Kat's body flushed hot and then utterly cold. Everything fell suddenly into place. She and Jacky had missed the entire point – in the myth it wasn't about fitting the whole Greek army into a ridiculous, hollow horse, out of which they emerged and kicked Trojan ass. It was about getting inside the impenetrable, god-fashioned walls of Troy and opening the gates.

Kat stared at the levers and at the two men who guarded them. No way would they allow anyone to get close enough to them to trip the chain and open the gates. But a princess of Troy was not just anyone.

'I am the Trojan horse,' she whispered, and the words sent a terrible shiver through her body.

Chapter Thirty-two

Kat lifted her hand to grasp the heart-shaped pendant that still hung from around her neck, but a movement just outside the city walls caught at the edge of her vision. Gold and scarlet flashed, drawing her eyes. The Greek army had already pulled back and was disappearing into the olive grove. Only one warrior remained.

'Achilles! Oh, god, no.' Horrified, Kat shook her head back and forth, back and forth. He was driving a chariot, lashing the horses into a frenzy as he drove past the city gates again and again, dragging the bloody, brutalized body of Hector behind him.

That terrible scene decided her. Kat was going to do whatever it took to end this. Resolutely she went back into her chamber, opened the locket and called to Venus.

'Venus, come to me.'

This time the glittering of the goddess's divine cloud was markedly subdued as she materialized.

'I know,' Venus said. 'Hector is dead. I heard Andromache's cries of grief. They were very much in love.'

'Do you know about this?' Kat gestured to the balcony. The goddess walked close enough to gaze out. Kat saw the jolt of shock that went through her body as she realized what she was witnessing.

'Achilles is desecrating Hector's body.'

'It's not Achilles.'

'It's unthinkable.'

'It's *not* Achilles!' Kat drew a deep, steadying breath. 'I need you to get Hera and Athena here. Oh, and Thetis, too. I know how to end this, but you'll all have to play a part.'

'I don't know if it's possible for Hera to come. She's keeping Zeus busy.' Venus's gaze briefly went back to the balcony before she continued. 'And she needs to keep him busy. If he knew what was going on out there you would never have a chance at saving your Achilles.'

'But it's Zeus's fault that the berserker is here at all! He cursed Achilles with him,' Kat said angrily.

'Darling,' Venus said gently, 'it was Achilles' choice – Achilles' responsibility. That's why this is so terrible for him. He picked this fate.'

'I'm changing it. Love is changing it.'

'Me?'

'Us. And by changing Achilles' fate I'm ending the war.'

'You figured out a way,' Venus said.

'I'm the Trojan horse,' Kat said.

'Darling?'

'Just trust me.'

'Implicitly. What do you need?'

'I'm assuming that Thetis, being a sea goddess, can conjure up some fog?'

'Naturally, darling.'

'Good. In the hour before dawn have Thetis make fog roll in from the sea. I need a lot of it – enough to hide the Myrmidons. Tell Athena to have Odysseus lead Achilles' men to the city gates. And I mean right up to them. I'll have them open.'

'You?'

'Trojan horse, remember?'

Venus nodded slowly. 'You truly are.'

'I am.' *Or maybe a better analogy is that I'm Judas*, Kat thought, then shook herself mentally. That line of reasoning wouldn't help her or Achilles. 'Be sure Athena tells Odysseus to have the Greek army waiting just out of sight – the entire Greek army. This is their only chance.'

'Done. And what do we do about Achilles?'

'Nothing. He's my diversion.' Kat retreated into her clinical persona – calm, dispassionate, free of clogging emotions like despair and guilt and fear. 'If anyone looks from Troy, they'll be looking at him. The fog should do the rest. This is going to get the Greeks inside the walls of Troy – they should be able to end the war then, right?'

'One would think so,' Venus said. 'And what will you be doing?'

'I'm going to be getting Achilles back.'

Venus hesitated before speaking. 'I should probably warn you against trying to reach him. It didn't work today. It probably won't work tomorrow.'

'But . . .' Kat prompted.

'But I believe in the power of love,' she said simply.

'I'm finding that I have a newfound appreciation for the power of love myself,' Kat said.

Venus smiled. 'I knew I'd made the right choice in you.'

'Let's hope so. Okay, I need one more thing: a sleeping potion that works quickly. A really strong one.'

Without any hesitation Venus held out her hand, wiggling her fingers. Almost immediately a tiny crystal bottle filled with a clear liquid appeared in a glittering of dust.

'Careful with this. It's a little something the gods use when they need oblivion. It's made by nymphs from the Island of the

322

Lotus Eaters. If it so much as touches mortal skin you will feel its effects.'

Kat took it gingerly, setting it down on the polished surface of a vanity desk. 'Thanks, that's perfect.'

The wind suddenly increased, causing the gauzy curtains that framed the balcony to billow diaphanously into the chamber, bringing with it the berserker's insane roars. Venus stepped closer to Kat and cupped her face with a smooth palm.

'Katrina, I leave you with Love's blessing.' Venus kissed Kat's forehead softly, and Kat felt a delicious surge of warmth and tenderness rush into her body.

As the goddess raised her hand, Kat suddenly remembered to ask, 'Venus, is Patroklos still alive?'

The goddess smiled. 'Alive and recovering from surgery with Jacqueline nursemaiding him.'

'Don't bring them back unless I get this mess worked out,' Kat said, although it hurt her heart to think about Jacky being a world away from her.

Venus nodded solemnly.

'If – if something happens and I don't make it out of this, will you promise to take care of Jacky?'

'I will,' Venus said. Then she lifted a slim brow. 'Anything else, my delightfully demanding mortal?'

Kat chewed the side of her cheek and then decided, what the hell, she might as well go for it. 'Yes. If I die – this time for good – would you let me go wherever it is that Achilles' soul goes? He's going to be lonely without me.'

'You have my oath on it, Katrina. Should you die tomorrow I will personally escort your soul to the beauty of the Elysian Fields,' Venus assured her.

'Okay, well, that makes me feel better.'

'You won't die tomorrow, Kat, darling.'

'Do you know that for sure?' Kat asked hopefully. 'Like did a goddess oracle thing show you my future?'

'Let's just call it Love's intuition. I see a happily ever after coming on.' Venus raised her arm again, flicked her wrist and disappeared in a puff of glittery smoke.

Kat sighed. 'Great, and now I know the origin of the saying: Love is blind.'

Odysseus felt utterly hopeless. He'd failed the princess who called herself Katrina, the Myrmidons, his own men and Achilles. Disquiet ran deeply through the army. No one, not a single man, approved of what Achilles was doing to Hector's body. The desecration of any dead angered the gods – the desecration of an honorable warrior, a prince of royal blood, would doubtless cause retribution to rain upon them from Mount Olympus.

All of that was bad, but Odysseus had angered the gods before and never felt as he did that night. He knew why. It was Athena's betrayal that had sliced him to the bone. It didn't matter what Katrina had said. He recognized her words for what they were – a kind attempt to reassure him. He knew better. Of course Athena had known about Patroklos's masquerade. She was Goddess of War. How could she not have known?

Odysseus sat heavily on the simple chair in his sparsely furnished tent. He stared into the goblet of wine he'd poured himself, wishing he could divine answers from the blood-colored liquid.

The air in the tent changed, got warmer, sweeter, right before she materialized. It didn't matter that Odysseus braced himself before he gazed at her. His reaction was still the same as it had been since he'd had his first glimpse of her when he was a young boy. Longing for her heated and sweetened his blood, just as it had the air around him.

'My Odysseus,' Athena said.

She came to him and offered her hand. Odysseus took it in both of his. Dropping to one knee before his goddess, he closed his eyes, pressed his lips to her skin and inhaled her scent.

'My Goddess,' he said. Then he opened his eyes, let loose her hand and stood. 'I'm honored by your visit.' His voice sounded as empty as his heart felt.

Odysseus had forgotten that his goddess knew him very, very well. Her gray eyes narrowed as she studied him.

'You haven't washed or changed your clothes from today's battle. You look terrible. What has happened?'

Odysseus refilled his goblet, using his actions as an excuse not to meet her gaze. 'I think you know what happened today, Great Goddess. Achilles believes Patroklos to be dead. He has given himself over completely to the berserker. The princess, who told me today her real name is Katrina, tried to reach Achilles and she was *rescued*' – he pronounced the word sarcastically – 'by Hector and his Trojans, and then Achilles cut down Hector. He is currently desecrating the prince's body.'

Athena had gone very still. 'You're angry at me.'

He did meet her gaze then. 'I thought you loved me.'

Odysseus saw the jolt of surprise his words caused the goddess to feel as she snapped an immediate response. 'I do love you!'

'If you loved me you would not have lied to me.'

Athena didn't speak, but Odysseus saw the truth in her eyes. He'd been right. She'd known.

'Were all the goddesses in on the joke you played on Achilles, or was it just Venus and you?'

'It wasn't a joke,' Athena said, gray eyes flashing in anger. 'It should have worked – it should have ended the war.'

'It might have worked if you had told me! Had I known I could have protected him!' Odysseus shouted, all his pent-up emotions finally exploding. 'Am I worth so little to you that you do not trust me at all?'

'So little!' Athena began, then when her words caused the ground beneath them to shake and the sides of the tent to quiver dangerously, she drew a deep, calming breath and began again. 'You are the only mortal man I have ever loved. Every day I live in fear of your mortality because I know that I must eventually surrender to Fate and lose you.'

'But am I truly a man to you – with a heart and soul and mind worthy of respect – or am I simply your favorite plaything?' he asked bitterly.

Her fair face flushed. 'How can you say such a thing after what we have known together?'

'I say it because all mortals know the capriciousness of the gods.'

'Not me. I do not take human lovers on whim. I do not take any lover on whim. I thought you knew that – I thought you knew me better than that.'

'I thought I did, too.' He sounded defeated, and his wide shoulders slumped. 'But you did not trust me with your confidence.'

And then Athena, Goddess of War and Wisdom, shocked him utterly. She met his gaze and said, 'I was wrong. Forgive me. I should not have lied to you.'

'Athena, I—' He paused, struggling with joy so overwhelming that it clogged his throat and choked his words.

The gray-eyed goddess came to him and lay her head on his shoulder. 'My Odysseus,' she murmured.

Odysseus held his goddess and forgave her. And then, while she lay beside him, Athena told Odysseus everything about Katrina, Achilles, Venus and Hera, and for the first time the Goddess of War discussed battle plans *with* a mortal, rather than commanding a mortal to obey her whim.

And Odysseus's heart soared.

Kat was so nervous her legs were wobbly. When the black of night had just begun to be relieved by a hint of gray, she poured the sleeping potion into a clay pottery jug half full of red wine, grabbed two goblets from a bedside dresser and left her room.

It was a mourning palace – a palace of muffled tears and melancholy silence. The halls were deserted, lit only dimly by an occasional wall sconce. Unimpeded, Kat wandered, doing her best to keep heading in what she thought was the right direction. Her sense of direction had always been pretty good, but she was starting to believe she'd never find the way to the niche in the wall when she turned a corner and saw a simply dressed middle-aged woman coming out of a side room.

'My lady, are you well? Is there something I can get for you?' the servant asked, bobbing a quick curtsey and looking worried.

'I'm lost,' Kat blurted. She'd rehearsed in her head how she would react to the many different circumstances she could get herself into that night, and she'd opted to stick as close to the truth as possible, deciding it would cut down on mistakes, if not babbling. 'I know it's silly, but I've gotten confused. It – it must be because I haven't had enough sleep since . . .' Kat let her voice fade, finding it easy to look upset and scared and completely disoriented.

'Oh, my lady! Of course you're not yourself. Let me take you back to your chamber.'

'Could you lead me to the warriors who are watching over the gates instead?'

'The gate warriors? I don't understand, Princess.'

'I heard that the two men guarding the, uh, levers that open the gates' – Kat mentally crossed her fingers, hoping that she wasn't saying anything too wrong – 'were key to my rescue.' The servant's face was still an utter question mark, so Kat did the only thing she could think to do. She burst into tears. 'I have to thank them! Hector would want me to. It's just all so terrible.' Kat sobbed.

'Oh, Princess! Please don't cry. You're home now, my lady. All will be well.' The servant reached out hesitantly, as if she wanted to take Kat into her arms, but wasn't sure she dared.

'Will you lead me to the gate warriors, please?'

'Of course, Princess. You're tired and overwrought, and you've simply gotten yourself turned around. You'll see – the gate room isn't far from here. You were almost there.'

Keeping up a steady stream of soothing chatter, the servant led Kat around a turn in the hall, down a fork to the right and then stopped before a narrow archway. A door was open to a stone catwalk on which was built the wooden platform and the niche carved into the Trojan wall. Just as she had seen from her balcony, one warrior was positioned on guard on the platform, and another stood between the chain and the levers.

Kat sniffled and smiled. 'Thank you.'

'Shall I wait for you, my lady, and be certain you find your way back to your chamber?'

'No. Thank you, but no. You were right. I'd just gotten confused and upset. I know where I am now.'

'Very good, my lady.' The woman curtseyed, gave her one more worried look, and then retraced the path they had just taken, disappearing around the bend in the hallway.

Kat wiped her eyes with her sleeve, put on her best damsel-in-distress face, and went out onto the catwalk.

Both warriors snapped to attention. Neither of them spoke. Kat cleared her throat, pitching her voice to sound as young as possible.

'Hello. I came to thank the two of you.'

She saw twin flickers of confusion in the men's eyes.

'For saving me from—' She broke off and began to sob.

The men's confusion turned to panic.

'Princess Polyxena, there is no need. We did not—'

'Oh, but you did! You saved me! I could still be there, with the Greeks, in that horrible camp where they . . .' Kat dissolved into unintelligible blubbering.

Both men looked helpless and rather pale.

'Princess,' said the warrior who had been standing in the niche, but who had now joined the other warrior on the platform. 'You are safe now. Our sacred walls will always protect you from the Greeks – you have our oaths on that.'

Feeling like the biggest ass in the known universe, Kat smiled innocent adoration at them through her tears. 'Thank you, darlings,' she said, sounding weirdly like Venus. Then, for the coup de grace, she finished with, 'I brought you wine from my own chamber.' Kat handed them each a goblet and quickly poured a generous splash of wine for both. 'To Trojan warriors!' She shouted tearfully, raising her fist in the air.

The men glanced at each other. Kat could almost see their emotional shrugs. Then they repeated, 'To Trojan warriors!' and upended the goblets.

'I feel so much better now,' Kat babbled. 'Here, have some more.' She'd just begun to lift the jug to the first man's goblet when a look of shock widened his eyes. Kat glanced at the other man. His brow was furrowed, as if he had a question he'd like to ask, but had forgotten what it was. Then both men swayed, and with surprisingly little sound, fell backward as if a giant hand had smacked them. Kat bent over them only long enough to see that they were snoring peacefully, then she retrieved one of their swords from where it had clattered on the platform between them. As she gripped the hilt Kat was surprised at how heavy it was, and was glad of the weight in her hand. Maybe it would help keep her trembling under control. She approached the levers and peered out of the long, narrow window onto the battlefield.

The night had gone from coal to slate, and with the gloaming had come Thetis's fog. It drifted across the battlefield like waves of mist, lapping against the olive grove, then, unhindered, poured out into the blood-crusted emptiness that surrounded the walls of Troy. It was dreamlike in its otherworldly beauty, but for whom the dream would morph into a nightmare was yet to be seen.

Kat saw shapes moving within the fog, darkness against darkness – spectral forms that could be mist, men or madness, and before it all was the creature who had been Achilles, and was now the ultimate expression of nightmare.

He hadn't left the battlefield. He'd driven the horses all night, around and around the walls of Troy dragging the prince's body, halting only when they fell to their knees and could go on no longer. Then he'd demanded a new team. Automedon had brought fresh horses, and he'd continued his grisly, monotonous journey. Kat knew, because she'd watched from her window all night. She'd felt like she had to. Someone who cared about Achilles, someone who believed in him, needed to keep watch over him.

Kat put her hands on the levers, closed her eyes and pulled them down.

The sound of the massive chains coming alive was jarringly loud in the guilty silence. She kept her eyes trained on the ghostly shapes she'd glimpsed within the mist and soon she was sure she could make out the distinctive figure of Odysseus leading them closer and closer to the slowly opening walls. Even hidden by the magical fog, he had a light that seemed to surround him that had to be evidence of Athena's favor. Kat whispered a prayer to the goddess while she stared out at Odysseus. *He's a good man, and he loves you very much. Try to keep him safe, Athena.*

And then there was a shout below Kat. At the street level of the gate a man noticed the massive walls opening, even though there was no sight of the Trojan army mounted and ready to take to the field.

Kat hastily ran back to the door that opened to the catwalk and closed it, dropping a bar into place to secure it. Then she pulled the sleeping warriors inside the niche and pressed herself against the inner wall, trying to be inconspicuous, but the shouting got louder and louder as the gates, Sisyphus-like, pushed themselves relentlessly outward. Kat could see that already three men abreast could enter through the gates.

'Close them! Fool! No one has ordered the gates open until midday!' came the command from a powerful voice below her.

Kat shut them all out of her mind and counted slowly to ten: 'One – Mississippi, two – Mississippi, three – Mississippi, four – Mississippi . . .' When she finally got to ten – Mississippi, men were pounding on the door to the catwalk.

Kat glanced down at the gates. Myrmidons, led by a shining Odysseus, were plunging into the city. Satisfied, Kat lifted the sword over her head with both hands, and then she brought it down with all her force, smashing it into the system of gears and chains and balances that the city had so meticulously refined over several hundred years. With a scream that sounded like a mad woman, the chain locked into place, and the wide open gates came to a groaning halt.

Now all that was left was Achilles and the final battle for his soul.

Chapter Thirty-three

The door to the catwalk burst open. Kat had positioned herself between the bodies of the two sleeping warriors. At the first sight of the men, she drew a tremendous breath and let loose the most ear-shattering girl scream she could conjure. Then she rolled her eye-balls up in her head and fell down in a faint worthy of Scarlett O'Hara.

She continued to play possum as a warrior lifted her and carried her from the room amid much discussion of what could have possibly happened – the general consensus of which was that there must be divine mischief afoot. Kat slitted her eyes and peeked over the warrior's shoulder to see the other men milling impotently around the broken gears.

Halfway to her chamber Kat roused. 'What has happened?' she asked faintly. Then she gasped and began to struggle. 'Put me down! Where are you taking me?'

The warrior put her down as if she'd caught on fire. 'Princess, you were found in the gate room. You and the warriors were unconscious.'

'The gate room?' Kat looked hysterically around, letting her eyes fill with tears. 'What are you talking about?' Noise from the battle that was raging in the city drifted up to them. Kat clutched at her throat, looking like she was going to faint again. 'What is that sound?'

'Princess, the gate was opened. The city has been breeched.'

Kat let out a shriek and swayed dramatically.

'Princess, let me take you—'

'No! You have to go help them keep the Greeks from the palace! Go! I'll find my father.' When he hesitated she added, 'Hurry!' turned and whirled away down the hall. Thankfully he didn't follow her.

Kat's heart hurt as she made her way, playing the hysterical princess, from the palace. It was easier than she imagined it would be. Chaos ruled. There was mass panic. Women screamed, darting hysterically into and then out of the streets when they glimpsed Greek warriors. The women needn't have worried, at least not at that moment. The Greeks were too busy engaging in bloody pockets of fighting with desperate Trojans to bother with the raping part of raping and pillaging. The stones of the city streets were slick with blood. Fire colored the dawn, turning the world scarlet.

The great front gates were wide open, belching Greek warriors. Kat pressed herself against the wall of the city, searching desperately for a familiar face. Finally she noticed a knot of Myrmidons fighting not far from her and she pushed herself through the seething mass of warriors, swallowing down debilitating fear as she dodged bloody swords and dismembered bodies.

'Myrmidons! Help me!' she cried as she struggled to get closer to them.

First one helmeted head lifted, and then another. She saw eyes widened as they recognized her.

'It's Achilles' princess!' Diomedes shouted. As one, the Myrmidons moved to her and surrounded her in a protective circle.

'Get me to Achilles. I have to try to reach him again.'

Diomedes' incredulous look was mirrored in the other men. 'Princess, Achilles is gone. No one has been able to reach him.'

'I can,' she said firmly. Kat grabbed the young warrior's bloody forearm. 'You have to let me try, and we have to hurry.'

'Princess, let us get you safely from this place. You can return to Phthia with us, and be honored there for the love our lord had for you.'

'Diomedes! Don't give up on him!'

'Take her to Achilles,' said one of the warriors whose name Kat couldn't remember.

Automedon stepped forward, nodding briefly to her. 'I say take her to Achilles, too.'

'Aye,' said another man.

'Aye,' chorused several others.

'Very well,' Diomedes said. 'Let's get her to Achilles. Form up!'

Moving inside the phalanx of men was an eerily familiar sensation. With the Myrmidons surrounding her, Kat pushed easily through the gates, glad that the broad shoulders and protective shields of the men shielded her view of the mayhem. *Caused by me*, her mind berated her. *But I'm ending the war!* she shouted back at herself. *At what cost?* her guilt whispered.

The berserker's roar shattered her internal struggle.

Kat pushed on Automedon's shoulder. 'Let me though – let me see him.'

The men parted enough for Kat to see that Achilles was still dragging Hector's deteriorating body behind his chariot, but he was also engaging in the battle by picking off any unfortunate Trojan who had managed to fight his way through the city gates.

'You have to force him out of the chariot.'

'How—' Automedon began.

'Encircle the chariot. The princess and I will do the rest.' Kat looked up to see Odysseus had joined the Myrmidons. 'Now. Spread out around him. I'll protect her while you're getting into place.'

The Myrmidons obeyed Odysseus, leaving her alone with the warrior.

'I know how you can reach him,' Odysseus said.

'Tell me,' Kat said.

'It has to be through love. Don't think about calming him – it's gone beyond that. Don't try to reason with him and explain about Patroklos – he won't listen. Just make him know that, no matter what else has happened and will happen in your lives, he can count on your love. He has to believe that you value him above everything else. That you see him as truly worthy of you will be what reaches him.'

Kat looked into the famous warrior's eyes and knew that he was speaking from his heart, soul and experience. She smiled. 'She loves you.'

In the midst of chaos, Odysseus's eyes sparkled as if he was a worry-free boy again. 'She does, indeed.'

'Princess!' Diomedes called.

Kat and Odysseus glanced up. The Myrmidons had Achilles circled. He'd stopped insanely driving the horses. Now he stood in the chariot, growling at his men.

Odysseus held out one hand to her. 'Ready?'

'As I'll ever be.' Kat took his hand, gripping it hard as if Odysseus's strength could be transferred into her body through their palms.

Odysseus led her through the circle of warriors. He stopped just inside the line of men.

'Achilles!' he shouted. 'I have something that belongs to you!'

Snarling, Achilles whirled to face them. His blazing red eyes narrowed as he caught sight of Katrina. With terrible speed he stalked forward.

Kat gave herself no time to think – no time to hesitate – no time to reconsider. She squeezed Odysseus's hand, then dropped it and stepped forward to meet the beast. She saw the flash of surprise in those blood-colored eyes, and then the surprise was replaced by satisfaction. He reached her quickly, grabbing her shoulders.

'Now, woman, I will taste you.'

Kat gazed up into his ravaged face. It had gotten worse over the past twenty-four hours. The berserker's possession had become even more physically pronounced. His skin was stretched tight, his lips were permanently curled to expose teeth that were more fang-like than human. His head appeared bulbous, as if it were literally trying to change shape. And covering this nightmare visage was gore and filth and the putrid odor of death.

She stepped into his arms, sliding her hands up and around his grotesquely misshapen shoulders. 'There is no reason for this rage, Achilles. There is no battle here.' The monster hesitated. She could feel the tremor that quaked through his body. Kat focused all the love and desire and need she had for the complex soul who was still within the tormented body – her Achilles, the man who believed he had never been good enough and only thought of himself as *almost* a leader ... *almost* a husband ... *almost* a hero ... and not ever truly worthy of love. She smiled. 'I love you, Achilles. It isn't a dream. Come back to me.' Then she pulled his ravaged face down to hers and kissed him.

* * *

337

That Agamemnon had pronounced Patroklos's death and had been the mouthpiece that had sealed his fate had, by that time, been but an irony and irritant to Achilles. He'd known he couldn't escape his destiny. Yes, for Katrina's sake he'd pretended to believe in the dream, but it had been only that, just a waking dream he'd been allowed to visit temporarily. Like all dreams, by its very nature, it must end.

He let his despair at losing Katrina couple with the pain his cousin's death caused, breeding rage, and then Achilles gave himself over to it. For the first time he didn't hold on to his humanity. Instead he welcomed the glowing scarlet fire of the berserker, letting the creature fill him and burn away his agony. Achilles became rage, embracing the fate that had haunted him for more than a decade. The man retreated to the farthest reaches of his soul where he waited for inevitable death to free him.

The light of consciousness had nudged him once and the man had stirred, but then rage exploded, searing humanity and blinding him again.

When the light returned it came not simply in the form of a brightness that shined through the darkness of the berserker's red rage. This time it was Katrina's voice, a shimmering beacon of cool water that extinguished the berserker's fire, washing a path of love from the external to Achilles' spirit, the man within the man.

Achilles' vision returned to him in a shocking rush. Katrina was standing within his arms.

Completely disorientated, Achilles could feel the wrongness in his body and the hideous changes the berserker had wrought. He wanted to fling her away from him and then find a place deep within the seas where he could hide himself forever.

And then Katrina smiled. 'I love you, Achilles. It isn't a dream. Come back to me.'

When she pulled his face down to hers and kissed him, Katrina kicked away the crutches of rage that had sustained him, leaving Achilles with only his humanity and her love as his support. He wrapped his arms around her and returned the kiss.

She leaned back enough to look into his eyes. He knew what she would see. Though his consciousness had returned, his body had been ravaged, permanently changed by the complete possession of rage. He braced for her rejection, promising himself that he would fight off the berserker until he got Katrina to safety.

She smiled again, this time followed by a beautiful, joyous laugh. 'I knew you would come back to me!' Kat threw herself into his arms, hugging him hard. 'Achilles, Patroklos isn't dead. I give you my word – he's alive and well and with Jacky.'

Elated, Achilles held her fiercely. Patroklos was alive and Katrina loved him despite everything!

Then his brain processed what his eyes were seeing and he pulled gently away from her, looking disbelievingly at a world utterly changed. The Trojan gates were open wide and the city was afire. And he remembered none of it. Always before when he'd returned to himself Achilles had remembered everything the berserker had done, as if it had been a play he'd been observing. This time, there was nothing, only a charred spot burned out of his memory.

Dazed, Achilles realized he and Katrina were standing in the center of a circle of his warriors. Behind him was his chariot and tied to the rear of it was a bloody body that—

'Achilles! My friend!' Odysseus was suddenly there, grasping his forearm. 'It's true. He's returned!' He shouted to the ring of Myrmidons, who broke ranks and approached him more hesitantly.

'What has happened?' Achilles asked.

'The princess opened the gates. Troy has fallen,' Odysseus said.

'You did this?'

'Well, I had a little help from the goddesses, but basically, yes,' Kat said. Achilles thought she looked extremely uncomfortable and wondered about the full story, hoping he would have years, decades, to ask her about it.

Then his eyes were drawn to the desecrated body. There was something about the dead warrior . . .

'Who is that?'

Odysseus hesitated. Kat looked obviously upset. And he knew.

'Hector. I killed him.' Achilles felt a sweep of horror. 'And then I descrated his body.'

'*You* didn't,' Kat said firmly. 'It wasn't you.'

'Ah, gods! Why was I allowed to do this?' Achilles walked slowly over to Hector's body. He bowed his head, warring with his feelings, refusing to allow the berserker another opportunity to spread more destruction. He spoke to the body. 'You were a valiant warrior and honorable prince. I give you my oath that I will make this right. I will build a funeral pyre to you so great that even Mount Olympus will feel its heat.'

The stabbing, terrible pain in his leg shocked a cry from Achilles. He tried to turn around, to crouch defensively, but the spear had skewered him through the ankle, pinning him to the ground. Clutching uselessly at the deeply imbedded spear, he

340

twisted his body and saw the young, slender man, eyes wide with hatred and madness, draw the bow and let fly a flaming arrow covered in tar.

'Die, monster!' Paris screamed.

Chapter Thirty-four

The arrow hit Achilles in the middle of his chest, impaling itself to the flaming quill, spilling molten tar down his body like overflowing lava. Through the agony, Achilles heard Katrina scream and saw her rushing to him as the Myrmidons converged on Paris, burying him under an avalanche of swords and blood.

The berserker, so newly banished, slammed back into his body. Achilles fought the possession, but as his body began to burn, the pain overwhelmed him. Then Katrina's face swam before him, and through the red haze he watched her snap the golden chain from around her neck and wrench open the locket.

'Venus! Hera! Athena! I call the three of you to me to claim the boon you swore you would owe me!'

The air shimmered, like mist rising from a morning field, and the three goddesses appeared as Achilles was driven to his knees. Body and mind afire, he still struggled against being lost to the berserker.

'I fulfilled my part of the deal,' Kat said. 'The boon I want is Achilles. I claim the man and ask that you save him from the monster.'

Achilles began to lose hope when the goddesses exchanged surprised looks. It was too much. Katrina had tried. He had tried. His fate was unavoidable – what had been purposed by the gods could not be changed, not even by the gods themselves.

He closed his eyes, concentrating on maintaining his humanity. He wanted to die a man, not a monster.

'Please.' Kat looked pleadingly at each of the goddesses.

'Darling, if you choose this you cannot return to your old life,' Venus said.

'You will live and die in this ancient world,' Athena said.

'Be very sure this is your wish,' Hera said.

'I've never been surer about anything in my life,' Kat said. 'Please save him.'

Venus smiled. 'You have already saved him. Take his hand and call him to you.'

Venus blew a kiss at her, and Kat felt the shock of divine power fill her body. She hurried to Achilles. His body was completely engulfed in fire, but she didn't hesitate. She reached through the flames and grasped his hand. She felt no heat, no pain, only the surety of her love for him.

'Come to me, Achilles.' Her voice reverberated across the Trojan plain, magnified by the magic of the goddesses.

Kat felt Achilles shudder. Something gave under her hand. Automatically she pulled, and from the burning, ruined body of the berserker-ravaged warrior stepped a golden man. He was smaller in stature than Achilles, and he looked years younger. His body was free of scars. His eyes were a brilliant, clear blue. Gone were the pain and despair, regret and guilt that had been his companions for more than a decade. He gazed at Kat with an expression of happiness so complete that her heart felt as if it would burst with joy. Achilles pulled her into his arms and kissed her tenderly. Then, still holding her hand, he faced the three goddesses. Achilles dropped to one knee. The men around him followed suit. The fighting stopped and all eyes turned to the goddesses.

'My name will not be remembered for thousands of years, but I pledge that my children will honor goddesses for as long as my blood runs through their veins.'

'Actually, darling, your name will be remembered forever,' Venus said.

'No, Goddess.' He pointed back at the burning body that had been reduced to smoldering ash. '*That* is Achilles. I am only a man, not a legend, not a myth and definitely not a god.'

'I have discovered that being a man means being more than any of those things,' Athena said, her gray eyes finding Odysseus.

'Go with our blessings, mortal man. And know that when love is strong enough it can even cause Fate to change her course,' Hera said.

Still clasping hands, Achilles and Katrina walked from the battlefield with the Myrmidons silently following them. The armies, Trojan and Greek, parted to let them pass. The fighting, after almost a decade, was finally over.

So it was with no little sense of shock that Kat heard an earpiercing scream. They were in the middle of the dunes between the Greek and Myrmidon camps when a small party of soldiers stumbled into view. There were two women with them. One was being led by a rope around her slender, white neck. She held her head high and ignored everyone and everything around her. The other woman was hurling herself against the man leading the others – it was she who was shrieking and crying.

Kat recognized the hysterical woman instantly. 'Holy crap, it's Briseis.'

'After all I've done for you, you *dare* cast me aside for Cassandra! A witch!' Briseis railed at Agamemnon.

The king called the line of warriors to a halt. 'Briseis, I have already assured you that I will arrange for your return to your father and will send with you a handsome bride price. Your father will be able to make an excellent match for you.'

'My father is a reprobate! The reason that I'm here is that I fled his house.'

'And again I say that is not my concern.' Agamemnon motioned to his personal guard. 'Escort my lady to the ship I have provided, and see her safely off with the next tide.'

The warriors saluted him. With utterly blank expressions, they began to drag Briseis away.

'I curse you, Agamemnon! You reject love, so love will be your downfall!'

Agamemnon yawned. 'I'm afraid you're too late. I've already been cursed by love once.'

'Fucking asshole,' Kat murmured.

As if he heard her, Agamemnon's gaze turned her way. Kat watched his eyes glance past Achilles, discount him and then widen in disbelief and return to him. She looked up at her lover. His lips were curved up in his little half smile as he met the king's shocked gaze.

'Make that three times you've been cursed by love,' Achilles said. He didn't shout, but his voice carried easily over the dune. 'You deserve no less than to be destroyed by that which you thought to use against others.'

Agamemnon paled, called an order to his men and the group hurried away toward the Greek camp.

Achilles glanced at Kat as they continued walking. 'Was it you who cursed him the first time?'

'Absolutely,' she said.

'I'm glad of it,' Achilles said with a chuckle.

'I wish I could remember what happens to Agamemnon,' Kat said softly to Achilles as they came to the Myrmidon beach where the black-sailed ships were docked just offshore. 'Well, I suppose I mean what happened to him according to Greek mythology. You know, Jacky is just as bad at mythology as I was, which is . . .' Kat ran out of words as the heartsick truth hit her. Jacky was still in the modern world.

'Remind them,' Achilles said.

'Huh?' Kat said.

'Didn't the goddesses grant Jacqueline a boon, too? Remind them, and if it is her wish, they will return her.'

Kat grinned. 'And Patroklos.'

He mirrored her smile. 'And Patroklos.'

She opened the locket that she still gripped in her fist. 'Uh, Venus. Sorry to bug you again, but I think the three of you forgot that Jacky gets a boon, too. And I know for a fact that she would like to come back here with Patroklos. So, if it's not too much trouble I'd really appreciate it if—'

With an abrupt *pop* Jacky and Patroklos materialized on the beach in front of them. Jacky was wearing an exceedingly short, tight, nurse's 'uniform.' The kind that can be found in smut shops, especially around Halloween, complete with white thigh highs, garters and red come-fuck-me pumps. She was obviously in the middle of a very nasty bump and grind and was caught midfling of her long, waving, blonde tresses. Patroklos, who materialized sitting on his butt in the sand, was wearing an open-backed hospital robe. He was sporting several different sizes and shapes of bandages, the most evident of which was wrapped around his neck. Patroklos was very obviously alive and very, very obviously firmly in the middle of a recovery stage.

Jacky blinked and looked around, eyes widening. 'Oh, Jesus wept! Could you not have waited a few minutes or so?'

'Jacky!' Kat cried, hurling herself into her friend's arms while

Achilles and the Myrmidons descended upon Patroklos, thumping him not so gently on the back and commenting on his strange manner of dress.

Kat was happily telling Jacky how utterly stank she was when the sea began to boil. Achilles moved swiftly to her side, pushing the complaining, mostly naked Patroklos behind him with Kat and Jacky and shouting for the Myrmidons to form ranks as the god arose from the cove.

Kat had never seen, never even imagined anything like the being who towered out of the sea over them. He was huge. Instead of skin he had scales that were shaded all the colors of the oceans. His white beard curled down to his massive chest, matching his thick hair that fell in ringlets around his shoulders. Barnacles made of diamonds and sapphires and aquamarines decorated his body. He was carrying a trident carved from red coral, which he lifted and then thudded against the sea floor, causing waves to froth in the normally placid cove, and making the Myrmidon fleet bob precariously like a petulant child's bathtub toys.

'The walls of Troy have been breeched!' His voice boomed across the water. 'They no longer keep out the Greeks, so they will also no longer keep out the sea. This is one oath old Priam cannot ignore.' The god lifted his trident again, as if he was getting ready to lead a charge, but the clearing of a lovely voice from behind him had him hesitating and looking around.

The beautiful Thetis of the Silver Feet stepped delicately forward, gliding over the top of the waves as if she was strolling on dry land. 'Poseidon, wouldn't you like to reward the mortal who has finally given you Troy?' she said.

Poseidon lifted his bushy white brows. 'I would, indeed, lovely Thetis.'

Thetis glanced in their direction. Achilles gave his mother a respectful nod and then took Kat's hand and moved up to the shoreline. He bowed deeply to Poseidon.

Poseidon inclined his head familiarly. 'Achilles, it is with glad eyes that I see you have shaken off my brother's curse. For your mother's sake I am pleased that the berserker is no more. So what reward do I owe you for breeching the walls of Troy?'

'Great God of the Seas, I thank you for your kind offer, but it is not me to whom you owe a reward.' Achilles took Kat's arm and presented her to Poseidon. 'This mortal woman is responsible for delivering to you the walls of Troy.'

Poseidon stared down at her. Kat wasn't sure of correct protocol, but she bobbed a nervous curtsey.

'This small mortal woman did what an entire army of Greeks could not?'

'I did,' Kat said.

Poseidon bent so he could get a better look at her, then his eyes widened. 'You! But you are the Trojan princess, Polyxena.'

'It would appear I am,' Kat said calmly.

'Then it also appears I owe you a double boon – one for bringing me the walls of Troy and another for a slight, ur, misunderstanding earlier that could have ended very badly without divine intervention.' The god actually seemed chagrined, giving Thetis an apologetic look. Then he turned his attention back to Kat. 'So, Princess, what reward do you choose? I offer you anything within the wide seas of the world as yours.'

Kat's gaze met Achilles'. 'Choose for us, my princess,' he said. She looked over her shoulder at Jacky and Patroklos, who nodded and smiled at her.

She drew a deep breath. 'I know exactly what I want. I want you to give me an island that can be hidden from the world – a separate place of unimaginable beauty dedicated to healing and peace and the goddesses.'

Poseidon stroked his beard while he considered. 'I believe I do have such an island, but it is far from here. In another time – another place.'

Kat squeezed Achilles' hand. 'The farther away, the better.'

'Then come!' Poseidon waved a hand over the cove. The black-sailed Myrmidon ships scattered like autumn leaves as a shining ship made of pearl surged to the surface from beneath the ocean depths. The waters of the cove parted, leaving a sidewalk of dry land leading to the glistening iridescent ship.

Achilles faced his men. 'I can no longer lead you. That Achilles died in flames on the Trojan battlefield. I want no more battles – no more glory. I want only the magic of peace. If that is what you want for your lives, you are free to join me.' His half smile flickered. 'But only if you are willing to bow to the goddesses.' Then he took Kat's hand, and they started down the god-made path, with Jacky and Patroklos following immediately behind them.

Kat glanced back and was pleased to see that almost every Myrmidon and several of their war-prize brides, Aetnia included, were choosing to take the path to the pearl boat, too.

'Um, Poseidon?' Jacky called as the last of the Myrmidons boarded and she and Kat, Patroklos and Achilles had moved to the bow of the ship.

The God of the Seas peered down at Jacky, his bushy brows lifting when he saw what she was wearing. 'Yes, mortal woman with the unusual costume, you have a question for Poseidon?'

'Yeah. I was wondering, does this island you're giving the, uh, princess have a name?'

'It does, indeed. The mortals call it Avalon.'

Kat and Jacky exchanged stunned looks.

'Jesus wept,' Jacky whispered, fanning herself and leaning weakly back against Patroklos. 'My heart! I feel my heart going again.'

'Holy fucking shit,' Kat said, shaking her head numbly.

'My god, Kat! I can't wait to meet the locals,' Jacky said, laughing softly.

Achilles' arms went around Kat. 'Is all well? Do you know this island called Avalon?'

Feeling dazed, Kat looked into his beautiful eyes. 'I do. And it is utterly, completely, perfect.'

She pulled Achilles down to her and kissed him while Poseidon waved his hand over the cove and the waters returned to normal as the pearl ship began to glide seaward into a bank of fog that shimmered and rippled magically. 'I wish you a good voyage and a blessed future!' the God of the Seas called.

'Kat, stop making out and look at this. I do believe we're sailing into something that is less than normal,' Jacky said, thumping Kat on her back.

Kat turned, but stayed within Achilles' arms, and looked out at the rippling magic of their future. 'I think we'd better just forget about what we used to think of as normal,' she said.

Jacky snuggled against Patroklos's side. Kat was glad to see that the warriors had pieced together something for him to wear – although the hospital gown had revealed a nice view of his firm backside.

'Fine with me. I've never liked normal,' Jacky said.

'You mean you've never *been* normal,' Kat teased.

'You're going to have to rename me,' Achilles said abruptly. 'I don't want anything to taint our new life, so Achilles is a name that must forever die at Troy.'

'I have an idea,' Jacky said. Three sets of eyes turned to her. 'I think you should name him Angel.'

'You know, you are a very troubled woman. Get over your *Buffy* addiction – it's just not right,' Kat said while the two men looked confused.

'I did not mean Angel as in *Buffy*. I meant Angel as in fallen. Please! He doesn't even have dark hair,' Jacky grumbled.

Kat shook her head in disgust. 'I seriously do not think so. Anyway, I have a better idea.'

'What will you call me?' Achilles asked.

Kat turned in his arms. 'What do you think of Kirk?'

'Kirk . . .' Achilles tested the name. 'I think I like it.'

'Sounds like the name of a leader,' Patroklos said.

'Well?' Kat asked Jacky.

'I cannot believe you give me a hard time about my *Buffy* issue, Ms. *Star Trek*,' Jacky said.

'But you think it's a good choice, don't you?' Kat grinned mischievously at her best friend.

Jacky laughed. 'What I think is that our future is going to be anything but boring.'

And the magical fog closed around the pearl ship, carrying them away to a new time . . . and new place . . . and a future that was definitely not boring.

Epilogue

The battle was over. Straggling remnants of the Trojan army were being rounded up and, under Odysseus's direction, treated with mercy. Athena had ordered Greek warriors to go to all of the temples outside the Trojan walls and be sure that the priestesses and priests were not harmed. When Poseidon showed up with his army of Oceanids and began ripping apart the walls, the three goddesses, rolling their eyes, moved to a safer position in the grove of ancient olive trees.

Hera was restless and kept jumping at every twig crack and leaf flutter.

'What is it with you?' Venus asked. 'The war's over – we got what we wanted.'

'I realize that. We very *visibly* got what we wanted, *clearly* showing that the three of us orchestrated all of this.' Hera waved a hand sweepingly at Troy. 'At any moment Zeus will awaken from sleeping off the exhaustion caused by our days of magnificent love-making and he will learn of our interference here. Angry is an understatement about what he will be – and you know how he is when he's angered.'

'Wow, you exhausted him? Well done you!' Venus said.

Athena sighed. 'Love missed the point, as usual.'

'I didn't miss it. I just liked the other part better,' Venus said.

'He's going to be so angry,' Hera said softly. 'And we'd been getting along so well, too.'

'Then there is nothing to do but to make sure Zeus does not hear of the parts we played here,' Athena said.

'What do you suggest?' Hera said. 'And keep in mind I really don't think I can keep up the sexual calisthenics. For a few days it was fun. For eternity it would be . . .' She paused and grimaced. 'Painful.'

'We'll simply bespell them,' Athena said.

'Huh?' Venus said. 'Bespelling the genitals of the King and Queen of Olympus is going to be far more difficult than—'

'Would you please get your mind off everyone's genitals? I'm talking about the Trojans and the Greeks. It should be no problem if the three of us join our powers. Let's wipe the mortal's memories clean of everything that happened after the berserker was killed.'

'Could we really do that?' Hera said, beginning to brighten.

'I don't see why not,' Venus said. She gave Athena a considering look. 'You know, all this sex is really having an excellent effect on you. Of course I hate to say it again, but I told you so.'

'While it pains me, it does appear that you were right.' When Venus's face blossomed into a victorious smile, she added, 'This time, that is.' Then the gray-eyed goddess looked out on the battlefield. Her eyes were unerringly drawn to the tall warrior she loved so dearly. Not raising her voice above a whisper, she said, 'Odysseus, come to me.' Even from that distance she could see that he looked at her, smiled and began closing the distance between them.

'Why are you calling him? We're supposed to wipe their memories,' Hera said.

'Not his,' Athena said. 'I don't care about the rest of them, but Odysseus will always remember everything.'

'It's only right,' Venus said. 'She loves him. Messing with his memory would dishonor what they've shared together.'

For once Athena smiled at Venus with genuine appreciation. 'Thank you, Goddess of Love.'

'Not a problem, Goddess of War.' Venus gave her a snappy little salute.

'So if we wipe their memories clean, what are we going to put in place of what really happened?' Hera said.

'We could blame it on Poseidon,' Athena said. 'He's already here and obviously has issues with the Trojans.'

'No, everyone knows that he couldn't touch the Trojan walls until they were breeched. He made that deal decades ago with King Laomedon. If it could have been broken, he would have done so by now. Plus we really don't want to anger the sea god. You know how ugly it can get when the seas are in turmoil,' Hera said.

Then Venus burst into giggles. 'I've got it! And it's perfect. Remember the stupid Trojan horse that that ridiculous author made up along with the whole Achilles' heel thing?'

'Of course we remember it. It's just like that horrid rumor about the three of us starting the Trojan War.' Hera shuddered. 'It's simply unconscionable!'

'Well let's use the asinine rumors and the verbose fictionalizing to our benefit. Let's zap the Trojan horse into the city and put that memory in the mortals' minds,' Venus said.

'It's brilliant,' Hera said.

'I do like it,' Athena said.

'What is a Trojan horse?' Odysseus asked.

Athena smiled lovingly at him. 'And we're giving Odysseus credit for thinking of it.'

Athena and Venus shrugged.

'Whatever,' Venus said. Hera nodded.

'What is a Trojan horse?' Odysseus asked again.

'I'll explain all of it to you later,' Athena said. 'Right now perhaps you should step aside.'

The three goddesses joined hands and together they walked onto the ravaged battlefield. As they got closer to the Trojan walls, the goddesses began to glow with combined power. Each woman's voice rang throughout Troy, washing the mortals like a cleansing rain.

'*Our task is complete. The Trojan War is done,*' Athena began.

'*But the memory of we three shall fade with today's setting sun,*' Venus said.

'*And with the dawn new memories and a new era will have begun,*' Hera concluded.

Then the goddesses raised their arms and, in perfect accord, flung their powers out to Troy. A massive wooden horse materialized just as, behind them, the sun set into the bleeding ocean.

'Well, that's that,' Venus said, brushing her hands together as if wiping off the crumbs of a job well done.

'I have to get back to Zeus before he wakes up,' Hera said. 'You know, this has invigorated me. I may be ready for some more calisthenics.' She lifted her hands to bless them. 'Goddesses, it has been a pleasure.'

'My Queen,' Venus and Athena said together, bowing respectfully as Hera disappeared.

'I really should explain everything to Odysseus,' Athena said, her eyes already seeking out her lover.

'Go with Love's blessing, Athena,' Venus said.

'Thank you, my friend,' Athena said, and then she hurried away.

Venus sighed happily, thinking about her virile husband, Vulcan, who she had definitely not spent enough time with since this whole adventure had begun. Already her mind was humming with the romantic rendezvous she would plan for that very night. 'Hera was right – I feel invigorated,' she said. 'After all, Love does adore a happily ever after.' Venus lifted her smooth arm and, with a snap of her fingers, disappeared, leaving a cloud of diamonds that turned into fireflies that filled the silent grove like beacons of hope.

Historical Notes*

Agamemnon returned to Greece and Clytemnestra, the wife he had left behind. He brought Cassandra with him, arrogantly believing Clytemnestra would have to bow to his will and ignore the fact that he flaunted his new lover. Instead of submitting to him, her love for Agamemnon turned to hatred and Clytemnestra killed him alone, in his bath, after binding him with a silk cloth. She also killed Cassandra.

Briseis, also known as Hippodameia, returned to her father, King Oenomaus of Pisa. She functioned as his queen. Court rumor was that she and her father were lovers. He did everything he could to avoid his daughter getting married and challenged all her suitors in a horse race. When they lost they were killed. Pelops was the twentieth suitor and with Briseis's help (some say she was aided by Hera, who believed she owed the mortal woman a boon), he beat her father, who was killed in the process. They got married and ruled Pisa, and had many children together, but Pelops also had a son by a previous wife. He loved him dearly. Filled with jealousy, Briseis manipulated two of her sons into killing the boy. Pelops rejected Briseis and then cursed both sons. In utter despair Briseis committed suicide.

---

* Gentle reader, please understand that by "historical notes" I mean history as translated through my eyes. More specifically, I decided how I wanted the story to end for each character and then I made it up.

357

It takes ten years for Odysseus to return to his home in Ithaca. Athena was with him during the entire journey, and it was even rumored that she stayed with him afterward, but *that* is a whole other adventure . . .

TURN THE PAGE TO READ AN EXCERPT
FROM ANOTHER SENSATIONAL NOVEL IN
P. C. CAST'S GODDESS SUMMONING SERIES

Goddess of the Sea

COMING SOON FROM PIATKUS

Part One

Chapter One

Arms filled with groceries, CC struggled to pull her key from the lock and push the door shut behind her with her foot. Automatically, she glanced up at the clock in the foyer of her spacious apartment. Seven thirty already. It had taken her an eternity to finish things up at the Communication Center and then stop by the package store and the commissary. After that, fighting the traffic from Tinker Air Force Base had been like driving through axle-deep mud. To add to her frustration, she had tried to take a shortcut home and had ended up taking a wrong turn. Soon she was hopelessly lost. A kind soul at a Quick Trip had given her directions, and she had felt compelled to explain to him that she was lost only because she had been stationed at Tinker for just three months, and she hadn't had time to learn her way around yet.

The man had patted her shoulder like she was a puppy and asked, 'What is a young little thing like you doing in the air force?' CC had treated the question rhetorically, thanked him and driven away, face hot with embarrassment.

Understandably, her already harried nerves jumped at the insistent sound of her ringing phone.

'Hang on! I'm coming!' she yelled and rushed into the kitchen, plopping the bags unceremoniously onto the spotless counter and lunging for the phone.

'Hello,' she panted into the dead sound of a dial tone that was broken only by the rhythmic bleat of her answering machine. 'Well, at least they left a message.' CC sighed and carried the phone with her back to the kitchen, punching in her message retrieval code. With one hand she held the phone to her ear, and with the other, she extracted twin bottles of champagne from one of the bags.

'You have two new messages,' the mechanical voice proclaimed. 'First new message, sent at 5:30 P.M.'

CC listened attentively as she picked at the metallic casing that covered the wire-imprisoned champagne cork.

'*Hello, Christine, it's your parents!*' Her mom's recorded voice, sounding a little unnatural and tinny, chirped through the phone.

'*Hi there, Christine!*' More distant, but similarly cheerful, Dad's voice echoed from an extension.

CC smiled indulgently. Of course it was her parents – they were the only two people on this earth who still insisted on calling her by her given name.

'*Just wanted to say we didn't actually forget your big day.*'

Here her mom paused, and she could hear her dad chuckling in the background. Forget her birthday? She hadn't thought they had – until then.

Her mom's breathy voice continued. '*We've just been running ourselves ragged getting ready for our next cruise! You know how long it takes your father to pack.*' This said in a conspiratorial whisper. '*But don't worry, honey, even though we didn't get your box off, we did manage to fix up a little surprise for our favorite twenty-five year old.*'

'*Twenty-five?*' Her dad sounded honestly surprised. '*Well, good Lord. I thought she was only twenty-two.*'

'*Time sure flies, dear,*' Mom said sagely.

'*Damn straight, honey,*' Dad agreed. '*That's one reason I told you*' *we should spend more time traveling – but only one reason.'* Dad chuckled suggestively.

'You certainly were right about that reason, dear.' Mom kidded back breathlessly, suddenly sounding decades younger.

'They're flirting with each other on my message,' CC sputtered. 'And they really did forget my birthday!'

'Anyway, we're getting ready to leave for the airport—'

Dad's voice, even more distant, broke in. *'Elinor! Say good-bye, the airport limo is here.'*

'Well, have to go, Birthday Girl! Oh, and you have a nice time on your little air force trip. Aren't you leaving in a couple of days?'

Her little air force trip?! CC rolled her eyes. Her ninety-day deployment as noncommissioned officer in charge of Quality Control at the Communications Center at Riyadh Air Base in Saudi Arabia to support the war on terrorism was just a 'little air force trip?'

'And, honey, don't you worry about flying wherever it is you're going. You're old enough to be over that silly fear by now. And, my goodness, you did join the air force!'

CC shuddered, wishing her mother hadn't mentioned her phobia – airplanes – since she would soon be flying halfway around the world over oceans of water. It was the only part of the air force she didn't like.

'We love you! Bye now.'

The message ended and CC, still shaking her head, hit the Off button and put the phone on the counter.

'I can't believe you guys forgot my birthday! You've always said that it's impossible to forget my birthday because I was born right before midnight on Halloween.' She berated the phone while she reached into a cabinet for a champagne flute. 'You didn't even remember my box.' She continued to glare at the phone as she wrestled with the champagne cork.

For the seven years CC had been on active duty service in the United States Air Force, her parents had never forgotten her birthday box. Until now. Her twenty-fifth birthday – she had lived one-fourth a century. It really was a landmark year, and she was going to celebrate it with no birthday box from home.

'It's a family tradition!' she sputtered, popping the cork and holding the foaming bottle over the sink.

CC sighed and felt an unexpected twinge of homesickness.

No, she reminded herself sternly, she liked her life in the air force and had never been sorry for her impetuous decision to join the service right out of high school. After all, it had certainly gotten her away from her nice, ordinary, quiet, small town life. No, she hadn't exactly 'seen the world,' as the ads had promised. But she had lived in Texas, Mississippi, Nebraska, Colorado and now Oklahoma, which were five states more than the majority of the complacent people in her hometown of Homer, Illinois, would ever live in, or even visit.

'Apparently that doesn't include my parents!' CC poured the glass of champagne, sipped it and tapped her foot – still glaring at the phone. It seemed that during the past year her parents had gone on more Silver Adventure Tours than was humanly possible. 'They must be trying to set some sort of record.' CC remembered the flirty banter in their voices and closed her eyes quickly at that particular visual image.

Her eyes snapped back open, and her gaze fastened again on the phone.

'But Mom, none of your homemade chocolate chip cookies?' She sipped the champagne and discovered she needed a refill. 'How am I supposed to cover all the food groups without my birthday box?' She reached into the other bag and pulled out the bucket of Kentucky Fried Chicken, original recipe, of course. Pointing from the chicken to the champagne, she continued her one-sided discourse. 'I have the meat group – KFC – mixed with the all important grease group for proper digestion. Then I have the fruit group, champagne, my personal favorite. How am I supposed to complete the culinary birthday ensemble without the dairy/chocolate/sugar group?' She gestured in disgust at the phone.

Lifting the lid off the KFC, she snagged a drumstick and bit into it. Then, using it to punctuate her hand gestures, she continued.

'You know that you guys always send something totally useless that makes me laugh and remember home. No matter where I am. Like the year before last when you sent me the frog rain gauge. And I don't have a yard! And how about the GOD BLESS THIS HOUSE stepping stone, which I have to hang on the *wall* of my *apartment*, because I have no house!' CC's disgruntled look was broken by a smile as she recounted her parents' silly gifts.

'I suppose you're trying to tell me to get married, or at the very least, to become a homeowner.'

She chewed thoughtfully and sighed again, a little annoyed to realize that she probably sounded fifteen instead of twenty-five. Then she brightened.

'Hey! I forgot about my *other* message,' she told the phone as she scooped it back up, dialed her messages, and skipped past her parents' voices.

'Next new message. Sent at 6:32 P.M.'

CC grinned around a mouth full of chicken. It was probably Sandy, her oldest friend – actually she was the only high school

367

friend CC still kept in touch with. Sandy had known her since first grade, and she rarely forgot anything, let alone a birthday. The two of them loved to laugh long distance about how they had managed to 'escape' small town Homer. Sandy had landed an excellent job working for a large hospital in the fun and fabulous city of Chicago. Her official title was Physician Affairs Liaison, which actually meant she was in charge of recruiting new doctors for the hospital, but she and Sandy loved the totally unrealistic, risqué-sounding title. It was especially amusing because Sandy had been happily and faithfully married for three years.

'Hi there, CC. Long time no call, girl!'

Instead of Sandy's familiar Midwestern accent, the voice had a long, fluid Southern drawl. 'It's me, Halley. Your favorite Georgia peach! Oh, my – I had such a hard time getting your new phone number. Naughty you forgot to give it to me when you shipped out.'

CC's grin slipped off her face like wax from a candle. Halley was one of the few things she hadn't missed about her last duty station.

'Just have a quick second to talk. I'm calling to remind you that my thirtieth birthday is just a month and a half away – December fifteenth, to be exact – and I want you to mark your little ol' calendar.'

CC listened with disbelief. 'This is like a train wreck. It just keeps getting worse and worse.'

'I'm having the Party to End All Parties, and I expect your attendance. So put in for leave ASAP. I'll send the formal invite in a week or so. And, yes, presents are acceptable.' Halley giggled like a Southern Barbie doll. 'See y'all soon. Bye-bye for now!'

'I don't believe it.' CC punched the Off button with decidedly more force than was necessary. 'First my parents forget my birthday. Then not only does it look like my oldest friend has forgotten it, too, but I get a call from an annoying non-friend inviting

me to *her* party!' She dropped the phone back on the counter. 'A month and a half in advance!'

CC shoved the unopened bottle of champagne into the fridge.

'Consider yourself on-deck,' she told it grimly. Then she grabbed the open bottle of champagne, her half-empty glass, the bucket of KFC and marched purposefully to the living room where she spread out her feast on the coffee table before returning to the kitchen for a handful of napkins. Passing the deceptively silent phone she halted and spun around.

'Oh, no. I'm not done with you; you're coming with me.' She tossed the phone next to her on the couch. 'Just sit there. I'm keeping an eye on you.'

CC picked out another piece of delightfully greasy chicken and clicked on the TV – and groaned. The screen was nothing but static.

'Oh, no! The cable!' Because she would be out of the country for three months, she had decided to have the cable temporarily disconnected and had been proud of herself for being so money conscious. 'Not tonight! I told them effective the first of November, not the thirty-first of October.' She glanced at the silent phone. 'You probably had something to do with this.'

And she started to laugh, semihysterically.

'I'm talking to the telephone.' She poured herself another glass of champagne, noting the bottle was now half empty. Sipping the bubbly liquid thoughtfully, CC spoke aloud, pointedly ignoring the phone. 'This obviously calls for emergency measures. Time to break out the Favorite Girl Movies.'

Clutching the chicken thigh between her teeth, she wiped her hands on the paper towel before opening the video cabinet that stood next to her television set. Through a full mouth she mumbled the titles as she scanned her stash.

'*Dirty Dancing, Shadowlands, West Side Story, Gone With the Wind.*' She paused and chewed, considering. 'Nope, too long – and it's really not birthday material. Humm . . .' She kept reading. '*Superman, Pride and Prejudice, Last of the Mohicans, The Accidental Tourist, The Color Purple, The Witches of Eastwick.*' She stopped.

'This is exactly what I need. Some Girl Power.' She plunked the video in the VCR. 'No,' she corrected herself. 'This is better than Girl Power – it's Women Power!' CC raised her glass to the screen, toasting each of the vibrant movie goddesses as they appeared. They were unique and fabulous.

Cher was mysterious and exotic, with a full, perfect mouth and a wealth of seductive ringlets that framed her face like the mane of a wild, dark lioness.

CC sighed. She couldn't really do anything about her own little lips – if she did, they would look like a science experiment. But everything else about her was so small. Maybe it was time to rethink her short, boyish haircut.

Michelle Pfeiffer – now there was a gorgeous woman. Even playing the role of Ms. Fertile Mom, she was still undeniably ethereal in her blonde beauty.

No one would ever call *her* cute.

And Susan Sarandon. She couldn't look frumpy even when she was dressed like an old schoolmarm music teacher. She oozed sexuality.

No guy would ever think of her as *just a friend*. At least no heterosexual guy.

'To three amazing women who are everything I wish I could be!' She couldn't believe her glass was empty – and the bottle, too.

'It's a darn good thing we have another.' She patted the phone

affectionately before rescuing the other champagne bottle from a life of loneliness in the fridge.

Ignoring the fact that her steps seemed a little unsteady, she settled back, grabbed a fourth piece of chicken and slanted a glance at the ever-silent phone. 'Bet it shocks you that someone who's so little can eat so much.'

It answered with a shrill ring.

CC jumped, almost choking on the half-chewed piece of chicken. 'Good Lord, you scared the bejeezes out of me!'

The phone bleated again.

'CC, it's a phone. Get it together, Sarg.' She shook her head at her own foolishness.

The thing rang again before she had her hands wiped and her nerves settled enough to answer it.

'H-hello?' she said tentatively.

'May I speak with Christine Canady, please?' The woman's voice was unfamiliar, but pleasant sounding.

'This is she.' CC clicked the remote and paused *The Witches of Eastwick.*

'Miss Canady, this is Jess Brown from Woodland Hills Resort in Branson, Missouri. I'm calling to tell you that your parents, Elinor and Herb, have given you a weekend in Branson at our beautiful resort for your twenty-second birthday! Happy Birthday, Miss Canady!' CC could almost see Jess Brown beaming in delight all the way from Branson. Wherever that was.

'Twenty-fifth,' was all she could make her mouth say.

'Pardon?'

'It's my twenty-fifth birthday, not my twenty-second.'

'No.' Through the phone came the sound of papers being frantically rustled. 'No, it says right here – Christine Canady, twenty-second birthday.'

'But I'm not.'

'Not Christine Canady?' Jess sounded worried.

'Not twenty-two!' CC eyed the newly opened second bottle of champagne. Maybe she was drunk and hallucinating.

'But you are Christine Canady?'

'Yes.'

'And your parents are Elinor and Herb Canady?'

'Yes.'

'Well, as long as you're really you, I suppose the rest doesn't matter.' Jess was obviously relieved.

'I guess not.' CC shrugged helplessly. She decided she might as well join the madness.

'Good!' Jess's perkiness was back in place. 'Now, just a few little details you should know. You can plan your weekend anytime in the next year, but you will need to call to reserve your cabin . . .'

Cabin? CC's mind whirred. What had they done?

'. . . at least one month ahead of time or we cannot guarantee availability. And, of course, this gift is just for your personal use, but if you would like to bring a friend, the resort would be willing to allow him or her to join you for a nominal fee – *or* for totally free if he or she would be willing to attend a short informational meeting about our time-share facility.'

CC closed her eyes and rubbed her right temple where the echo of a headache was just beginning.

'And along with your wonderful Woodland weekend,' Jess Brown alliterated, 'your parents have generously reserved a ticket for you to the Andy Williams Moon River Theater, one of the most popular and long-running shows in Branson!'

CC couldn't stop the bleak groan that escaped her lips.

'Oh, I can well understand your excitement!' Jess gushed.

'We'll be sending you the official information packet in the mail. Just let me double-check your address . . .'

CC heard herself woodenly confirming her address.

'Okay! I think that's all the information we need. You have a lovely evening, Miss Canady, and a very happy twenty-second birthday!' Jess Brown cheerfully clicked off the line.

'But where *is* Branson?' CC asked the dial tone.

GODDESS OF LOVE

Pea Chamberlain needs help. Her shoes, hair, clothes, make-up are all disasters and she really needs a makeover – especially if she wants to attract sexy fireman Griffin DeAngelo at the firemen's masked ball. And who better to coax Pea out of her pod than the Goddess of Love, whom she invokes when she gets her hands on a book of enchantments.

Sure enough, Venus works her magic on Pea, which is what she has been doing for eons – helping others find love. But who will help the Goddess of Love when she finds herself falling head over heels for the same sexy fireman she is trying to land for Pea? Could it be that Venus needs a love makeover herself?

978-0-7499-5356-0

Do you love fiction with a supernatural twist?

Want the chance to hear news about your favourite
authors (and the chance to win free books)?

Keri Arthur
S. G. Browne
P.C. Cast
Christine Feehan
Jacquelyn Frank
Larissa Ione
Sherrilyn Kenyon
Jackie Kessler
Jayne Ann Krentz and Jayne Castle
Martin Millar
Kat Richardson
J.R. Ward
David Wellington

Then visit the Piatkus website and blog
www.piatkus.co.uk | www.piatkusbooks.net

And follow us on Facebook and Twitter
www.facebook.com/piatkusfiction | www.twitter.com/piatkusbooks

piatkus